THE MERCILESS LADIES

Ross Poldark
Demelza
Jeremy Poldark
Warleggan
The Black Moon
The Four Swans
The Angry Tide

Night Journey
Cordelia
The Forgotten Story
Night Without Stars
Take My Life
The Little Walls
Fortune is a Woman
The Sleeping Partner
Greek Fire
The Tumbled House
Marnie
The Grove of Eagles
After the Act
The Walking Stick
Angell, Pearl and Little God
The Japanese Girl
Woman in the Mirror

The Spanish Armadas

The
Merciless Ladies

WINSTON GRAHAM

THE BODLEY HEAD
LONDON SYDNEY
TORONTO

British Library Cataloguing
in Publication Data
Graham, Winston
The merciless ladies.
I. Title
823'.9'1F   PR6013.R24M
ISBN 0–370–30237–0

All rights reserved
© Winston Graham this edition 1979
Printed in Great Britain for
The Bodley Head Ltd
9 Bow Street London WC2E 7AL
by William Clowes & Sons Ltd, Beccles
This edition first published 1979

Foreword

I have resisted suggestions that this novel should be reissued because there were one or two scenes in it that did not seem to me quite right, and I was waiting to find time and the mood to do something about them. These, I hope, have now been improved. Although the book was not contemporary when written, I have taken the opportunity of this revision to double-distance the events described by giving them the perspective of today.

W.G.

Chapter One

I

Three full-length books and a variety of articles have been written about Paul Stafford attempting to evaluate his life and work. To all of them I have refused to contribute or to offer co-operation. As I was his best friend, and remained so through all the vicissitudes of his career—and through I might say the perhaps greater vicissitudes of my own—it wouldn't be unnatural if I were supposed to have something to add to the comments he made about himself and to the history of his career as it appeared at times in the newspapers.

The reason I did not is an obvious one. At the beginning everyone I could have written about was alive; then many; then most; then a precious few. But now I am an old man. It's the privilege of an old man who has outlived his contemporaries to speak freely of a time now gone. (Though not, it seems to me, *so* far gone.) It is also his duty and his responsibility to be sure that his memory is clear and to get his perspectives right. My memory happens to be excellent—and is reinforced by many notebooks I filled during the two years I was withdrawn from the world. Perspective is another matter. I can only aim for that, knowing that, however long I live, I can't achieve true detachment.

But as Paul might have said in another context: 'To hell with perspective: that's for amateurs.'

II

Even so I'd better begin with the Lynn family, as their part in all that happened is so important.

I met the two boys, Bertie and Leo, at my prep school and we went on to Turstall together. Turstall folded up between the wars, but at the time I speak of it was a flourishing if minor public school on the borders of Montgomery and Shropshire. It was probably one of the cheapest public schools in England and so attracted two different sets of parents—those who were making sacrifices to give their children a better start than they had had in life, and those who had come down in the world and yet would go to great lengths to see that their children, if not old Etonians, would be able to claim to be old Something-or-others.

In the very stable world of that time, and in such a school, it meant that an intense degree of snobbery existed, to which most of the masters themselves notably contributed.

Yet for a minor school it was not such a bad place. When one reads the accounts by famous authors, still living, of the goings on in the major schools they went to, one doesn't feel too upset at being deprived of their privileges. Of course at Turstall there was bullying and sneaking and surreptitious sex and terrible food, but none of it on the majestic scale they describe.

Practically run by the two housemasters, the school was presided over by a fierce old cripple called Marshall who seemed to do very little except take the Sixth in Greek and Latin, read prayers, smoke Woodbines in his study, and occasionally emerge to limp along the corridors and through the classrooms like a tattered grey bat with his gown flying, handing out lines and raps with his cane at the least excuse. Yet it was really all his doing that life there was tolerable.

If thirteen were a reflective age I might have wondered what the Lynns were doing following me to Turstall. Their father was attached to the new university of Reading and was doing research of some sort. One might have supposed him more ambitious for his sons. Bertie, the elder, was a quiet, modest, easy boy with a fair skin and long legs that always looked as if they'd just been washed. He was a keen runner and a good and stylish bat. Leo, the younger by eleven months, had dark hair that grew, Caesar fashion, over his big head and down his muscular neck. He was keen on music, talkative and self-absorbed, very generous, and quite without a sense of humour. He was also a romantic and prone to self-dramatisation. Even at that age he loved abstract talk about quest-ions which didn't much matter except as pegs on which to hang an argument. His problem was never lack of a subject but lack of someone to take him seriously.

They lived, I found, in a stone-built Georgian house standing in its own overgrown grounds on a tributary of the Thames. When I first went to stay with them it was not so much that Dr and Mrs Lynn had forgotten I was coming that was disconcerting for the conven-tional thirteen-year-old son of conventional parents, it was that when I arrived and surprised them they didn't seem concerned to do anything about it. And all through the week they were constantly forgetting to lay a place for me at the table, or ordering one cutlet too few from the butcher. Had I stayed a second week the position might have improved, and this was later confirmed in a letter from Leo, who wrote, 'Mother has been laying plates for you all this week and seems quite worried when you don't turn up.'

They were not really absent-minded, for they could remember things they needed to remember; casualness was at the root of the trouble and an ill-developed sense of responsibility.

That first night, after helping Bertie to make up a bed in the spare room and eating a supper even more frugal than those at Turstall, I didn't try to reason out their lack of hospitality. Dr and Mrs Lynn were awful, the house was worse than anything I had ever imagined, the child sister a wizened little gnome of a creature peering from behind monstrous spectacles. I couldn't imagine how they had bothered to write me an invitation. The sooner I made an excuse and went the better. Perhaps even an excuse was unnecessary. Nobody would notice I'd left.

But it happened that the following day was hot and sunny; flies buzzed against the window; we had fresh eggs gathered that morning; and through the trees a silver knife of river gleamed. So one day became two, two three, and soon the week was up and I'd rather enjoyed myself after all.

Dr Lynn was not of course old at that time, although he looked old to me. He was extremely tall and his appearance was disreputable. There was a workhouse at Felbury, and the main road from there to Reading ran near Newton. When Dr Lynn went for a stroll along this road, passers-by frequently mistook him for a tramp making his way from one institution to the next. His hair, already thinning, was seldom cut, and fell over his ears and over a collar freckled with dandruff. His pockets always bulged with notebooks. He was alive with pencils. His eyes were very keen and small and grey, his jaw long and his mouth wide with the lips narrow and clever. He had a dry wit of the type peculiar to scholars.

The most striking characteristics about Mrs Lynn were her height, her long jaw and her disreputable appearance. Husband and wife were sometimes taken for brother and sister. But Mrs Lynn was proportionately taller for a woman, and her untidiness in a woman was more noticeable. She had blue eyes, of a startling, vivid blue, wispy fair hair and a very high colour. Her voice was high-pitched and less attractive than her husband's. To see these two strange long-legged creatures gardening together like angular scarecrows, and conversing in English as it should be but seldom is spoken, was a study in the incongruous I was then too young to appreciate.

Mrs Lynn played the violin and took a few special pupils in advanced Greek and Hebrew. Dr Lynn had just resigned his post at the university in order to give his full time to research. This must have been a financial sacrifice and I think was the reason for Bertie and Leo's presence at Turstall. Money always seemed tight at Newton.

They had no domestic help. 'Maids are such a bore,' said Mrs Lynn. As a matter of course nothing was ever put away. Dishes and cutlery were washed when next needed. Books were thrust back on the shelves when there was no more room on the table for them. the grate was cleaned when the next fire became necessary. Curtain-rods and pictures generally contrived to be aslant, and carpets would get a kink in them which nobody bothered to put right. The house was lit by gas produced from a private plant in an outhouse, which Dr Lynn tried to keep in order. The innumerable candles propped up and stuck to the mantelpiece in every room testified to his failures.

Empty soda siphons were everywhere: nobody touched intoxicants, but everyone drank fruit juice or barley water 'fizzed up'. Crockery was much cracked and most cups were without handles. In every corner was dust. A certain amount of work was done in the house, but it was undertaken to remove a nuisance and, like the gardening, was always an attempt to catch up, never the anticipation of necessity.

As for Holly, their daughter of nine, one imagined her as an after-thought in the biological experiment which had produced Bertie and Leo. As a tiresome afterthought, too, since long before she was born Dr and Mrs Lynn had passed to a consideration of the De Broglie theory of the electron. She had been brought up in a home in which meals were never to time and usually makeshift; she breathed an atmosphere in which the academic idea was everything and the practical fact of the moment nothing. She had long spindly legs and arms, an anaemic face, and spectacles and boots sizes too big. Her hair was lank and greasy, and the solitary redeeming feature was a clever mouth like her father's but without its accompanying long jaw.

For the first two days she stared at me through her great spectacles with an air of intense curiosity, as if I were a fish in an aquarium; but later I grew grudgingly to admire the gameness with which she joined in her brothers' sports and pranks. Her elder brother Bertie did far more for her than her mother, and it was not cheering to think of the life she must have led when they were at school. They treated her as a boy of their own age and by dint of much perseverance on both sides were already teaching her to bowl and bat in an orthodox manner.

Mentally she was a precocious child, a not uncommon result of being the youngest of a family; but Holly's precocity was a monstrous thing. She already knew more of elementary physics, biology and simple chemistry than her brothers would ever know; but of the ordinary commonplace joys of childhood she knew practically nothing.

By the spring of the following year the disadvantages of a week spent at Newton had faded into the background and I was looking forward to another invitation. Its atmosphere of freedom from restraint was not like any other house I had ever been in. I used to wonder sometimes why the three children had not turned out little savages. Presumably they were born civilised.

Of Paul Stafford's existence I suppose I'd been aware since the September before, when he came to the school, but only as one of the hundred and sixteen other boys enjoying the dubious advantages of education at Turstall. Then in April he moved into my form and into my dormitory. He was two years older than the boys he had been working with, and the school had decided to push him up a year so that the disparity in ages was not so great.

Of course, as everyone knows, he was born near Lancaster, the son of the village grocer, and at thirteen was serving behind the counter and running errands, his thoughts of schooling already done with. But Mr Stafford had come in for a little money and with determined ideas of betterment had decided his son should continue his education, and at a place which would lay its own veneer on him. Hence Paul, and hence his unpopularity. Today it would hardly matter, but in those days the idea that a boy should finish his education at a council school and then begin it again at Turstall was more than some of the more delicate-minded of us would accept. And some of the masters too.

He was a tall boy, which emphasised his backwardness, but also a strong and muscular one, which prevented the fact being too loudly commented on in his presence. No photographs of him remain of this particular time, except the small-scale school photographs, but I remember him with a shock of brown hair, cut short and standing up in a brush like a prize fighter's. He had light blue eyes and very long lashes which persisted even into middle age. Sometimes his eyes could be very cold, steely, when he encountered opposition; but more often they were intent, concentrated on the object before them, and then rather engaging. He had a strong Lancashire accent with a trace of Westmorland burr, which was easy to mimic.

We got friendly. I was tall and reedy, shy and self-contained, a poor mixer. I was hopeless at all games except cricket, and I couldn't box however much they put me in the ring. I could fight if necessary but then only with an effort of violence which might leave me the winner but for which I paid in nervous strain for hours after. He was older and had grown up in a community where one learned to look after oneself. But without fuss. In those days I thought he had no nerves. He was without talent for or interest in any games. He would sometimes commit bloomers in speech or behaviour which much diverted his classmates. I helped him to avoid these, although he never seemed too embarrassed when they happened.

The stories of his extreme poverty are well known and authentic enough; of his going to his first school with ill-patched and threadbare trousers which were a source of diversion even in the neighbourhood in which he lived; of his first pair of shoes that he wore all day on the wrong feet; of a two-roomed tenement without fire or food; of his mother's early death from over-work and malnutrition; of his father being helped by his brother to start the tiny shop that later just maintained him.

He was not a clever boy, which made more pathetic his father's determination to spend his small legacy so fruitlessly. Stafford senior could well have enlarged his shop or moved to a more prosperous village, or even made some provision for his old age. But no. He put down all his own troubles to lack of education. Paul must be different. Paul must work and get a scholarship to carry him to some university where he would take a degree. Stafford senior, Paul said, spoke of 'a degree' as if it were some charm to ward off want. A peculiar inflection always came into his voice when he referred to it. The qualified man, in whatever relatively humble capacity, would never, he believed, fear unemployment. A teacher, a civil servant, even—rising higher—a lawyer or a doctor. Paul must get a degree.

It might have been kinder if, after a term or two, Dr Marshall had told Mr Stafford that Paul had little or no hope of getting a scholarship anywhere, or any further education unless the legacy would run to it. Stafford senior would no doubt still have persisted and hoped, having overlooked the one inclination his son had shown by tanning the hide off him for stealing crayons from a stationer's shop. To say that when I first met him Paul had no ambition was almost true, for it had hardly dawned on him that the only thing he really wanted to do in life might be accounted a profession—of a sort—too.

No doubt it would have come to him sooner or later. Even had he had no further education beyond thirteen his talent would have surfaced and found its own level. Someone would have 'discovered' him. You cannot ignore or overlook or fail to notice something so powerful and so purposive. But as it happened it was the innocent affair of Dogden and the paper darts that gave it outlet and direction.

III

By now the war was raging. Paul had already been home twice with me to Grimsby, where my father had bought a practice ten years before. On the second visit my father was already in the RAMC and there was a total black-out in the port, against the risk of Zeppelin raids and enemy cruisers—for Scarborough and Hartlepool had already been bombarded. But my mother still allowed us to use our dinghy, and in that fine August of 1915 we seemed scarcely ever to be out of the boat. It was on his visits to us and in these troubled years that Paul developed his love of the sea and of small craft. And it must have been those holidays which, when the war extended long enough to draw him in, made him opt for the Navy.

When we returned to Turstall its staff, exiguous at the best of times, had been depleted by the loss of four masters, and three women only had so far come to take their place. Dogden, the maths master, of uncertain temper anyway, was in a vile mood. In fact, although he looked to us a man far gone in age, he was thirty-four and a bachelor, and during the holidays two separate ladies with bright smiles but hard eyes had presented him with a white feather.

Paul, slow at any but the simplest of sums, and coming from a background that Doggy despised, was an obvious butt, and I remember distinctly the first words addressed to him that morning. 'Stafford, stand up when I speak to you. You're lazy, you're idle, you're insubordinatious, you never have cared the toss of a button whether you do your work or not! I don't believe you even know what a square root is, unless you suppose it to be something your father grows in his vegetable garden!'

There was much laughter at this, and much laughter followed. If Doggy cared to entertain us with his sarcasms, well and good, so long as they were not directed at us. And it all helped to get through the forty-five minutes. But soon another diversion occurred. Dogden hated summer flies and of late had been suffocating his class by keeping the windows shut. The Headmaster chose this moment to put in one of his rare appearances. He came in noisily, banging the door, and stumped with his club foot across to the desk.

'Mr Dogden, pardon me; I came to ask you about— mm—mm—mm—mm—Infernally stuffy in here— mm—mm—mm—mm—Why don't you open the windows? mm—mm—mm . . .'

'Well, Dr Marshall, that is what I have always maintained—mm—mm—mm—it's largely a matter of a group decision . . .'

While they were talking Marshall limped across to the long window at the end of the room and Dogden went with him. So they had their backs to us. Paul had a talent for making paper darts, which he had passed on to me. We often practised at home, and now, perhaps to assert himself after a bad few minutes, he threw a dart across the room at me.

It came beautifully—I can see it now—describing a graceful arc like a glider of the future. Hoskin, the boy in front of me, tried to grab it, but I got there first.

17

There was a slight scuffle but the two masters were too occupied with their conversation to notice it. I barely took in that the dart was coloured before I straightened the tail and threw it back.

At that moment Marshall had opened the window and a fresh westerly breeze came into the room. The dart, homing moderately well—I was not as good at it as Paul—was caught by the breeze, swerved upwards and landed at Dr Marshall's feet as he turned to walk back.

All masters are particularly sensitive to anything which goes wrong in front of the Head—particularly anything which suggests they cannot keep their class under control. Dogden went purple. He snatched up the dart.

'*Who*—is responsible for throwing this—this thing?'

No one spoke.

'Unless the boy who threw this does not immediately stand up, the whole class will come back here after school and do an extra half hour of maths.'

There was a groan and a murmur and everyone looked expectantly at me. I stood up.

'*You*, Grant,' said Dogden ominously. Then he noticed the colouring on the dart and began to unfold it. On the piece of paper, drawn in crayons, was an insulting caricature which even he could not fail to recognise as being of himself.

The drawing was really of a satyr—though I doubt if Paul had heard the word at the time—in which a naked body covered with red hair from the waist down was surmounted by a head unmistakably Mr Dogden's. It carried a pitchfork in one claw, and impaled on the prongs was a struggling schoolboy.

Although I would have taken the blame, Paul was

soon on his feet too, to Dogden's obvious satisfaction. What made matters worse was that, followed by Dr Marshall, who I swear was hiding a faint smirk of amusement under his yellowing moustache, Dogden went to Paul's desk and instructed him to turn it out. So the sketch-book came to light.

I had known from the time of his first holiday with us of Paul's interest in sketching, but it had made no great impression on me. It was similar to knowing a boy who liked strumming on the piano: a quirk of character, a little talent. Sometimes he had shown me his sketches and they seemed rather good. There was one of me on our mantelpiece at home, but I thought I looked too lean in it and too melancholy.

Of particular interest in the sketch-book turned up by Dogden were crayon drawings of almost every master in the school, and quite a number of the pupils. They were not caricatures in the ordinary sense of the word, being more insulting in their near likeness and their loving care for detail. The most unfortunate part of the matter was that the three lady teachers had been drawn without any clothes on.

Being in a sense implicated in the first place, I was present at the interview in Dr Marshall's study.

'What you must appreciate, Stafford,' I remember Dr Marshall saying, 'is that your father is not paying your school fees with the idea that you should occupy your time making insulting studies of your headmaster and his colleagues. Nor do we exist and draw our salaries for the purpose of acting as models and butts for every young puppy who comes here with a talent for sketching. I trust you will come to realise that.'

'Yes, sir.'

'Indeed, I should feel I had failed in my duty if I allowed you to leave this establishment with such an impression. How old are you?'

'Sixteen, sir.'

'Old enough to know better. The more offensive juvenile antics should be behind one by then. Where did you learn your drawing?'

'Nowhere, sir.'

'Who taught you draughtsmanship? Not Mr Harper, surely?'

'No, sir. I could draw as long as I can remember.'

'And what did Mr Harper think of you? Alas, I shall not be able to ask him as he has answered his country's call.' A pause while the pages of the sketchbook crackled. 'Ever heard of Adrian Brouwer?'

'No, sir.'

'Dutchman. Lived in the seventeenth century. Died in Antwerp when not much more than thirty ... The un-beautiful on canvas ... One sees the best of him in Dresden and Munich ... Tell me, who informed you that I had one shoulder lower than the other?'

'No one, sir.'

'Yet I wear a pad which makes it unnoticeable to outsiders. Or so I thought. A perceptive young man. It disturbs me to punish such diligence.'

I was there standing just behind Paul, but at this stage I might not have existed. There was a strange concentration between the boy and the man. I remember staring at the ink pots on the desk—there were six or seven of them—and wondering what Marshall did with them all. Different colours for different moods?

'How many boys have seen this sketch-book, Stafford?'

'None, sir.'

'Grant?'

'No, sir.'

'You see, Stafford, there are two offences here. One is impudence, and an insult may be expiated by a few strokes of the cane. The other is the matter of the—hm—the drawing of Miss Atkins and the other two ladies. And that is altogether more serious.'

'Yes, sir.'

'You appreciate that?'

'Yes, sir.'

Dr Marshall took out a large grey handkerchief—grey perhaps from blackboards—and wiped his moustache.

'If you go on to an art school—and this would seem the obvious course—you will no doubt come to paint the nude figure many times. All artists do. All great artists have. It is their prerogative, and as an art form it is not considered to transgress the limits of decency. Nor perhaps would I have taken great exception to nude figures in your sketch-book had the faces been merely—figurative. But as it is, drawn with the faces of ladies known to us all, and all recent additions to our staff, it becomes grossly obscene. For that expulsion seems the natural punishment.'

There was a very long silence, during which the school clock chimed something.

Dr Marshall said: 'I am reluctant to do that for two reasons. First that the sketch-book was essentially private and there is no actual *evidence* that you intended to show it to others—though the fact that you had it in the classroom suggests otherwise. The second is that, in this holocaust we are now enduring, the minor indecencies of growing boys are dwarfed by the sacrifices they may shortly be expected to make for their king and country. That giant shadow falls over us all . . . So I shall cane you, Stafford, and for the moment leave it at that. But I have to warn you that if Miss Atkins or either of the other ladies should learn of this matter I may still have to dismiss you at a later date ... Now as to you, Grant ...'

IV

Thereafter Paul Stafford was a more amenable pupil. If he could never be talented at the more conventional subjects, he was at least no longer idle. His inability to grasp simple principles of learning seemed less evident. I was surprised. I hadn't thought a mere caning would wreak such a change. It was some months before I learned that Dr Marshall, in the absence of anyone capable of teaching art in the school, was himself taking Paul for two hours a week. It made all the difference.

I got to know this after Christmas when Paul told me he had been to London and had had an interview with a M. Becker who was the principal of the Grasse School, and that he had the half promise of a place when he was seventeen. When I speculated as to what Mr Stafford thought, Paul said: 'Father doesn't like it. He thinks I'll end up in the gutter where I came from. But old Marshall has persuaded him to go along with the idea.' He turned and stared at me with his pale long-lashed eyes. 'It's not going to be easy, Bill. But once I'm away from these patronising louts ...'

'They're not really so bad,' I said. 'It comes natural to some people to poke fun at what they don't understand. That's all there is to it.'

'Which is enough,' he said. 'Which is enough. Well ... Marshall's shown me a way, and I shall take it. I'm told there's money in commercial art. Maybe that's the way I'll go about it. Become the *success* that Father so earnestly desires. Who knows? Anyway, I'm not going to let anything or anyone stand in my way now.'

I looked at him and with the confidence of youth believed him. I sensed great purpose in him. It didn't then seem to me at all a peculiar attitude of mind—an 'I'll show them' attitude—with which to approach a vocation.

V

As the war advanced my summer stays with the Lynns became longer. Their company, abnormal on first encounter, became, by failing to change, more normal in an atmosphere of bloodshed and hysteria. The war was scarcely ever mentioned except as a passing inconvenience, a world aberration that even if it could not be avoided was best ignored. Fortunately for Dr Lynn, his work was considered of sufficient national importance for him to be left unmolested. And with the arrival of conscription the white feather ladies disappeared.

As the Kennet ran almost at the bottom of the garden, there was constant bathing for the young and much paddling about the reach in an old rowing boat and a leaky canoe. Mrs Lynn would also immerse herself in the river every morning at seven o'clock. The irreverent Holly, when she was older, said it was her mother's spiritual Ganges.

The four of us would scrape together a snack lunch and go off for the day to some shady spot further up the river, to bathe and play wild games and fish for trout. Then we would return about seven, ravenously hungry, to find the kitchen fire out and the breakfast things unwashed. Mrs Lynn, in a much darned jumper, short skirt, ankle socks over lisle stockings, and red morocco slippers, would be in the study playing over one of Bach's unaccompanied sonatas for the violin; and Dr Lynn would be upstairs in his room working out some theory to do with the relativity of acceleration.

The strange part of such a discovery would be that Holly would forget her hunger and cling with one arm round her father's neck wanting to know in simple terms what he was about, and Leo would immediately begin to argue dogmatically with his mother on just how the sonata should be played, leaving the only practical one, Bertie, and myself, to gather together a semblance of a meal.

When she was eleven Holly climbed an oak tree at school, and fell out of one of the branches. She was laid up for some time and was sent home where she would receive 'the best attention'. Thereafter she bowled, batted and walked with a slight limp.

'On my birthday too,' she said. 'Mummy had sent me a birthday cake she'd made herself. It'd caved in in the middle the way Mummy's cakes always do, but it was frightfully rich. I got none for a week.'

'I thought your birthday was at Christmas. Otherwise, why the name?'

'Oh, didn't you know? It was Daddy's doing. He decided to call me Horace after his favourite poet. When I wasn't a boy he made it Horatia, which was the nearest he could get. But the boys thought it foul, so everyone calls me Holly.'

'Yes, Horatia is a bit awful,' I agreed.

She stared at me a moment. 'And if you want to know, Bertie is called after Einstein and Leo's real name is Galileo. Only don't ever tell them I told you.

Who were you called after?'
'My mother's father.'
'Did he wear a kilt and paint his legs yellow?'
'Don't be a young ass,' I said.

Holly was twelve the year Leo and I were seventeen. Boarding school had given her a chance of regular meals—however stark and unappetising, they were more use to her than what she got at home—and regular hours, and she grew and strengthened under the regime. But she was not remotely good-looking; her legs, it seemed, would always be like the cricket stumps she so regularly bowled at; her face had filled out sufficiently to make her spectacles seem less disproportionate; but her complexion was sallow and her large eyes were a muddy grey. And her hair grew no less lank as the years passed. She would make an excellent teacher like her parents, for she had more brain than the two boys put together, and even a certain sense of responsibility that her parents lacked. Nature had made one of its frequent mal-arrangements; if Holly had had Bertie's looks and Bertie Holly's brains they would each have been better fitted for the world.

But we were the lucky generation. The young men who had been our immediate seniors at school were dying at Passchendaele, La Bassée, St Quentin, Péronne. It would soon be our turn to fill the gaps. Yet of the four of us, although we were called up, only Paul and Bertie saw active service. Leo and I were training at Kinmel Park when the Armistice was signed. Bertie survived his six months in France, Paul nearly twelve at sea.

One of Paul's biographers, A. H. Jennings, has supposed that he had some influence to get into the Navy, for, by the time he was called up it was the

Army's desperate shortage of manpower that overrode all other considerations. That he could have had any influence at all is of course nonsense; nor did we at Turstall even have a branch of the naval cadets. Paul never would tell me how it had happened. I believe he refused any other form of service and was prepared to go to prison as a conscientious objector if he didn't get his way. In some matters he had a mulish determination, and this must in the end have impressed the authorities. He had a tough time in the Navy, on a minesweeper, but about this too he had very little to say after. I only learned from another source that he had been blown up once and spent some hours on a raft in the North Sea.

But the Armistice came, and presently we were all 'demobbed', and the world began to lick its wounds, to bury its dead, to try to return to sanity after four years of manic-depressive psychosis. And we picked up our lives again, or tried to, from where they had left off. But nothing was the same again.

Chapter Two

I

So the world fit for heroes to live in was born, and the Jazz Age, and the day of the Shimmy, the One-Step and the Charleston. The age of the League of Nations, and Reparations and Disarmament. The age of Unemployment, and Votes for Women, and the Flapper, and the White Russians, the Locarno Pact, the Dawes Agreement. The age of disillusion and the dole.

Yet for four young men, and for many others like them, it was the beginning of a new life, life unshadowed by prospects of early death or mutilation, a life of opportunity and limitless years ahead.

Bertie, the first demobbed, showing no particular desire or aptitude for any of the expected things, was offered a job in an insurance firm in Reading and gratefully took it. The prospects were unexciting but, in a world where so many could find nothing, it was *work*. Leo still rather sulkily wanted to be something in the musical scene, but his mother said he had ideas bigger than his head: he could never become a front-rank pianist; as for composition, he had *some* talent, he might do some good for himself if he worked hard but it would take time. Meanwhile he stayed at home, desultorily answering advertisements for clerks and bookkeepers.

At nineteen I got a job as a cub reporter on the *Sheffield Daily Telegraph*; and Paul, the last to return to civilian life, finally took up his scholarship at M. Becker's Grasse School of Art in Chelsea.

Thereafter I lost touch with him for another year, and it was not until a chance assignment took me to London that I was able to look him up. I found him in a lodging house in the Bayswater Road, in which, conventionally, he had a top room with a dormer window and a fan-light. In the room was an easel, a single bed and two tables, everything possible cluttered with sketch pads, palettes, tubes of paint leaking basic colours, rags, sheets of glass and half-finished boards and canvases. The intervening years had changed him, and there is a self-portrait in the Walker Art Gallery that shows very much how he looked then.

In some ways Turstall had been bad for him. The war, and his return to a new, young society in London had helped to soften the combative inhibitions. The resentfulness had gone, but he was still very purposive, very self-contained. And much less uncouth. He was surrounded by portaits, one or two of which I tried to admire, but he was genuinely dismissive of them, contemptuous of his own work, not because in his view it was bad but because it ought to have been better.

In a pub round the corner we talked for an hour. He was hoping to get to France for a while: there was some sort of an exchange system between pupils of the Grasse School and the Ecole des Beaux Arts. He was working five nights a week washing dishes in a restaurant and had saved a few pounds: he hoped it would be enough. He wanted to be back for Christmas: in spite of the lure of Paris, London was the place where everything happened, the only place he really wished to be, to live, to work. He had 'sold' two portraits to friends and had one or two other small successes. With an optimism rare in him, he saw himself as able to make some sort of a living in a year or two. When was I coming to Town so that we could share a flat?

Chance, I said, was a fine thing, and I meant it with all conviction; for what he said was absolutely true: to a young man working on a provincial newspaper, or indeed to anyone interested, however peripherally, in the arts and in letters, London was the only place to be. Post-war London had, it seemed to me, every-thing—except the job to keep me there.

Before I left, Paul introduced me to a dozen of his friends: young, lively, talkative, knowing about the things that 'mattered', admirably emancipated. And two pretty girls who had an eye for him. One of them was called Olive Crayam. That meant nothing to me at the time. I went home terribly discontented, envious of his life, though it was clear that it was still the monthly supplement from 'the old man' that enabled him to exist.

Although on that visit there were obvious signs that his work was maturing, I was absolutely dumbfounded to hear that one of his paintings was to be in the Summer Exhibition at the Royal Academy. In a single year he had made the step from total obscurity to being among those who counted. It was, of course, the portrait of M. Becker himself—now in the Columbus Gallery of Fine Art, Ohio. That M. Becker had consented to sit was a sufficient guide to what he thought of his pupil.

In those days the importance of art and literature rated much higher than they do today. Well-known authors were invited to contribute centre-page articles on current topics; their opinions were sought and their opinions were news. Similarly the Royal Academy Summer Exhibition never opened without a full two pages in the quality newspapers, devoted to illustration and comment. And Paul Stafford's portrait (of a well-known teacher with a following), well hung, and the work of a newcomer, attracted a lot of attention. John Grey, writing in the *Morning Post*, went over the top about it.

'There is about this work the decided accent of a young man born to paint portraits, born to draw from each sitter perhaps the one unforgettable and vital impression which is waiting to be set down. Mr Stafford has a remarkable future.'

Others were more cautious but the over-all impression was that a new talent had arrived.

Sir Laurence Bright, who made a fortune out of army belts during the war, wrote a rather pedestrian autobiography which, published at his own expense, soon sank from sight. But I came across a second-hand copy on a bookstall the other day, and in it he mentions his visit to Burlington House that year and his reactions to Paul's picture. He wrote to the unknown artist, and suggested that he might commission him to paint the writer's twin daughters. Paul was then in Paris, so replied that he would be willing to do this on his return, and a price and date were agreed without their ever having met.

Sir Laurence goes on:

'Mr Stafford arranged to be in Hertford by the 9.30 train, and I sent my chauffeur to fetch him from the station. I and my daughters, too conventionally, expected to meet a youngish man, perhaps bearded, with a pale sensitive face, a velvet jacket, a glowing black bow tie. Instead a clumsy, ill-dressed youth of twenty-one was shown into the drawing-room. He might more properly have been an apprentice engineer or an omnibus driver. My first thought was that Mr Stafford was ill and had sent a servant to present his apologies. The anti-climax for Elizabeth and Pamela was profound. However, this first bad impression soon wore off. Mr Stafford had a way with him, particularly, it seemed, with young ladies.'

Later Paul spoke ill of his first commissioned portrait, but I believe it is still in the Bright family home where he painted it. And it made him money and it was a beginning.

Not that he was remotely out of the wood. It was still his father's help that kept him above the level of poverty.

However, that soon changed when he met Diana Marnsett.

II

The Hon. Mrs Brian Marnsett was the second daughter of Lord Crantell. She had married young—just before the war—and her husband, Colonel Marnsett, twenty years older than herself, was a rich and distinguished man. Apart from being a director of the Westminster Bank and of the White Star shipping line, he owned one of the best art collections in the country and was a notable philanthropist, having bought a number of well-known and valuable pictures for the nation. He was, however, a dull stick, and since the Crantells were still trying to recoup on the third baron's dissolute extravagances, it was not unnaturally supposed that Diana had married her husband less for love than for money. She confirmed this view by becoming a leader of a smart set which led fashion in London and dispensed patronage to the arts.

When I first met her, which was a year or so later, I thought her one of the most beautiful women I'd ever seen. Born in India when her father was governor of Bengal, she had brought home with her a certain duskiness under the eyes which contrasted in a marvellous way with the extreme pallor and purity of her skin. She was tall and slender with a mass of fine ebony hair and dark, wide-set eyes that could be either soulful or imperious. Her profile was not so good, and she knew it. People could close their eyes to a suggestion of sharpness here, just as her husband must have closed his eyes to a good deal in her behaviour. She accepted admiration as her right. She had favourites but generally tended to change them quickly. She was a born hostess. When Paul first met her she was thirty.

It's quite difficult in this permissive age, when everybody leaps into bed with everyone else—at least, according to the media—when certainly a man and a woman can live together without benefit of clergy and no one really lifts an eyebrow to judge, to remember a state of affairs where, in spite of the emancipating effects of the bloodiest war in history, morality was only slowly shifting its values away from the rigid codes of the Victorian age. Of course there was a lot of immorality—if that is a word that can still be used— as there has been at all times—but it had to be hidden, kept quietly under cover, not flaunted or publicised. If it was so publicised it could still do a great deal of harm, to one's social life, to one's financial expectations, to one's actual career.

Paul at this time was involved with Mary Compton—one of the two girls I had met on that first visit to him in London—but to what lengths I have no means of knowing, and Mary Compton, who married shortly afterwards, clearly never had any wish to say more about it. Her attachment with Paul broke soon after he met Diana.

Diana Marnsett's interest in Paul was immediate. Through her husband and some of her friends she knew enough about painting to see his obvious talents; and, to a woman jaded with the attentions of smooth young gentlemen, his blunt, uncompromising maleness must have made a special appeal.

He had not known her a month when she offered him the advice that it would pay him to have some of these rough corners 'rounded off'. There was an elocutionist in Hanover Square: a couple of lessons a week would make all the difference. Her husband's tailor in Cork Street would fit him out, and he was never in a hurry for his money when someone came in with the right introduction. As for his hair, Brown of Bond Street was an artist in his own way too and would wreak an interesting change.

He did. They did. They all did. When at the beginning of the following year to my delight I was offered a job—though at no higher wages—in the London office of the then *Manchester Guardian*, and went to see him after the interview I was astonished, aghast at the change.

Presumably it was Mr Brown of Bond Street who had divined the trouble with his hair. He now wore it long—or long for those days—and it had ceased to stand up like an aggressive brush at the front, but curled away from his forehead in a good glossy mane. He hadn't adopted 'arty clothes', but wore well-cut, heavy tweeds with a suggestion of flair. Most surprising was his voice, from which most of the flat vowels had disappeared. No doubt Mr Shaw's Professor Higgins would have been able to tell not only that Stafford came from Lancashire, but exactly what part. For normal people that didn't apply. For normal people he had a new voice.

I remember at the time being not only aghast but disappointed. For eight years our friendship had run very true, without flaw. I thought highly of his talents and believed he would become famous. This pandering to snobbery lowered him. I didn't say so but commented simply that he had taken Mrs Marnsett's advice to heart.

He said sharply: 'Of course I have, because it's the soundest I've ever been offered. I have a supreme contempt for people who judge by such things, but since ninety per cent of the people I shall be mixing with think that way, it's common sense to do it. If I can't change them I can at least change myself.'

'Which means,' I said, 'that you have a supreme contempt for ninety per cent of the people you mix with.'

'Well, eighty-nine,' he said, with a gleam in his eye.

By now gossip was linking his name with Diana Marnsett in a way that went beyond friendly advice.

I noticed that he didn't renew his suggestion that we should share a flat. He was somehow contriving to live a smart life—into which I perhaps would no longer easily fit—and yet was painting six and seven hours a day. The occasional commission came his way. A young woman who didn't like him implied that Mrs Marnsett was supporting him, but I felt I knew him better than that.

One day we had lunch together and Paul told me he had just had a brush with Adrian Becker. What about? I asked in surprise.

'I showed him my three entries for this year's Academy. He doesn't like them.'

'He liked his own portrait, didn't he?'

'Oh, yes. But after seeing this later stuff he referred me to the Bible and its statement that you cannot serve both God and Mammon.'

I waited, expecting more.

'He says I'm talented enough to know the difference between gold and gilt. He says these paintings are too facile. That I'm not a great portraitist anyhow, that I have other fields to plough. That portraiture comes easiest to me and that, having now done little else for two years, I should drop it and concentrate on other things. He didn't actually bring up the question of my birthright and a mess of pottage, but I was afraid any moment he might.'

'Well . . .' I said. 'What's your view on that?'

'I think probably he's right—though I don't see it in such black and white terms.'

'And what are you going to do about it?'

Paul's long lashes veiled the expression in his eyes. Certainly the new grooming had improved his looks.

'Nothing.'

'Nothing?'

'Nothing. I've told you long ago, Bill, where I'm going. So far I haven't let anything stand in my way. D'you think I'm prepared to let my own talent—if that's what it is—do so now?'

'No,' I said, looking at him.

'No, indeed. I've seen people do that sort of thing before. Casting away the substance for the shadow. What's the good of fame after you're dead, if you live your life in poverty, and empty-minded, half-literate snobs are able to patronise you and get the best of everything?'

'The trouble is to decide which is substance and which is shadow,' I said cautiously.

'Nonsense. It's perfectly plain. When I get to the top maybe I shall be able to please myself. People are like sheep. Once you get ahead of the flock the rest of the flock will follow.'

'I hope you're right.'

'Anyway, I must earn my living. I've bled Father white and can't expect more. I don't *want* more. With luck I shall manage.'

Soon after this I took a week's holiday at Newton. Leo had been unable to follow Bertie into commerce and was still beating out his life on the piano. But, in spite of her severe words, Leo was his mother's ewe lamb, and she had so far shaken herself out of her preoccupations with Greek, the violin and the latest vegetable seeds to take a long journey to see her brother Frederick and put Leo's plight to him in her high-pitched fluty tones. The result was that Brother Frederick had come up to scratch and Leo was shortly coming up to London.

Holly was away at school on this visit, but I saw a good deal of Bertie, who was still living at home and playing cricket for Berkshire. He had also developed an interest in Toc H; 'Some sort of a secret society,' Mrs Lynn explained, a view to which she adhered in spite of all efforts to correct her.

Chapter Three

I

If you turn to the press reviews of the Royal Academy Summer Exhibition of the following year you will find some diversity of opinion over Paul Stafford's second really important picture, the portrait which was to be probably the most discussed painting of the season.

Pride White in the *Observer*, summing up the show, commented:

'Painted as this is by a young man only just twenty-three, Paul Stafford's "Diana Marnsett" is a work which must make a critic of imagination anxious about the future. It offers, at least so far as portraiture goes, the uncanny spectacle of a talent which on the very threshold of its career seems to have nothing more to learn.'

Alfred Young in the *Daily Telegraph* did use the word 'facile', but on the whole the comments were favourable. As it happened, the *Spectator* had invited the French critic René Buerchel to review the exhibition for them, and he, after some half-hearted praise of Paul's painting, went into a long discourse on the psychology of women who become 'professional beauties'. He argued that Stafford had treated the portrait of Diana Marnsett in this light: he had not so much idealised Diana as depicted the idol which men saw and which women came to see in themselves.

Paul became a name. Noel Coward—roughly the

37

same age as Paul—wrote somewhere of living and having his being 'in extreme poverty among wealthy friends'. This was exactly Paul's position. Talked of, photographed, attender at first nights, guest at parties at Deauville and St Moritz, the money he made went on clothes and keeping up a front. He had moved to a small studio in Chelsea—not far from the Grasse School, with whose principal he was no longer on speaking terms—and there he sometimes held court, usually with Diana at his side.

Yet he never lost touch with old friends, and whenever he could would contrive some benefit on their behalf. When Leo came to London to study at the Royal College of Music he invited him to a couple of his parties. Not that they had ever been entirely 'simpatico'. Leo never understood Paul's self-contained manner, his lack of any outward sign of temperament. He thought Paul dull, without spark. And Paul had little patience with Leo's ebullient enthusiasms, his love of discussions that didn't seem to matter. If Paul thought a thing he said so, and that was the end of it: no point in going on. Leo loved to have a case to argue, to put it one way, then another, according to the response he got, even to do an about-turn if it suited him. He chattered and assumed attitudes and was always concerned with ethics and social significance.

So it was partly as a concession to me that Leo was invited, and very soon I wished he hadn't been. Paul had introduced me to Diana Marnsett four months before, commenting satirically that perhaps I would divert some of La Marnsett's attentions from himself. There may have been by then a grain of truth in it, for Paul was becoming notoriously fickle with his women; but Diana rightly would not be diverted. Unfortunately Leo achieved the end playfully set for me.

Leo might not be going to hit any headlines; but at a piano, which by now he could play very well, with his handsome Roman head set with its black curls, and his great muscular white body, Diana found him irresistible. There was in fact little resistance on either side. Leo fell for her instantly, and was far too self-absorbed to be respectful or subtle about it. He grasped the forbidden fruit with both hands.

Paul was not jealous, only amused. With a greater sense of responsibility for Leo's welfare, I was a bit anxious and eventually tackled him about it. Paul's affair had at least been discreet. His, being Leo, naturally was less so; and Colonel Marnsett, long-suffering though he might be, could probably turn nasty if too obviously provoked. It wouldn't be a happy beginning, I pointed out to Leo, if he were to be involved in a divorce case at the very outset of his career.

'I should welcome it,' said Leo. 'Lord, man, d'you think I like seeing her tied to that withered old bounder? If she were free I'd marry her tomorrow!'

'On prospects and a family allowance?' I suggested.

He flung out of his chair. 'You know damned well I can't earn more or I would! I'll earn presently. But she has money of her own. Yes, I'd even sponge on her rather than see her tied to him.'

'What does she feel about that?'

He looked at me with a sort of angry hauteur. 'Good God, man, d'you think we talk about money when we're together, when every minute's precious?'

'No,' I said. 'Sorry. But these prosaic details may crop up if you're not careful. I'm only trying to be helpful.'

'Well, shut up and talk about something else, then.'

Paul smiled when I discussed this conversation with him.

'Diana's been a good friend to me,' he said, 'but I never got too deeply involved. It doesn't do with her. Actually I *don't* much like the way she's treating Leo. I know she says she's in love with him and all that— but hers isn't the same kind of love. Women are funny that way, I think. You imagine them the most romantic of creatures, but really they're intensely practical.'

'Speaking from experience,' I said,

He smiled again. 'Speaking from experience. Also from painting them. A good portrait is a kind of wooing. People begin by trying to hide themselves behind the subterfuge of their best behaviour. But after a while it slips. Of course, it's easier for an artist to see through a woman than it is for a lover.'

'Diana's having a whale of a time.'

'Well, Diana is intoxicated with her own beauty. She's no more capable of resisting Leo than a glutton is of taking the biggest and juiciest chocolate. She's become even more lovely this month—have you noticed? But mark you, she's perfectly level-headed underneath. Only let her get some danger signal from the Colonel and she'll drop Leo flat. At least, that's how I see it. I may be doing her an injustice.'

'All I hope,' I said, 'is that she sees Marnsett's danger signal in time.'

Leo naturally enough was responsible for the sudden termination of the affair. Since talk, argument, deep humourless discussion were the very breath of life to him, could he be expected to keep quiet about the greatest experience of his existence? Not at all. At one time I was afraid he might even write home with details of the whole affair.

Actually little of the truth reached Newton; though such was their inconsequence that one wonders if this news would have shaken the academic calm.

And then, true to Paul's prediction, Diana saw the red light. A concert of Bela Bartok music she had promised to attend found Leo alone and an empty seat beside him. The next day it was known that Colonel and the Hon. Mrs Brian Marnsett had left for a holiday in Scotland.

. . . We all thought Leo had taken the matter pretty well. After all, it's not pleasant to come up to London, an intense and unsophisticated young musician, to be taken up by one of the most beautiful women of her time and the leader of her set, to have a presumably passionate affair with her, to exchange Heaven knows how many protestations of undying devotion, to bask in the glory of being the one chosen above all others, and then to find when it comes to the pinch that she prefers her husband after all. One needs a cool head, a good sense of proportion and, maybe, a sense of irony. Leo was deficient in all three.

Later I learned that he had written to her every day, having assured himself that her attitude was a manoeuvre to deceive her husband. It kept him going. He even went so far as to deride us secretly for imagining the affair was finished.

But when she returned she refused to see him, and when they met once in public she turned her back on him. It was hard then not to realise that the only victim of one's deception was oneself. I think he convinced himself that everybody was now going to laugh uncontrollably at his downfall. And that was insufferable.

One morning I was sitting at my desk wondering

if the League of Nations would be able to prevent war between Italy and Greece over the murder of an Italian general, when I was connected to a professor at the Royal College of Music, who seemed concerned to know whether I was as close a friend of Mr Leo Lynn as he had been told.

'Why? Is anything wrong?'

'Well, we're not sure. He's been absent for the last week without explanation or apology. A friend thought you might know where he might be.'

'No . . . I suppose you've sent to his lodgings?'

'They say he's not been there since Monday. We wired his home but they've heard nothing from him.'

'Oh,' I said, frowning my disquiet at the receiver.

'I'm afraid there's not much left for us to do but inform the police. His attendances, of course, have been irregular for some time, and we're not anxious to raise an unnecessary scare. . .'

'Can you give me until this evening? I may or may not be able to help, but I could try. There are one or two places . . .'

'Of course. But if you could let us know. I think we must do something more positive by tomorrow morning at the latest . . .'

When he had hung up I rang Paul and fortunately he was free. He said he'd meet me at Leo's lodgings in half an hour.

When we got there a middle-aged woman opened the door. She had enlarged eyes and a thick neck and seemed indisposed to let us in.

'Have you no idea where he might have gone?' I asked.

'He's only in for breakfast usually and I see nought of him besides, except when I goes up to clean his room. And a regular mess it is too. There he sits

42

strumming on 'is piano while I pushes the carpet-sweeper round 'is feet.'

'Does he—did he ever bring a lady back with him?'

'Not if I knew anythink about it he didn't! I don't have no loose behaviour in this 'ouse. But last Sunday Gertie, that's the maid, did see 'im leaving with a young woman, and told me. I was going to tackle 'im with it but I've not 'ad the chance.'

Under pressure she summoned Gertie, who confirmed this information. She had not seen the visitor's face but had heard her speak with a foreign accent.

Nebulous ideas of Diana using broken English to disguise her identity moved through my mind and were expelled. Diana surely would not come to such a place under any guise.

'May we go up to his room?' I asked.

'I suppose so. You won't find much there.'

She was right in that the ancient grand piano dominated the rest of the shabby furniture and left little space for manoeuvre. I wondered what her other lodgers said about the noise. Easier to be a painter.

While the landlady was shouting something down the stairs I said: '*Another* girl? Surely to heaven he's not been keeping two going.'

Paul shook his head. 'The Diana affair has been over for all practical purposes for five weeks. He may have been seeking consolation.'

'The same consolation so soon?'

Paul rubbed his chin. 'We had a dog at home that used to sit up and beg to Father for his supper every night. When Father was laid up with a broken leg we used to find the dog sitting up and begging to a broomstick that stood in the corner behind Father's chair.'

'You've got a nasty mind,' I said.

Paul wandered aimlessly round the room, staring at himself in the mildewed mirror, smearing a finger with the dust of the mantelpiece, taking in the battered gas fire, the unemptied ash-trays.

He said: 'Suppose I go down and get Mrs What's-it to let me phone Diana. After all, she might have some knowledge of his movements.'

'There are some letters here,' I said. 'D'you think it would be all right to read them?'

'Please yourself.'

While he was gone I picked up the letters and glanced through them. Presently he came back.

'Sometimes,' he said, 'I don't think Diana is a very nice character. I mean is she *really* prepared to give herself to a man and then drop him like a discarded toffee paper?'

'You prophesied that.'

'But there are ways and ways. I hold no brief for Leo; I know he's made a fool of himself. What I implied was that when you scratched a woman's security you found underneath a cool common sense, an eye to the main chance, which is not altogether admirable but is certainly excusable. But when you scratch Diana you get granite—or maybe it's cheap flint.'

'There's nothing in the letters. There's this card: "*Mlle Jacqueline Dupaix, Teacher of Ballroom Dancing, 4 Markham Mansions, Paddington.*" I wonder . . .'

'Near my old haunts,' said Paul. 'It's not the sort of district Diana would approve of. Bring that card along and let's try Miss Dupaix.'

We bade goodbye to the landlady, who was waiting suspiciously on the steps, and took a tube.

Markham Mansions was even poorer than Leo's address, and we climbed four flights and pressed the bell without much hope of finding the lady at home at this hour. But a girl came to the door and answered to the name we inquired for.

I let Paul do the talking. By this time experience had done far more than tuition or cultivation to give him an easy manner.

Mlle Dupaix was very young, with dark eyes and a sulky mouth and a habit of flinging back a lock of black hair from her brow. She would not admit us, even when our mission was made known, and kept a hand up to the neck of her dressing-gown as if she suspected our intentions.

She made no secret of the fact that Leo had been there, but said he had left that morning. Leo had been sharing her room since Sunday night. She gave dancing lessons both here and in Greek Street, where she had met Leo. She had known him a month. He was very unwell, very upset, suffering from a malaise. He had said he was coming and had come. He had stayed and not gone out. They had cooked their meals together. This morning he had said he was going and had gone. No, she did not know where. Possibly home; who could tell? Now, please, she was busy.

We stared together at the door where a moment before her dark, sulphurous but attractive face had been.

'Is she telling the truth?'

'Yes,' said Paul.

'I got that impression too.'

We went down the stairs.

'Well,' I said, 'Leo's particular broomstick isn't a common prostitute.'

'No, indeed,' said Paul. 'A distinctly uncommon one. I'd like to paint her as Madame de Montespan. I've always wanted to paint Madame de Montespan.'

I glanced at him. 'Yes, what is this idea you've got?'

'What idea?'

'Someone told me you were thinking of painting a series—famous courtesans, they said. Using, I presume, present day models.'

'That's the idea.'

'With what end in view?'

'What end could there be except the usual? To exhibit. Probably to sell. It seems to me an interesting notion.'

I kicked some mud off my heel. 'It isn't exactly a forward step, is it?'

'What d'you mean?'

'Well . . . it's *illustration*, isn't it? It's not quite the—the creative art I thought you were aiming at.'

'You'll sound like old Becker soon, Bill. Serving God and Mammon etc. Anyway that objection is *rubbish*. Plain *rubbish*. What about Rubens and his "Rebecca" and his "Sarah", and five hundred other people out of the Bible? What about "The Last Supper"? Is that illustration? What about Vermeer's "Diana at her Toilette"? Or "Christ in the House of Martha and Mary"? Illustrations? Or Rembrandt's allegorical paintings? Or just a few thousand others?'

'You out-gun me,' I said. 'Sorry I spoke.'

'No need to be. But don't join the crap-brigade. There are one or two critics have got me in their sights—I was too good too young. The fact that I'm going to paint a series of high-class prostitutes doesn't accord with accepted ideas quite as well as if I was painting the twelve thousandth allegorical portrait of the Virgin Mary. That's all.'

We had been walking back towards the tube.

I said pacifically: 'So what's the next move about Leo?'

46

'I suppose we could telephone again, see if by any chance we've crossed in the post. Though my general feeling is to let it drop.'

'We'll telephone,' I said.

We entered a near-by call-box and I rang Leo's lodgings. The now familiar voice of Leo's landlady came crackling through the wire.

Who? Mr Who? Never heard of him. Oh, Mr Lynn. Yes, he'd just come in, just after we'd left. See him? No, she hadn't seen him. She knew his footsteps. Speak to him?

The line faded out, became clear again. Speak to him? Hold on: she'd see.

A long wait. Hullo. Were we still there? She'd been up to his room but he wouldn't come down. Yes, she'd given the name. Well, there it was; it wasn't her business if we'd fallen out over something . . .

Contact ended, and I hung up and explained the position to Paul.

He gave a shrug of impatience. 'Oh, blast the fellow; if he wants to nurse his grievance, let him. Anyway, you can phone the school. I'm going home to do some work.'

I didn't move. 'I've got a hunch, Paul.'

'Well?'

'I'd like to see him.'

'Well, go and hold his hand if you want to; I've done with the fellow, leading us all over London.'

'Can you spare another half-hour?'

'On a good purpose, yes. Not on consoling a sulky idiot.'

'Come on,' I said. 'One sulky idiot is enough.'

I don't know if I had any inkling of the truth at this stage, but certainly some very strong impulse persuaded me to go.

Leo's goitrous landlady stood exasperated, knuckles on hips, as we mounted the stairs. I went to Leo's door and knocked. There was no answer, so I tried the door. It was locked. I knocked again. Paul suddenly wrinkled his nose. 'Out of the way, Bill.'

He went back, took a run, butted into the door. It creaked and complained, but held firm.

He raised a foot and kicked violently at the panel just below the handle. after a few kicks it began to splinter, and he was able to get a hand in and upwards and turn the key. Amid shouts of protest from the mounting landlady we opened the door and entered a room full of gas.

II

We dragged Leo out on the landing. He was breathing still but was a very bad colour. We knelt there on the ragged linoleum trying to apply what resuscitation we could think of while the landlady moaned complaints about the damage done to her door and, when she could spare the time, offered useless advice on getting a doctor. In the end Paul shouted her down with a demand for water. I think it was his furious face more than anything that sent her scurrying.

I've seldom seen anyone so angry as Paul was that afternoon at Leo's action. In spite of his humble origin and the apparent ease with which he was at present adapting himself to a sophisticated way of living, he had certain ingrained values that his social behaviour didn't touch. Even a sense of form. This incident to him was bad form. He couldn't stand the hysterical in any guise. That anyone should try to put an end to himself for the inadequate reasons that moved Leo;

48

that anyone should take himself so seriously; particularly that it was Leo—and over a woman *he* had introduced him to . . .

We worked on Leo for a few minutes, but as soon as it became clear that the suicide attempt was going to be as much of a failure as the love affair that had provoked it, Paul got up, dusted his hands and left the rest to me. Then he limped off—having bruised his foot in breaking the door—before Leo had properly come round.

Later, at Leo's request, I went to Newton and told the Lynns a faked story to explain his absence from the Royal College of Music. They swallowed it without question. But Leo was so down I was a bit afraid that, despite promises to the contrary, he might give a repeat performance with greater success. It was with relief that I saw him begin to take an interest in his music again, and at the end of the year he left for Paris to continue his studies there.

Paul never afterwards mentioned the matter to me in any way. It was as if it was something indecent he had witnessed. Nevertheless I believe this was very much a motivating force—and one which has never been mentioned before—in the notorious quarrel in which he was to become involved.

But before that he married.

Chapter Four

I

This is not meant to be a biography of Paul Stafford. It is the story of my relationship with him and those nearest to him. It is not meant to be the story of *my* life; yet inevitably something of my life must come in. That is what I mean by lack of perspective. Although often the observer, it was impossible for me to be the detached observer.

Thus with Olive Crayam. She'd been a student of M. Becker's at the Grasse School, and Paul had known her there. I had met her through Paul, and we had taken a fancy to each other. We'd been out together a number of times; twice I'd gone back to her apartment which she shared with two girls; the other girls were out; but little happened to match the lurid fancies of today. With Olive I think nothing *would* have happened, even if it had got that far. She was careful that nothing should occur before marriage. To some girls that is a matter of principle, and then in my out-dated view it is admirable. Olive's carefulness was more a matter of calculation.

Paul had been commissioned to do the designs for *A Midsummer Night's Dream* at the Old Vic—another feather in his cap—and although all this work was initially figurative, he extended his commission to paint a half dozen of the main characters personally. Little Mark Alderson, who was playing Puck, was unavailable, so Paul asked Olive to sit for him.

She was right for it: very small, with small bones, lovely rounded limbs, unnoticeable breasts, a mischievous, gay expression. Auburn gold hair cut short—it was the day of the shingle—large and very beautiful ice-green eyes, a milky skin, small delicate ears.

So she sat for him, and the next thing they were engaged. Knowing him very well as I did and her better than most, it never seemed to me to be 'on' as a likely match. Others of course have pointed out the advantage to them both. Paul was a rising man in the profession in which she had a fair talent: although of working-class origin he was quickly becoming one of London's most successful portraitists; he might become another Sargent; certainly he had an entry into the sort of society she would seek and enjoy. For his part, aside from her looks which probably suggested a dozen different poses, she came of a county family which traced its ancestry back to the Wars of the Roses, and in her turn she could bring him a society, and commissions in that society, which otherwise he wouldn't attain to.

If one had been able to overlook a mere matter of temperament it might indeed have been the perfect match.

Her father, Sir Alexander Crayam, was a tall, thin, desiccated man high in the Civil Service, with an absent manner, glazed eyes and a habit of moving his lips when he was not talking, as if dictating everlasting memos. Her mother was dark and neurasthenic, hated enclosed spaces, and complained of blinding headaches and lassitude. There had been three children, and the two eldest, both boys, had been drowned in a boating accident in Scotland.

Olive was twenty-one and Paul twenty-four. There was no cause for delay. It was going to be a grand wedding, and almost every guest was to be a potential sitter. Sir Alexander rented them a small house in Royal Avenue, and it was there that I frequently met them in the days before the wedding.

Olive went out of her way to be nice to me, in a sisterly way, of course, as if anxious to make it clear that she had no intention of coming between Paul and his best friend; and I appreciated this; though I remember at the time being ashamed of myself for wondering if it all rang true. One day, I know, we were leaving at the same time, while Paul was staying on to lock up after a plasterer had finished. It was raining, and she offered me a lift in her little Riley.

After we had driven for a while she said: 'You're a dear man, Bill. I sometimes think I wouldn't have minded marrying you too.'

I looked at her fingers on the wheel. 'Polygamy is not a proper subject for a would-be bride.'

She laughed. 'OK. I'll spare your blushes. It was just a thought.'

'Of course,' I said, 'as best man I shall be standing next to Paul at the wedding, so perhaps we can whisper our vows on the side.'

She let in the clutch. 'Let's try.'

The screen-wipers stopped as she accelerated sharply away, then began to move again as she half-released the pedal. I looked at her composed face with its bow lips, tightly curling hair, skin of incredible fineness. The inscrutable Puck. I'm not sure that anyone has satisfactorily explained the psychology of smallness. Because small people feel themselves ignored, they tend to become thrusters: the Napoleons of the world are made as well as born. Legends too grow round them. When, a few years later, Chancellor

Dolfuss was murdered by Hitler's thugs, few people knew enough of him to decide whether his good deeds more than balanced his ill, all they knew was that 'little Dolfuss' had been foully done to death, and a wave of indignation swept Europe. In her own way Olive had the same advantages, and she made the most of them.

I said: 'What do your parents think of the marriage?'

'Disappointed.'

'They're hiding it well.'

'Oh, yes. But I was their remaining ewe lamb. Of course they weren't *too* fussy. Any old duke would have done.'

'Paul's going a long way.'

'And how far are you going, Bill?'

'Remains to be seen.'

'Not as far as you should if you stay in Paul's shadow.'

'I don't think that applies.'

'Be sure it doesn't. Were *you* disappointed?'

'What about?'

'The wedding, of course, you silly boy.'

I was on the point of replying as if the question was meant, was I disappointed for Paul; just in time I avoided the awful bloomer.

'I shall be envious on Tuesday.'

She laughed, pleased with the answer. 'Diana Marnsett is furious. But really furious.'

'I'm not surprised.'

'She looked on Paul as her special *protégé*, her special possession. She wanted him always dancing attendance.'

'I don't think his worst enemies could ever see Paul as a dancing man.'

'How far did it go between them, do you know?'

'Afraid I don't.'

'Dear Bill, always so loyal.'

'It's not a question of loyalty,' I said, irritated. 'I'm not his keeper.'

We stopped at a traffic policeman. 'Light me a cigarette, will you?'

I did this. She said: 'Well, if La Marnsett has any girlish fancies about keeping tags, she'll have to think again.'

'Olive,' I said. 'Diana Marnsett was invaluable to Paul a couple of years ago. He wouldn't have got where he is so soon without her. It's common sense and common manners to remember that. But that's all. That's it. Forget the rest.'

'How wise you are.' This was not meant.

I began to speak again, and then stopped.

'What were you going to say?'

'No matter.'

We drove on to my lodgings. The car stopped and I turned up the collar of my raincoat before dashing for the steps.

'What were you going to say?'

'It wouldn't help.'

'Try me.'

'No advice is more unwelcome than the well-meant. It's just that—knowing Paul—and wishing you well, I would say, don't shackle him. You'll get your own way better with a loose rein—one he's not aware of. That way I think he'll be very indulgent—and kind.'

'Thank you, Uncle Bill,' she said, showing her pointed eye-teeth in a wide warm smile.

I left her with a feeling of unease. She still in an odd perverse way attracted me physically—perhaps always would—and, since the Puck painting, I for ever seemed to see her in the revealing boy's clothes. I could understand Paul's feelings for her, his wish to use her as a model again and again, his desire to paint her naked—if she would let him. Sensually she was a presence, inescapable. But what went on in that precise, cool, feminine mind? How far was she *committed*? At times these last weeks I had felt the first faint prickings of dislike. Or was this just jealousy? Because I was afraid she would come between Paul and me? Of course, that *must* happen. But would it break my association with them altogether? Behind her warmth there was an unwarmth. Behind her openness there was calculation. Behind her friendliness there was possessiveness. How far, subjectively, was I misjudging her?

A couple of days after this I went round to Paul's old place and found him working on a portrait, so waited in the kitchen drinking coffee until he had done. To pass the time I looked through a bunch of newspaper reviews of the year's Royal Academy exhibition. Paul had had his full quota again. It was becoming customary. I noticed the critics on the whole concentrated on 'Puck' as the work most worthy of mention. I picked out the adjectives. 'Brilliant.' 'Ingenious.' 'Savoury.' 'Enchanting.' Who could have wished for better? Almost the only dissenting voice was again Alfred Young in the *Daily Telegraph*.

'Mr Stafford has been the victim of a reputation too easily acquired. He does his obvious talents injustice by neglecting taste in every element in these pictures, except that brilliant sense of tonality in which he generally excels. Despite the advantage of a very striking model, his "Puck" is hard, the painting is metallic, the foliage is raw, there is no taste in the expression, air, or modelling.'

I put down the cuttings and picked up a list of wedding guests. As I was glancing down it Paul came in.

'Some people say children are difficult sitters, but I prefer them. They've so much less to hide.'

'Your father's name isn't here,' I said. 'Shouldn't it be, just to plan the seating arrangements?'

Paul helped himself to coffee. 'I must go back in a minute: there are a few things I want to add now the boy's gone. Father? Oh, Father's not coming.'

'Why, is he ill?'

'No. I've not invited him. I've written to him, of course, to explain why.'

'Write to me on the same subject,' I said.

Paul stared into his cup, then dabbed a spot of paint off his index finger. 'Aren't the reasons fairly clear? He'd be like a stranded fish.'

'Isn't that for him to decide?'

'I don't think he would realise.'

'He'd come to his son's wedding, that's all that matters, surely.'

'Look, Bill.' Paul pointed his stained finger at me. 'At the moment that part of my life is behind me. I'm like the lady of sixty: sensitive about her age. In another ten years she'll begin to brag about it. Well, in another ten years I shall be able to brag about my origins. Not now.'

'In another ten years,' I said, 'what difference is it going to make who was at your wedding?'

He shrugged irritably, finished his coffee and went back into the studio. I followed, and sat for a while watching him add a brush-stroke here and there to the portrait of Patrick Munster.

Suddenly he put his brush down and said: 'Oh, for

God's sake, Bill, don't squat there like my nonconformist conscience! D'you think I don't know my obligations? My father came in for a bit of money and was stupid enough to blue it all on his undeserving son. As a result I am where I am. What would be the point of his coming down now and undoing what he's helped to build?'

'Damn it,' I said, 'you underrate even the people you mix with! Nobody cares that much. Opie came to London a rough country boy and painted the best people in the land.'

'The trouble is, I'm not a rough country boy any longer.'

'Nor need you be. Nobody would take more than a passing account of your father.'

'Thanks,' he snapped. 'When he comes I *want* them to take more than a passing account of him. Anyway, I'll choose my own wedding guests.'

The telephone rang and we had time to cool off. Of course I knew his anger was not because I was raising fresh arguments but only those in his own mind he had narrowly overcome. And of course I knew it was not so much his prospective clients he was sensitive about as his prospective in-laws. He knew he was marrying outside his class. This may all seem derisory in the present day, when a crude accent and an ignorance of syntax rank as a status symbol, but it was not so then.

All the same, I thought I understood. Only later did it come to me that the thing Paul could not and would not have stood for was any patronage of his father, any snide remarks just out of his hearing, any sarcastic glances. Perhaps his was the greater wisdom, for had his father been there and the subject of any such dislikeable display, Paul would have reacted in a very downright manner; and this could have set off his relationship with Olive on the wrong foot from the start. He was in love with Olive but he rightly judged the family she came from.

Chapter Five

I

Soon after the wedding the opportunity arose for me to go out to Rome as Jeremy Winthrop's right-hand man, and I took it. So for two years, instead of watching at close quarters the progress of Paul Stafford, I witnessed the progress of the Fascist movement and the emergence of Benito Amilcare Andrea Mussolini as master of Italy. The 'Sawdust Caesar', as my old friend George Seldes called him. It was difficult work, trying to report objectively on a resurgence of national pride and national discipline which, so good in itself, was being welcomed throughout the world; but which had a sort of corruption at its heart. Anyway, by December '25 our reporting of the scene, however objectively intended, had so far displeased the authorities that both Winthrop and I were 'invited' to leave the country, and in the new year I found myself back in London trying to pick up old threads and old friendships.

The break-up of Paul's marriage has been described elsewhere. Superficially, as I have said, everything was set fair. They were in love. Their tastes were the same; they were full of vitality, both night-birds, fond of life and society; they were both artists; they were both climbers. But Paul's only real concern in life was to paint; everything else was a means to that end. Olive wanted a part in every aspect of his life and he was not willing to cede it.

After a honeymoon in Paris they settled into Royal Avenue and things went well for six or seven months. Rifts first began to appear as she sought to influence whom he should mix with and whom he should paint. She was too demanding of his interest and he too untactful in his inattention. I sometimes wonder if possessiveness is not one of the nastiest of minor sins.

To her great annoyance he continued to see something of his old friends—even occasionally Diana Marnsett—yet there was never any suggestion at the time, whatever Olive may have implied later, that he was unfaithful to her. Nor that their love suddenly cooled. It sputtered and sparked, irritation and attraction like two chemicals that would not coalesce or interblend.

There would have been more chance for the marriage if he had been a lesser painter and she a better. She expected to have the run of his studio; she expected to paint there alongside him, so that they could work together, maybe have breaks for coffee and mutual admiration.

A. H. Jennings describes one of the scenes that led to the break-up. Where his information came from I don't know.

'Paul had been working all day on a difficult portrait. The sitter was not now present but the artist knew that somewhere behind the self-conscious mask was an expression he was seeking but could not find. Unless he found it now, by himself, he knew in the morning when the lady came back he must start again. Olive had that morning been to a show by a contemporary painter at the Kalman Galleries, and over a sandwich lunch she wanted to discuss it. Her standard, like that of many amateurs, was impossibly high (for others) and she condemned everything she had seen, perhaps supposing that Paul would be pleased with her criticisms. But Paul, aware of his own difficulties and short-comings, found himself drawn into a defence of a rival whose work he didn't actually like.

'After lunch Olive came into the studio and began painting a still-life of some peaches in a dish, and during the afternoon her occasional remarks were nagging at the outer edges of his mind, pulling him back from absorption. His answers became shorter, and presently she tightened up into an icy silence. When he stopped to make tea from the studio kettle he knew that she had finished her painting.

'Throughout the two years of their marriage he had humoured her about her own work, praising where he could and turning away the point where he could not. It was unlikely that his words ever quite satisfied her, for she was used to lavish praise in her own family and among the many young men who thought her beautiful. But this afternoon, still unable to grasp the secret of his own failure, his tongue would not frame the syllables for another evasive reply. He was exasperated, tired of her demands on his nervous energy.

'But perhaps whatever he said it would by then have been useless. She had seen his gaze and rightly interpreted it.

'"Well," she said. "So you think I'm no good. Is that it?"

'"Not at all." But his voice was empty of denial.

'"Perhaps not worthy of a place in your studio."

'"As my wife you've every right to come in here."

'"But not as a painter, is that it?"

'"Look, Olive—"

'"Not as a painter. You would like me to give up, be the little helpmeet, bringing in the food and drink for the great man."

'"You're fully entitled to paint just as much as you want. But—"

'"But what?"

'He threw down his brush. "Leave it at that."

'But she would not. "Don't you *really* feel you're the only one entitled to be creative? Aren't you jealous and grudging every time I pick up a palette? There can't be two suns in one house both attracting attention—and you have to be it!"

'He considered this, but now it had to come. "All right, if we can't go on as we are, let's come to an understanding about it. I begrudge you *nothing*, Olive—certainly not the talent you've got. I wish for it everything you could wish yourself. But I'm tired— yes, dog tired—of trying to pretend to admire a talent you haven't got, and never will have—"

'"You being God, who knows all—"

'"Of course there can be differing opinions; but not over fundamentals. You—you've a considerable talent for sketching—your line is always good—and once in a while a watercolour comes off because it's almost all drawing and no colour. But so far as that goes"—and he gestured towards the still-life—"how can you expect me to take it seriously? I would put the ability to *paint* there if I could, willingly and thankfully; but I can't. Really, Olive ... I could do better with that sort of subject when I was ten. And Matisse could paint better than I ever shall if I live to be eighty. What's the use of shirking the facts?"

'Olive Stafford turned on her heel and left the studio. She never entered it again.'

I tend to doubt whether Paul would ever have been quite so eloquent as that, but I'm pretty sure the gist is correct. Anyway, by the time I returned they were not living together. She had moved into a small but expensive apartment in Mayfair on the generous allowance Paul made her. By now Paul had reached the fullness of his success. His income had gone up and up, and thanks to Olive his expenditure had kept pace. Not that he was frugal himself. He was a popular man in his way, a member now of two exclusive clubs, a frequent attender at the theatre, at concerts and the opera. But he was careful not to run into debt. It was almost the last sign of his frugal North-country upbringing: during the 'tightrope' period when he was dancing attendance on Diana Marnsett and her group, he had been acutely miserable, for ever owing money, and he told me he would never let himself get into such a situation again. There was now no need. While general economic depression began to creep across the country those who made money like him were, because of the stability of prices, rich indeed.

Absent for so long, I was able to look at him with new eyes; yet the changes were not in direction, only in degree. He had taken his new direction while under Diana Marnsett's influence, and success had only brought a hardening and a strengthening of the drive. To be seen at the first nights of *The Vortex* and *Saint Joan* were as important to him as knowing a fair sprinkling of the fashionable audience on first-name terms. In an age when advertising had hardly begun and television was a spectre of the future, this was a way of becoming and remaining a name, in newspapers and on the pens of gossip-columnists. In the middle-Twenties too, led perhaps by Coward, it was the fashionable thing to pretend decadence—a sort of Wildean a–morality—however hard and devotedly one in fact worked when one was out of the limelight.

He was painting portraits exclusively now, and always had them in the Academy show; but whereas three years ago he had idealised his sitter only on rare occasions—as in the first portrait of Diana Marnsett—and often had been unsentimental and quite unflattering, now he seemed always to try to produce a painting that would please the sitter.

A few of the other critics were beginning to follow Alfred Young's lead in their attitude towards his work; Paul said this was simply because they were always looking for someone new; now he was an established success he could be disparaged. They for their part could be ignored. At least, I said, they did not ignore *him*. And it was true: even if his style showed signs of becoming facile, there was a quality in it that couldn't be overlooked. Many of these works are still in private hands, but a particularly good example of this period came up in Sotheby's last year and was bought for a record price by an American bidder: it was a painting of young Beatrice Lillie in the costume in which she appeared in one of André Charlot's revues, and the vitality of the original has been exactly captured—which so very few of her portraits succeeded in doing.

In February of that year the Grosvenor Gallery had an exhibition of modern portraitists, and I got the usual invitation to the 'Private View 6–8'. I hoped to skip it, but Paul telephoned and said he would call for me. My flat was on the first floor, and he came up before I could meet him.

He said: 'I thought I'd better warn you. It's La

Diana's car. She insisted on calling for me at the last minute, so who am I to disappoint a lady?'

He was looking as well-dressed and as composed as ever.

I said: 'I didn't know you were still riding that horse.'

'Dear boy, the company of journalists is coarsening your language.'

'Well, you know what I mean.'

He smiled. 'Roughly, yes. And the answer is roughly, no. But now that Olive has gone she considers she has a residuary interest.'

'Any other legatees?'

'It's a moot point. Come on: we're late as it is.'

Diana greeted me coolly but pleasantly. I was not of sufficient importance to rate big in her world, but I was a pre-Olive friend of Paul's and therefore might possibly be on Diana's side of the court. She was wearing a very short sheath-type black moiré frock with a high neck and short sleeves, and a blue-fox fur. A cloche hat partly hid the eton crop. The silky legs were carelessly crossed; a cigarette in a long cigarette holder decanted ash on my coat. In the partial light of the limousine she might have been twenty-one.

We drove to the exhibition and made a royal entrance. Paul and Diana were surrounded by admiring friends, and I drifted away to look at the pictures. Three of Paul's nine exhibits were of royal mistresses: Louise de la Vallière, Diane de Poitiers and Nell Gwyn. I noticed that Mme de Montespan was not there and wondered if Paul had made any attempt to persuade Mlle Jacqueline Dupaix, Teacher of Ballroom Dancing, to sit for him. The last time I'd seen Leo had been six months ago when an orchestra with which he was working in some minor capacity paid a visit to Rome. Leo had looked quite unchanged except that his forehead was higher. He had asked about Paul, but the name of Mrs Marnsett had not come up.

As I drifted round the gallery snips of conversation came to me from others on the same parade, and I noted those which referred to Paul.

'Yes, that's him over there. Still terribly young. And good-looking, my dear, in a sort of way.'

'Did you see his "Frederick Arthur Marshall" at the Academy last year? Reminded one of Whistler's "Carlyle" . . . No, it's on show in Paris at the moment.'

'They say the old man had done him some favour when he was at school . . . Dropped several commissions and went up and did it without charge . . . Hurry? I don't know. The old man was due to retire, or something.'

I moved on.

'Well, personally, Nigel, I find the whole collection here quite nauseating. We're in the Nineteen-Twenties, not the Eighteen-Eighties. These people who toe the academic line . . .'

'Well, some of them don't know any better, my dear, just not any better. But in the early days one had had hopes of Stafford.'

I moved on again.

'. . . They say the one thing Sargent couldn't do was paint a pretty face. Well, very soon that'll be all Stafford *can* do . . .'

'I don't know. I think one can pardon him the juggler's tricks. His work always has such a distinct personality . . .'

A hand touched my arm and I turned to face Jeremy Winthrop, my 'boss' in Italy, with whom from that country I had had to beat an ignominious retreat, not even quite sure until we had crossed the frontier that some thugs from the OVRA might not come along with belts and truncheons to help us on our way.

'What,' I said, 'are *you* doing here?'

'Passing an hour. And deciding whether to go to Washington.'

I'd heard that he had been offered the post.

'Why not?'

'Oh, it's a plum job but it's too far *away*. Europe is where it's still all going to happen over the next few years, Bill. I've a feeling in my bones.'

'Well, I'm stuck here now for a bit, chained to the desk, whether I like it or not.'

'And picking up on culture.'

'Sort of.'

'Stafford's a friend of yours, isn't he?'

'Yes.'

'Ever read Stacy Aumonier?'

'Occasionally.'

'In a recent short story he called success a beautiful, merciless lady. One woos her at one's own risk. A sort of modern La Belle Dame Sans Merci, pursued by all and gained by few. And she has a knack of destroying those she accepts as lovers. They flourish and flower for a year or two and then suddenly it's all gone to the devil.'

'I think,' I said, 'if I were Paul I might point out that failure is another merciless lady. Only she's not even beautiful; she's an ugly hag. Who wouldn't prefer the beautiful whore?'

'Who indeed? Give me the tart carrying the champagne every day.' Winthrop looked at me. 'You've faith in Stafford, haven't you?'

'Faith? I don't know. But he's a tough nut.'

'Maybe it's not just success I mean as such *quick* success. What is he going to do with the rest of his life?'

'Paint, I imagine.'

'But you think we're wasting our metaphors.'

'I believe so.'

Chapter Six

I

During my absence a very strange thing had happened to the Lynns. Dr Lynn had been given a knighthood. This occurrence might have shaken a lesser man, but Sir Clement bore the affliction bravely and refused to be put off his stroke.

As Bertie said to me in a letter, the KBE would have been more welcome if it had had a few golden guineas dangling from the ribbon.

In fact, the breadwinner seemed capable of many things but not of earning bread; and in the end, reluctantly brought to face up to the question of his finances, Sir Clement had been persuaded much against his will to make a lecture tour of America. Lady Lynn—save the mark with her horse's bonnet and ankle socks—refused to accompany him. She had, she said, far too many interests in Reading and district to jettison them at short notice and catch the first boat to New York like a girl of twenty. Let Holly go. Holly had got her expected scholarship for Oxford and her mathematical progress was absurdly rapid. Missing one term wouldn't hurt her. She seemed to enjoy looking after Clem and was just the right age.

So they left England the month before I returned and I didn't see them.

Bertie had left England at about the same time. The story sounded typically eccentric, so I went down to Reading on my first free week-end to discover what it was all about.

I found Lady Lynn there with her sister to keep her company. Lady Lynn greeted me effusively but vaguely, and her sister, tall and ragged as a fir-tree, offered me a limp hand.

'Clem's away,' said Lady Lynn. 'He's in Cleveland, I think. Lecturing on Röntgen rays. As if he knew.' She pulled down the front of her jumper, which was too short and immediately sprang up again. 'Holly's gone with him to see he changes his collars. Leo—'

'What's this about Bertie?' I said. 'Giving up his job and—'

'Yes, he wrote to you, I'm sure. Perhaps it's gone to Turkey, or Rome, is it? He told us over tea one Sunday. "I'm giving up this insurance racket," he said. Those were his words. Slang phraseology was always one of his weak points.'

'But West Africa,' I said, 'to work among lepers?'

'Put the kettle on, dear. We can have tea now. It's this Toc H, Bill. They called for six volunteers from all over England. They'd only funds for six, and Bertie was one of the chosen. Sounds like the New Testament, doesn't it? He's looking forward to it frightfully; he says he'll be the only white man in the camp.'

'There's no gas,' said her sister.

'I must have forgotten to wind it up this morning. We'll light a fire. There should be some sticks somewhere.'

'How do you feel about it?' I asked.

'Well, Clem said, had he really looked at it all round and did it justify giving up a steady living, and Bertie said yes, so of course there was nothing more to be done.'

'How long has he gone for?'

'Two years, to begin. Of course Holly said to Bertie, "Suppose you get it," but Bertie says hardly anybody ever *dies* of leprosy. They've some new thing now, the juice of some tree. Works wonders.'

'Does he know anything about medicine?'

'He's been going to night-school. Unknown to us. Very secretive of him. Could you lend me a match, Bill?'

I pictured Bertie arriving home hours late for dinner two or three nights a week and nobody bothering to ask what he'd been doing.

'All this unrest,' said Lady Lynn. She had picked up an old newspaper to use in the fire, but had become engrossed in the leading article. 'Why don't they build the *Queen Mary*? Bankers think man was made to fit money, not money to fit man. One thing I'm pleased about, this Toc H thing has a Christian basis. Some sort of a secret society, founded by the early Christians. Double cross of the catacombs.'

'I'm sorry I wasn't able to see him before he left.'

'I'm all alone,' said Lady Lynn. 'Except for Vera, who doesn't count. Have you put water in the kettle, dear? No, well, it's burnt its bottom. How was Leo when you saw him?'

'He told you about his job in the orchestra, I suppose?' I said. 'Pot-boiling, he called it, in order to work at composition in his spare time.'

'Holly's growing into a big girl,' said Lady Lynn. 'Strange how all the angles become curvilinear. Don't know quite what we're going to do with her. The trouble with Leo, of course, is that he wants to find a short cut to success. All glory, like that artist friend of yours.'

'Paul Stafford?' I said cautiously. 'Have you met him?'

71

'Leo and Bertie were at the same school, didn't you know? Vera and I went to a show of his pictures last week in Bond Street. Very dull, I thought. So many faces.'

Lady Lynn, I reflected, had a talent for summary. But a couple of months afterwards, when Paul Stafford's second portrait of Diana Marnsett was to be seen, I wondered if Lady Lynn would have used the same adjective.

A couple of days after Newton, Olive Stafford rang me and said she was having a few people for drinks next Friday, would I come? All my preferences were to think up a hurried excuse, but I weakly accepted, hoping something would really crop up at the office to stop me. Of course it didn't, and I went along, and about two dozen people were there and we drank White Ladies and talked the usual nonsense that is the lingua franca of the cocktail set.

I hadn't seen the flat before and realised that Paul *must* have been generous with his money if with nothing else. It was all white rectangular furniture with expensive fur rugs on a parquet floor; an easel tastefully decorated one corner and in the other, scintillating with photographs, a baby grand on which at the moment a man called Peter Sharble, who I understood later was an MP, was strumming a tune or two. When I was about to take the first polite opportunity to leave she whispered: 'Stay on a bit, Bill. You've not got a date? I want to talk.'

So I was stuck until the last guest left and she said: 'I'm going to change my drink: how about you?'

I joined her in a stiff whisky and we talked in a desultory way in the smoke-laden room. The conversation turned to Paul. She treated it lightly. Pity the ice had cracked so quickly: the thaw had come unseasonably fast. Was it true Paul was painting Diana Marnsett again? He must be getting short of ideas. Or was it just short of money? She hadn't been to the exhibition at the Grosvenor Galleries. It all seemed *vieux jeu* to her.

Olive was growing her hair. The tight chestnut auburn curls—they had been darkened a shade—were falling out, becoming softer; they gentled her face, made her less elfin, more feminine. The stresses of marriage, and a failed marriage, had done no harm to her looks at all.

She said: 'It's *good* to have you back. I *rely* on you. Did you know that?'

I smiled. 'Come off it.'

'Well it's true! We were—sweethearts for a time, if one can still use the expression. I like—*après* Paul—to think I still have my friends.'

'You must have many, Olive. You're better looking, more glamorous than ever.'

'Oh, that. Yes. Well, I have my little side-amours. But that's not quite what I mean. You're something *more.*'

I sipped my drink again, wondering where this was leading.

I said: 'Does it have to be *après* Paul?'

'Well, what do you suggest? I can tell you he's hell to live with.'

'You didn't give it a very long try.'

'Two *years*. It seemed a lifetime!'

She was sitting with a puckered frown, her face tightened as if to resist inquiry. I said: 'These things don't always fall right the first time. Why not give it a second throw?'

She shrugged. 'Did he tell you he was willing?'

'No.'

'No. Nor is he likely to while he's got that bitch Marnsett in tow.'

'But *you* might be willing?'

She got up. 'What d'you think I am, Bill—a squaw, waiting for the Big Chief to lift his finger? To hell with him and his cheap entourage!'

I looked at her standing by the window in her flimsy emerald-green frock and wondered—not altogether idly—if Paul ever *had* painted her naked. She was a very attractive woman. And could be a dangerous one.

'What are you thinking, Bill?'

The question came sharply. 'Thinking? About myself.'

'That must be quite a change.'

'Don't you believe it. I'm constantly in my thoughts. But sometimes you intrude on them.'

'Do I?' She smiled. 'Tell me.'

I shook my head. 'It's time I went. Is Maud still here?'

Maud was a plump spotty woman who had let me in and handed round the drinks.

'Why? D'you need a chaperon?'

'No . . . She put my coat away somewhere.'

'She's in the kitchen. I'll call her in a moment.'

We looked at each other. Olive came across and stood on tip-toe, hands on my shoulder. I bent and kissed her, my hands moving up and down her back. She gave her whole body to me, like something without bone. After a long time she used her hands to push me away.

'Yes,' she said, 'I see what you mean. You *do* need a chaperon.'

I said: 'Perhaps you need Paul.'

It was a queer note to part on, half sexual, half antagonistic, but that was the way it went between us.

II

I was busy for a while and did not see any of them. I was sent up to cover one of the Jarrow unemployment marches, and after that the prosperity and the quarrels of my friends did not seem quite real for a while. When I *did* call on Paul, Diana Marnsett was there and had just been sitting for him, so I proceeded to back out, but Paul gripped my arm.

'There's a drink behind you, old boy. What's the worst the Press can do these days?'

'I'm an amateur,' I said. 'Refer you to the society editor.'

'It must be healthy to be a journalist,' Diana said, blowing smoke rings. 'One can work off one's lower nature in print. Sort of spiritual purge taken daily. I wish—'

'One thing,' Paul said. 'Printer's ink smells better than turps. My stomach is beginning to turn.'

I raised my eyebrows. It seemed as if I had come at a time when feelings were roused.

'Is this the conventional complaint of a rich man?' I asked. 'Or is it some special private gloom I've intruded on?'

'D'you know John Connor?' Paul asked.

'The yachtsman? I think I've met him once.'

'We were talking at the Hanover Club last night. He's sailing to the Canaries later this summer and asked if I'd like to go with him. I'm seriously considering it.'

'It's the idea of a simpleton,' said Diana. 'At the first

75

storm you'd be swamped—or pooped—or whatever the word is.'

Paul stared at her. 'You forget, woman—or maybe you don't know—that in another incarnation, before I became the darling of the *beau monde*, there was a war. And in the war I sailed in boats. And even in wartime the sea took absolutely no notice but was just as temperamental, just as difficult, just as stormy as—'

'I know what you're going to say,' Diana interrupted. 'And you needn't say it. I hate to be compared to rather dirty salt water, even as a generality. Please shut up.'

'Well . . .' Paul moved restlessly about the room. About him were evidences of his increasing wealth and taste—paintings by other artists he admired, some very fine ceramic ware—a long way, I thought, from the Jarrow marchers, though at one time he had been scarcely different from them. 'I'm off balance,' he said. 'I've been working too hard. Or too closely. I want time to look at myself—to look at my work—to have time to think. Just a month or so's break.'

'There are plenty of good ordinary cruises,' Diana said. 'Fresh air, a change of company, a decent degree of comfort.'

'And mixing with all the best tweeds? Thanks, no.'

'Well . . .' Diana said shortly, 'the remedy's in your own hands. Don't let your present company bore you.'

Feeling that the exchange was becoming personal I said: 'That portrait of Lady Blakeley, Paul. Is it finished? I'd like to see it.'

He stared at me as if not seeing me. 'Oh, that. Yes, go ahead. It's face to the wall by the window. The painting on the easel is covered and I charge you not to uncover it.'

'OK.'

'And,' he said, as I was about to leave them, 'you may find answers to more than one of your questions up there.'

I raised my eyebrows in inquiry but he waved his glass and would say no more. I went up to his studio. The room was very striking with its ivory coloured walls and black velvet curtains and black carpet—designed to impress the sitter—and I could detect Olive's hand in the decor. But more surprising was the presence of an elderly man staring at one of the paintings.

He turned to give me roughly the same assessing treatment with his very direct blue eyes. A good-looking old man with white hair and a short beard. And roughened skin with a net of tiny veins about the nose. I said good evening and he answered in a rough North-country voice. The shiny blue suit, the stiff white collar, the bootlace tie; I instantly knew.

I said: 'Paul sent me up, but he didn't tell me anyone was here.'

'Well, yes. I'm 'ere, as you might say. Is Paul still with Mrs Marnsett?'

I nodded. He moved slowly back to one of the pictures. All his movements were ponderous: he stood squarely on strong reliable legs. The beard was becoming.

'What d'ye make of this?' he asked.

I went up. As it happened I had been in the studio when Paul painted it a month ago. He had had a few minutes to spare before we went out together and had taken up a piece of strawboard and made a few swift lines on it in charcoal. Over it all he had painted evenly a coat of dark grey so that the thing looked like a greyish blackboard. Then he had mixed yellow ochre with a little white and, while the grey was still wet, had painted in this second colour. In a matter of three minutes something had come to life: a distorted window showing light from a derelict woodman's cottage squeezed down among tall trees which bulked about it as if to crush it out of existence. The two colours were all he had used, but the result was grim and crooked and overpowering, a Hans Andersen fairy story which had taken the expected turning.

I said: 'I think it's marvellous.'

He transferred his unblinking gaze to me. 'Do you know owt about it?'

This wasn't to take me down a peg but a simple question requiring a simple answer.

'Not much, except what I've picked up from Paul. You're his father, aren't you?'

''Ow d'ye know that?'

'A likeness perhaps. My name is William Grant.'

'Ah ... so you're Bill Grant. Where he used to go and stay for 'olidays.' He put out a slow swollen hand. 'Nay, he's nowt like me. I can't draw. Can't even paint shop wi'out dripping t'paint down my sleeve.'

'Is this your first visit to London, Mr Stafford? I mean to see your son.'

He took a pipe from his pocket and began to fill it from a battered old pouch.

'We've 'ad one or two differences o' late years ... He's changed a lot, 'as Paul. But he's been good; paid back what I spent on 'im to the last farthing. Now 'e allows me two hundred a year. I didn't *want* 'is money; first off I said nay, nay; but times are bad in the North ... 'E always pays his debts, does Paul.'

Yes, I thought, even to painting the presentation for old Dr Marshall.

'D'you know,' said Mr Stafford, 'wi' the money Paul

78

makes me have, and me bit of capital back, I'm quite *rich*. Sometimes it makes me fair ashamed.'

'Why ever should it?'

'Folk around us—that's why. I help where I can but it's too big. People can scarce live. Cousin of mine in Great Harwood. Forty-one she'll be. Nay, I'm a liar: forty-two this January. Married to a mill-worker, got four kids. Mill's closed. They got to manage on thirty-two shilling a week. *And* they pay nine shilling a week rent. I help *them*. But it's hard. And they don't like being 'elped.'

'Does Paul know?'

'It's not for me to remind him. He pays 'is debts.'

We took a pace or two together.

''Is wife,' said Mr Stafford. 'I never met 'is wife. What's amiss between them? Can't be right for a husband and a wife to live separate.'

'They're both artists, Mr Stafford. They're temperamental—didn't get on.'

'Should've found that out before they wed.' A match flickered up and down, blue smoke rose. 'Is it permanent?'

'I don't know.'

'And no children on the way?'

'No.'

'Children bring folk together ... There's never been a divorce in our family. In the North it's looked on as a disgrace.'

He took out the pipe and examined the stem. That at least gave him satisfaction.

'And this Mrs Marnsett. What's she after?'

'Diana was a friend of Paul's before he married. She helped him a lot. I think they've become friendly again since he and Olive separated.'

'Friendly?' Mr Stafford said belligerently. 'What

79

does friendly mean?'

I didn't answer because his guess was as good as mine. We looked at one or two of the paintings.

'That's a fine boy,' said Mr Stafford, pointing with the stem of his pipe. 'Puts me in mind of my nephew in Morecambe.'

'Yes . . .'

'What did she do for him?'

I tried to explain something of the complicated process of getting known.

He grunted. 'She's the wrong influence, just the same . . . Not that folk influence Paul much so far as I can see. 'E goes his own way.'

There was silence.

'Was she why Paul's marriage broke up?'

'Not at all. I'm sure not.'

'Paul's very close,' said Mr Stafford, unblinking, as if to explain his questions. 'He don't talk things over with me. I've to mind what I say . . . But he ought to have got a degree. That's what I tell him. I was disappointed. He'd be safer with a degree.'

'I must be going,' I said. 'I'll see you again, Mr Stafford.'

'Nay, I'm off home tomorrow.' He rubbed the palm of his hand across his beard. 'He were always a queer lad, was Paul. Always drawing faces on the flour bags. I used to tan 'is behind.'

I shook Mr Stafford's hand and left him standing solidly where I had found him, puffing meditatively at his pipe. One felt that ideas did not come quickly to him but that when they came they stuck. I didn't bother Paul again or discover if Diana was still there, but let myself out. I had forgotten to see the portrait of Lady Blakeley after all.

Chapter Seven

I

The affair of Diana's second portrait, which became so notorious, started very quietly.

I had been surprised when Olive first mentioned he was doing another, but Diana's presence that day had confirmed it. Although Paul sometimes gave me the impression that he found her proprietorial attitude a bit oppressive, the ambiguous friendship continued. If they got on each other's nerves sometimes more like lovers than friends it was nobody's business but theirs. Presumably Colonel Marnsett tolerated it because it was discreet. As March advanced it became known that Paul's three paintings for the Summer Exhibition were to be a head and shoulders of Diana Marnsett, the portrait of Lady Blakeley, and one of his historical series, a painting of Maria Anne Fitzherbert.

Paul seemed in better spirits now. His paintings at the Grosvenor Gallery had attracted so much attention that he had been offered a one-man show at the Ludwig Galleries in King Street, to open in late April. Henry Ludwig was a man of prestige and usually only showed foreign artists of established reputation. Paul hoped to complete the last of his historical portraits in time for the opening. No more was heard of the yachting holiday; presumably Diana had got her way over that. Since I was not a member of the Hanover I couldn't be sure.

Paul still strictly adhered to his rule of not allowing

a sitter to see the portrait until it was completed. The events of the day in April when Diana saw hers have been related variously. Since I was not there I can claim no absolute authority for my version. Paul told me, that was all.

Before he showed her the portrait he said he explained to her that he had been breaking new ground and that she might find the result a bit startling. He was convinced, he told her, that he had succeeded in what he had set out to do; she might not necessarily *agree* with him or actually *like* his interpretation. It expressed something he had felt for some time, *not*, of course, specially about her but about portraiture in general, something he had not been able to put into a conventional work. All this she smilingly accepted as a sort of *hors d'oeuvre* to whet her expectation; she took no warning at all from his remarks.

So he lifted the cloth and she looked at it, and her face changed colour.

'You're joking, Paul.'

'I was never more serious in my life.'

She went nearer, he said, and stared again. Then she stared at him. She saw then he was absolutely in earnest, that there was no *real*, flattering portrait to be put up with a laugh in its place. She turned and picked up a palette knife and made for the picture.

He caught her just in time and they fought—like cat and dog, he said—for the knife. Forgetting her refined upbringing and sophisticated manners, she bit and kicked and wounded his hand before he got the knife away from her.

Then he carried her still struggling to the door of the flat and put her outside on the mat.

Four days later Paul received a letter from a firm of
solicitors, Messrs Berriman, Smith & Berriman,
informing him that they had received instructions
from their client, the Hon. Mrs Brian Marnsett, to
make payment for a picture commissioned by her.
They begged to enclose cheque for four hundred
guineas, the sum stipulated at the outset, and would
be glad to acknowledge receipt of the picture at his
early convenience. They were his faithfully.

Paul replied by the next post, returning the cheque
and stating that no agreement had been entered into
for the sale of the picture, that no price had been put
on it, and that it was not at present for sale.

There followed silence.

Two days later the three paintings were parcelled
up and sent in to the Academy committee. In the
ordinary course of time Paul received a communica-
tion accepting two of the pictures submitted: the
portraits of Lady Blakeley and the Hon. Mrs Brian
Marnsett. The third the selection committee found
unsuitable and returned with regrets.

It was unusual for Paul not to have all three
accepted, but the painting of Mrs Fitzherbert, differing as it did so basically from contemporary portraits
of the lady, might have been considered unacceptable
on those grounds.

'Good luck to them,' said Paul, 'it can go in Ludwig's
instead.'

A week passed, and then he had a visit from Colonel
Marnsett.

Colonel Marnsett was a small man, trimly dressed,
with white hair and a short grey moustache. Everything about him suggested he was used to command,

and that not just of a regiment.

'Mr Stafford,' he said. 'I believe you have recently painted a portrait of my wife.'

Paul inclined his head. 'That is so.'

'I have not seen this picture but I understand it is most objectionable.'

'Not from an artistic standpoint.'

'Ah. That is a matter I don't wish to go into. From my wife's point of view it is objectionable—yet she offered to buy it. You refused to sell. May I ask why?'

'Because I wish first to exhibit it. From her comments I imagine your wife would buy it only to destroy it.'

'But it was commissioned, Mr Stafford. If she pays the agreed price the painting is legally hers.'

'No price was agreed, sir. If she wishes to buy it after it has been exhibited I shall be glad to sell it at something like the price you mention.'

'Do you always take such interest in the fate of your commissioned work?'

'No-o. But some of my work I hold in greater esteem than others. This—this portrait—it isn't flattering, I agree. But I never undertook to paint another picture just like the last. She has one, as you know. This . . . this was an experiment. I think it was a successful experiment. I find it very satisfactory. Others may not think so—I don't know. But I *would* like to know what they think of it before it is—destroyed.'

Colonel Marnsett prodded the carpet with his rolled umbrella. 'Mr Stafford, you have been a friend of my wife's for some years. I don't know how you assess friendship, but my wife asserts that this portrait will make her the butt of half London. I gather she has helped you considerably in the past, with

84

introductions, with recommendations . . . Perhaps we could come to some arrangement. Provided it is not shown to the public . . .'

Paul got up. 'I'm not unaware of my debts—and I try to pay them. I'm truly sorry that Diana feels the way she does. At the moment the matter is out of my hands because the Academy has accepted it for exhibition. I understand it's to be hung on the line. But once it has been exhibited in this way she's welcome to it. I'll not sell it to her, I'll *give* it her.'

The Colonel stared through Paul with his icy eyes. 'You could still withdraw the picture. You could say that circumstances—er—had arisen which—er—made it impossible—'

'Colonel Marnsett, circumstances have *not* arisen. Personally I think your wife is greatly exaggerating the effect the painting will have on anyone else. *She* may see it as unflattering. Most people won't even *consider* it in that way.'

'But the effect on her is still as upsetting . . . Perhaps there's another approach I could make. Suppose I were to find a purchaser who would undertake not to destroy the painting. And within reason you could name your own price.'

'After the show I should be *most* interested.'

'I am talking of before the show, as you very well know. Would six hundred guineas interest you?'

'I'm sorry. At this stage the painting isn't for sale.'

Colonel Marnsett continued to prod the carpet. He was not a man lightly to be crossed.

'I appreciate that what you're really seeking is the sensational publicity. What is that worth to you?'

'The picture isn't for sale.'

Marnsett slowly picked up his hat, got to his feet. 'You'll not do yourself any good at all, you know. Do you know? I am not without influence in these matters. After this, few women will risk being held up to public ridicule.'

'That's a chance that must be taken. I'm getting tired of seeking solely to please.'

'I've long had my own opinion of you, Stafford. It has been against my wishes that my wife has associated with you. I know your kind: the upstart with a good command of the latest artistic catchwords to justify whatever he may choose to attempt. You bring your profession into disrepute.'

'At least,' said Paul, 'I confine myself to my own profession. I don't think this conversation is getting us anywhere, do you?'

Later that evening Paul told me what had passed. 'They can have the thing after the show,' he added. 'But I do—for once—want the reactions of the critics and the public. They've praised and blamed so much of my conventional stuff . . .'

'What's objectionable about it?'

'To Diana? I suppose the fact that she doesn't look as beautiful as she expected. The trouble is that although everyone has heard of Chagall and Picasso and Modigliani, nobody wants a portrait of themselves to look like that. Well, come to the preview and judge for yourself.'

By now Paul's exhibition at the Ludwig Galleries was just open. Downstairs was given over entirely to the historical series, and room had been found there for the rejected Mrs Fitzherbert. I confess I didn't think it one of his best works, and I believe he may have later destroyed it, for I've not been able to trace it today. Altogether, although he put some store by these, as it were, allegorical portraits I preferred his other work, which was upstairs. Among these was his portrait of Dr Marshall, back from Paris and shortly to be sent to the old man. Also, I was glad to see, that little fairy-tale fantasy he'd conjured up in ten minutes when I was there.

Three days before the opening of the Summer Show Paul received a letter from the Academy. It said that the hanging committee, after careful consideration, had been unable to find room for the portrait of Mrs Brian Marnsett after all. Pressure of space, they went on . . .

'Pressure of the Colonel!' said Paul, white-faced, and chewed the end of his pen for a few minutes. Then he wrote a reply. He took a taxi at once to Burlington House and brought the picture away, together with that of Lady Blakeley, and bore them straight round to King Street, where some of his other pictures were rearranged to make room for them. Then he telephoned the *Morning Post*, which had just given him a very good criticism of his own exhibition. The next day there was a paragraph in the paper headed:

ARTIST WITHDRAWS PICTURE AS PROTEST

'Last night, Mr Paul Stafford, well-known portrait painter, announced his intention of withdrawing his portrait of Lady Blakeley from the Royal Academy Exhibition, which opens to the public on Tuesday next, as a protest against the rejection of one of the pictures he submitted. In an exclusive interview given to our representative he states that originally two of his pictures were accepted and that only at the last moment was one of these arbitrarily returned to him. He described such treatment as without precedent and said that the present committee should be superseded by one abreast of modern ideas.

'The rejected picture is now on view at the Ludwig Galleries. It is a portrait of a well-known society lady, and our art critic, John Grey, suggests that it shows the influence of early Byzantine art.

'An official of the Royal Academy, interviewed later, declined to comment on the matter except to state that such an occurrence was not without precedent, and that the decision of the hanging committee must be accepted as final.'

That evening Paul had two other callers from the Press and while he was disposing of one, the telephone-bell rang. I picked up the receiver.

'Mr Stafford?'

'Mr Stafford is engaged at the moment.'

'Oh, is that Mr Grant? I thought I recognised your voice. This is Ludwig speaking.'

I had recognised *his* voice too. 'I don't suppose Paul will be more than ten minutes. Shall I get him to ring you back?'

'Well ... I wonder if you'd help me by putting a little matter to Mr Stafford? That you are his good friend I know. I am feeling a trifle uneasy—more than a trifle uneasy, I might say, about this portrait of Mrs Marnsett. From an artistic point of view it is beautiful, yes. But I do feel it would be better hung upstairs.'

'I don't understand.'

'I was not here when Mr Stafford came in yesterday, but he insisted, Mr Abrahams says, insisted it should be hung with his historical paintings.'

'Is there anything wrong with that?' I asked, knowing now what he meant.

'Well, Mr Grant, every one of his historical studies

88

is of a lady of light virtue. They comprise a series. To break up that series and insert one modern portrait. . .'

'Ye-es.'

'I gather—well, we all know, don't we?—that the painting has given some offence to the sitter. It seems a pity to make matters worse.'

'I'll speak to Mr Stafford about it as soon as I can and ring you back in half an hour.'

'Thank you. I'd be obliged.'

When I told Paul he stared at me and then laughed. 'Well, that's where Diana belongs, isn't it? And downstairs is the best light. She's where you can see in through the window.'

'Ludwig obviously thinks you're on delicate ground.'

'Let's stay on delicate ground. Fitzherbert was upright and decent and God-fearing. La Vallière would never have treated a man as callously as Diana treated Leo.'

'I suppose Ludwig feels that Marnsett is a man of influence and doesn't want to be involved in anything which will give him a grudge against his galleries.'

Paul got up and bit at his fingers. 'I'll ring him back now. But the exhibition is mine and he agreed to hold it. That painting's a good one and deserves the best position. That's all that should matter to him. Diana has only herself to blame for pulling strings.'

III

In reading the reviews of the Academy Exhibition for that year it's perfectly clear that most of the critics had taken the trouble, either before or after, to visit the

Ludwig Galleries, four minutes' walk away, and examine Paul's rejected portrait for themselves. Certainly most of them in one way or another referred to it. Alfred Young, who had so long been Paul's severest critic, was among those who said bluntly that the hanging committee had made a mistake.

'Portraiture [he wrote] follows conventional lines... Apart from these there is little to remark, and one misses the vigorous if facile work of Stafford. In rejecting his portrait of the Hon. Mrs Brian Marnsett they have done art in this country a notable disservice. This picture would never be a popular one with the public—some might consider it distasteful—but we feel that its honesty and strength and originality put it above everything which is at present showing at Burlington House. For Stafford himself it is a complete break with tradition, and will tend to encourage those who long ago saw in him the beginning of a new movement in portraiture and who of late years have reluctantly felt that prophecy to be misplaced.'

During the week I was at last able to snatch half an hour and take a look at the cause of all the trouble.

It's difficult, seeing a reproduction of it today, to appreciate the rather shocking impact it had when first shown. Art has moved far in fifty years. Not that the informed public was unaware of the brilliant and bizarre work which had been emerging from France and other parts of Europe for more than a quarter of a century—as Paul pointed out. Names like Braque, Picabia, Léger and Picasso were becoming known. But by and large they were still not accepted. It wasn't so many years since the first Post-Impressionist exhibition had opened in London and been greeted with derisive laughter.

Nor, of course, was there a lack of unorthodox and unflattering portraits in history. Goya had even guyed the royal family on whom he depended for his patronage. But he was one of the 'classics'. As of the mid-Nineteen-Twenties, in England, this sort of thing was not expected of a fashionable portrait painter exhibiting at the Royal Academy.

The picture was a half-length of Diana sitting beside a table on which was a spray of carnations. There was no true perspective, the figure being fitted into a background of sharply defined areas of colour, almost like stained glass. Although quite out of proportion, the face was marvellously recognisable. All that old gift of caricature had come out—the hairline, eton-cropped, was hard as a convict's, the plucked eyebrows described precisely the same downward arc as the sulky mouth; and lines on the pure dusky skin were where no lines yet existed but where, the viewer instantly saw, they were *going* to exist.

'It's not a picture,' I said to Paul, 'that will gain you many commissions.'

'Old John Grey says it reminds him of Velasquez's portrait of Queen Mariana. I've never seen it but I'll pin that up for a comparison.'

We talked of other things for a few minutes, and then abruptly he came back to it. 'Of course I know most of our set—or her set—will think I'm tired of her and been deliberately insulting. Let 'em say so. It isn't that, I tell you. She asked me to paint her and I did just that. I was bored with the idea at first—as I've begun to get stale and bored with the whole of my present job—but *not* bored with *her* particularly. I find her hardness, her shallowness, her selfishness, intolerable at times—but no more so than I find *myself. . .*'

'Why?'

'Why what? Why do I find myself shallow? Or rather *when*. When I contrast the money I make and the way I spend it with the Depression and the way maybe one in ten of the rest of us live. Of course, I don't think of it often, and when I do I know I can do nothing to alter it. But now and then it eats into me. So . . .'

'So you began to paint her.'

'I began to *paint* her. I won't inflict the word inspiration on you—especially something which may look—destructive—to you . . .'

'I didn't say so—'

'But sometimes, quite unexpectedly, things fuse, reluctance becomes inclination, inclination takes flight. Something happens and from then on everything moves to one end. You don't think of anybody else, I'm afraid; certainly not the sitter; and when it's finished you're *released* from the driving force; then you take the responsibility—get the praise or the blame, anything else that's going. Of course . . . of course I know Diana particularly well: if something of that comes out, an understanding of her tricks and conceits and her discontent—then I'm to blame for that. But I assure you, it came from too deep inside me to be called deliberate, and it's as much a criticism of myself as it is of her.'

He stopped for a bit then and ran a hand over his face, as if apologetic for having talked at more length than usual.

'Anyway,' he said. 'My show closes next Saturday. She can have it then to do what she likes with. Or I'll give it to old Marnsett as a parting gift.'

This good intention never came off. The forces to arrest it were already in motion. On the Thursday

Messrs Berriman, Smith & Berriman of Chancery Lane, acting on behalf of their client, the Hon. Mrs Brian Marnsett, issued a writ for libel against Mr Paul Stafford and claimed damages.

Chapter Eight

I

On a wet Friday afternoon in May I found myself sitting with Paul in the dingy offices of Messrs Jude & Freeman at an address mistakenly called New Square, EC4. Paul had asked me to go with him. The two gentlemen we were consulting were Mr Freeman and Mr Kidstone.

Freeman, the senior partner, was a wizened, grey-haired man with a high frail voice and a fastidious expression as if a lifetime of acquaintance with the secrets of his fellow men had left him nauseated. Kidstone was blond and dapper and fat and in the middle thirties. He was a member of the Hanover Club and Paul had taken the writ to him.

'Well,' said Mr Freeman. 'It's a very interesting case. Unique in the history of the law, I should think. Though there have been a few not dissimilar precedents. What surprises me is that the Ludwig Galleries is not jointly cited. I can't see Berriman issuing a writ without including the owner of the premises on which the alleged libel was published.'

'He must be acting on explicit instructions from the plaintiff,' said Kidstone. 'Though I don't know quite what her motive can be.'

'Perhaps,' said Paul, 'she looks on it as a private quarrel, to be settled privately.'

'Settled,' said Freeman, looking up hopefully. 'Yes. I agree with you there. This is eminently a case not to take to court. There are too many pitfalls.'

'When I spoke of its being settled,' said Paul, 'I didn't mean it in a legal sense. After all, if someone killed someone else in a duel, that would be called settled, wouldn't it?'

Mr Freeman coughed and turned over the papers in front of him. 'There's no doubt the writ has been skilfully and thoughtfully worded. Wouldn't you agree, Kidstone? Of course, Mr Stafford, it's unfortunate there should have been this initial quarrel over the painting between you and the plaintiff. It gives colour to the suggestion that malice entered into the hanging of the picture in that particular company. That would colour a jury's view—if it ever came to a matter of a jury, which I trust it will not. Feelings may cool, Mr Stafford; in spite of what you say, feelings may cool.'

'It would be for her to withdraw the charge,' said Paul. 'I'm not able to guess whether her feelings will change in the next few weeks.'

'Perhaps an adequate apology, phrased in words to be mutually agreed, might help her to—to salve present anger.'

'No apology,' said Paul.

'Ha—hmm. For the moment then we have to consider this little quarrel as if it *will* come to court. . . I take it from what you say that you wish us to enter a defence based on a simple plea of "no libel"?'

'I think so. As far as I understand it.'

'But—' I began.

Paul waved me to silence.

'I must tell you, Paul,' Kidstone said, 'that if you restrict the defence in this way you're very much limiting your chance of success. And I'm certain whatever counsel we approach will tell you the same.'

The bad odour under Mr Freeman's nose became

95

more unpleasant. 'Of course, I don't know the full circumstances, but Mr Stafford may not be entirely wrong, Kidstone. There are special dangers to a plea of justification.'

'Oh, I know. If it should go wrong, the plaintiff's damages will rocket. But how could it go wrong? Mrs Marnsett is a woman who's hardly been noted for her observation of the conventions. If properly handled the case wouldn't stand a chance of *coming* to court. The mere threat of justification would scare the daylights out of her.'

Paul said: 'Tell me again what justification means.'

'It means that the alleged libel is no libel because it is more or less the truth. It means a justification of the construction put upon the offending matter by the plaintiff. In this case, if reasonable proof is forthcoming that Mrs Marnsett is a woman of light virtue, the association of her name and portrait with the names and portraits of other women of light virtue constitutes no libel and that's that.'

'You mean if justification were forthcoming the case would collapse.'

'Like a pack of cards. But of course Mr Freeman is right in that the proof would have to *be* convincing. British juries dislike attempted justification, especially against a woman, and a failure in this case would be disastrous. My point is that the mere *threat* of justification—if she isn't a woman of impeccable virtue, and I gather she isn't—would bring the case to a halt before it got off the ground.'

'And if we stick to the other defence?'

'Then it's simply argued out on its merits. Is such an exhibition a libel or not? I tend to think a judge will say yes. But if we get a good KC he may be able to bring Mrs Marnsett's character into the issue without actually attacking it. I'd say we had a fifty-fifty chance.'

Freeman said: 'Certainly I would advise a few preliminary inquiries into Mrs M's character. That can do no harm and will give us a better view of the situation.'

Paul was silent for some moments, biting his lower lip. 'No,' he said. 'Leave the woman's character out of it. This is a straightforward quarrel over a painting. She's a fool, but no *libel* was intended, so let the defence be based on that.'

'Hm,' said Mr Freeman. 'Hm. Hm. Hm.'

'You may find chivalry expensive, Paul,' said Kidstone, 'but if that's how you want it, let's see how it goes. In the meantime we must brief the best man we can to look after it.'

'Whom do you suggest?'

We all looked at Freeman, who rubbed the place where his hair should have been.

'Sir Philip Bagshawe is the top man.'

Paul grunted. 'I've only seen him twice, but I don't like the frontal bones of his head.'

'One thing we ought to consider,' said Freeman, 'is that if we don't retain him the other side almost certainly will.'

Paul stretched forward for a piece of blotting-paper and made some pencil lines on it. This he handed to the senior partner.

'D'you see what I mean?'

'Ha. Hm,' said the senior partner, and blinked. 'Well, there's Bartlett and ... whom do you suggest, Kidstone?'

'There's Raymond Hart,' said Kidstone

'Hart?' said Paul. 'Yes, I've played poker with him. Not a bad fellow.'

'We'll approach him,' said Freeman. 'We've not done much with him but he's certainly a coming man. I'll make an approach and see what he thinks. Eh?'

'What's the normal amount of delay in a case like this?' I asked.

Freeman said: 'The lists are pretty full.'

'Not as bad as sometimes,' said Kidstone. 'I was looking yesterday. We might get on about the middle of the Michaelmas term.'

'Michaelmas?' said Paul. 'That's the *autumn.*'

'Yes. Possibly early November.'

'Good God.'

Mr Freeman smiled thinly. 'It will have to go on the special jury list. But, after all, it will give that much longer, won't it, for feelings to cool?' It was clear that he was firmly of the opinion that this case, one way or another, must never come to court.

Kidstone saw us down the dirty, narrow, creaking, uncarpeted staircase.

'The law has a funny lopsided sort of wisdom,' he said. 'Nothing quite works as one thinks it should, but the proper end is quite often achieved. The longer experience you have of it the more you come to see that. Will you be in the Hanover this evening, Paul?'

II

In silence we walked through the rain to where Paul's grey and silver Rover waited. We climbed in, and Paul offered me a cigarette.

'Well?' he said.

'Well, what d'you *expect* me to say? To congratulate you on your idiocy?'

'Idiocy?'

'Well, chivalry, as Kidstone calls it! For God's sake, Paul! I was sitting there like a kettle on the boil, wondering what the Hell you were up to!'

'And now you're letting off steam, eh?'

'Why did you invite me and expect me to be a party to this nonsense? Of course you must justify!'

He started the engine but did not at once drive off. 'How?' he said. 'Send for Leo to talk about a passion five years cold?'

'You know very well that Leo was not the only one—nor the last one.'

'And what proof have I? One hears a lot—and sometimes Diana talks too much; but I haven't kept tags on everything she's done. It's not been *that* sort of a friendship, Bill. Anyway, Diana had a shock over the affair with Leo. Old Marnsett dug in his heels, and she's been more circumspect since.'

'With you?' I said.

He turned his car out of the square and through the old gate. Then he had to stop while a lorry was turning.

'It takes two to make love as well as a quarrel.'

'But one can usually provoke it.'

He smiled. 'OK. True enough. Of course I was Diana's lover in the early days. Since the break-up with Olive we've been—just good friends. Though twice—I have to confess twice—the friendship has led us into the bedroom.'

'Well, it's damned *ridiculous*!' I said. 'It's ludicrous— a woman claiming that you have damaged her reputation by hanging her portrait among light women, when she knows you only have to open your mouth to prove that she is one!'

'It's not quite as easy as that, old boy. Even supposing I wanted to open my mouth, as you elegantly call it, what proof have I? We didn't exactly alert the parlour maid! And *wouldn't* the jury think me a fine fellow trying to justify without proof in *that* way! Great !'

We moved off again. I frowned out of the window. 'But—but ... Kidstone says—the mere *threat* should be more than enough. If she were to get away with this, the thing could cost you thousands ... See the name of this street we're going through now? Carey Street. I don't want to see you ending up here.'

'Nor do I. But we're a long way from that. Anyway, she may withdraw yet, as Freeman clearly hopes. That's if she's allowed to.'

'Who would stop her?'

'Shall I drop you at your office?'

'Please.'

'Who would stop her? I'm not sure she has gone all the way with this willingly.'

'You mean Marnsett himself?'

'Well, yes... Let's think it through. She was certainly beside herself with pique and fury when she first saw the picture. Obviously she got him to put pressure on the hanging committee to have it thrown out of the Academy. No doubt she foamed at the mouth when she'd heard where I'd hung her in my own exhibition. She may well have said, "I'll *sue* him!" and meant it. And there I suspect Brian Marnsett took her up on the idea. There are times, you know ... Generally she has enormous influence over him; he gives her almost all her own way. But he's not altogether a fool, and now and then he suddenly puts his foot down and takes charge. Their relationship hasn't been too good for some time.'

'You mean Diana's bringing this action against her will?'

'Not exactly. But she may have made so many complaints about me to Marnsett that she can't back down now even if she thinks better of it—that is, and retain some sort of married association with him. It may be something of a test case for their marriage.'

'For which you may suffer.'

'I don't know...' He suddenly looked very tired. 'I had a letter from Olive the other day.'

'Oh?... Suggesting a reconciliation?'

'Suggesting that I pay her more money.'

'Does she know about your quarrel with Diana?'

'Of course. It's the general gossip. She offers me her sarcastic sympathy. I sometimes wonder if she ever cared twopence for me.'

'I think she cared a lot. But that doesn't mean she wishes you well now.'

He looked at me. 'You've been seeing her?'

'I saw her a while ago. I suggested then that you might make it up, but she didn't take kindly to the idea.'

'Thinking back. Thinking back, I ask myself if I was not the one who was half-hearted—or not whole-minded anyhow. Perhaps I never have been whole-minded in any of my love affairs, that's the trouble.'

He stopped the car outside my office and switched off. The engine had a moment or two's over-run, suggesting it needed tuning. He said: 'Whistler wrote a book called *The Gentle Art of Making Enemies*. I don't need any lessons from him.'

'Two jealous women.'

'What I need,' he said, 'is a lesson in the gentle art of making friends. Human values usually escape me. I deal mainly in the values of paint. Coming round tonight?'

'I don't think I can. Having spent the morning with you ...'

He said: 'But one *does* need to be whole-minded where human beings are concerned. Otherwise all but the dimmest notice something missing. Sooner or later—usually sooner—people discover that burnt sienna is more important to me than blood ties; viridian seems to have a gentler influence than maidenly virtue ... Yellow ochre, ivory black, orange chrome, cobalt blue, permanent crimson: I live 'em and breathe 'em and *eat* 'em. And to what end? That's what I ask myself—to what end? Keeping a wife in a style to which she thinks she ought to become accustomed? And defending my nose-thumbing gesture in the law courts? I think I shall drive home and get drunk.'

Chapter Nine

I

The mild damp spring and summer slipped away, lit only by a sudden brilliant fortnight for Wimbledon. I saw little of Paul, as I was working very hard covering the effects of the General Strike. News reached me that Mr Raymond Hart had been briefed to lead us in the libel action, and that, true to Freeman's prophecy, the solicitors acting for Diana had briefed Sir Philip Bagshawe. Although there was talk of a settlement, nothing had yet come of it. Paul, through the columns of the *Spectator*, carried on an acid correspondence with two RAs on the subject of his criticisms of the selection committee; but it all seemed rather trivial and unimportant against the traumas of class strife.

I wasn't able to get down to see Lady Lynn again, but I learned that the lecture tour had proved such a success that it had been extended, and Holly and Sir Clement were not now expected back until late in the year.

One day at the beginning of August I lunched with Paul at his club. He gave me a large whisky and downed one himself. For the first time his skin looked unhealthy, and I wondered if he had spent a fair part of the last two months doing what he was doing now. Presently we were joined by John Connor, a big upstanding black-haired Irishman with a slow gentle way of talking that belied his fierce looks.

'Glad you could make it, John. You've met Bill Grant . . . Bill, we have a proposition.'

'So your yachting holiday's still being considered?' I said.

'With no dissentients this time. We hope to leave some time next week. For Madeira.'

'Good. I'll drink to that.'

'Actually,' Paul said, 'that was all decided a week ago. What's being considered at this meeting is *your* yachting holiday.'

I smiled. 'Week at Margate for me. With or without a blonde.'

Paul ordered another round of drinks. 'There are four of us so far. John and myself and two of a crew. There's plenty of room for a fifth, and personally I'd like you to come. What do you say?'

'Me? A veritable land-lubber?'

'Don't give me that. After all the mucking about in small boats we did in Grimsby.'

'Small boats? Just how small is this? It can't be exactly a dinghy.'

'She's a fifty-eight-ton cutter,' said Connor. 'I bought her last autumn. She's an ex-pilot cutter that's been converted. Fairly old, of course, but she's sound over every inch. I've made sure of that. I've had an auxiliary motor fitted for inshore work. I've been round Ireland twice this summer and she's a first rate little craft.'

'And how long,' I asked, sipping a second drink, 'do you suppose this little jaunt is going to take?'

'Six weeks, maybe. Of course it would depend a bit on the weather.'

I said: 'You both obviously have laughable ideas of the amount of leave given to struggling journalists.'

'You're not struggling any longer,' said Paul. 'I hate

104

mock modesty. Why not go to your editor and tell him the facts? You haven't had *much* time off.'

That was true enough. I'd been working fourteen hours a day some of the time.

Connor said: 'Let's go to lunch, shall we? It'll give him time to think. Anyway, don't persuade him against his wishes. You don't know how poisonous even the most willing partners may seem to each other after a month at sea. You'll maybe hate my guts in a fortnight.'

'I'm convinced of it,' said Paul. 'That's why I want a change of company.'

We went in and ate.

'Have we anyone else in view if Grant refuses?' Connor asked. 'It's a pity Doughton-Smith is out of England.'

'There's Parkins,' said Paul. 'He's inoffensive enough. But an eternal yes-man might equally get one's goat in the end.'

'No, thanks,' I said to the wine. 'I have to work this afternoon.'

'D'you know, I'm looking forward to it, John,' said Paul. 'Whatever pleasure we get, or whatever mishaps, at least they'll be *real*. I could do with being in touch with something real for a change.'

When we had finished lunch Paul said: 'Well, Bill?'

I said: 'I'll talk it over with my immediate boss. But it may mean going up to Manchester and seeing Scott. He doesn't believe journalists should have holidays. I'll ring you as soon as I know.'

Rather to my surprise when I put the idea up that I should like a break—and if I exceeded the time for a legitimate break the rest would strictly be unpaid—the paper didn't object. I'd been at the stretch for three years. They were pleased with my reporting and articles on the General Strike and its consequences. The miners' strike looked as if it was going on for ever, and there wasn't much new to say about that. Perhaps I'd like to write a couple of pieces on what it felt like to be shipwrecked in the Atlantic? It would be a change from recording the shipwreck of goodwill in England.

I phoned Paul next morning and told him I'd come.

II

It wasn't until I saw the *Patience* that I had second thoughts. Experience showed she was all Connor claimed for her, but that first afternoon in Plymouth she looked lifeless, cramped, insignificant and ugly of line, dwarfed by the vessels around her and ridiculously small for anything more adventurous than an afternoon's fishing off Salcombe. We went aboard, stared about the deck, examined the gear and the sails, and then climbed awkwardly down into the gloomy and cramped and smelly interior.

Forward of the main companion ladder down which we had climbed was the saloon, with its hinged dining-table, its small swinging lamp, two or three mahogany cupboards, a solitary bookshelf and a portable wireless set. Leading off from this forward was a double cabin with, beyond, a door leading into the forecastle, where the crew slept and the cooking was done, and which connected separately with the deck by means of a forward ladder. Aft of the main ladder was another double cabin, and this was separated from the tiny engine-room behind by a stout bulkhead. The engine itself, a four-cylinder Kelvin motor, was accessible from a third hatch just in front of the binnacle. A lavatory and store cupboard occupied the space on either side of the main ladder.

Connor carefully watched our faces for any signs of misgiving or distaste, but Paul was always hard to read, and I was at pains on this occasion to show nothing of what I felt. We went off and had dinner at the Royal. Over it we discussed additional stores and when we should start. Connor thought everything would be ready by the day after tomorrow. Paul was taking along a case of whisky.

'I like those brothers,' said Paul, referring to our 'crew'. 'They're the sort who'd have been useful to Drake.'

'They'll not let us down,' said Connor. 'It's not a lot of fun being the crew on a show like this. Great thing is to find people who won't get seasick or the sulks at the first sign of bad weather.'

Among the passengers as well, I thought he was probably implying.

'Even bad weather,' said Paul, 'would be a change for me from the atmospheres I've been breathing. I don't know whether I dislike more the smell of Mayfair drawing-rooms or of lawyers' offices.'

III

We left Plymouth on a damp misty morning in mid-August and put into Vigo on the following Wednesday. The sea in the Channel on the first two days was choppy, with the cutter kicking and bucketing about at unexpected moments, and our newness to the vessel made adjustment a bit difficult; but later the weather improved and we had a fresh following breeze.

We settled into our quarters uncomfortably enough. After a time they began to expand, as do all shipboard quarters, even the tiniest, and we ceased to fall over each other and bang our heads and kick into various obstructions. The table in the saloon was on gimbals with lead beneath it to give it stability, and when the cutter was driving hard the person on one side of the table would eat his dinner standing up, while the man opposite sat on the floor. Paul and I shared the centre cabin and John Connor had the rear one to himself.

Sam and Dave Grimshawe—or the brothers Grimm, as they were soon called—were tough, hardy, efficient old mariners, both men who had commanded their own small craft and been at sea since childhood.

From Vigo to Madeira everything was as favourable as it could be. We caught the north-east trades, the sun shone, and with such a leading wind the idea that there was something venturesome in sailing over a thousand miles across the Atlantic in a small pilot cutter seemed a quite misplaced one.

Despite all his concern to see that the case was safely shipped, Paul did not touch the whisky after the first day out. As the days passed we turned brown and leathery with the warmth of the sun and the whip of the wind. I saw the tight expression on Paul's face begin to relax. During the last few months or years there had crept over his features certain nuances which had been unnoted until they began to go. The life he had been living had left its mark. Something of the smoothness and polite insincerity of his normal speech showed itself in the way his mouth formed the words: they slipped out facilely, polished and rounded and impermanent. Something of the universal praise with which success had surrounded him could be noticed in his eyes. With some saving instinct he had withdrawn for these few weeks to take stock.

For there *is* something fundamentally searching to the soul in sailing a small yacht in deep waters, even in fair weather. A man should not essay it unless he's prepared to see and recognise his own stature and his own unimportance. It's a sovereign cure for egoism and smugness. The sun rises out of a silver-grey horizon, and the immensity of waters, unmarred by ship or rock or bird, colours and blooms into the familiar pigments of day. The sea is a long grey swell; even in fair weather it is always uneasy, always moving in low ridges towards one or another horizon bent on some strange purpose, as if there were a universal solution to all restlessness waiting over the edge of the world.

The wind freshens and shifts a point and the sun climbs, quickly at first, then it seems more slowly as the measuring rim recedes. We shave unsteadily and wash and eat breakfast cooked on the Rippingale oil-stove by Dave Grimshawe, while Sam Grimshawe takes the wheel. Then we make our bunks and tidy the saloon, and John Connor, having taken his sights, goes below and plots out our position and our course, with Sam Grimshawe peering over his shoulder to see that the job is properly done. We talk or read through the morning until the sun rises to its greatest height and pours down on a tiny white cutter dipping through the water with its three sails taut and on the man at the wheel and on the men lounging on her slanting deck—and on nothing else except the furrowed, glinting sea. The sun begins its downward journey and the wind shifts another point and slackens, and for a few minutes there is a bustle while the sails are trimmed.

Then we have another meal and turn on the

wireless to remind ourselves that all the other men in the world still exist; and the afternoon passes like the morning, with a few clouds moving across the sky to mark the difference and to remind us that fine weather is our good fortune and not our right. Then the wind shifts back and freshens again, and the sun finds it's late and moves more quickly towards the end of the day. Gold seeps into the ridges of the waves, slivers of light turning slowly bloodshot, the deepening shadows in the troughs like smudges of the approaching night.

A last meal and everybody on deck to see the sunset, pipes going and a sense of well-being, speech in monosyllables if at all. Barely noticed, the temperature has fallen as the sky reddens: one and then another of us goes below. Dave Grimshawe, bearded and silent, spits overboard, and moves forward to light and put up the sidelights in the rigging. The sun has gone down into a slate-grey horizon bare of any ship or rock or bird.

Stars appear, winking one by one unobtrusively in the pale sky, then quite suddenly they have begun to grow and multiply and glitter in a cave of cobalt. And in that great space of empty water two stars only wink and bob their way blindly through the encroaching darkness, those in the red and green sidelights which Dave Grimshawe has put up. Neither of the Grimshawes could live for one minute in a vessel without those lights, for the Mercantile Law is rightly the law to them. But being a miserable amateur I sometimes wonder at their value. They certainly don't show us our way. Of course, they are a valuable protection against our being run down. But run down by what? The ocean is emptier than it has been for four hundred years. All steamships keep to the sea lanes.

And we are quite alone and bobbing forwards into the loneliness of sea and sky.

Well, the day is done and we are for the night.

IV

One unnatural event spread a cloud over the last few days of the outward voyage. As Paul's spirits lightened so Connor's grew heavier.

This was all the more curious because he had been the one to mention, before we left, the danger of a small company palling on each other in cramped surroundings over a long period. But the weather had been so good and the voyage so pleasant, I began to wonder if this was a normal development on his part, that he ended every voyage quarrelling with everyone in sight.

So we endured his attitude in silence and tried to ignore it. When he was particularly glum we politely asked after his health, but this made him more snappy than ever.

We made a good landfall on the last day of August and reached Madeira later the same day. We dropped anchor in the roadstead outside Funchal, and I began to speculate on what excuse Paul and I could make to return by passenger ship and leave Connor to his private gloom.

Not until the little bearded Portuguese doctor came out to issue our *pratique* did the mystery begin to resolve. His examination of us was brief and perfunctory until he came to Connor. There he stopped, felt his pulse, shook an emphatic head and thrust a thermometer into the Irishman's mouth. This when retrieved showed the figure 103.8°, and we were all refused permission to land. Connor glowered at the doctor and said it was all nonsense, what he needed was a few days ashore and some fresh fruit to eat; then he glowered at us and said yes, well, he'd had pains in his belly ever since leaving Vigo, but it was no good squealing about them in mid-Atlantic, he'd be all right in a couple of days. We said why on earth didn't he let us know he was sick, and he said a fine lot of good that would have done, we'd only have prescribed what he'd already taken himself.

In about an hour the doctor returned with a hospital launch, and Connor was taken ashore. For the rest of that day and night we remained bobbing gently up and down at our moorings, full of anxious speculation.

Early the following morning the little doctor again appeared, this time with permission for us to land and with the story in his broken English that during the night Connor had been operated on for peritonitis. We went ashore in the bright sunshine, and spent the next eight days in the neighbourhood of the International Nursing Home where Connor hovered between life and death.

While September slipped away we watched Connor fight his way slowly out of danger. In the meantime we kept an eye on the calendar. The Michaelmas Law Sittings began on October 10. We had intended spending only a week in Madeira, whereas it would be at least a month before Connor was able to travel, and then it was very doubtful whether he would be fit to rough it in the *Patience*. Paul cabled Messrs Jude & Freeman and received the answer 'Expect about October Sixteen or Seventeen.'

In the end Connor himself provided the solution. He suggested that we and the Grimshawes should take the *Patience* home ourselves and that he should return at his leisure in November or December.

'You've both got calls in London, and there's no need to hang around for me. With luck we should get a month of tolerable weather yet. The brothers Grimm are first-rate navigators and you should be home by the first week in October.'

'All the same, she's your cutter,' said Paul. 'We can wait another fortnight. You may pick up very quickly now.'

Connor shook his head.

'Summer weather is unreliable enough, God knows; but the chance of trouble much increases when October comes. There are really two choices: (*a*) you leave for home this week in the *Patience*, or (*b*) you book a passage at your convenience and leave *Patience* here.'

'What then?' I said.

'Then I'd either sell her on the spot or leave her in one of the harbours in the Canaries until next summer, when I could come out and fetch her.'

Paul looked at me and then back at the sick man.

'Which would you do, Bill?'

'I'd rather take the *Patience* home.'

'So would I,' said Paul.

Connor nodded. 'That's what I hoped. Good luck. And this time you won't have someone trying to navigate the ship and forget the pains in his belly. In the meantime will you ask the Grimshawes to come and see me.'

It was still early when we left the hospital: the sun was gaining in heat every minute, but a pleasant fresh breeze blew and we had ample time to stroll back to our hotel for lunch. The nursing home was east of the town and our hotel west of it, on the cliff overlooking the harbour and the sea, so we had a walk ahead.

'This place,' said Paul, breaking a long silence, 'almost makes me regret not bringing a box of crayons. The colours are so rich. See the light there . . .'

'Why didn't you?'

'Didn't I what?'

'Bring a sketch-book. You know, this holiday is the first time in my life I've seen you without some sort of a pencil in your hand.'

'I feel I don't want to bother . . . I've been painting without a break for seven years.'

We strolled along, and I stared absently at a tall man walking in front of us.

'Where did inclination end and compulsion begin?' I asked.

'God knows. You can't partition things off in life. At first you're dead keen just to paint. Then you're dead keen to paint really well. Then you're all out to make a name. Then you're all out to maintain it. Then suddenly instead of being all out, you're all in.'

'Career in a nutshell. But it doesn't end there.'

'No . . . one breaks and rests and begins afresh. But this holiday has been such a change . . . Life's the size you make it, isn't it? I suppose it's at this point that the tussle with fate really begins.'

We had wandered down through the steep, twisting streets of the old town to the jetty and were now about to take the new road leading from the Pontinha, which runs across the Ribeiro Secco to the West Cliff. At that moment the back of the tall man whom we had been following for some time became familiar. There was also a tall girl limping at his side.

I muttered something to Paul and ran up alongside them. It was Sir Clement Lynn and Holly.

114

V

My grandmother used to say of a hot drink on a winter's night that it 'warmed the cockles of your heart'. In a world where overt friendship is so common and the real thing so rare the experience of meeting true friends after a long interval is similar. They were returning at last from the protracted lecture tour and had broken their journey at Madeira in order that Sir Clement could meet a German physicist who had made his home there.

I introduced Paul and we strolled along talking at a good rate. Except that his hands and face were clean, Sir Clement was little altered. In the four years since we had last met he had developed a paunch, which lay strangely under a badly knitted pullover and seemed not to belong to him; one felt that at any moment he might reach up a hand and pull out a scarf or other detachable cause. In manner he had not changed in the least from the day I first met him when I was twelve years old: scrupulously polite, vague, long-jawed, deeply intellectual, and still with some inherent irresponsibility in his dealings with ordinary men. His knighthood was a slight embarrassment to him, like an ill-fitting collar-stud.

But Holly had changed—perhaps more even than the average girl between the ages of fifteen and twenty. For at fifteen she had been mentally precocious but physically undeveloped. I felt like someone who has left England in April and comes back in the middle of June. Not that she was pretty or ever would be, but in the interval summer had come.

We talked about their tour and about our voyage; I told them our troubles; they had heard Leo was engaged to be married; was it true, did I think? As if

I were likely to know more than they did. How was Mummy managing without them? Her letters told one nothing except about the dogs. A great idea, coming here in one's own yacht; it was like being a millionaire without the cost.

At their hotel we stopped, and I put in an invitation to dinner that evening before they did. We arranged to meet at seven-thirty.

Paul and I walked on to our hotel in silence.

'So they're the rest of the Lynns,' he said at last. 'They're in a different league from the brothers, aren't they? Not that Bertie is too bad ... But these two—these two are the genuine thing. Like father like daughter, eh?'

'She's doing pretty well at Oxford,' I said. 'What time she spends there.'

Paul stared at an elderly woman with mascaraed eyelids, dressed in flowing draperies and carrying a pet dog.

'What was he knighted for?'

'Services to science. I think it was something to do with the wave theory of matter.'

Paul scowled at the woman to show that she offended his aesthetic sense.

He said: 'I'm so damned ignorant of everything except a few social graces and how to paint pretty women in a pretty way—sometimes.'

'You're miserably illogical.'

'Oh, I suppose so.'

'You set out to specialise. Everything else must go by the board. And now you're complaining because your education hasn't been more varied. And you set out to be a success. Nothing must stand in your way. You made that clear often enough, in all manner of ways. Well, now you've got there, all I hear is moans of discontent. You began by despising the people concerned with success, and now you've come to despise the state itself.'

He was silent for some time.

He said: 'The first part of that isn't quite true. I'm not altogether discontented. But in a sense I've come to a dead end; because the Marnsett picture was a flash in the pan. I can break other new ground. But it won't be easy. Or I can go on repeating. I can with the *greatest* ease go on *endlessly* repeating. That's simple. Terrifyingly simple.'

We were near our hotel now and looking down on the shallow curve of the bay. The sea was a brilliant aquamarine dotted here and there with the white of small craft and the yellow and grey of a larger vessel which had just arrived off the island. The land climbed steeply behind us and towards the east it jutted out into the sea, grey-purple and grey-green.

Paul mopped his forehead. 'And the second part isn't true either. I don't despise success. Why should I? It's given me all I have. I'm independent of fools and rogues. I enjoy comfort and good food and drink. I like having plenty of money and being my own master and mixing with other successful men just as much as I ever did. And I don't despise *them* either. I'd be a bigger fool to do that. Most of them have had to work hard to get where they are and most of them have to work hard to stay there. Most of them have a better right to the title than I have. Most of them have made the best of the brains and intelligence and artistic gifts God gave them. And I like their attitude towards life; they're tolerant and astute and disillusioned and kindly. And they don't care in the slightest whether you were born in Blenheim or Bermondsey or went to Harrow or Borstal. In fact, the second would be an added attraction. The snobs I have to pander to is another matter; but one of the really satisfying things is that I hardly need consider them now.'

He had been talking rapidly but now he stopped.

'Go on,' I said.

He looked at me. 'Did I tell you I spent the month of July in Paris?'

'No. I wondered at the silence.'

'I spent the month just wandering around—looking at pictures, other people's pictures. And visiting studios, other people's studios. What I saw didn't make me any more proud of myself.'

'You've been there before.'

'I *lived* there—for a short time. I must have gone about with my eyes closed. I was too *young*, or something. I spent my time whoring, sitting talking with other students at corner cafés, learning a bit of French—and of course painting. Painting out of myself, and being taught now and then, but not *seeing*, not *really* learning as I should have done. Look at it this way: you're a reader, I'm not: did it never happen to you that you opened some of the great writers before you were *ready*—so you didn't take them in, the sentences didn't mean much, so you turned back to *The Magnet* and *The Boy's Friend*?'

'I know what you mean.'

'That's how I've been feeling these last two or three months.'

After a bit I said: 'Perhaps it's what Henri Becker was driving at long ago.'

'What?'

'About serving God and Mammon.'

'Hell, that's too much of a simplification.'

'I wonder, Paul,' I said, 'how many of those artists

you so much admired in Paris were living as comfortably as you are—or if dead were not miserably poor when they were alive.'

We turned in at the gates of the hotel.

'Oh, I know, I know,' he said, his voice suddenly lighter. 'One gets moments of passing disillusion. No one with imagination escapes them. But don't make the mistake of thinking I'm not going to hold on to what I've got.'

I wondered if these words were addressed to me or to himself by way of reassurance.

'I shall be getting as self-engrossed as Leo,' he added. 'And as long-winded. It's a habit that must be sharply discouraged. What time did the Lynns say? ... D'you think Sir Clement would tell me something of his wave theory over dinner?'

'Unless you want to miss your dinner I wouldn't ask him.'

VI

Holly arrived in an almost smart dinner frock which made her look more mature than ever. She had somehow become comely without losing those characteristics which I should always associate with her, the lanky youthfulness, the good grey eyes and the expressive mouth. The straggly hair seemed to have a new life and gloss about it, and light horn-rimmed spectacles had replaced the old steel goggles which had never been the right size. There was a warmth about her which the other Lynns lacked. She might not be good-looking, but she was going to be very much better looking than one would have expected five years ago.

'I'd hardly have recognised Holly,' I said to her father. 'I might have passed her in the street.'

'I wouldn't have given you the chance,' said Holly.

'Yes,' said Sir Clement, heaping unnecessary sugar on his grapefruit. 'I suppose she has grown.'

'Daddy measures my change by inches,' said Holly gently. 'It's the sort of phenomenon he can understand.'

'My dear child, I do appreciate that you were twenty years old the month before last—'

'By the slide rule.'

'By the natural sequence of somatic development as the term is generally understood. By the passage and measurement of man-made time.'

'You can add a thing up different ways,' I said. 'You can put it that a butterfly is so many weeks older than the chrysalis, but that doesn't exhaust the subject.'

'Or so many younger than the caterpillar,' said Holly. 'Have you ever painted a caterpillar, Mr Stafford?'

Paul looked surprised. 'No . . .'

Holly said: 'Nobody ever seems to paint insects properly. They're too small to bother about.'

'What is your special line, Mr Stafford?' Sir Clement asked.

'Mainly portraits,' said Paul, looking pleased someone didn't know.

'Of course, you saw something of Leo when he was in London, didn't you? I remember his saying you had introduced him to some of your friends. I remember him speaking of the Hon. Mrs Holderness, was it? Or was it Montgomery?'

'Montgomery,' said Paul. He looked at Holly. 'I've

always fancied that my masterpiece will be a full-length study of an earwig.'

'Caterpillars are my favourites,' said Holly. 'Those big furry ones with eyebrows.'

'You mustn't mind my daughter's views on painting,' said Sir Clement. 'I have found her with peculiar notions even on important subjects.'

This was definitely the remark of the evening.

'Coming here from New Orleans,' Holly said, 'Daddy's cabin was very noisy and he was put off his work by a dance band and other things. We're leaving the day after tomorrow in a banana boat, so that should be quieter. I've told him he should wait until we reach England; there's plenty of time then.'

Sir Clement said: 'It's really a question of working while things are fresh in one's mind. Notes are never the same. And besides, I am fifty-three this year, which gives me the bare expectation and no certainty of another seventeen years. No certainty at all. Seventeen years, that's, let me see, around a hundred and forty-eight thousand nine hundred and twenty hours. Roughly dividing that into half leaves a general maximum of seventy-four thousand four hundred and sixty hours for work. I hope to progress a considerable way, but there's no guarantee I shall have that length of time and certainly there's no incentive for listening to those semi-negroid discords which dance bands make.'

'Well, bananas should be quiet enough,' Holly said. 'You can't even make a noise eating one.'

'Why don't you come home with us?' Paul said. 'We've the room and the quietness.'

She looked at him directly for a moment, then transferred her bright eyes to me. 'Do you mean that?'

Surprised at this reaction, I said: 'If we'd a commodious steam yacht of about a thousand tons we'd be only too happy . . . You haven't seen our gilded dinghy.'

'There's a spare cabin,' said Paul. 'With two bunks. It's as cramped as the devil, but there'd be nothing to disturb you.'

'Except being bobbed about like a pea in a can and probably being sick for a fortnight,' I observed.

Sir Clement dabbed his bald head with his table napkin. 'Very warm in here. When I was a boy,' he said, 'I went to Australia in a three-masted barque. I remember being sick, but it soon passed. The captain was a Glasgow man. He used to quote Burns when the weather turned bad.

> Drumossie moor, Drumossie day,
> A waefu' day it was to me!
> For there I lost my father dear,
> My father dear and brethren three.
> Their winding-sheet the bluidy clay,
> Their graves are growing green to see.

Are you making this as a serious proposition, Mr Stafford?'

'We can't go, Daddy,' said Holly. 'Bill doesn't want us.'

'Ridiculous,' I said. 'Withdraw the statement!'

'Oh, I'll withdraw it,' she said, 'if you'll invite us to come.'

I looked at Paul. How far he *had* seriously meant the suggestion I couldn't be sure, but now he seemed in earnest. They were all smiling at me.

'Unfortunately,' I said, 'I'm the only responsible person at this meal. You're all a lot cleverer than I am, but so far as common sense goes you're twelve-year-olds.'

Holly said to Paul: 'I love Bill when he's being fatherly.'

Paul put his head back and laughed. 'Give it up, Bill. They know you're shamming.'

'The trouble with a lecture tour is that one has to *wear* things,' said Sir Clement. 'It would be a great relief not having to *wear* things. We should necessarily travel light?'

'One suitcase each at the outside.'

He beamed. 'My papers will just go in one case.'

'Make it a waterproof one,' I said.

'Would you really mind, Bill?' Holly asked.

'*Mind*?' I said.

'Good!' said Paul. 'I think it might be arranged.'

'It's arranged that we should like them to come,' I said. 'But at the risk of seeming fatherly again, I must point out a few of the provisos. First, let the idea be slept on tonight; see what second thoughts the morning brings. Then these two—children must be given a thorough opportunity of inspecting the cutter, and perhaps of taking a short trip in her to give them every excuse for backing out. Then if enthusiasm still remains at the same level John Connor must be consulted, since it's his yacht. Finally, I suppose we should get the views of the brothers Grimm, whether they would feel like tackling the journey with two more passengers ... that is, with a net increase of one. They're all points to be considered, but the most important is whether you two have the slightest notion of the sort of voyage you may be taking on.'

'I think,' said Sir Clement, eating rapidly, 'that a certain fine balance of imagination is necessary at the outset of all ventures. Enough to make the enterprise seem desirable, but not too much or the enterprise would never be undertaken.'

'That's exactly how I feel,' said Holly.

'Fr'instance,' he went on, 'had I known all the discomforts of that voyage to Australia I should never as a boy have had the courage to embark. But I have always been glad that I went. Pass the pepper, will you, Bill?'

I passed the pepper and smiled at Holly and felt myself already defeated.

Chapter Ten

I

In dealing with the Lynns it was always useless to expect the rational behaviour of ordinary creatures.

Paul was delighted with them. Unpleasant memories of the last few months, the shadow of the impending action, the staleness of overwork, the sham suaveness of the social new arrival, all these seemed to slip away.

The Lynns went to see John Connor, and, after he had assured himself that they were in their right minds and had not been cajoled by us, he raised no objection. Nor did the Grimshawes. Except for the awkwardness of having a girl about, one extra would make little difference.

The weather remained perfect, a slight westerly breeze with hot sun and cloudless skies, and the trip we took the Lynns round the island as an experiment was a too-complete success. Their tour of America had not been conducted without a good deal of lavish hospitality, and the prospect now of some discomfort and rough-and-ready meals was like a breath from home.

So we laid in our stores. Water for a month, bread in tins, lime juice, milk and tongues and pressed beef in cans, potatoes, sugar, butter, honey and jam, dried eggs, a big shallow box of spring onions planted in soil, soap and paraffin and matches, all the stores we had brought on the outward journey with some additional quantity and in a little more variety. Some of the additional stores were packed in the fo'c'sle, and Paul made room for extra water by selling his case of whisky to the hotel where we were staying.

We parted from Connor with good wishes and expressions of regret and weighed anchor exactly at dawn the day after. While it was still dark we had rowed out and taken our dinghy aboard. Both sea and land were very quiet, and there was an air of excitement and conspiracy about it. Very few lights in Funchal, and the island behind brooded dark and mountainous. A breeze stirred and moved across the ripples of the harbour.

We raised sail and slipped slowly away from the land, the last land we should approach for a thousand miles, if all went well. As the night lifted, the sky opened its opal of early light, with delicate pale islands of cloud decorating the silent greens of the east. Then a few darker clouds gathered and the sun sprang up behind them like the opening of furnace doors.

We had a free wind all that first day. Holly and her father had taken Connor's rear cabin, which was the most private, the rest of the accommodation remaining unchanged. Paul, I noticed, had bought a sketching block and some crayons in Funchal, but he still made no attempt to use them. He talked a good deal to both Holly and her father, and the expression in his long-lashed blue eyes was more than usually intent. Undeterred by my warning, he began to ply them with questions about their own work, which was a new world to him. They were very patient with him.

The sun went down that night brilliant but brassy, and clouds assembled in twos and threes on the horizon, pink and gold, with patches of washed green surrounding them. Dave Grimshawe caught my eye and jerked his thumb towards it, but we didn't say anything. After all, we couldn't expect all fine weather, and a few showery days would do no harm. Everyone was very happy and content.

The night was clear and calm, with an old moon rising after midnight and the wind a gentle breeze on our port quarter. Morning dawned watery but fine, and the choppy sea changed in character. A long, dark swell began to come in from the west. Almost for the first time since leaving England we saw cloud and felt the strength of the element on which we sailed.

The wind had gone north-west, but so far there was little of it. But the swell grew all day, until to us, who were accustomed to the swells of the narrow seas, it seemed of tremendous proportions. What affected one was not only the height of the waves but the great distances between them. From furrows ploughed in a field they had become hills and valleys. The cutter would lift to the top of one, light and airy, and it seemed without weight; in front of it was a great sleek-sided valley; you were on top of a ridge which stretched away for miles on either side, on top of a world of swift-moving water, then the vessel would slide down the side into a dark green, bottle green valley, the sails would flap, she would yaw a little; the valley was wide and dark and deep and there was no horizon to see, but some way off and approaching rapidly would be a rushing mountain of grey, swelling mast-high. She would answer her helm and shift back on her course and begin a slow climb, until the last moment when she would rise heart-lurchingly up and up like a cork, like a sea-gull, until we were again on top and gazing over all the rushing sea to the rim of the world.

We had a light supper that evening in a quieter

mood. Everything in the saloon creaked and slatted and groaned. The cutter seemed to be travelling through the water faster than she really was, and at times would twist and shudder disconcertingly. Every time we went down into a trough the sensation was like that of the Grand Dipper at a holiday fairground.

Holly had spent the day on deck in flannel slacks and a grey jumper, but in honour of the evening meal had changed into a skirt and blouse. Her hair had grown wilder and more Holly-like as the day progressed, but this also she had restored to its recent semi-tidiness. Despite the self-levelling table, cups slid about all over the place and could never be more than a quarter full. Towards the end of the meal Paul rose and lit the hanging paraffin lamp, but this made things still more uncomfortable. It swung its light constantly and maliciously backwards and forwards, creating and reducing shadows every few seconds and giving a goblinesque effect to the scene.

No sunset this evening; just a darkening of the clouds and a loss of the periodic horizon. Dave Grimshawe lit the navigation lights, and the night fell upon us.

Holly went to bed with a sick headache. She said the lamp was giving her the jitters. I saw that Paul was feeling ill also, but he would not let me take his turn at the wheel. In fact I didn't think the Grimshawes would allow him to take the wheel on a night like this, but I didn't argue and, since there was nothing else to do, turned in. I remember hearing it begin to rain heavily just before midnight, but did not hear Paul come in and slept soundly until dawn.

Paul woke me being sick. I condoled with him while I dressed and then went on deck. It was blowing now from somewhere north of west and raining too.

We were scudding along on our fore canvas and a snugly-reefed mainsail. Sam Grimshawe was at the wheel and I struggled to him. Drips of water formed and fell from the ends of his moustache. I shouted that the glass was not falling any more, but he shook his head. Presently he removed his unlighted pipe and spat overboard.

'Arn—eck—ine—er.' His words were blown away. On my asking for a repetition he was understood to say that we couldn't always expect fine weather. This was the sort of remark to invite no response, so I told him I'd get some breakfast and then relieve him at the wheel for a bit.

On going below I knocked at the door of the rear cabin and was told to enter. Holly was up and dressed but looking pale. Sir Clement was sitting up in his bunk in vivid crimson-striped pyjamas, his long legs dangling almost to the floor.

'Rough morning,' I said. 'It's blowing a bit and wet. How are you both?'

Holly pulled her mouth into a wry shape. 'We've had a foul night, being sick in turns. I'm better at present, but Daddy's still in the middle of it.'

Sir Clement said:

'The boat rocks at the pier o' Leith,
Fu' loud the wind blaws frae the ferry.

I find I dislike the sensation of sea-sickness more now than when I was a lad. But it comes back to me like yesterday.'

'Stay on your back today, Sir Clement,' I advised. 'Don't try to work and it will pass off quicker. I'll get you a cup of tea with plenty of glucose in it.'

'My dear Bill, there's a hoodoo on my work,' he said. 'First a dance band and then bad weather. Both produce in me the sensation of not wanting to live much longer.'

'I need some air,' said Holly abruptly. She pulled on a béret.

I followed her up the companion-ladder, which dipped and jerked as we climbed it. On deck I clutched a stay and put an arm round her to steady her against the first fierce thrust of the wind. After a moment or two one became used to the pressure. I noticed again how bright her eyes had become since she grew up.

She shouted: 'How's Paul?'

'In the same boat,' I said.

'You needn't be humorous about it.' She looked at me. 'Are you never sick, Bill?'

'I feel queasy but nothing happens. That's so long as I keep eating.'

'Ugh! Well, it's better up here. The air's—fresh. It clears your brain.'

The swell had broken up during the night, and sometimes flying spray was indistinguishable from the rain as it swept across the deck. Even on the lee side there was little protection.

We stayed for about ten minutes, then went below; I brewed tea for the invalids and had a cup with Holly in the saloon. I judged she was feeling better because she was able to watch me eating a boiled egg and bread and butter without aversion. The conversation turned to Paul, and I told her something of his recent history.

'And what's he going to do when it's all over?' she asked. 'He won't get many portrait commissions if he paints them all like that.'

'I think it was just a freak; a sudden break-away that won't be repeated.'

'It must be a bore to be famous,' she said. 'And dangerous. If everyone kept telling me how wonderful I was I might in the end come to believe it. I wonder if great men have any sense of humour.'

'It depends on the type. All embryo dictators ought to be sent on a voyage like this. It might save the world.'

'You mean if the yacht foundered.'

I laughed. 'Not necessarily. If the wind merely blew hard enough and they found themselves bobbing about in a very empty sea.'

She nodded. 'Most sailors have a feeling for religion.' She thoughtfully screwed a drip of water out of her béret and was silent. 'I wish I had more.'

I regarded her quizzically. 'More religion? What's the matter with it?'

'I don't know. It's like this beastly yacht, there one minute and not there the next. I've been dragged up in such an odd way, Bill. I've always been told the basic truth about everything. Truth in its component parts, so to speak. Food was so many calories and carbohydrates and proteins. Life began more or less with the slipper animalcule. The bloom on grapes had something to do with parasites or microbes. One had a bath in two parts of hydrogen to one of oxygen. The reason beech leaves were such a glorious green was that they absorbed all the colours of the spectrum and rejected only blue and yellow. Father Christmas was a fairy story told to old-fashioned children to keep them good. Intelligent children didn't need such a bribe. Religion by definition seems the same sort of story to keep adults good, and intelligent adults don't need it.'

Just in time I rescued my egg, which had decided to slide off towards the fo'c'sle.

'This comes of being tipped about in your bunk all night.'

Holly wrinkled her brows at me. 'The funny part is, Mother's a good *Christian* in spite of it all. A really good one; even though she taught me little enough. And Daddy . . . I think he feels that on his death-bed in a moment of perfect insight he'll suddenly find himself able to express God in the terms of one pure, beautiful equation.'

'I can't help you, Holly,' I said, feeling depressed that I could not.

'I know, Bill, nobody can. But I like talking to you. It's such a rest from being sick.'

'You've not really changed, you know,' I said. 'You're still the same horrid little girl who used to follow me about the place asking awkward questions when I came for holidays with Bertie and Leo.'

'Aren't I?' she agreed with pleasure. 'One doesn't alter much inside.' She went on: 'I've always—ever since I can remember—I've always wanted to know where I was going, wanted an aim and a purpose, and never really had one. I suppose I was born awkward. Some people just don't seem troubled at all. Whereas Bertie seemed to find exactly what he wanted and go off to it without a thought. He doesn't know as much as I do, but I think he's much *wiser*.' She stopped and made a face. 'I wish we didn't get so much of that going-down-in-a-lift feeling.'

'The great thing is—'

The door from the forward cabin opened and Paul came staggering in. He looked distinguished but incongruous in a black silk dressing-gown which would have been more suitable among the exotic decorations of the *Normandie*.

'Hullo,' said Holly. 'Are you feeling better too?'

132

He shook his head. 'I wish the damned ship would sink. I wish this damned infernal jigging and jerking would stop.'

'Keep in your bunk,' I said. 'You'll get over it quicker that way.'

'I heard Holly's voice.' He waved a foot-square piece of strawboard he was carrying. 'I finished this last night before the worst began. It's yours, Holly, both the responsibility and the result.'

She took the strawboard from him looked at it and coloured.

'Oh, Paul, how silly ...' She half laughed. 'Thank you so much. I didn't mean you had to do one. Look, Bill.'

It was a crayon sketch. Against a background of blue leaves was a great green caterpillar. It was such a caterpillar as never had been seen on land or sea. However, one could not doubt its identity; the thing fairly crawled with life.

'And now', said Paul, staring hard at my empty egg-shell, 'I'm going back to be sick.'

II

Before noon the wind had shifted to north of north-west, and it stayed there without a break for five days. At the beginning there were heavy hail showers, but these stopped later and conditions were that much less unpleasant. The wind never approached a gale, but there was always the danger of a gale developing.

The difficulty was to make any satisfactory headway without shipping green water. Most of the time we were beating into the wind, mainly on a north-easterly tack with three reefs in the mainsail, a reefed foresail

133

and a storm jib. Two nights we hove to and lost some of the hard progress made during the day. And all this time there was the swell. Never a moment's cessation from movement, from climbing and falling, climbing and falling. An endless succession of millions of hills to be surmounted and defeated, high ridges all hurrying heedlessly away to pour themselves out over the edge of the world.

The main hatch, protected by both sliding and folding doors, was the one used by both passengers and crew during this period; the fo'c'sle hatch proved to be not entirely watertight and, even when we battened it down, continued to let water in.

On the fourth day Paul slipped in the saloon and sprained his wrist. On the sixth day about noon the sky began to clear and the wind shifted north-east. Sam Grimshawe took his sights—always an unsatisfactory business in a vessel plunging about like a cork—and said we were about two hundred and ten miles north-east of Madeira. As the wind was not so strong, we set all sail and altered course to a north-westerly tack, which we maintained all through that day and the next night, which was clearer and intermittently starlit.

Dawn broke quickly that morning and was over soon. The upper ridges of cloud in the east were lit with undreamed-of lights, mainly tangerine and chocolate brown. Round the horizon the broken clouds were edged with pink and orange above the dark, empty sea. Then in a space of seconds the warmth went out of the colour and the upper ridges split into a raw, vivid yellow.

I was up in time to help Dave Grimshawe take two reefs in the mainsail. We were doing this none too soon. The wind was becoming squally and the cutter was plunging too much in the steeper seas. We staggered to the mainmast as the cutter dipped. Sam Grimshawe at the wheel eased her up into the wind a little to spill the wind out of the sails.

I took a turn with the topping lift to take the weight of the boom. A hail of sea-spray swept over us.

'Let go,' said Dave.

I lowered the throat halliard and then the peak.

The wind roared through the rigging, but Dave took in no sail. As the gaff came down a few inches the sail slapped and slatted.

'Go on!' I shouted.

Salt water dripped from Grimshawe's beard. 'The blamed thing's stuck,' he shouted back.

The mechanism which worked the roller reefing of the mainsail had jammed and the handle would not turn. I tightened the halliards again. Sam Grimshawe at the wheel saw something was wrong and luffed the cutter farther up into wind hoping this would help to clear the trouble. She dipped more wildly than ever and water came aboard and nearly swept me off my feet.

'I'll get ... screwdriver,' Dave shouted at me, and began to crawl back to the engine-hatch. Waiting a favourable moment, he dived down it, while I clung there with the spray like a flail.

She was getting her nose into them now, and as I watched she hit head on into the tip of a wave, like butting into a milestone, as Sam afterwards put it. When I had rubbed the water from my eyes the deck was awash and the cutter was heavy in the water and was not rising as she normally did to the oncoming seas.

After what seemed an age Dave Grimshawe reappeared again and crawled forward with Sam

135

shouting instructions after him. Fortunately at that juncture the first squall passed and we were able to make our adjustments before a second came up. But the cutter had taken in a lot of water, and it would be necessary to put somebody on the pump.

A few minutes later I found Sir Clement Lynn sitting in the saloon smoking a damp cigarette. He had a chair wedged under one end of the table so that it could not slide about, and his feet on the rail beside the cupboards. He had made very few appearances during the last days.

'Sorry about all the water,' I said.

He put out a rubber boot and stirred an eddying pool with his toe. 'The important thing is to view minor discomforts in their true perspective. The immediate present in time is apt to loom too large. What one should do is get a pencil and make a dot and say, "There, that is me at this instant, no more and no less." What is the tobacco the Grimshawes smoke?'

'Digger Plug.'

'Hm. Do they cook all the food in it? Perhaps I imagine these flavours. I wish Ethel could see me now. She always says I eat too much.'

At that moment Holly and Paul came into the saloon. Holly actually looked better for her eight days at sea; she had recovered more quickly than the other two, and the constant wind had tanned her normally pale skin. Paul, his wrist bandaged and with a considerable growth of beard, had not come off so well, but I had a feeling that he was more content than he had been for years.

'I'll clean this up in a few minutes,' said Holly, looking at the water which was slopping about the floor of the saloon.

I followed Paul's eyes to the barometer. 'I know,' I

said. 'It's still low and we haven't made very good progress. We'll be six weeks on the passage at this rate.'

Paul said: 'The Grimshawes want to make for Vigo. They say Sir Clement and Holly could travel overland from there.'

'That would be admitting defeat,' said Holly, taking off her mac and béret and shaking them.

'And the weather may improve at any time,' said her father.

'I suppose we've plenty of food?' said Paul. 'We shouldn't have used even our normal rations this week.'

'Food's all right,' I said. 'The question, with the wind in this quarter, is how long would it take to make Vigo?'

Paul draped his dripping coat over the end of the table, but said nothing.

'What of this court action of Stafford's?' asked Sir Clement. 'It's—hm—the first of October tomorrow.'

Paul said: 'It won't come off until about the fifteenth, and if I'm not there they can postpone the darned thing until I am.'

'Of course,' I said, 'the obvious resort would be to go about and run before the wind back to Funchal.'

There was silence.

'That *would* be admitting defeat,' said Holly.

I patted her head.

'Whom would it be admitting defeat to?' Paul asked.

'Ourselves,' she said. 'They're the only people that matter.'

He looked at her. 'Yes, you're perfectly right.'

Sir Clement climbed slowly to his feet, holding to a cupboard. 'This change of position has done me good. I'll go back and do a little work. That will complete the cure.' He rubbed the week's growth on his chin. 'I have seldom felt my kinship more with the Anthropomorpha. One develops the simian desire to scratch.'

When he had gone I said: 'He's the one we have to consider.'

Holly nodded. 'I know. And Paul's wrist. Don't be influenced by me; turn back if you think it best.'

'Let's see today out,' suggested Paul. 'There's a good chance that the weather will moderate. It should do on the law of averages.'

III

The law of averages is not one which has much influence on wind and weather. It blew steadily all that day, and we remained hove-to under reefed mainsail and small jib with a sheet to windward, bobbing up and down like a cork. With sails trimmed this way there is always a certain amount of drift, and some of our progress in the previous twenty-four hours was likely to be lost.

An hour before sunset, the wind having dropped, we sighted a tramp steamer. She was a biggish ship, eight or ten thousand tons, and was making heavy weather of it, burying her great blunt nose in the seas and spouting them across her decks. But her progress was steady and she rapidly came up with us. When she was about a mile away she signalled; but every few seconds she was hidden from us by the next wave and we couldn't read what she said. Dave Grimshawe got out a storm lantern and signalled I.M.I.

Through a flurry of rain we saw that she was

approaching nearer and had again altered course with the apparent intention of making a circle round us. Both Holly and Paul had come on deck, and the five of us watched her with interest.

'Wish she could give us a tow,' said Paul.

'She's all adrift if she thinks *we* want her help,' said Sam Grimshawe.

With the glasses we were able to read *John Armitage* and *Liverpool*. Homeward bound. She made no further signal.

After a complete circle she came in suddenly, on our lee so as not to interfere with our wind, and soon we were barely two hundred yards apart. She was wallowing now, fairly wallowing in the sea like a great animal, scuppers under.

We saw a man on the raised deck beneath the bridge. He put a megaphone to his lips, but the words didn't carry. Holly waved as if to show appreciation. Then a man appeared on the bridge-deck and began to semaphore.

'What is it?' I said.

Dave Grimshawe wiped the salt water from his mouth with the back of a hairy hand.

'He says, we seem to be in trouble; can he be of any assistance?'

'Looking for salvage,' growled Sam. 'Tell him, no. We're right 'nough.'

I said: 'I suppose he's not used to seeing little cutters in this latitude. Thank him, Dave, and say that we're going on quite nicely. But,' I added, 'ask him if he can take off a woman passenger and two sick men.'

'Bill!' said Holly. 'That's not fair! I—'

'One sick man,' said Paul.

'Go on,' I said to Dave. 'See what he says.'

I caught a glimpse of a smile under Dave's beard as

he began to signal.

'Bill, *why* should I go?' said Holly. 'I can see—'

'Sh . . . he's answering. Well?'

'He says the sea is too big at present, and it'll be dark in 'alf an hour. He says he'll try an' keep in contact with us tonight and see what the weather's like at dawn.'

'All right. Thank him and say we shall be pleased if he can do that.'

'I'm not going,' said Paul.

'You must,' I said. 'You don't want that action postponed.'

'I don't see why *anyone* need go,' said Holly. '*We* haven't complained, have we?'

'Your father isn't a young man,' I said, 'and he's had a tiring lecture tour. It was a great idea, but the weather's been against us. And if he goes . . .'

'Oh, yes.' Holly took off her glasses to wipe the spray from them. 'You're right there. I couldn't possibly desert him now.'

'If one goes we all ought to go,' said Paul. 'But then I don't suppose the brothers Grimshawe . . .'

'They couldn't manage it themselves,' I said. 'It wouldn't be fair either. It won't matter about my being a bit late back. Three can manage the cutter in comfort.'

'Or four,' said Paul.

'Three,' I said. 'With that wrist you'll be a passenger anyhow for another month.'

'Um,' said Paul. 'What do you think, Sam?'

The man at the wheel did not remove his suspicious eyes from the *John Armitage*, which had drawn away into the gathering dusk and was once more nudging her way into the oncoming seas.

'She'll have lost us long afore morning.'

140

Dawn found the horizon bare. Wind and sea had moderated, but still were much against us. We set some sail and decided that a useful compromise between all the conflicting suggestions was to try to make Vigo.

At noon to our surprise we sighted the *John Armitage*. We learned later that she had heaved to during the night and had taken the opportunity of making an engine repair. She had given us plenty of sea room and had fallen well behind.

As soon as the tramp was sighted Paul went into an excess of indecision. I had never known him so irresolute. I told him that the issue was plain: if the master of the *John Armitage* would agree to take anyone off, then he must go. Very well to say that he did not care if the libel action was put down in the lists again; that wasn't true, the thing had been at the back of his mind all summer. I didn't mind being left alone, it would be rather fun.

'I know, I know,' he said. 'It's all very pretty the way you put it. But I invited you on this trip. What sort of a mouse do you think I am to desert you in mid-Atlantic after a few days' bad weather!'

'Well, damn it, we're in no *danger*. I should certainly go if I were in your shoes. You ought to know me well enough to be sure I wouldn't say so if I didn't mean it.'

'Oh, you mean it,' he agreed. 'And thanks for the suggestion. It seems to be a question of my own conscience.'

'Your own what?'

'Anyway, don't congratulate yourself on losing me yet. This rusty old tramp will probably consider the sea is still too rough.'

Fifteen minutes later we began to exchange messages with the *John Armitage*. Then we dowsed our head-sails and took a few more rolls in the mainsail, leaving just enough to steady her in the swell while under motor. It was strange to feel the beat of the Kelvin engine.

The *John Armitage* signalled again.

Dave shouted: 'He wants fur us to go in further under his lee before he lowers a boat.'

'He'll not get me any nearer,' shouted Sam, his moustache drooping. 'If we got in too close he'd knock us to bits. Tell 'im no.'

More semaphoring passed.

'He'll lower a boat,' said Dave.

The big tramp came slightly more into the wind, and we edged round until we could feel some protection from her great iron sides. Two of her davits swung out and a small boat was cautiously launched, one moment relatively steady as she swung from the ropes, the next sweeping up and down by the side of the mother ship. Then she crawled away like a beetle from under a protecting wall and came towards us through the broken water.

Paul went. We said goodbye, Holly and Sir Clement and Paul and I. At the last moment I almost regretted having persuaded them to go; there might be a month of hard sailing ahead, and the change after they had left would be drastic. Sir Clement shook his head at me and took my hand while he clutched his suitcase of papers.

The transfer was an anxious one. Getting into the ship's boat with its crew of seven was the least difficult part. Through the glasses I watched them come under the shadow of the *John Armitage* and thought they were drowned twice in unsuccessful attempts to board her. But at last it was done. I saw three figures standing by the rail of the upper deck aft of the funnel as the *John Armitage* hooted once and slowly turned and began to draw away from us. I took the wheel while the Grimshawe brothers raised sail. Then through flying spray I watched the bulk of the tramp steamer dwindle until it disappeared into the grey heaving patchwork of the distance.

I went below and made an entry in the log. 'Mr Stafford, Sir Clement and Miss Lynn left for England. Remaining in *Patience*: Grimshawe, Grimshawe and Grant.'

For the rest of the morning I was below, tidying up the saloon, wandering through the unaccustomed emptiness of the three main cabins, wondering if now, in the ironical way things happen, we'd have fair weather all the way home.

Dave Grimshawe came below, paused, wedged in the door of the saloon to light his pipe.

'Be wondering what you'll have for your midday meal, Mr Grant. Tin of tongue, maybe?'

I agreed.

'Thur's a few of them spring onions left. As well t'eat them before the soil goes sour.'

'Yes,' I said. 'We'll have those.'

'Glass has gone down again,' he said. 'Didn't like the green in the sky this morning. Reckon we haven't seen the end of it yet by no means.'

'Well,' I said. 'I'm very sorry to lose my friends, but this was the best solution.'

'Aye. 'Tis just a question of ridin' out this stiff breeze o' wind.'

'Did you check the rest of the water?'

'Yes. 'Tis right enough.'

Dave Grimshawe stayed in the doorway drawing

at his juicy pipe. He had got on well enough with all those who had left, but their going had unlocked his tongue.

'That was a queer young lady,' he said. 'First night we was out she came and stood by me at the wheel. I started telling her about the stars. I felt a fool, fur it turned out she knew more about 'em than me.'

'She knows a good bit,' I said. But, I thought, she doesn't know Bertie's secret of happiness. Very few of us do.

'She don't make a show of it,' said Dave. 'But she told me one of them stars, Beetle-something in the Hunter, was so big that if you put the earth at its edge the earth wouldn't go round it in three hundred and sixty-five days. I suppose that couldn't be true?'

'If she told you,' I said, 'it is. They're a great family for telling the truth.'

'Be they engaged, Mr Stafford and her?'

'Engaged?' I said in surprise. 'Good Lord, no. They only met in Funchal. What makes you ask?'

He shifted and looked round for somewhere to spit, but thought better of it.

'Oh, nothin'. Twas just an idle thought.'

'But something must have made you think it. What was it?'

He stared at me from under bushy eyebrows.

'Lord, I don't know. I thought from the way I caught them looking at each other now and then that perhaps they was engaged. I say 'twas just a notion. That was all.'

Chapter Eleven

I

To a man not fond of his own company it might seem obvious that twenty-two days spent beating into head winds in a small cutter in the Atlantic with two taciturn seamen for company would become very tedious. But I hadn't expected that it would be so. I like being on my own. This has long been regarded as a major eccentricity by my friends.

Of course the persistently adverse weather was to blame. The cramped surroundings, the never-ceasing lifting and ducking of the boat, heavy rain, the awareness that we were making painfully slow progress; all these wore down patience and stamina. Of course, I was very disappointed at missing the libel action. The whole thing would be past history and stale news when we reached home.

... I dismissed from my mind Dave Grimshawe's curious assumption about Paul and Holly. Obviously there could be nothing in *that*. The thought recurred, and I wondered how he could have come to make the mistake ...

We did not run into Vigo but made the journey direct.

Off the Bishop a fast motor vessel passed so close to us that I could have given them the message I had promised Holly, but at that time we were almost becalmed, and reaching Plymouth might be a matter of one more day or two. So eventually we crept into the Sound one late October evening unheralded and unexpected.

Getting our clearance papers was not a difficult matter, and now that we were at last here I was anxious to go ashore. I parted from the Grimshawes, who both had homes to go to, and made an appointment to meet them again the next morning to see about the arrangements for the winter care of the cutter and such other minor matters as needed the attention of the owner. Then I went off to the Royal and booked a room for the night.

The sensation of being on solid ground again after so long a voyage is a peculiar one. I couldn't get used to the spaciousness of the hotel, to the fact that everything remained in exactly the same place minutes on end, to the absence of the sound of the sea and the thrust of the wind, and the creaks and groans of straining wood. My eyes, unused to the stability about them, began to supply movement by some mal-mechanics of their own. The floor of the dining-room persisted in going up and down before my eyes. I began to feel seasick.

I asked the waiter if he could get me an evening paper. He failed to do this but brought a morning paper instead, and I was able to subdue my dizziness and get abreast of latest developments in the world of affairs.

The miners had gone back at last. Mr Baldwin was predicting an era of industrial peace. Unemployment had reached a new peak. My old friend Mussolini had been making a belligerent speech at the League of Nations. The new football season was in full swing and I didn't know even who had won the cricket championship.

Then I stared at the paper, not quite able to believe

146

my own eyes. A paragraph said:

'The suit for libel, which the Hon. Mrs Brian
Marnsett, daughter of Lord Crantell, is bringing
against Mr Paul Stafford, the well-known portrait
painter, is due to open today before Mr Justice Freyte
and a special jury. Sir Philip Bagshawe, KC, and Mr
J. K. Fearborne are appearing for the plaintiff. Mr
Raymond Hart, KC, and Mr John C. Starbell are
representing Mr Stafford. Mr C. D. A. Cressigny is
holding a watching brief for the Ludwig Galleries.'

I looked at the date of the paper, and then went to
the reception desk and told them I'd not be requiring
my room tonight. A train for London left at 11.30. I
went into the writing-room and wrote to David
Grimshawe, explaining my reasons for leaving Plymouth without seeing them again and giving them
what advice I could for the laying up of the cutter and
the disposal of the remaining stores.

I phoned North Road Station and was lucky
enough to get a sleeper. Then I went out and tried to
get an evening paper for myself, but was only able to
buy a *Western Evening Herald*, which didn't mention
the libel suit. Then I went back to the hotel and
repacked my battered little suitcase.

Time passed, and I caught the night train for
London.

II

The libel suit is perhaps the most notorious event in
Paul Stafford's life, and it has been variously recounted
in his biographies and elsewhere. In retelling it here

147

it didn't seem enough to rely on these or on my own fairly vivid memory, so I have referred constantly for verification to the almost verbatim account which appeared in *The Times*. In those days *The Times* thought nothing of devoting several full pages to the processes of the law, and their reporting was meticulous.

When I reached Paddington, London, like me, was not yet properly awake: even so its noises impinged on my ears and I couldn't get used to them. The air smelt stale and as if everyone else had breathed it first. I took a quick bath, changed into a respectable suit, and decided the office could wait another day. Paul's flat at a quarter to nine, and the woman who came in every morning let me in.

'Bill!' Paul said, his face lighting up when he saw me. 'I was getting worried. Why didn't you let me know?'

'We only reached Plymouth yesterday afternoon. What's this about the lawsuit?'

'You're just in time. It only began yesterday.'

'So I saw. What caused the delay?'

'Some cases before ours took longer than expected. How did you manage after we left?'

I told him. No, I hadn't let Holly know yet. The news of the action had brought me up as quickly as I could make it. What had happened so far?

'The case for the plaintiff is about half through. But Diana hasn't given evidence yet. Tell me more about the trip. It must have been tedious.'

We talked while he brushed his hair and put on a jacket and waistcoat. He still looked tanned from his holiday and more rested and at ease. About him in this expensive flat were the ceramics he had collected, the pieces of good sculpture, the altogether handsome furnishings of a rich and successful man. The tramp steamer, he said, had deposited the Lynns and himself in Liverpool. He had been down to see the Lynns last week and what a ménage!—and had also seen Holly in Oxford. It was too early to say how the case was going—only the preliminary guns had been fired. Mr Justice Freyte was an odd character, who seemed to like practising his sense of humour on the court. Raymond Hart was able enough. He'd worked his way up, Paul had learnt, from a poverty hardly less complete than his own, so that at least established a bond.

'I suppose you're keeping to the defence you stipulated? No mud-slinging, I mean?'

Paul looked at his watch. 'Time we left. I've got my car round the corner ... Mud, you ask? Well, mud seems to be a sort of suspensory agent in all law cases. There won't be any direct mud-slinging if I can help it, Bill. But I can see there's going to be plenty of insinuations flung about, and nothing I can say will make the least difference.'

Just before we reached the Strand we stopped at a post office, and I sent off a telegram to Holly telling her of our safe arrival.

The Courts were fermenting with life, and reporters tried to get a statement and took photographs as we entered. Mr Freeman and Mr Kidstone were waiting in the gloomy Monastic-Gothic central hall; I shook hands with them and we went straight into court. We had to thread our way through numbers of well-dressed people who, on the grounds of various remote and largely imaginary connections with the case, were attempting to get into the body of the court, the public gallery being already full. Some of them greeted Paul hopefully, but his responses were brief and without encouragement.

We took seats just below the judicial bench. Freeman and Kidstone sat on each side of Paul, and I sat next to Kidstone. Further down Mr Henry Ludwig was passing the time flipping through a Sotheby's catalogue.

Already the court was nearly full. One was conscious all about one of a stir of expectancy. Pervading everything was that strange smell, books and breath and old leather.

Diana Marnsett came in, took a seat at the other end of the row in which we were sitting and began to confer with her solicitor. She didn't glance in our direction. She looked austere and irreproachable, dressed in black with a white flower to give the ensemble relief, and with a close-fitting black hat. I realised how wrong an impression I should gain of her if I were on the jury.

At this point a rich throaty voice broke in from behind and Paul turned to reply to it. Our counsel. I didn't like to turn round and so only received an impression of a red face and hooked nose with the curled grey wig tilted forward over it. So this was Mr Raymond Hart, KC, who had 'worked his way up'.

Beside him gowned figures were talking together in undertones, and at the other end of the bench I recognised Sir Philip Bagshawe from photographs, the heavy black-rimmed spectacles, the plump cheeks, the receding chin. There were three women on the jury.

Paul leaned across to me.

'I'm glad you're here, Bill. I feel more comfortable with you about.'

'What d'you make of the case so far?' I asked Kidstone.

Kidstone crossed his legs. 'Yesterday's witnesses were not impressive. Mr Hart succeeded in nullifying the effect of the doctor who said Mrs Marnsett had been ill as a result of the libel. And the employee of the Ludwig Galleries who came forward to testify that Mr Stafford was furious when he took in the portrait to be hung ... well, a man who has been discharged for drunkenness ... The sort of witness who comes forward and testifies from spite isn't much good to a litigant. Of course, a lot will depend—'

The rap of the hammer stopped him in mid-stride, and we rose to our feet as the judge came in. We bowed to each other and he sat down. The business of the day was ready to begin.

III

The sharp, thin, ascetic face under the wig didn't look a healthy face, but it looked a very alert one. Mr Justice Freyte was well known for his summings-up. Silence fell on the court. Sir Philip Bagshawe was on his feet.

'Call the Hon. Mrs Brian Marnsett.'

We watched her rise and walk with feline dignity into the witness box. With her beauty and poise she would be a hard witness to handle roughly, if one wished to keep the sympathy of the jury. Our Mr Raymond Hart would have his hands full.

Sir Philip led his client through her evidence: it was all courteous, deferential. The beautiful society woman, dignified and refined, second daughter of Lord Crantell, one-time governor of Bengal. Wife of Colonel Brian Marnsett, the well-known philanthropist and art connoisseur. This painting commissioned from Mr Paul Stafford. On completion a dispute arose as to the disposal of the painting. Mrs Marnsett had naturally understood it was to be her property at the price agreed.

Where *was* Colonel Marnsett? I wondered. If he was partly behind this action, as Paul suspected, there was no evidence of it by his presence in court.

... Astonished and deeply hurt at the news. Could hardly believe it, so she went round to the Ludwig Galleries and saw for herself. Certainly she felt that such a hanging was a grave and deliberate affront to her moral character—and made by a former friend. So upset had she been that she had been taken ill the following day, as Dr Sowerby had testified, and her health had been impaired for some time.

The gentle, courteous voice went on and on, coaxing its responses from the witness. The jury could not help but be convinced by the frank and modest manner in which the story was being told. The judge was leaning forward writing down the replies which Mrs Marnsett made. The light was shining across the lenses of his spectacles, and one got the impression that he was writing with his eyes shut. Unlike most of his colleagues, he didn't hold up the hearing every few seconds while he completed his notes, and I wondered if he used shorthand.

The voice of Sir Philip Bagshawe ceased, there was a stir in court and another stir behind me. Sir Philip had sat down and Mr Hart had risen to his feet. I saw Diana put one hand on the edge of the box and raise her head to meet the prospective challenge.

Mr Hart began to speak. A peculiar voice. Rich and rusty and aggravating.

'Mrs Marnsett, is it true that you are generally accepted as a beautiful woman?'

Diana stared at him a moment.

'Possibly.'

'Many men have told you that?'

'Some.'

'Sufficient to make you feel that there was some truth in their statements, eh?'

'Yes.'

'But you would not, I should say, describe yourself as a conceited woman?'

'Certainly not.'

'Just, shall we say, one with an adequate appreciation of her own charm and beauty?'

'I am not ashamed of being considered good-looking.'

'You are not ashamed. Certainly not. Now is it true, Mrs Marnsett, that in the last four years you have been painted eight times by various artists?'

Diana looked rather feline. 'What has that to do with it?'

'Please answer my question.'

'I can't remember off-hand. Probably seven or eight.'

'In fact you make quite a practice of it.'

'Not at all. It has just happened that I have been painted several times.'

'I see. It has "just happened". And these portraits: were they all commissioned by you?'

'Not exactly. In several cases the artist has expressed a wish to paint me and I have agreed.'

'In which case I suppose he has done the portrait without fee?'

'Yes. If I have liked it I have generally bought it.'

'And if you disliked it?'

Diana hesitated. 'Then I have not bought it.'

'And so the poor artist got nothing?'

'If you wish to express it that way.'

153

'Rather putting a premium on flattery, don't you think?'

'Not if an artist is honest.'

'An honest artist, you would say then, paints what he sees irrespective of what the sitter will think?'

Diana bit her lip. 'I didn't say that. But an honest artist will not descend to flattery.'

'Now this latest portrait by Mr Stafford. Did that, like the others, just happen?'

'No, it was commissioned. He agreed to paint my portrait for a sum of money, as he would anyone else's.'

'Did he appear reluctant to execute this commission?'

'Not at all.'

'You did not pester him until he accepted it?'

'I certainly did not.'

'He was in fact eager to paint your portrait?'

'I didn't say that. He was quite willing.'

'Even though he had painted you once before?'

'It's not unusual to do that.'

'Did the suggestion to paint your portrait again come from you or from him?'

'From me.'

'I put it to you that he was somewhat unwilling to accept this commission but that you would not leave him alone until he agreed to do it.'

'That isn't true.'

There was a moment's pause; then the rusty, well-fed voice began again. Question and answer, question and answer. The judge had stopped writing and was sitting with fingers clasped patiently listening to the long interchange.

'You have stated that you did not see the portrait until it was finished?' said Mr Hart.

'That is so.'

'May I ask what your feelings were when you did see it?'

'I was—annoyed. I didn't consider it lifelike.'

'Sufficiently—annoyed to attack the painting with a knife?'

A faint flush appeared in Mrs Marnsett's cheeks.

'A palette knife. I was annoyed. At first glance the painting seemed to be a deliberate insult. I made some gesture towards it as if to strike at the face. That was all.'

'Meaning, of course, no harm to the picture?' came the sarcastic voice.

'Oh, I might have cut it; I don't know. Mr Stafford took good care I shouldn't get near it.'

'Was there a struggle?'

'A slight one.'

'Did you stab Mr Stafford in the hand?'

'Certainly not.'

'Yet Mr Stafford's hand was rather badly cut, was it not?'

'Possibly it was scratched. I didn't notice.'

'Too beside yourself with fury?'

'If he cut his hand he did it himself.'

'Would it interest you to know that he had to have two stitches in the wound? Surely not the sort of thing one does oneself.'

'He obviously took my movement seriously and jumped on the knife. He was very offensive in his attitude. I left immediately.'

'Nevertheless, you later offered to purchase the picture. Why was that?'

Diana lifted her shoulders slightly. 'I wished to keep my part of the contract.'

'You mean you wished to buy the painting in order to destroy it?'

'I didn't say that.'

'That is the natural inference, isn't it?'

'If you like.'

'You were not concerned with any artistic value it may have possessed?'

'I didn't consider it had any.'

'That is your opinion. I will call expert opinion to the contrary. You are aware, of course, that this portrait was submitted to the committee of the Burlington House exhibition and accepted for their annual summer exhibition, and that later without good reason it was abruptly rejected.'

'I am aware that it was rejected.'

'Is it true, Mrs Marnsett, that your husband is a trustee of the Royal Academy and a trustee administrator of various bequests connected with that establishment?'

There was a pause before Diana replied. 'I and my husband had no influence over the rejection of the picture from the Academy exhibition, if that is what you suggest.'

'What *I* suggest?' said counsel. 'No, madam, the suggestion comes from you. If you choose to put your own construction on the question, the jury must decide why such a denial leapt to your mind.'

The judge moved his head.

'Frankly, Mr Hart, that would seem to me the natural construction to put on your questions.'

'As your Lordship pleases—'

'Or I should say,' went on Mr Justice Freyte, 'the natural inference to draw from the juxtaposition of the questions. Considered separately, of course, the questions impute nothing of the sort, and had they been asked with some interval between, it is unlikely that the witness would have drawn from them the

156

inference that she did.'

'I am indebted to your Lordship for correcting me ... May I put it to you this way, Mrs Marnsett. In all the numerous portraits which have been painted for you, have you ever made it a condition that the portrait when finished should not be publicly exhibited by the artist if he had the chance?'

'No.'

'Might it be said that an artist would take it for granted, even in the event of a commissioned portrait, that he would first have the right to exhibit?'

'I have no idea of the law on the matter.'

'Would you have objected to this unflattering portrait appearing before your friends in the Academy show?'

'Of course I should have disliked the idea,' said Diana, her voice raised in exasperation. 'It was only natural to dislike it.'

'Even though, even though if it had appeared as intended on the Academy walls, *there would have been no question of any moral imputation in the pictures with which it was associated?*'

I glanced across at the jury. For the most part their faces were expressionless. They seemed to be watching the counsel more than Mrs Marnsett. Diana was now holding the edge of the witness box with both gloved hands.

'Now, Mrs Marnsett, turn your attention, please, to the actual fact of the exhibition of the picture at the Ludwig Galleries. You have said that a friend first told you of this portrait being exhibited, and that you went there yourself and were deeply upset at what you saw.'

'Yes.'

'Who was this friend?'

'A Mrs Simon Armitage.'

'Why has she not appeared in this court?'

'My Lord,' said Sir Philip Bagshawe, half rising, 'I thought I had already explained that Mrs Armitage was in America. My learned friend must appreciate that her evidence is unlikely to influence the result of this suit.'

Mr Hart said: 'This Mrs Armitage; when she told you, she was shocked, I suppose?'

'She told me out of friendship,' said Diana. 'People were already talking about it.'

'She didn't treat the matter lightly?'

'No, certainly not.'

'Not as a joke?'

'No. It was not a matter for laughter.'

'You are a great friend of this Mrs Armitage?'

'I know her fairly well.'

'Moves in your circle, I suppose?'

'Yes.'

'Did you know that she had been divorced twice before marrying her present husband and had also been cited in another case?'

'I knew she had been divorced.'

'Hardly the sort of person to take much notice of a thing like this, was she? I mean, except as a source of amusement.'

'It was not her reputation which was affected; it was mine.'

'She was shocked and upset on your behalf?'

'Not shocked. She was concerned.'

'But you were shocked when you heard?'

'I was concerned and upset.'

'You were thinking of your reputation?'

'Naturally.'

'In other words, what your friends and acquaintances would think of you?'

'In a way. That's what a reputation is, isn't it?'

'Exactly. One is held in repute or otherwise by one's friends. Now, Mrs Marnsett, it is true to say, is it not, that you move in London society?'

'A part of it.'

'Can you tell us what part of it?'

'I don't know what you mean.'

'Well, would it be true to say that you move in what is generally known as "the smart set"?'

'It depends what you mean by that.'

'I mean the younger set, the artistic set, that section of society which particularly prides itself upon being go-ahead, sophisticated, bright and witty, modern in its ideas?'

'Perhaps. There are various such circles.'

'And you belong to one of them?'

'Yes.'

'Are you, in fact, one of its acknowledged leaders?'

'I suppose I am.'

'You suppose you are. You mix with the modern sophisticates who pride themselves on their advanced ideas?'

Diana's big dark eyes showed a spark of anger.

'There's no virtue in being old-fashioned these days.'

'*Thank* you, Mrs Marnsett. I could not have summed up the position half so well myself. There is no virtue in being old-fashioned these days. Might it even be true to say that in your opinion, taking a broad, abstract view of the matter, there is no virtue in virtue these days?'

'No, certainly not.'

Diana had moved back a little from the edge of the box. She knew she had been induced to make a false

159

move, and seemed to be seeking a better defensive position.

'My Lord,' said Sir Philip Bagshawe, rising, 'may I inquire if my learned friend is attempting to justify without having put in a plea of justification?'

Mr Hart looked at his opponent. 'My Lord,' he said, as if the port had been served slightly corked, 'I have been careful, and shall continue to be careful, not to question witness about her own moral character, which, as Sir Philip is aware, the defence is not attempting to assail. But I submit that it is vitally important to obtain a full view of the witness's mental attitude and the attitude of those with whom she associates.'

His Lordship gazed over their heads for a moment.

'I think, in so far as that is your aim, Mr Hart, it may be considered a legitimate one where a question of damages is likely to arise. You will, however, appreciate that in putting such questions dealing with the moral outlook of the plaintiff you are treading on the borderline of justification.'

'I fully appreciate that, my Lord, and I shall be happy at any time to accept your Lordship's correction—should you deem that necessary. I would, however, remind Sir Philip that I cannot be responsible for the admissibility of the witness's own answers.'

'That's a nasty one,' Kidstone muttered.

'Perhaps it would be better if you stated your question again, Mr Hart.'

'With your Lordship's permission I will frame it somewhat differently. Mrs Marnsett, are you a close friend of Gabriel Stentworth?'

'I know him quite well.'

'Would you call him a member of your circle?'

I saw Diana's eyes flicker momentarily in the direction of the public gallery, as if to ascertain which of her friends were sitting there.

'Yes, probably.'

'Are you a close friend of Noel Coward?'

'I would like to think so.'

'Is it also true that before Michael Arlen published *The Green Hat* and became famous—one might say scandalously famous—you helped him with money and hospitality and encouragement?'

'Yes, that is so.'

'And Ashley Prieff, whose views on the unnecessary shackles of marriage frequently appear in the popular press?'

'I don't subscribe to all the views of all the people I associate with.'

'But you admit some of them are extreme?'

'Extreme by some standards. The leaders of modern thought are often ahead of their time.'

'You consider these gentlemen the leaders of modern *thought*?'

'Opinion, then.'

'In your view, Mrs Marnsett, would you say that the general trend of the fashionable set with whom you mix is to treat fidelity to one's husband as rather a bore, a subject for humorous comment, to consider virtue and moral standards as fusty and out-of-date conventions to be set aside with the crinoline and the straw boater?'

'I've told you I don't agree with all the views of all the people I mix with.'

'But aren't you asking the court to believe that it is these people who are so concerned for the moral character of a friend?'

Diana passed the tip of her tongue along her upper

161

lip but did not reply.

'Tell us plainly, Mrs Marnsett, do you ask us to believe that the people who move in your circle would really be upset or concerned or disturbed, or be anything but amused at the very vague imputation contained in the hanging of this portrait?'

'All my friends are not of that sort.'

'So we are being asked to consider some other friends now. It is some small minority, outside the circle of which you are an acknowledged leader, whose opinion matters now?'

'Everybody's opinion matters.'

'Name some of these people, Mrs Marnsett, people outside the smart set whose opinion really matters to you ... Take your time; don't let me hurry you.'

'There's my husband.'

'And is he the only one you can think of?'

'There are his friends.'

'Does he not belong to this smart set?'

'No.'

'Does he approve of your mixing with these advanced sophisticates?'

The judge put down his pen. 'I don't think, Mr Hart, that we can necessarily assume a wife knows all that a husband thinks. Even though many of them believe they do.'

There was a ripple of amusement across the court.

Mr Hart bowed. 'As you say, my Lord. In this case I should have been particularly careful to avoid such an assumption ... Mrs Marnsett, has your husband ever given you reason to believe that he approves of your mixing with these advanced sophisticates?'

'I don't agree with that description of them.'

'Answer my question, please.'

'He certainly does not disapprove.'

'He has given you no reason to believe that he disapproves. Would you say that he tacitly approves?'

'Yes, certainly.'

'Would you not agree, then, that a husband, by approving his wife's mixing with a certain set of people, tacitly condones their sense of values?'

The judge moved again.

'Mr Hart, as I said before, we can't expect Mrs Marnsett to give us her husband's views on the matter. If necessary you may call Colonel Marnsett as your witness.'

'No, my Lord, I was putting a general case. If, for instance, I had a daughter or a wife who, with my approval, mixed with a certain set of people, I should expect my approval to be taken as some condonation of their sense of values.'

'So what exactly are you suggesting?'

'I am suggesting that Mrs Marnsett moves in a section of society which would consider the imputation so vague and so trivial by modern standards as to be worth no more than a passing joke.'

His Lordship looked at the tall woman in the box. 'You have heard what counsel says. What is your answer to that?'

'It isn't true, my Lord.'

'She says it isn't true. Now where does her husband come into the question?'

'I am suggesting, my Lord, that this small section of her friends, whose opinions Mrs Marnsett says is of so much more importance to her, doesn't in fact exist outside her imagination, and that her husband, who is the only one she can mention by name, has no such different standard of values from herself and those she mixes with.'

'What is your answer to that, Mrs Marnsett, so far

as the question concerns yourself?'

'It isn't true, my Lord.'

Mr Justice Freyte stared reflectively at Sir Philip Bagshawe.

'Is it your intention to call Colonel Marnsett, Sir Philip?'

'—er—no, my Lord.'

'Very well. Go on, Mr Hart.'

Mr Hart resumed.

'Let me put a simple question to you, Mrs Marnsett. In your experience, which would you consider of the greater importance in society today: a beautiful face or a beautiful character?'

I could see that Diana was really angry now.

'It depends,' she said, 'what you mean by a beautiful character.'

'Oh, precisely. I mean a moral character with old-fashioned views on respectability.'

There was no response. Diana looked at the judge.

'Must I answer that, my Lord?'

'Not if you don't wish to.'

'I shall be happy to be more explicit,' said Mr Hart. 'Moving in society as you do, madam, would you consider it a greater insult for, say, a painter to portray one of your women friends as unprepossessing and ugly, or for him, say, to boast of having made her his mistress?'

'It depends on the painter,' said Diana from between tight lips. The last word was almost inaudible.

The judge turned his head.

'What did you say?'

Anger had forced out the response before Diana could stop it. She put up a hand to her head as if fatigued.

'I beg your pardon. What I meant was, it would

depend on the people concerned whether—which would be considered the greater insult. How can I answer for other people?'

The judge continued to look at her for some moments. 'What counsel is suggesting, you know, is that you yourself would feel more resentment at some insult to your beauty than at some slur laid upon your moral character.'

'It isn't true.'

His Lordship nodded to Mr Hart.

'Furthermore,' said Mr Hart, 'I suggest that you have in fact brought this action, not because of some fancied smirch attaching to your picture being hung among those of famous courtesans but out of outraged vanity and pique because the painting itself offends your *amour propre.*'

'No!'

'That in fact, if the painting had been exhibited at the Royal Academy as originally intended, your feelings in this matter would be precisely, entirely and exactly the same.'

'That isn't so.'

The *frou-frou* of the old gown and the creak of the bench informed me that Mr Hart had sat down.

IV

There was a murmur and a stirring about the court. Paul's face was expressionless.

Diana had moved as if about to leave the box, but paused as her counsel rose.

'I take it, Mrs Marnsett,' he said, 'that you have a very wide circle of friends?'

'Yes.'

'Spread, generally speaking, over a considerable section of society?'

'Yes.'

'You have relatives as well as a husband?'

'Yes, quite a lot.'

'Is it likely that you number among your acquaintances not only those who, say, take a broad view of moral obligations, but also those who in both precept and practice adhere without question to the ordinary standards of moral behaviour?'

'Of course. A great many do.'

'Is it their opinion and that of your husband which you value most highly?'

'Yes.'

'Now is it true, Mrs Marnsett, that your relationship with your husband is one of mutual esteem?'

'Yes.'

'I take it he does not himself mix in any society to the extent you do, but that he raises no objection to your friendship with modern, artistic and intelligent people?'

'None whatever.'

'Have you ever given him cause to feel that mixing with the advanced intelligences you do has tended to result in the adoption by you of a lax moral attitude?'

Diana's eyelids flickered.

'Never,' she said.

'Thank you. That is all.'

Chapter Twelve

I

Over lunch Kidstone explained that before the case opened the jury had been shown photographs of the wall at the Ludwig Galleries with the pictures as they had been hung, and also an arrangement as far as was possible in an ante-room of the court of the actual pictures that had been exhibited. Unfortunately, Kidstone added, there had been a notice outside the galleries which said: 'Exhibition of the paintings of Paul Stafford. Modern portraits and water colour sketches. Also, Room 1, the complete series of his "Portraits of Famous Courtesans".' The picture of Mrs Marnsett had not of course been mentioned in the catalogue.

Paul said: 'I suppose Hart's opening this afternoon. When am I likely to be called?'

'Late today or first thing tomorrow. It's not a bad idea, in fact, to span two days if one can—makes it less tiring.'

'The sooner the better from my point of view. The quicker it's over the quicker we can pay up and move on.'

'Supreme faith in one's legal advisers,' I said. 'Incidentally, do we know where Brian Marnsett is?'

Kidstone said: 'He's believed to be at their place in the country. Hart did well with that. There are various rumours and I don't think Bagshawe will risk calling him.'

'Diana's righteousness made me pretty sick,' I said.

'I'm afraid one gets used to the hypocrisies of the witness box.'

Paul said: 'I should like to know what his Lordship privately thinks of it all.'

'We shall hear in due course,' said Kidstone grimly. 'And juries on the whole are more ready to take judicial direction in a civil suit than in a criminal trial.'

As we walked back to the Courts and reporters began to converge, Paul said: 'Are you free for Sunday?'

'I doubt it,' I said. 'Why?'

'Because I've accepted an invitation for you.'

'Well, there'll be a lot of work accumulated! Where do you want me to go?'

'Down to the Lynns.'

'Are you going?'

'Yes. Holly will be there. I promised to bring you the first Sunday you were back.'

'Oh,' I said. 'Well, I suppose I can manage it by working all Saturday. Do you still find them interesting?'

'I still find them interesting,' said Paul.

II

We were back in our seats in time to hear Mr Raymond Hart open for the defence. He wished to make it quite clear at the outset, he said, that, since the plaintiff's counsel had seen fit to introduce the issue of malice, it would be his first concern to produce witnesses to refute this. He would, he said, call witnesses to counter the suggestion of malice in the painting itself—then he would call witnesses to dispute malice in the hanging; and finally he would bring witnesses to refute the suggestion that its hanging had in fact the effect the plaintiff claimed, which was, he would remind the jury, the real question at issue.

He seemed to be going over much the same ground covered in his cross-examination of Mrs Marnsett, and several of the jury looked as if they were feeling the effects of a not-yet-fully-digested meal. But at length the speech was done and the first witness called.

Mr Vincent de Lisle, RBA, was himself a portrait painter of some eminence. In his opinion, the painting 'Diana Marnsett' conformed with the best canons of the art, and the suggestion that its peculiar technique should have been used out of spite or ill-will for the sitter would be a ridiculous suggestion to anyone who understood portraiture.

Cross fire developed between him and Bagshawe. Sir Philip established that the witness and Paul were well acquainted, 'were in fact friends', and then, finding himself worsted on the technical front, asked de Lisle did he not agree that ill-will must have been shown when the portrait was deliberately hung in a gallery of notorious women.

Mr de Lisle said sharply: 'It's surely a question of *honi soit qui mal y pense*. People who go to a gallery do so to view the pictures from an artistic standpoint, not to gossip about some fancied insult in the hanging, like salacious scullery maids.'

'I wish you would not obscure the issue,' said Sir Philip.

'I'm not obscuring it. Because in my view there is none.'

'Perhaps you would explain to the court what you mean.'

'Certainly.' De Lisle screwed in his eyeglass. 'I don't consider that Mrs Marnsett was seriously maligned by the company she was placed in.'

Sir Philip glanced at the jury. 'Go on, Mr de Lisle.'

'Well, these women, these courtesans, were generally speaking women of refinement and taste. The fact that they were mistresses of a ruling king doesn't stamp them as common whores: it only marks them as the ancestors of a large proportion of our present aristocracy.'

There was a gust of laughter through the court.

'If I may cap your quotation with another,' said Sir Philip, acidly aware that he had not got the answer he hoped for, 'I think the court will agree that it is a question of *autres temps, autres moeurs*. It might in the old days have been considered a mark of distinction to be pointed out as a king's mistress: it is not so today. Therefore with your permission the issue remains.'

But he didn't detain the artist much longer.

J. J. Paynard, another artist, was next in the box, and then Henry Ludwig of the Ludwig Galleries. He was there a long time under cross-examination but did not give away that he had phoned Paul asking him to move the picture. As the afternoon went on it became clear that Paul wouldn't be called that day, so I eventually muttered an excuse to him and slipped out of the court. I had a moral obligation to report to my paper *sometime* within twelve hours of my return; and if I got in now and picked up some of the loose odds and ends I should have a better conscience about spending another day in the Courts tomorrow.

I paused at the entrance to the central hall, carefully avoiding the eye of a reporter who was looking at me hopefully. Late October sunshine lit the Strand with a hazy light. The sky was colourless, the street fume-filled and noisy. This time yesterday we had been coming into the Sound. So little time ago, and already the city and its concerns had closed in.

A voice said: 'Can I give you a lift, Bill?'

Little Olive. I had not met her since the evening before all the trouble with Diana started. And then we had separated in that peculiar way.

She was as usual well dressed. I don't think she ever spent a fortune on clothes, but she knew exactly what to buy and what suited her and what would look just as smart in two years' time. Paul said she was a terror in the dress shops.

'Olive,' I said. 'How nice. But I'm only walking to my office down the street.'

'Oh.' She looked disappointed. 'I'm just back from Rome. I met friends of yours there. The Paladinis. And the Bellegardes.'

We fell into step. She had heard about the trip to Madeira. At the entrance to Essex Court she said: 'My car's just down here. Isn't it time you gave up your old work for a bit?'

'Gave it *up*!' I said. 'I haven't begun yet! I only arrived in Plymouth this time yesterday!'

'Do they know you're home?'

'They soon will. Were you in court today?'

'Of course. I wouldn't have missed it for worlds.'

'You came out early.'

'I saw you leave and thought we might have a chat.'

'Really?'

'Yes, and don't sound so disbelieving! It's the truth. The Bellegardes have sent various messages. Also I wanted—to talk about Paul.'

I foolishly hesitated. Did I really want this meeting?

Surely not. I glanced at her, hesitated again, and was lost.

'All right.'

She made a little *moue* at my lack of enthusiasm, and we walked to her car.

She said: 'Where are you living now?'

'The same old address. Afraid it's not looking its best because it's been empty since August. I stopped in this morning just to dump my things and get a change of clothes.'

'Let's go to my place. Maud's out, but I mix a good Scotch. Can even if pressed produce an *omelette al prosciutto* that wouldn't disgrace a *taverna*.'

'What took you to Italy?'

'What takes everyone there: the light, the sun, the sea, the architecture. Even, believe it or not, a few tawdry paintings they have on the walls of their palaces.'

'And Signor Mussolini?'

'Oh, him. I'm sorry for people like the Paladinis who are very political and very anti. But for the rest, nothing much has changed except that everything is slightly better run. Are you very intense, Bill?'

'About what?'

'About politics. I find them a bore. The glory of Rome won't change because one man is in power and another out.'

'I'm not all that interested in politics. But I'm interested in the dreary old word democracy—which somebody said the world was being made safe for. Russia never had any, so that isn't much loss. But Italy has had for the last fifty odd years—since Garibaldi, I mean—and it's sad for many reasons if it fails there. Because one strong man who's successful can lead to other strong men trying it on: in Germany, in France, in Spain.'

We drove off and, presently, for the second time that year, I found myself in her white rectilinear flat.

'Tell me,' she said, as she poured the drinks, 'I must say I find this action diverting. Diana suing Paul for telling the truth about her! It's—*incredible*! Why is it being fought on such pure lines? Since when has Paul decided to behave like a gentleman?'

'Since he became one.'

'Perhaps Paul's afraid to prove his case because of all the things Diana could tell about him in return!' Laughter bubbled in her throat. 'Everyone I speak to who knows them is dying with amusement!'

She took off her coat and hat and threw them on a chair. She was wearing a brown silk frock with transparent sleeves and short pleated skirt. She sat on the settee and curled her legs under her.

'Tell me about your adventures in the Atlantic.'

'It was really all quite dull. Just bobbing about for hours and making practically no progress.'

'Is it true that Paul couldn't stay the course and had to be taken off by a luxury liner, leaving you to struggle home more or less alone?'

'Paul had to be home for the libel suit, otherwise he wouldn't have left.'

'Didn't you have some professor and his daughter with you?'

'Yes. Friends of mine. We met them by chance in Madeira.'

'Pretty girl?'

'Not particularly.'

'They also left you, didn't they?'

'The weather wasn't suitable for them to stay.'

'You're very brown,' she said.

'It'll soon be gone.'

'Yes. Pity.'

We sipped our drinks. It was still rather early for drinks. The light was only just fading.

I thought of the similarities and the differences between the two principal women in Paul's life. They were both beautiful, intelligent and spoiled. But Diana, fundamentally, was ruled by her emotions, whether they happened to be amorous or the contrary. When she erred she did so from an excess of human nature not from a lack of it. Olive seemed always to be ruled by her head. She would take all and not, like Diana, give in return.

'Does Maud live with you now?' I asked.

'Oh, yes. Devoted. Not that that's unwelcome in an unfriendly world. But there's times when it cloys.'

'How did you first employ her?'

'Oh, she was my brothers' nanny. When they died she became a sort of general factotum for the family. After Daddy retired last year they cut down on help, so I came in for her.'

'Do your parents give you an allowance?'

She looked at me. 'Since you ask, no. Why should they?'

'. . . I just wondered.'

'They're *comfortable*. But there's no real *money* in our family—not lying about, not available to bail out a daughter who has made a botch of her marriage, if that's what you're thinking. Anyway, Paul can continue to do that.'

'Have you ever thought of marrying again?'

'Supposing I were free, who?'

'Ah, that I don't know.'

'You?'

I finished my drink.

'I couldn't support your life style. Besides . . .'

174

'Besides, we're not really meant for each other, are we? Perhaps a little affair in bed, but . . .'

Her eyes were cat-like in the fading light.

I said: 'Do you go in for that sort of thing?'

'Frequently.'

After a moment I said: 'I don't believe you.'

She laughed. 'Do we know each other so well?'

'Well . . . we've known each other a fair time. I took you out before Paul ever did.'

'And you think I'm a moral woman?'

'By present-day standards, yes.'

'By Diana's standards. By Paul's, certainly.'

'Paul isn't *that* dissolute. Was he ever unfaithful to you while you were living together?'

'How should I know?'

'That's precisely what you *would* know—would have known.'

She laughed again. 'It's beside the point. Anyway, I've told you—I do have affairs.'

I smiled back at her.

The smile faded. 'Is this a ploy, Bill?'

'A ploy?'

'A sort of challenge. You tell me I don't and dare me to prove the opposite.'

'No. That wasn't the idea.'

'I suppose being at sea for a month might give a man thoughts.'

'Oh, it doesn't need a voyage at sea for that.'

There was a long silence, and she began to speak of her visit to Rome. She'd been there with Peter Sharble, the MP, and a couple I knew vaguely, called Alexander. She gave me the messages from my friends, but they were little more than affectionate greetings and told me nothing of how these distinguished members of the old ruling classes were faring under the new regime. One day soon, if I could get a *laissez passer*, I must go again and see.

She stopped. 'What are you thinking of?'

'What you've been saying, of course.'

'Well, I *asked* you here to talk about Rome.'

'And Paul, you said.'

'To hell with Paul.'

I rose and refilled her glass. Then I took some myself. But I didn't immediately sit down again.

She said: 'And what about your life? You never tell me about your life.'

I knew what she meant. 'There's not much to say.'

'You tell me *I'm* moral, by today's standards. What are you?'

'The same... Oh, there was a girl in Italy. *Ravishing* to look at—like some artist's dream of perfection. *Not* very bright, in fact. But very sweet. The family, of course, *watched* her—the mother and the two brothers. There was nothing I could do ... Perhaps there was nothing I was absolutely certain I *wanted* to do. Why bring her down to earth, make a woman of a saint? Someday soon somebody will, some dark-eyed, ego-centric Italian lad. But not me. Not me.'

'You sound like an aesthete.'

'Well, I'm not that.'

'Sure?'

I sighed. 'Anything you say ... I'm hungry. Let's go out and have an early supper.'

'No. I'll cook something. You're surprised? Think I can't? Another challenge?'

'Ham and eggs?'

'Right.'

She didn't move.

She said: 'Are you human, Bill?'

'Quite probably.'

'So am I. You still doubt that, don't you?'

'No ... I think you've got very strong feelings but they're usually under such careful control.'

'As now?'

'I can't answer for now.'

A few lights were coming on outside. They didn't illuminate the room so much as emphasise the growing dusk.

She said: 'Have you ever made love in the early evening?'

'No.'

'Would it be different?'

'Sight would be different. Touch would be the same.'

She finished her drink.

'Would you like to give it a try?'

'Yes,' I said.

III

Later that evening she said: 'You're damned right, you bastard, how do you understand me so well?'

'I wish I understood you better.'

I might not have spoken. She was sitting by the dressing table in a white gown, brushing her hair, which was longer than I had ever seen it.

She said: 'There's been no one since Paul. Why? For just the reasons you say. I don't like pawing for the sake of pawing—louts demonstrating their manhood, to their own satisfaction if not to mine. Men who—'

'This lout included?'

'No ... No, not that. You have always been— different. But don't think ... don't think this is the

177

beginning of an affair. It might even be a once only. Don't think something has been started.'

'So why did it happen?'

She paused in her brushing, slim-boned wrist poised with silver brush, slowly lowering it.

'Because . . . as I said, you are something different. I'm not sure I even *like* you. But I have always wanted—in a half subconscious way I have always wanted what has just happened. I half desire, half dislike you.'

Good God, I thought . . . Has it ever happened before—if so isn't it rare, rare—that two people should regard each other so similarly?

I said: 'Well, don't regret this.'

We were silent for a time. It was probably only about seven-thirty. She got up and sat on the bed beside me. I put my hand over hers.

'And Paul?'

'Paul?'

'You said when we first met that you wanted to talk about him.'

She shrugged. 'Does it matter?'

'It could.'

'Does it matter that deep down I suppose he's the one?'

'The one you care most about?'

'I don't know.'

'*Do* you?'

'Yes . . . I suppose so.'

'More than yourself?'

'Don't bitch at me. I suppose when we met outside the Law Courts I thought of saying to you, what chance is there of getting him back? Reaction of the primitive female. Pity I didn't.'

'Why?'

'Because then this wouldn't have happened.'

'So you do regret it.'

She shrugged. 'There's something in me that always resents having to yield to this need. To be at the beck and call of another person, to be in a way dependent, to have to surrender one's sovereignty over one's own body, if only for a brief time. Regret it? No, that would be stupid. Besides, since no doubt you would like to know, you gave me satisfaction.'

'I wasn't unaware of that.'

'More satisfaction than Paul, sometimes. His commitment was seldom absolute.'

'But you'd like him back.'

She made an irritable gesture. 'Not in those *words*. It's too crude—in those words. But after all . . . setting aside any special significance in the wedding ceremony . . . we did agree, we gave our solemn word. He's mine—by right, by agreement, by law. Why should he—throw me *over*—as if I were something he could discard, dispose of, when he so chooses?'

I said: 'Would you think that attitude a suitable one for resuming a marriage?'

'Why not? What's wrong with it?'

I hesitated, aware that our love-making, if you could call it that, was over. Yet she was vulnerable, in spite of her hardness. And she was sitting beside me, small and pretty and as tense as a wire.

'It's an attitude of mind, Olive.'

'What is?'

'D'you remember before you married I said not to try to shackle Paul too closely. He's an impossible man to do that to.'

'I know you were full of wise old saws.'

'Possessiveness,' I said. 'It's a vice we all have and give way to. But you perhaps more than most. After

179

your brothers died your parents must have given you almost anything you wanted. Didn't they? And since then—you're so *pretty*, so intelligent, so young and determined—haven't you nearly always got what you wanted? And *owned* it. I think you tried too hard to own Paul. You can't expect a man like him to become your possession, to think what you think, to dislike what you dislike, to have the opinions you feed him. Your grip was too tight. So in the end you lost him. Sooner than have a part title you gave up ownership altogether.'

'What a journalistic imagination!'

'Maybe.'

'Are you saying I got what I wanted tonight because you couldn't resist me?'

'Yes.'

'Rubbish. You could have—'

'Not rubbish at all. But you know I've always wanted you—in the same way that it seems you have wanted me. That was what it was.'

'And now we can spit in each other's face. Is that it?'

'I hope not . . . But you said you brought me here to discuss Paul. I'm discussing him. Nothing would please me better than to see the marriage back on the rails. But if that's the attitude of mind you're bringing to it I don't think you have a hope, Olive . . . Maybe you're both too individual even to *live* in the same house. Really, you need a man you can dominate. I don't know what *he* needs but certainly tact, certainly freedom, even perhaps more love.'

She looked at me and then got up.

'Go to hell,' she said.

Chapter Thirteen

I

The court was just as crowded next morning, but I could not see if Olive had managed to squeeze in. The case resumed with a legal argument concerning the admissibility of some letters, and this dragged on long enough to produce a surreptitious yawn from the foreman of the jury. One wondered how far a juryman's private life affected the outcome of an action involving perhaps many thousand pounds. Had the foreman for instance had a sudden satisfactory/unsatisfactory affair the evening before with a pretty young woman who was soft of body and hard of mind and who had stretched out naked in the twilight on her white oval bed and later turned him out brusquely, contemptuously, as if dismissing not only him but the encounter for ever from her mind?

Witnesses went in and out of the box testifying to this and that, and it was eleven-thirty before Paul was called. As he rose and walked without haste to the witness box he showed no signs of nervousness, nor of the distaste and anger that this action had caused him. Shades of a gawky youth!

Mr Hart was all kindness, his rusty voice having quite lost that irritating quality he reserved for the opposite side. The examination went on about fifteen minutes, and then, having led Paul to answer one or two questions requiring a straight denial, Mr Hart said: 'In conclusion, Mr Stafford; in choosing the position you did to hang this portrait in the Ludwig Galleries, were you *at any time* or *in any degree* actuated by spite or ill-will towards the plaintiff?'

'No,' said Paul.

After all, one had to expect hypocrisy on both sides.

A silence had fallen, as one gown folded itself and another was unfurled.

'My Lord,' said Sir Philip Bagshawe, 'may I ask your permission to have the painting of Mrs Marnsett brought into the court.'

Mr Hart was on his feet at once. 'M'Lord, throughout this case my learned friend has constantly tried to muddy the waters by introducing irrelevances. The libel he is attempting to prove is concerned with the *arrangement* of the portrait in relation to certain others. It has nothing whatever to do with the portrait itself.'

'My Lord,' said Sir Philip, 'no one can have failed to notice that counsel based a very considerable part of his cross-examination of the plaintiff upon the issue of her resentment at the sight of the portrait. I submit therefore that it cannot be irrelevant for the jury to be in a position to refresh their memories.'

'The merits of the portrait,' said Mr Justice Freyte, 'have been an issue in this case from the beginning. It is indeed a two-edged sword which can be manipulated by both sides. I'm sorry, Mr Hart, but I can certainly see no objection to its being seen again. I take it you are not going to introduce fresh evidence regarding it, Sir Philip?'

'No, m'Lud.'

The painting was duly carried in and propped against the stenographer's desk. To anyone who could see the original sitting in the second row, the portrait must have looked like a caricature. I thought of Paul's schoolboy efforts with the nude Miss Atkins.

'Now, Mr Stafford,' said Sir Philip. 'In the course of this action a good deal of contradictory evidence has been given, and, I expect you'll agree, a good deal of animosity has been shown.'

'It depends whom you mean it has been shown by.'

'Never mind that for the moment. Shall we say that this painting of yours has given rise to a good deal of heart burning and ill-feeling?'

'If you wish to put it that way, yes.'

'In fact it might have been better all round if your original reluctance to paint this portrait had never been overcome.'

'It would not,' said Paul, 'have been better for the legal profession.'

There was a ripple of amusement in the court.

'Tell me, Mr Stafford, why were you reluctant to paint your good friend, Mrs Marnsett?'

'I did not say I was reluctant. An artist accepts a commission in much the way, say, that a barrister does, not necessarily because he is in sympathy with his client but because it is his job.'

'And in this case you were "out of sympathy" with Mrs Marnsett?'

'No. The result may have distressed her, but personally, after an initial reluctance, I found the commission stimulating.'

'Got a kick out of it, one might say?'

'I found it stimulating.'

'A bit of good fun, I suppose.'

'Fun doesn't enter into it.'

'No,' said Sir Philip reflectively, staring at the picture. 'On consideration fun is too harmless a word.' He left his seat and walked over to the picture. Then he beckoned an usher to hold the painting where it could be seen by both the witness and the jury. 'This is a modern painting, Mr Stafford?'

'In style, d'you mean? Not particularly.'

'You will surely admit that it is unconventional?'

'Well, a portrait can be painted in a number of ways. It can be photographic, merely trying to copy the camera. Or it can simplify detail, giving an impression of the sitter rather than a meticulous transcription. Or the portrait may give rise in the artist's mind to a creative expression which doesn't conform to normal portraiture at all.'

'I am indebted for the explanation. Which of these three ways have you followed here?'

'To some extent the second, but mainly the third.'

'So I should imagine!' The barrister glanced at his client, who was sitting on the bench near him. 'You don't, I suppose, deny that the portrait is an unflattering one?'

'So far as its exact reproduction of the sitter goes, no. But all portraits should be good paintings first and good portraits second.'

'You consider this a good painting, Mr Stafford?'

'Witnesses today have said so.'

'I'm not concerned with them. I'm concerned with your own opinion. Do you consider this a good painting?'

'Well, I like the carnations.'

There was another ripple of laughter in the court.

The judge had also been looking at the picture. 'The trouble is,' he said dryly, 'that you put the bloom in the wrong place.'

The laughter was less restrained this time, broke, died away.

'My Lord,' said Paul, 'I put the bloom where my instinct told me it should be.'

'And the plaintiff, I think,' said his Lordship, 'apportions the blame by the same process.'

While the rising murmur again filled the court Sir Philip stood patiently, arms folded on chest. I remembered Freeman saying: 'Bagshawe hates his examinations to be interrupted.'

'Did it never occur to you,' said Sir Philip at length, 'that your old friend might be deeply hurt at this—this insulting portrayal?'

'I didn't consider it insulting.'

'Come, Mr Stafford, look at the plaintiff. Don't you see a beautiful woman? How could you have expected any woman to be pleased at this extraordinary representation of beauty upon canvas?'

Paul hesitated. 'It didn't occur to me that she would be either pleased or insulted. I was too deeply absorbed in the painting to consider the feelings of the sitter.'

'You are, I suppose, a pretty successful artist, are you not?'

'Yes. On the whole.'

'Make a pretty good income, I suppose?'

Paul turned slightly towards the judge. 'My Lord,' he said, 'if my income will in any way influence the result of this case I shall be pleased to furnish the court with details.'

His Lordship put down his pen. 'Hardly likely, is it, Sir Philip, that his income will affect the outcome?'

More laughter.

Sir Philip cleared his throat loudly to gain silence.

'You are still young, Mr Stafford. You started, I understand, at the bottom of the tree. Your rise, in fact, has been exceptionally rapid?'

'Fairly, I suppose. But I have been painting many years.'

'Cast your mind back over this brilliant career of

yours. Is there any one incident in it which stands out as a milestone on your road to success?'

'There are a number. I don't think one specially.'

'No one portrait?'

'Several have been very successful.'

'What was the first portrait of yours to be hung on the line in the Royal Academy, the first to bring your name fully before the public?'

Paul pursed his lips. 'The first portrait of mine to be hung on the line was my earlier portrait of Mrs Marnsett. But I had had a portrait in the previous year's show, before I met her.'

'I suppose you will admit that that earlier portrait of her was a special success?'

'Oh, yes. Certainly.'

'Do you consider that it would have been such a success if it had resembled the extraordinary portrayal which we have here?'

'Quite possibly.'

'With Mrs Marnsett?'

'No, I see it would not with Mrs Marnsett.'

'You were wiser then, eh?'

'No, I don't think so.'

'But you were poorer, less successful?'

'Naturally.'

'Naturally. With an eye to future recommendations?'

I saw a steely glint come into Paul's eyes. 'Five years ago I painted Mrs Marnsett as I saw her then. This year I painted her as I see her now. I couldn't in any case have painted her this way the first time, for I had not then the technique.'

'Or the success. Success is necessary before one can take the risk of being insulting. Would I be right in suggesting that throughout the earlier period of your career Mrs Marnsett was constantly helping you by recommending you to her many friends and by offering you all manner of advice?'

'She was certainly very kind at the time.'

'You felt grateful to her?'

'Of course.'

'And you have shown your gratitude, I suppose, by painting her a second time in such a way as to make her look old and ugly?'

'Not exactly.'

'But you did do that, didn't you?'

'My dear sir,' said Paul sharply, 'one doesn't paint a picture with gratitude, one paints it with oil on canvas.'

'That is a frivolous response and an excuse for evading the issue! Please answer me.'

'I think, Sir Philip,' said Mr Justice Freyte mildly, 'I think that the witness means that a work of creative art, once begun, is not dictated by the homely emotions of affection or dislike for the subject painted. One follows deeper impulses of the spirit.'

'Thank you, my Lord. The court is much indebted to you for the clarification of that point. With deference, however, I should like to pursue it one stage further. How long, Mr Stafford, did it take you to paint that picture?'

'About five days, I believe. That is not including a few preparatory sketches.'

'And can you honestly tell the court that during the whole of the time, while you were painting, and while you were resting and sleeping in between, it never occurred to the non-artistic side of you, the ordinary human side of you which deals presumably in ordinary human emotions like friendship and gratitude, that this painting you were doing might hurt and upset your old friend and bring her great unhappiness?'

Paul hesitated, frowned. He suddenly began to look tired and older. 'I can only repeat what I've already said: this was a normal professional engagement, just as you are in court on the engagement of the plaintiff. Would you expect her to retain a permanent grievance against you if you didn't conduct this case exactly as she expected? Would you not consider yourself the better judge of law, as I am of paint?'

'Well, answer me this, then. Would it be true to say that in this portrait of Mrs Marnsett gratitude and friendship never entered your thoughts at all? Answer me, yes or no.'

'Yes, certainly. It would be true of every one of the portraits I have painted.'

Sir Philip exhaled a deep breath and stared at the jury. 'So far we have progressed at last. So far. When you paint a portrait, whosesoever it is, you are carried away on the wings of artistic passion so that you are dead to any of the ordinary human feelings which govern the life of lesser mortals?'

Paul stared steadily at his baiter for some moments. 'If you wish to put it so offensively.'

'Well, tell me this, Mr Stafford: are you also in the grip of such an artistic passion *when you come to arrange about the hanging of a picture in a private show*?'

'Naturally not.'

'So that in the course of such an occupation you might be expected to have some consideration for the feelings of your friends?'

'If the occasion arose.'

'I suggest to you that such an occasion arose in April of this year when you took Mrs Marnsett's portrait round to be hung in the Ludwig Galleries.'

'I don't think so.'

'Why?'

'I don't know. I don't think the occasion arose.'

'Shall I offer you a suggestion why? Because by then Mrs Marnsett was no longer your friend.'

'That was not the reason.'

'Do you assert that on April 30 of this year, when you hung the picture of Mrs Marnsett in the Ludwig Galleries, that on that date she was still your friend?'

'Possibly not.'

'Indeed not! I suggest to you that you had what you conceived to be a strong grievance against her.'

'That certainly isn't true.'

'Then just why did you hang the picture in that room?'

'I have said, because it is a picture which needs a strong light to bring out the tonality, and in that room the light is much better than in the other.'

'These historical paintings of—hm—famous women of fortune; you were proud of them?'

'I liked them.'

'That, I suppose, was why they were given the best room?'

'They too needed good light.'

'They are a sort of series, I suppose?'

'They're a number of paintings with a connecting idea.'

'Exactly. A historical series. Yet you were prepared to break up this series, of which you admit you were proud, in order to interject in their midst one single modern portrait of an entirely foreign mood and conception. Come, Mr Stafford. We shall need a better reason than that.'

'I have told you the truth. I can give you one other

189

reason only: that the exhibition had already been open a week and the total effect, as it were, of the historical paintings had been absorbed by a fairly large section of the public. What I wanted now was to give this portrait prominence.'

'Why?' demanded Sir Philip.

'Why?'

'Yes, why give it this prominence?'

'I've already told you. Because in it I had been breaking new ground.'

'No other reason?'

'Not so far as I can remember.'

'You were not annoyed at the time?'

'Annoyed?'

'Well, this painting had just been summarily rejected by the Academy. Tell us your feelings when that happened.'

'... I was disappointed.'

'Not annoyed?'

'Yes ... annoyed.'

'So annoyed, in fact, that you withdrew your other painting from the Exhibition as a protest and gave an interview to various reporters on the supposed decadence of the Academy selection committee.'

'In the circumstance I think my annoyance was reasonable.'

'And what did you do with the other portrait—of Lady Blakeley?'

'I hung it in the Galleries.'

'Where?'

'In the upstairs room.'

'Why? Did that not need the light too?'

'It was a more conventional painting. But in any case I had to divide them. There was not space in either room for two more paintings. So I hung one upstairs and one down.'

'Were you not very angry with Mrs Marnsett because you thought she had persuaded her husband to put pressure on the hanging committee to have her portrait rejected?'

'The idea may have occurred to me.'

'And as a result of this unfounded suspicion did you not conceive such a hatred—yes, hatred—of your benefactor that you looked around for how best you might give her further offence? And with a row of royal harlots to place her among, the opportunity was not lacking! The chance was too good to miss. There: hang her, let her be pilloried and scorned!'

'You are entitled to your own view of the facts.'

'So is the court, Mr Stafford. So is the jury.'

II

Mr Hart was standing up.

'Please tell us again, Mr Stafford; how long is it since you painted your first portrait of Mrs Marnsett?'

'About five and a half years.'

'During this intervening period, did your relationship with Mrs Marnsett remain one of consistent, unbroken friendship?'

'No, I wouldn't say that.'

'It fluctuated on both sides?'

'Yes.'

'You too have many friends?'

'Certainly.'

'A rising young artist, I imagine, has even in the early stages many acquaintances among the moneyed and pseudo-artistic classes who like to constitute themselves mentors and friends of the brilliant new star, get in as it were on the ground floor of friendship and take to themselves a little of the reflected glory of his success, some of the kudos of being able to boast that he was one of their discoveries?'

'Yes. That's so.'

'Did you feel under any *special* obligation to Mrs Marnsett in the matter of her earlier—hm—sponsorship?'

'I felt a measure of friendship—a due measure.'

'Do you consider that you owe your present success to her?'

'Good Heavens, no!'

'Did you feel any animosity towards Mrs Marnsett at the time when you began to paint her second portrait?'

'None whatever.'

'Did you, rightly or wrongly, feel any animosity towards her after your picture had been rejected by the Academy?'

'It's unusual to have a painting rejected by the Academy after it has once been accepted. I couldn't help but feel annoyed.'

'Towards Mrs Marnsett specially?'

'No, not towards her specially.'

'I put it to you: did you feel sufficient annoyance towards her at any time to wish to cast any imputation on her moral character?'

'Of course not. I wouldn't be so petty.'

'Thank you, Mr Stafford.'

III

The closing speeches had been made, and the case would end that afternoon as Kidstone had predicted. It was still the only prediction he had made. The clock pointed to the time at which I had slipped out yesterday, but there was no air of somnolence about the present proceedings. The court was more crowded than ever, for word had spread that the case was near its end and a number of extra barristers had pushed their way in to listen to the judge's summing up.

The jury seemed to pull itself together for this final effort of concentration. Paul sat quite still without a muscle moving in his face, and his long lashes hid any revealing expression there might have been in his half-closed eyes. He had been in this mood during lunch, suffering no doubt, as we all do on such occasions, from staircase wit, the knowledge of how much better one might have answered the question if one had had a few more seconds to think.

Mr Justice Freyte said: 'I have considered the unusual features of this case at some length. Libel, we are accustomed to think, concerns the written word. No man shall write of another that which is untrue and which shall bring him into loss or disrepute. Nor any woman. No man shall be able to injure another's business or profession by making false statements to his discredit. These are the axioms of our law.

'But in the present case we have no written word, and no slanderous utterance. The plaintiff alleges libel by imputation in the arrangement of certain pictures in a public exhibition of the defendant's paintings.'

Mr Justice Freyte went on to restate the main facts of the case.

'If we ask ourselves,' he continued, 'whether the circumstances as here presented can in fact constitute a libel, the answer is, yes. Libel by effigy can exist, and libel by imputation and arrangement has in fact many times been conceded. It has, for instance, been ruled

193

as libellous for a man to exhibit a red lamp outside a neighbour's house, thus suggesting that that house is one of ill repute. In a case which has a number of close resemblances to the present one—I am referring to Monson *versus* Tussaud, 1894—it was held as libellous that the effigy of a man recently charged with murder and acquitted should be exhibited in such proximity to the Chamber of Horrors as to impugn his innocence. Indeed, so obvious a libel was this considered that an interlocutory injunction was granted to restrain further exhibition of the effigy pending the hearing of the action—a course which so prejudges the outcome of an action as to be resorted to only in the most flagrant of cases.

'In Monson *versus* Tussaud, of course, the libel implied that Monson was an unconvicted murderer. The present alleged libel concerns the morality of the plaintiff. The similarity lies in the circumstances, not in the imputation. But the imputation of unchastity in a woman is deemed so serious that by a comparatively recent statute it is made actionable—and rightly so—without proof of specific damage sustained by her. The circumstances of this case, therefore, are in no way incompatible with a verdict of libel. It is your duty, members of the jury, to decide from the evidence whether such a verdict should be found. Now let us consider the evidence that has been put before us.'

The three women jurors seemed the most absorbed. One had a deep frown of concentration and was tapping a pencil between her teeth. I remembered a lecturer saying to me once: 'Never forget the public—any public—has only so much capacity for absorption. You've got to give them breathing space—even repeat yourself—otherwise half is lost.'

'What you must ask yourselves, members of the

jury, is this. Was the arrangement such that it would suggest to a normal beholder—not a member of any particular set but any average beholder—that Mrs Marnsett's portrait was included among the courtesans? Would you yourself take such a hanging to have such an imputation?

'If you consider that the arrangement of the pictures as set out for you is such as to impugn the plaintiff's moral character, then you are *in duty bound* to return a verdict of libel. Remember particularly that the defence has not been based on a justification of the alleged libel. The defence doesn't claim that Mrs Marnsett is an immoral woman. It merely contends that no libel was intended and that no libel was in fact committed.

'The fact that the defence has tried to show that Mrs Marnsett moves in a circle which would treat such an assertion lightly mustn't have the slightest effect on your *verdict*: it can only affect the question of damages or the allocation of costs. Similarly, counsel for Mrs Marnsett has attempted to prove ill-will on the part of Mr Stafford. But the issue of libel or no libel is not affected by the question of ill-will either. A man may libel another without ever having heard of him. Innocence is no excuse. If the arrangement of the pictures was such as to cast a smirch upon the reputation of the plaintiff, irrespective of intention on the part of the defendant, then you must bring in a verdict of libel unswayed by any other consideration.'

I glanced sideways at Kidstone. Aware of my glance, he pulled his mouth down at the sides.

'If,' said Mr Justice Freyte, 'having weighed the relevant facts—and no others—you come to a clear decision that a libel has been committed, then, and then only, can all the other circumstances of this action be taken into account, for the question of damages then arises. Now in the majority of cases where libel is proved, damages can be computed upon some basis provided by the evidence—loss of trade and the like. Where, however, reputation only is involved, no such basis exists. It doesn't follow for that reason that they need be less. Mr Justice Best in an early judgment said: "If we reflect on the degree of suffering occasioned by loss of character and compare it with that occasioned by loss of property, the amount of the former injury far exceeds that of the latter." It's on this point that the rest of the evidence you have heard has such a vital bearing.

'So far as actual evidence of mental distress is available, you have, of course, the evidence of the plaintiff, corroborated so far as physical symptoms go by the evidence of her doctor. You must, however, remember that Doctor Sowerby in cross-examination has admitted that the symptoms complained of by Mrs Marnsett were of a character identical with those for which he had treated her last year. All you have got therefore is evidence of the *recurrence* of a physical ailment in the plaintiff which may or may not have been brought on or aggravated by the worry and distress of this case. If, however, the plaintiff is a woman of good character and responsible position, mental distress may be fairly assumed to have resulted.

'Now the defence has been at pains to suggest, and the plaintiff at pains to refute, the idea that Mrs Marnsett moves in a circle in which a comparatively vague imputation of immorality would be treated as of no importance whatever, that, in fact, Mrs Marnsett herself in other circumstances would treat the imputation with levity and disregard. Mrs Marnsett has admitted that she mixes with an advanced set, but she claims that she doesn't associate herself with their most advanced ideas. This would seem a reasonable claim in so far as there is a considerable difference between condoning immorality in others and being accused of it oneself. Nevertheless, in weighing up any question of damages this is a very pertinent question: the society in which the plaintiff moves is very much a part of the plaintiff's life and background. The mental distress resulting to a woman who mixes with the "bright young people" of today can safely be assumed to be very much less than that, say, resulting to the wife of a clergyman or one whose part in society serves different and more substantial ends.

'With this in mind, the defence has put forward another suggestion: that what the plaintiff in her heart is really claiming damages for is not the alleged insult to her moral character but the insult to her facial beauty, that her outlook and vanity is such that if this portrait were a flattering one she wouldn't have objected wherever and in whatever company it had been hung.

'But for one circumstance I should be inclined to dismiss this argument of the defendant as lacking any corroborative evidence. Mrs Marnsett's annoyance on seeing this portrait cannot be taken as proof of an *overweening* vanity. A certain *natural* vanity, when not carried to excess, is becoming and even desirable in a woman; and with the portrait and the original still before you it is not necessary for me to point out that the painting is unflattering in the extreme. It is indeed only to be expected that Mrs Marnsett should dislike the picture for itself. It is not unnatural that the picture should become the subject of a quarrel between her and Mr Stafford. But the one circumstance, it seems to me, which entitles this argument to be considered with careful attention is the fact that Mrs Marnsett attacked the painting with a palette knife. The testimony is at some variance, but there seems to be no doubt that such an incident did take place. What I ask myself, and what you must ask yourselves is this: is such an act, of attacking a finished portrait with some intention to deface it, the act of a reasonable woman deeply hurt and upset by what she considers is a caricature of herself, or is it the unreasoning reaction of a vain society woman accustomed to the flattery of men and suddenly overcome with rage and disappointment at being confronted with this strange cynical vision instead of the idealised portrait she expected?'

His Lordship sorted out his notes and glanced round the court.

'For the purpose of assessing damages it is relevant to consider whether any malice existed on the part of the defendant, and for the purpose of assessing whether such malice did in fact exist, evidence of almost anything that can throw light on the relations between the parties is admissible. What further facts have we to weigh?

'Counsel for the plaintiff has also emphasised the initial quarrel over the portrait, and claims that the portrait itself is proof of the state of the defendant's mind, further that it was spite and ill-will arising out of this quarrel which induced Mr Stafford to hang the portrait in the Ludwig Galleries and to insist on its being hung among the courtesans. Mr Stafford has admitted that Mrs Marnsett twice offered to purchase the portrait at a high price and that he refused. Did he do this out of ill-will towards her or out of a desire to see his painting hung and commented on? Mr Stafford in evidence has said: "I paint what I see." Are we in a position to draw inferences from an artist's creative vision?

'Furthermore, if a measure of vanity is natural in a woman it is also natural in an artist. We have had the evidence of other artists that this portrait in their opinion is a work of high merit. There's no reason to believe that Mr Stafford didn't feel the same. He has said that he wished to obtain the reaction of the critics—a natural and understandable wish. He has given as his reasons for hanging the portrait as he did, first the quite unanswerable one that it had just been returned to him by the committee of the Royal Academy, second that only in that position in the Ludwig Galleries did the portrait catch the strong light it required. He has said that it never occurred to him that any objectionable imputation should arise out of his hanging the picture where he did.

'On this point I am inclined to believe him. Artists are notoriously people—can I say it without offence?—with single-track minds. What I mean is that they do one job at a time with complete concentration, that is a necessity of creative work. Well, is it not possible to conceive of Mr Stafford going to the Ludwig Galleries, the picture in his hands, and deciding instantly where it must be hung, all other considerations being ignored?

'Besides, if malice and not impulse had actuated him, would his revenge have not been a far simpler matter? We have it admitted that Mrs Marnsett took strong exception, and reasonable exception in my view, to the public exhibition of this portrait. Would not a man actuated by malice have taken care simply to *exhibit* the portrait? Against that Mrs Marnsett would have had no reasonable redress. Why invite a lawsuit when a free revenge lay ready to hand?

'Weighing up the testimony of all the witnesses most carefully, it seems to me very doubtful, despite the existence of the original quarrel, whether any malice existed in the hanging of the picture.'

I glanced at Kidstone, but this time he gave no answering sign. He in turn was watching the jury.

'Therefore consider your verdict,' said the judge. 'First, does a libel exist in the fact of the picture's exhibition as presented to you? For this decision clear your mind of all consideration of the degree of injury sustained and the possibility of malicious intent. If in your opinion a libel does not exist, then no question of damages arises; and it is customary to award full costs against the plaintiff. If in your opinion libel does exist, then consider the amount of the injury suffered by the plaintiff. If in your opinion libel does exist but no injury has been suffered, contemptuous damages may be brought in with full costs against the plaintiff, or a division of costs between the contestant parties. If in your opinion some injury has been suffered, the costs will go against the defendant with such damages as you, as representatives of the public, see fit to award.'

IV

We all got up while the judge left. Then we watched the jury file out. I wondered how I should feel if I were one of them and had brought a completely unbiased mind to the case.

'Very fair,' I heard Mr Hart say behind me. 'Very fair, Mr Stafford. We certainly can't complain.'

'You can always rely on his Lordship for that,' said his junior in an undertone. 'Mind you, he didn't leave much for the jury to decide. Mm ... mm ... mm ... mm ...'

I glanced sidelong at Kidstone again. Damn these lawyers with their polite poker faces! Paul was still talking to Hart, but I couldn't overhear their conversation. I sat quiet and said nothing and asked nothing, listening to the murmur of conversation and the stir of the court.

The graven image beside me stirred.

'Shouldn't be long now,' said Kidstone.

'Oh,' I said. 'What if the jury disagrees?'

'It shouldn't.'

'I suppose you know what they're deciding,' I said unpleasantly.

'Yes, probably. Damages and costs.'

'So we've lost the case?'

'Technically, yes, I think so. There wasn't much chance of anything else. Morally, no; unless the jury goes against the judge.'

I glanced over to where Diana sat gently bending the fingers of her gloves. Did she also anticipate the verdict? How would the outcome affect her? Sir Philip Bagshawe was packing up his papers before departure. Probably he had another case to scan in preparation for the following morning. Somebody else's grievance, spite or cupidity couched in the formality of legal terms. Strange how these men could work up a temporary and superficial interest and if necessary passion for each separate suit. They were like actors with a large repertory to draw upon. "When I played Bassanio, laddie, I shall never forget ..." "Now in the case of Greengraves *versus* Greengraves and Long, old boy ..."

There was the rap of the hammer, and I got up as the judge came in. The jury filed back. Well, Kidstone had at least been right as to the length of time they would take.

The clerk of the court addressed them. The foreman looked very self-conscious, standing there with the eyes of the whole court on him.

'We have,' he replied in answer to the question whether they had reached a unanimous verdict.

'Do you return a verdict for the defendant or for the plaintiff?'

'For the plaintiff.'

'And what damages do you award to the plaintiff?'

'We think the defendant should pay her fifty pounds damages and bear the costs of both parties.'

V

As we came out of the Law Courts some twenty minutes later a small crowd of Paul's friends raised a cheer. Reluctantly but with tolerant good humour he allowed himself to be surrounded. These people had 'come to his libel action' in the way they would come to his play, if he ever wrote one. In a sense they were his fans, so now for a little while he must bear their opinions and comments. This was the price of fame. He had already arranged to see Kidstone in the morning and now he jerked his head at me to intimate that I should rejoin him in a few minutes. But I shook my head and pointed Citywards and mouthed at him, 'See you Sunday.' He nodded and then turned smiling to answer the question put to him by one of the people near him.

I walked down Fleet Street. Hart and the others seemed well satisfied with the outcome, but it seemed to me that, although we had in a sense secured a moral victory over Diana, the fact that all the costs would descend on Paul rendered the decision punitive without anyone being better for it except Mr Hart and his colleagues.

Although Paul's sea voyage had done him an amazing amount of good and the consequences had not yet expended themselves, yet his return to London must sooner or later surely obliterate its effects. The rough, lonely holiday had given him the break he desired, the complete change he needed.

Yet his return to his normal social round, his coming back immediately and more fully than ever into the public eye, meant that he had stepped once more into the very centre of the stream.

Unreasonable to expect that he would not be carried along.

Chapter Fourteen

I

Paul called for me at ten on the Sunday and we set off for Newton. As we drove out through the suburbs I said: 'Have you heard what the costs of the action are going to be?'

'Freeman thinks about nine hundred pounds.'

'Diana's done nobody but the legal profession a good turn.'

'Still, I don't altogether regret it now it's over. I'm thinking of painting a series of famous stooges and hanging Brian Marnsett in the middle of them.'

'Well, it's an expensive form of pleasure.'

'You never know how things will turn out,' said Paul. 'My net loss is going to be negligible. De Vere's, the New York art dealers, approached me yesterday through their London office. They've a client who wants to buy the picture. I thought I'd choke them off and said seven hundred guineas, and to my surprise they cabled an acceptance. The picture's good, but it isn't worth that. But then, it isn't really intrinsic merit which counts in a case like this, it's publicity value.'

'You'd have got a thousand if you'd asked it. Then the affair would have shown a profit.'

'It'll show a profit as it is,' said Paul. 'I'm snowed under with commissions. Painting portraits is like rolling a boulder down a hill; the merry devil to get to start, and then when it really gets going you just can't stop it.'

'What are you going to do?'

He smiled. 'It's a shame to turn away good money.'

'Well, I'm glad you no longer feel stale.'

He didn't confirm or deny this. 'I shall have to engage a private secretary or something for my correspondence. Some tin-pot society has asked me to go and lecture on Van Gogh. As if I knew anything about Van Gogh. I don't even know where he was born. I've a notion of what he was trying to do in paint, but I haven't the gift of the gab to put it in words.'

'Get Lady Lynn to write it for you,' I suggested. 'You'd be hailed as the revolutionary artist of the age.'

We drove on. It seemed a good time to talk to him about Olive. But what to say? 'I slept with your wife last week and she wants you back?' 'I saw Olive last week and she's willing to try again?' 'Now that this beastly action is out of the way and we can forget all about Diana Marnsett, why not try to repair your marriage? It would be common sense, it would be good economics, and I'm pretty certain Olive would co-operate?'

Would there be any sincerity in any of this? My encounter with Olive made it harder for me to intervene. The *event* stood between Paul and me, even though only I knew of it. And the *memory* of the event was a deterrent. Although there had been pleasure enough and satisfaction in it, particularly the satisfaction of uncovering the mystery of her appeal, there had been a sour edge to it, the edge of her personality, which left the memory a little ragged and raw. She had warned me that it was not the beginning of an affair between us, and with that, privately, I was in entire agreement.

On any grounds, how could I advise Paul to try

again when I felt certain the attempt would only lead to more acrimony and failure? So we drove on unspeaking, and later in the drive I discovered it would have been a useless attempt anyway.

We made good time to Reading, and stopped for petrol there. There had been morning mist with a heavy dew that looked like frost. Now a fitful sun was helping the trees to push through, some already gaunt, others still heavy with the old leaves they were beginning to shrug off. It was good to be away from London noise again.

As we got in the car again Paul said: 'I want to talk to you about Holly.'

'Oh?'

'Yes . . . I—want to marry her.'

He changed up and took his foot off the clutch. The mileage of the speedometer was only 4,176. As I watched, the six changed to a seven. The petrol gauge now registered eight gallons. The oil pressure was forty pounds.

'How do you mean?'

'We fell in love,' said Paul, 'almost as soon as we met. I can't explain. She's just—Holly. She represents something . . . that I haven't found before.' His voice was unsmooth.

We separated a village; yellow stucco pub, cars outside; square-towered Norman church, people coming out in their best clothes; thatched cottages; a village shop with green blinds drawn.

'Do we turn here?' he said.

'No, the next one.'

'I went wrong last time.'

Presently we turned.

'She's just twenty,' I said.

'I'm only twenty-eight.'

It wasn't age that made the obstacles. Holly bowling off-breaks with a straggle of lank hair and thin drumstick legs. The blossoming Holly of Funchal and the *Patience*. But as a sophisticated society woman . . .

'What about Olive?'

'Olive will have to divorce me.'

'You're not going to bring Holly into . . .'

'Good God, no.' He spoke irritably. 'I can provide the normal phoney evidence.'

It was a narrow road now and winding, and when we had to pass another vehicle the camber made the car tilt sharply.

'Olive didn't give me the impression she would be willing to divorce you.'

'When was that?'

'Last week . . . We met outside the Law Courts.'

'She'll have to change her mind.'

'Supposing she won't?'

'She will.'

I watched the altering numbers on the speedometer. Were the miles trailing behind us as quickly as it said?

'I can't see your proposition quite straight,' I got out. 'I've known Holly, of course, all my adult life. And you. Something one of the Grimshawe brothers said suggested that he thought you were—interested in each other. I didn't pay much attention at the time. I confess I didn't notice it. Perhaps you were—didn't show it—when I was there. How does she . . . Does she feel the same?'

He nodded. 'She seems to. At least I think so . . . I knew it would be a surprise to you, Bill. In a way it was a surprise to me—to us both. It isn't the sort of thing one looks for. You're going to have to be patient with us . . .'

'If she feels the same . . .' I said.

'Does that surprise you?'

'No ... Many women have found you very attractive.'

'This is not many women. This is Holly.'

'Paul . . .'

'Yes?'

'Oh, it doesn't matter.'

The muscles of his face moved. 'Say what you have to say.'

Still I hesitated. 'We've been good friends a long time. And running our own private lives. The fact that you've had a number of love affairs and one crash marriage is no business of mine—except when you've cared to discuss it with me. But this is different. I've known the Lynns longer even than I've known you.'

'So you've said.'

'In dealing with the Lynns—all of them—you're dealing with innocents and children. I've long since taken up a voluntary responsibility for them. To say that I'd be sorry to see Holly's life mucked up for the sake of a passing attraction just isn't making use of the possibilities of the language.'

'One thing,' Paul said. 'Tell me before we go any further. I hope you haven't got anything else at stake in this affair, Bill?'

'In what way?'

'In the only way you could have.'

Olive naked on her oval bed half lit by the street lights outside; Olive brushing her red-gold hair, delicate wrist raised, silver brush glinting; Olive smiling, teeth alive in the semi-dark . . .

I said: 'What I want most is Holly's happiness.'

'You haven't answered me.'

I stared at the patchworked Berkshire fields.

'If I felt like you suspect, I should already have put my claim in ...'

Paul let out a breath. 'Thank God for that. It hadn't occurred to me until ... But you were going to say more.'

I was oppressed by the futility of my own life, everything I was and thought and did.

I said sharply: 'I can't *preach* at you, Paul. But if you value my friendship don't let this be another snarl up.'

'I can't predict the future, can I? All I can say is that this is different from anything there's ever been in my life before.'

We were almost there. Fortunately a flock of sheep blocked our way and this gave a breathing space.

He said: 'Did Olive say much? How was she?'

'Well enough in health.'

'No change in her feelings towards me?'

'No change.'

Paul shut his mouth tightly. 'I can't go on tied to her all my life, Bill. It was an honest mistake. I don't *owe* her anything. What advantage does she get out of clinging to the empty position of being my wife?'

'Cat in the manger. I can't, you shan't.'

'Something's got to be done. Can't I divorce her?'

'If she gives you grounds.'

'I must go and see her sometime. Horrible thought. But it's got to be done. We have our own separate lives to lead.'

I said: 'Holly's led a secluded, studious, careless, desperately untidy existence. Are you expecting her to come out of the shade of a small country house and a study at Lady Margaret Hall into the limelight of society with all its business of sophisticated gossip and cocktail parties and entertaining and first nights as the wife of a well-known artist—'

'I'm only asking her to *marry* me. That's all. D'you think I should want to marry her for what she is and then ask her to change into something else? I could get ten better than her in Mayfair any day! I fell in love with her because she is what she is ... careless and intelligent and untidy and shy and charming. That's how I want her ...'

'In a Mayfair drawing-room.'

'Damn a Mayfair drawing-room! I'm at the top and nobody's going to dictate how I shall live!'

'Nobody but yourself,' I said. 'Can a leopard change its spots?'

'Of course it can't,' he said. 'But I wasn't born with mine.'

Through the moulting trees the shabby square Georgian block of Newton lay ahead. As we turned in at the gate I wondered what else lay ahead. Time only would show, and by then the thing would be done and it would be too late for second thoughts, too late to wish you'd acted otherwise. Fired by his own immutable determination, Paul would drive on towards whatever lay ahead, undeterred by the obstacles in his way.

What was that old problem about the irresistible force and the immovable object? Did Olive constitute the immovable object? And even if she could be moved, what sort of a future could Holly and Paul build together?

The bright October day seemed shadowed with the presentiment of winter as clouds sidled up to cover the sun.

All the Lynns were delighted to see me, and we spent what should have been a pleasant day together. Holly went out of her way to make me welcome; she was happy and talkative and apparently carefree. She and Paul were obviously close friends, but this didn't stand out in a company where all were on the best of terms. I didn't even know if the elder Lynns knew of Paul's designs and was doubtful whether their sketchy idea of parental responsibility would prompt them to any action if they did.

Not until it was nearly time for us to leave did Lady Lynn resolve this question by drawing me aside into the abominably littered drawing-room and pouring out all the doubts and fears of an anxious mother.

'Bill,' she said. 'Clem told me to ask you something. I wonder what it was?'

'I hesitate to imagine.'

'I remember; it was about Paul Stafford. He seems quite personable, don't you think?'

'My best friend.'

'Yes. Just so. I like him better than his pictures. Less genteel. He and Holly, you know. They seem to be striking it off. But what's all this about his being married?'

'It happens, you know.'

'H'm. Very temptatious, being a portrait painter. All those females.'

'He was married about three years ago, but they never got on. They've been separated quite a while.'

'Whose fault was it, d'you think?'

'I should say largely hers.'

'I remember my great-aunt marrying a divorced man. Very shocking in those days. And she was rising forty. She died of arterio sclerosis. Often happens with these hot-blooded people.'

'Paul isn't divorced,' I said.

'No. He says he'll arrange it. Can one arrange adultery?'

'The courts frown on it as collusion, but it's often done. The question is whether his wife will be willing to free him.'

'Roman Catholic or something?'

'No. She just feels vindictive.'

'Jealous as a Barbary pigeon. I know the type. Well, what's he going to do?'

'Try and persuade her, I imagine.'

Lady Lynn rubbed her long pink cheek thoughtfully.

'I shouldn't like Holly to be illegal. So upsetting for everyone. They seem quite to have struck it off.'

'It will be a big change,' I said warily. 'Paul's life has been very different from hers.'

'So he told me. He says he wants to live differently. *Mutatis mutandis*, so to speak. Have you any weight with this wife of his?'

'I wish I had. Paul may succeed. He's an extraordinary fellow for getting his own way.'

'Puppy, puppy, puppy!' said Lady Lynn. 'Come here.' She sighed. 'You know, I always pictured Holly marrying a curate. I rather fancied that. I want lots of grandchildren, and curates are generally fertile.'

'What about her own work?' I said.

'Well, she should be able to do some after she's married. Anyway, it's for her to choose. Women do marry, Bill; it's their nature. Most of 'em go all domestic then, but the few that matter carry on.'

'You won't raise any opposition, then?'

'Not if Paul gets rid of his obstruction. If he doesn't I don't know what will happen. I never took any notice of *my* mother. I'd have married Clem even if he'd been a Mormon.' She bent down and raised a struggling, wriggling cocker spaniel to her face. 'Holly must live her own life, Bill. Ethelred's tail is getting quite out of hand.'

'You're very broad-minded,' I said.

'He must have it clipped. Is it true that some dealers bite 'em off? Disgusting! Christianity was not broad-minded in my young days. Nor tolerant. It's time it became so.'

'Surely it's become so,' I said. 'The question now is where tolerance ends and indifference begins.'

'Dear Bill. I believe you're a Presbyter at heart.'

'Far from it. But while we're on this subject, tell me something I'm curious about. Holly said to me recently that you never taught her much of religion. I wonder why that was.'

The puppy made a substantial meal off Lady Lynn's face, and presently she set him down on the table among all the books and papers and candles and siphons and scientific magazines. He stood there looking up at her uncertainly, waving his top-heavy tail, then began a cross-country journey over the litter to the other side of the table.

'Dear Bill,' she said again. 'I taught Holly a certain amount about Christianity; as much as I taught any of them; so that they could approach the subject with an historically informed and perfectly open mind. I didn't teach them religion, because nobody can do that. Religious life is a matter of *a priori* experience.'

'Oh, God!' I said.

She darted round the table in time to prevent

Ethelred from committing suicide over the other edge. I wondered if she would have done the same for her daughter.

'Naughty boy! Naughty boy!' She picked up the puppy and set him down on the floor, whereupon he squatted and made a pool. 'Naughty boy,' she added perfunctorily. 'You know Paul better than we do, Bill. Do you think he could make Holly happy?'

I hesitated. 'I don't know quite what he wants to *do* with his life. As you say, he talks about changing, somehow. Well, what is that going to mean? I'd put nothing past him if he made up his mind to it. But he's overflowing with commissions, overflowing with engagements, overflowing with invitations. It isn't human nature to refuse them. But Holly may like all that.'

'You remind me of Old Moore,' said Lady Lynn. 'He generally contrives to say that there may be war next year, but if there isn't there'll be peace.'

'Well, I don't charge twopence for my prophecies.'

'No,' she admitted reasonably. 'Now where did I put that rag?'

'This it?'

'Thank you, dear.' She bent down and dabbed half-heartedly.

'Let me do it.'

'Thank you, dear.'

'Do you train your dogs?' I said. 'Or do you allow them to learn house manners by *a priori* experience?'

'Now, Bill, you're being rude. I should be furious with you. Thank you, dear; give me the cloth and I'll hang it out of the window to dry.'

I followed her slowly to the window. Holly, Paul and Sir Clement were standing by the sundial in the centre of the lawn. Sir Clement was talking. Paul's large well-groomed head was bent slightly forward as he listened; the cheek-bones had become more prominent with maturity. One seldom attains to a detached view of a close and constant friend; I thought, in ten years he'll have the head of an apostle or a satyr, I don't know which; God help Holly, for no one else will.

Holly was standing beside him, as tall as he, still lanky but with a pleasant suggestion of shapeliness. Sir Clement, long-jawed and bald and full of pencils, was emphasising his point by gesturing with a long bony hand. He often made these gestures when lecturing; they helped to illustrate his meaning or gather up the threads of an argument.

I thought of the many times I had played about that dial in the past with Holly and Bertie and Leo. Lady Lynn, characteristically, had for many years used it as a bird table, so that the figures were now obscured.

'Perhaps,' said Lady Lynn, 'you'd find out for us what he's—er—aiming to do about things. Speak as an old friend of the family. Of course *we* could ask him, but we don't know him well enough to see into his answers, if you follow me.'

'Nobody can,' I said; 'because he can't himself. I'll do my best. I'm convinced he's in earnest. That's all I know.'

'Clem's hair needs cutting,' said Lady Lynn. 'Did you ever see anything so ridiculous as that beard he came home with? He looked like Uncle Sam.' She stared down penetratingly at the puppy rolling at her feet. 'I mustn't forget to write to Bertie and Leo about Holly. I always forget these things when I take a pen in my hand. I wonder why dog breeders are so conservative. If they'd only allow all dogs to mix together, just separating them into large, medium and small, look what variety there would be. Eventually, too, one would achieve the mean average dog.'

'Mr Everydog,' I suggested.

'Exactly. The Dog-in-the-Street. Just like human beings. Most interesting. You'll not forget to ask Paul, will you, Bill?'

'I'll do my best.'

III

If there was some truth in the suggestion that Holly was as much in earnest as Paul I didn't learn it that day, for by luck or good management I didn't catch her alone. In any event I should not have known what to say, for she would have been needle-sharp to detect any reservation on my part. If she was happy then the last thing I wanted was to cast any damper on her happiness.

Might it last.

IV

On the Wednesday I flew to Ireland with a couple of other journalists. It was my first flight. I think it was a de Havilland 50 J. Anyway it was the type of plane in which Alan Cobham had just flown to Cape Town and back, and it was thought an interesting thing to write about. For my part, as we wobbled up out of Croydon and droned across England and the Irish Sea, with plenty of cloud to provide the bumps, I decided that a fifty-eight-ton cutter was much more to my liking.

Of course I personally had no business to grab this fairly trivial assignment, but I had told the editor I wanted to get out of England again for a spell. ('You've only just come back,' he said plaintively. 'Scott won't like it when he gets to hear.') But having seen my set expression and having presumably some wish to keep me on the paper, he decided to square his conscience by arranging an interview for me with Kevin O'Higgins, who had done so much to put the Irish civil service on its feet after Independence; this I accordingly did—not knowing then that his life was soon to be cut short by assassination. I also sent back an article on the Abbey Theatre, and two on the partition problem; so in the end it was three weeks before I lacked an excuse to stay on. Then I worked at the head office of the paper for three more weeks before returning to London.

I had only been home two days when Paul called at my flat.

'You didn't write,' he said. 'I wondered what had happened.'

'I wrote to Holly. I thought she'd tell you.'

'Later she did. But she's been in Oxford and she's not on the telephone . . .'

I said: 'So what news?'

'D'you mean? . . .'

'Have you been to see Olive?'

'Yes. I went that first week after you left, but I didn't get much encouragement. Not then. Since then she's changed her mind.'

'D'you mean about a *divorce*?'

'Yes.'

I stared at him. 'I don't know how you ever persuaded her!'

'I didn't have to!'

I lit a cigarette and leaned against the mantelpiece, thinking this through, trying to feel pleased about it.

'Have a drink,' I said.

'No, thanks.'

I raised my eyebrows but said nothing further.

He said: 'The first meeting was pretty grim. You're right: she hasn't changed much.'

I waited.

'I went to see her on the Thursday. I knew it wasn't any good going and telling her the exact truth: that I'm keen to marry again, that I feel I'm at a sort of cross-roads and need—need Holly to help me change direction, that I want to cut out so much . . . and can't do it without her help. On the other hand I knew she wouldn't believe me if I started telling her a pack of lies . . .

'So I began according to plan, saying I felt it was time we both had our freedom, and that of course I'd provide her with the evidence if she was willing. She laughed at me.'

'That's what I would have expected.'

'We talked for a while, argued. In the end she said: "Well, Paul, I'm afraid you're going to have to stay married to me for a bit yet. Get used to the idea. If you've any little starlet lurking round the corner hoping she's going to become the second Mrs Stafford, tell her to forget it. Explain to her what fun it is living in sin."'

I could hear Olive's voice saying this. I could see her sitting on her white settee, carefully moistening her lips each time she spoke.

'So what has happened to make the difference?'

'Last week she rang me and said she'd changed her mind and would I like to go round? I dropped everything and went. She said she'd considered it and had decided we'd both be better free, so if I made the necessary arrangements she'd do her part.'

'Any reason?'

'Yes, thank God. She's remarrying herself. I suppose it was the natural thing, but I could have shouted with joy! Apparently some Member of Parliament wants to marry her. I've forgotten his name, but it seems they've known each other for quite a while—'

'Peter Sharble.'

'That's it. How d'you know?'

'She's mentioned him more than once. And I met him at her flat soon after I came back from Rome.'

'Well, God bless him, that's all I say! Poor devil, I hope he makes her happy.'

I put out my cigarette. 'So it's all going to come straight after all.'

'Apparently. I've already been to see Kidstone, made arrangements about hiring some woman; it's just a routine one has to go through. I confess I'll be happier when it's done.' Paul ran a finger under his collar. 'You know, Bill, it's all going so well I'm scared. I'm scared of Olive in a way I've never remotely been before. There was a smirk about her expression that suggested she was enjoying some secret joke. I didn't live with her two years and not learn to know her rather well. I'm trying to persuade myself it's a smirk of self-satisfaction. After all a rising politician of good family is a much better proposition than a successful artist with no background. I looked up Sharble's constituency and he's in a safe seat. Olive will absolutely love being the Member's wife. I hope to God that's what it is; but I shall be happier when it's all through.'

V

A letter from Holly, dated 7 November but not delivered until late in the year, having twice crossed the Irish Sea. I have it before me now, much smeared and the ink faint for having been so often exposed to the light.

Dearest Bill,

Thank you so very much for your letter about Paul and me. Do write again, as, while I'm at Oxford, I get out of touch with things. One lives in a fortress—or is it just an ivory tower?—which keeps the world at a respectful distance.

I can count up quickly enough all the letters I've ever had from you—total six, and one of those was abusive, so it's time you made up a bit of leeway.

I do appreciate your good wishes. But to read your letter one would think the whole thing sealed and settled instead of very much in abeyance until Paul can get his freedom. Write and tell me sometime what sort of a woman Paul's first wife is.

You say in your letter that perhaps this—this being my prospective marriage to Paul—that perhaps this is what I've really needed, what I spoke of in the *Patience*, a lack of a sense of purpose, having no direction or object in life. Well, if it is I didn't know it then! All I know is that Paul says he needs my help. How can I help him? Perhaps I shall find out. What's wrong with us all, Bill, that none of us seems to fit into life as it is set out for us? People are like a litter of puppies, all struggling over each other and trying to edge someone else out and squeeze down into the corner that just suits them. And when they get there they find it doesn't really suit them so well after all.

Should I except you from this view? You always seem so quiet and level-headed and unperturbed by other people's strugglings. You're the puppy in the corner that takes no part in the scramble but ends by getting the most comfortable place. Am I right, Bill; or have you your own secret sorrows and your own special discontent?

I must stop now. Write me a long letter next week.

Love,
Holly

In December I had arranged to have dinner with Paul at the Hanover Club, where he was now anxious to put me up for membership. It may be remembered that some of the newspapers reporting the lawsuit had made a lot of that part of Paul's evidence dealing with the rejection of the picture by Burlington House and the implication that this rejection could have been on politic rather than artistic grounds. So there had been more angry correspondence both in the newspapers and out. Paul's break with the Academy was now absolute. Since there had always been an influential number of artists who scorned the Academy anyhow, this didn't bother him, especially as he was now so well known that he no longer needed a showcase.

I called for him at Royal Avenue and we had a drink there first. As we were leaving to get into his car a tall man in a bowler hat asked for Mr Paul Stafford, thrust an envelope into Paul's hand, said 'Good evening, sir,' and walked off. Paul tore open the envelope, saw it was the divorce writ Olive had agreed to serve on him, grunted with satisfaction and drove off.

'I'm happier now it's really under way,' he said.

He was at his best that night, lively and young-looking, and even witty. The influence of club life over a matter of eight or nine years, and the companionship of clever, successful and amiable men, had encouraged him to relax his guard, to join in their conversation, to be one of them, and had encouraged his personality to flower.

It wasn't until after dinner that I met him in the passage, thinking it was time I left, and saw a change had come over his face. He put the long envelope in my hand.

'A lesson to teach us to read what we're given. Olive's had her secret little joke after all.'

I took the writ and read it and saw what he meant. The formal, artificial evidence which Paul had been at pains to provide had not been made use of. The co-respondent cited was the Hon. Mrs Brian Marnsett.

Chapter Fifteen

If this tale of my relationship with Paul Stafford were to have proper shape and design it would now be necessary to go through the next year month by month and event by event. I don't want to. I want to tell things just as they come to my memory. Shape and design are poor bedfellows if they bring back what is better forgotten.

First let me explain what puzzled us greatly at the time but which I learned later, explicitly, from Olive. She said that after the break-up of their marriage she had heard that Paul was associating with Diana again, and purely for her own satisfaction had paid to have him watched. 'After all, it was his money.' She had had no real intention of using the evidence for she had then had no intention of divorcing him. She was saving the information to confront him with if the occasion arose. But later, when he came and asked for a divorce, and Peter Sharble asked her to marry him, the chance to use this evidence was too glorious to miss.

It put Paul in an impossible position. Through the stilted phraseology of a solicitor's letter it became plain that Diana Marnsett wanted to defend the suit. He could only refuse. It would be ludicrous to become involved in the defence of Diana's good name, having recently forfeited almost a thousand pounds for having defamed it. But much more importantly, if he defended and won he would still be tied to Olive.

He went to see Olive, but Olive had discreetly

disappeared on a cruise.

Although she now wanted her freedom too, he was fearful that she might change her mind—or that Peter Sharble (poor fellow) might change his. Paul's need of Holly grew no less with delay. Diana would have to fend for herself.

The cause lists were full. Waiting was tedious and a nervous strain. Then a second blow fell that we might perhaps have anticipated. Colonel Marnsett sued his wife for divorce and cited Paul. What was more, he claimed damages. Olive was getting full value for her money.

Paul must have felt he would never be free of the shackles of the law courts and solicitors' offices and writs.

This year I eventually yielded to pressure from the north and agreed to operate from Cross Street, Manchester, for an experimental period. 'C.P.' was obviously determined to keep an avuncular eye on me. In one of my articles I had misused a gerund, and it wouldn't do.

And Holly stayed on at Oxford, working occasionally for her first, which inevitably she got. Paul and I spent two Sundays with her in June. These are the islands on which remembrance dwells with pleasure. We took a canoe up the Cherwell, paddled it to a shady spot high up the river and picnicked and talked and bathed and talked again, and nothing was further from us than Chancery Lane and vindictive women and the stale old legal language which dries up, as it records, the quicksilver of human passion. Every detail of those two days remains in my memory. They will live as long as I do.

I was not at either of the divorce hearings, but I gather the first ran its predestined course. The second was complicated by Colonel Marnsett's claim for damages. After commenting unfavourably on the claim, since it had become distasteful to the modern Englishman to assess the loss of a wife in hard cash, Mr Justice Buckley said that, never the less, since it had been put forward, he was legally bound to make an award. He assessed the damage sustained by Colonel Marnsett at one thousand pounds. Judgment would be entered accordingly.

While this was going on Paul's and Olive's solicitors were battling with each other as to the amount of maintenance Paul should be bound to pay her when the divorce was made absolute. Since Olive was likely to marry within the year, this was largely a matter of form, but the legal argument went on just the same. Paul said this was because both firms of solicitors were anxious to refurnish their dingy offices out of the proceeds. He was becoming more and more inclined to nod his head wearily at any suggestion put forward. It was an expensive tendency, but he was making enough money to feel that a few hundred pounds one way or the other weren't worth the worry and delay. Anything to have done with it.

Yet with all the delays and disappointment eventually a day for Paul and Holly's wedding really could be fixed, and, having been fixed, really did arrive. The date, as everyone knows, was 12 April 1928.

As was to be expected, their wedding conformed to no conventional standards. No one was present but immediate relatives. The vicar of the parish in which Newton was situated had agreed, rather against his principles but out of friendship for the Lynns, to marry them in church, and he did this with a great deal of dramatic vigour as if to cover up his own heart-searchings. He was a little man with an ovoid bald head, dark glasses to assist his near-blindness, and bird-like movements.

Sir Clement, against all advice, had resurrected a professorial morning suit with a green tinge from among the accumulated lumber in his bedroom; but his recent paunch made the waistcoat too tight, and Lady Lynn had to slit it up the back.

Lady Lynn strode uncertainly about in a passion of vagueness, her long blue frock, relic of some garden party of thirty years ago, flapping about her heels like a cassock. Her sister was there, tall and bony as a Grenadier Guard, and an uncle—the one who had financed Leo—played the organ. That was the sum of Holly's relatives—Bertie being in Africa and Leo in Paris—and I, again, most reluctantly, his best man, was the only outsider. Paul had no other representative present. His father had been invited but was ill with jaundice.

Holly was in grey, neat and fresh and tall, though happily dwarfed by her two female relatives.

No sentimentality was encouraged. Everything was done with the utmost decency and despatch. One went to church and saw them married, properly married in the sight of God, thank God; that was over, good; hurry up and sign the register; now everyone had better come home—everyone being eight—for tea and sandwiches. You'll come, Vicar, of course? Good. A busy man, but able to spare an hour. We would just go nicely into two cars.

In the dining-room Sir Clement said, 'Sit down, sit down, help yourself to the sandwiches;' and at once took his own advice. He had boiled himself an egg for breakfast, but since then his wife and sister-in-law had been too busy to see about any food for him.

'No, no, sit down, Holly dear,' said Lady Lynn;

'you mustn't wait on yourself today of all days. Vera, we've forgotten the lump sugar; you'll find some in the three-pound mustard tin in the first cupboard, marked rice. Paul, you don't take sugar, do you? So sorry we haven't any whisky for you, but we don't usually drink it, and the wine merchant in Reading must have forgotten to deliver what I ordered. Plenty of soda water and lemonade and barley water. Holly ... no, Clem: be a dear and fetch the soda water.'

'My dear Lady Lynn,' said Paul. 'I'm as ardent a tea drinker as anyone here.'

'Best way to drink tea,' said Uncle Frederick, 'is with no milk or sugar and a slice of lemon. When I had a duodenal ulcer ...'

'When you had a duodenal ulcer,' said Aunt Vera, reappearing from the kitchen, 'you wrote the best fugues of your life. I wonder what connection there is between inspiration and ill health. What do you say, Mr Stafford?'

Paul said: 'It's probably much easier to create masterpieces when underfed. I suppose that was the idea behind mortification of the flesh. The old monks knew how to achieve sanctity.'

'I remember when I was a student,' began the Vicar in his pleasant chirping voice, 'a friend of mine who—'

'Sanctity,' said Sir Clement, helping himself to another sandwich. 'The odour of sanctity became known as that, being a familiar smell upon the breath of monks, you know, and was associated by ignorant people of those days with holiness and shaven heads. (I beg your pardon, Vicar, but yours is not *shaven*.) In actual fact, when the stomach has been empty for so many days—anybody's stomach—the digestive juices create a distinctive sourness which lends itself to the breath—'

'Daddy,' said Holly, 'suppose you concentrate a bit more on that sandwich and less on—'

'What sandwich?' said Sir Clement.

'This one,' said Paul, passing the plate.

'Don't eat them *all*, Clem,' said Lady Lynn. 'After all, it isn't *your* wedding day.'

'So, of course,' said the Vicar, 'I said to my friend, "You may be a student of theology, but I hesitate to imagine what sort of a student you would—"'

'Eat up, Bill,' said Paul. 'Meals at weddings are provided solely for the parents and the best man. Don't contradict me, it's an acknowledged fact.'

'When I had a duodenal ulcer,' said Uncle Frederick, 'certain forms of meat were plain poison to me . . .'

'A very interesting old church, Paul,' Lady Lynn said. 'Unfortunately it was restored by Sir Philip somebody or other in Victoria's reign. Most distressing. Those pitch-pine pews.'

'. . . the operation,' said Uncle Frederick. 'On the table for three hours. Of course they found more than they expected. Sir Giles Landsdowne, who performed the operation, described to me afterwards . . .'

'Unfortunately,' said the Vicar, 'there is a good deal of beetle in that part which has not been restored. We opened a fund last year. If we may, I should like to put your generous donation to this, Mr Stafford. There is much that is worth saving. The Norman screen. I wonder if you noticed . . .?'

'What was the name of the man who spoiled so many churches about that time?' asked Lady Lynn. 'The fellow who would have built those Government offices in Whitehall pure Gothic if Lord Palmerston hadn't put his foot down and said Italian Renaissance or nothing.'

'This cutting up fashion,' said Sir Clement, swallowing tea, 'seems to me greatly overdone. Where, of course, the trouble cannot be cured any other way—'

'Mine could not,' said Uncle Frederick.

'I'm not asserting that it could. But in so many minor cases—'

'Lord Palmerston spent a long life putting his foot down,' said Paul.

'I wonder why?' said Aunt Vera, who frequently used this opening gambit. 'I wonder why the Victorian era produced so many great men? Now—'

'Because it lasted so long, Auntie,' said Holly gravely.

'Not at all. You speak from ignorance, child. Darwin, Ruskin, Browning, Gordon ...'

'The cutting away of living tissues,' said Sir Clement, 'is a fundamentally artificial process which must create a profound and incalculable reaction on other parts of the body ...'

'The reaction in my case,' said Uncle Frederick, 'has been entirely beneficial. But I do not contend that in other instances ...'

Surrounded by these amiable eccentrics, Paul might have exhibited some signs of boredom in view of the usual company he kept. Or as a compromise he might have talked and listened exclusively to Holly, letting the others chatter among themselves. Instead he joined in with them as one of the family without effort and with a genuineness and gentleness which one could not begin to doubt.

The meal over, they were soon ready for off. They were to spend their honeymoon in the Channel Isles, where they hoped to do some more sailing.

No sentimentality now. Especially none now. Kiss

and goodbye. 'Goodbye, Daddy; look after yourself. Don't forget to take your bi-focals when you give that lecture on Saturday. Goodbye, Ma; bless you; I'll write. Goodbye, Bill; I don't know why you're left to the end.'

Her lips were on mine for some seconds. 'Pistol's gone,' I said. 'The race is to the swift. Goodbye, my dear.'

They were in the big Chrysler Paul had recently bought. Paul's self-contained eyes met mine. These last months he had lost weight. The change suited him; he looked less worldly.

'This is it,' he said. 'You've helped, Bill. I'll not forget.'

'No point in looking back,' I said. 'Look ahead now.'

'I'll do that,' he said, and glanced at his wife. 'This is it, Holly.'

She nodded distantly. 'Go on. Don't make me make a scene now.'

He touched my hand, which was on the door, then leaned forward and started up the engine. A few moments later the grey car had disappeared down the drive.

Chapter Sixteen

A selection from among the letters that lie on my desk, and one news cutting.

From Holly Stafford to William Grant at Via Caglioni 21, Trastevere, Rome.

Royal Avenue
1 May

Dearest Bill,

I'm writing to say how disappointed we were not being able to see you again before you left. We missed you by only two days: the weather in Guernsey was damp and windy so we didn't prolong our h/moon, there being so much to see in London.

I thought you'd *refused* the offer. I know it's short term and may lead to something better—what: do we know?—but you're back writing of a regime you don't *like*, and, from what you tell me, that can't be altogether without risk. Also, does it mean you've left the M. Guardian permanently?

I'm now comfortably settled in here and feeling quite good about it, though one cannot help noticing a few differences from Newton and Oxford. Still not got used to being called Mrs Stafford. Also I've never known before what it is not to be short of money!

The people we meet are very quaint and have quite a different standard of values from normal people like Daddy or Mother. Paul wants to become a recluse, but I refuse to be pampered and insist that it's good business to mix with a few people, even though he may at present feel sick of them. He's always refusing invitations.

I had a letter from Bertie yesterday. He seems very happy among the lepers. He enclosed photographs of people covered with sores and says in six months he'll send me some snaps of the same people after treatment. Leo remains in Paris. A pity you missed him on the way out. He's still disgruntled at the necessity of earning a living and thinks of marrying some rich widow in order that he could devote the rest of his life to composition.

Paul is at present very deep in a portrait of Mary, Countess of Doughmore. I hope it will not be like the one of Mrs Marnsett. Paul tells me you said that was a wicked portrait, and from the reproduction, I agree. I told him my sympathies were entirely with Mrs Marnsett.

Mummy has just bought a new cocker spaniel which she has christened Mussolini, because she says it is always barking up the wrong tree.

I go to Newton about once a fortnight, to see them both, Mother and Daddy I mean. I hope you are happy in Rome but won't accept an extension of stay. Now that I'm married and living in London I should like to see more of my third brother and best friend.

Ever yours,
Holly

Letter from Holly Stafford to William Grant, at same address.

232

Dearest Bill,

Thank you so much for the lovely Venetian bag. It was sweet of you. I do hope you had a good Christmas.

We were lucky and managed a family reunion at Newton. Bertie is back on holiday, as you probably heard, looking very well and not dried up with the climate, and no sores. He has formed a cricket team out there and they play in the morning before the sun gets high. He's discovered a left arm spin bowler, and seems upset that he can't bring him to England until his few remaining patches are cured.

And Leo came from Paris! He's having his first concerto performed next month and is very much the composer now. He rather got on Paul's nerves, who as you know is always so matter-of-fact in his dress and behaviour; but we all really managed very well together. Mother had a cook in for the week, some friend of hers who is hard up; but when she came we found she couldn't cook after all; so Bertie and I (mainly Bertie) did the Christmas dinner.

These days it takes me most of my time looking after Paul in one way or another: arranging appointments, answering letters and invitations. So far I haven't had as much leisure as I'd planned for helping Daddy with his physics, but we maintain a correspondence. Anyway Paul is still dead keen to cut out a lot of his present work. I'm dissuading him from any change at the moment because I'm afraid it might be an *emotional* change, all bound up with marrying me etc. Any new direction in his life has to be taken coolly and in detachment.

I met Olive entirely by accident last week—at least I think it was accident. She's quite *beautiful*, isn't she? But *probably* a little uncomfortable to live with.

I have never seen so many plays in my life, some marvellous but others so inane that one wonders what the critics saw to praise in them or the audiences to laugh at.

Write soon, *please*.

Love,
Holly

Extract from a letter to John Nichols in Scotland, from his wife Madge, later passed on to William Grant. Dated 12 April 1929.

... I must tell you about Mavis Hammersley's latest party, where I met—at last—Paul Stafford's new wife—and on her own! Seeing they've been married nearly a year, she'll soon cease to qualify for that description; but at least she's new to *me*, so closely has Paul kept her under his wing.

They say she's brainy—but so *young*, like a schoolgirl almost—not good-looking, with horn-rimmed glasses, nice eyes—straight of body but with a sort of hiccup of a walk. Someone said she looked like an awkward colt suffering from under-feeding. Out of her depth at this party, which was the usual thing, bridge, tea, gossip. She couldn't play bridge, or wouldn't, stood or sat (figuratively) with her back to the wall for an hour or so, not sulky or defiant but self-contained and mute unless spoken to.

And then who should come in but Olive Stafford. Mavis swears she wasn't invited, but Mavis is such a harebrain that you can never be sure. Anyway from the moment she got there Olive was not in a *good mood*. Something had got in her—long before she knew her successor was there. You know what Olive's like—slightly smaller than life, tip-tilted face, those eyes. And you know how she dresses. The way I'd like to dress if I had the figure and *you* gave me the *money*! Mrs Stafford II was wearing a tweed skirt and a cream lace blouse. Terribly correct for a suburban afternoon.

Of course in that company it wasn't possible to keep them apart for long, and of course in most circumstances it wouldn't much matter. After all, if divorce can't be treated as a civilised expedient these days it's just too bad for everybody. But because Holly S is *not that type* we did our best. Alas, no go. Olive soon got the message from somebody and at once went across and said something about how glad she was to meet Mrs Stafford in such pleasant surroundings as she'd fully expected to encounter her in the divorce courts.

Holly S didn't quite take this in, as no one had told her who Olive was, but naturally she could see she was being got at.

'But tell me,' Olive said, sweet as arsenic, 'how is dear Paul?'

Mrs Stafford II still didn't cotton, and said to Olive: 'You know Paul well?'

Olive laughed at this and said: 'I ought to, my dear, I slept with him long before you did.'

So far, a little rancid, you'll agree, but not exceptional in that company. But then Olive really let rip—and there are standards, my love, even in that job-lot of Mavis's friends, who I know you don't think too highly of yourself. Out came the poison pills, coated with sugar. Paul and his working-class manners and his eccentric vices; the dreariness of life with him, his habit of sucking his teeth when asleep, his dislike of changing his socks, his . . . well, I can't remember it all, but it got nastier and nastier. Until now I've always thought Olive rather good *value*—but I must confess I was somewhat sickened.

The second Mrs Stafford, who had been going whiter and whiter, suddenly forced a smile and said: 'Well. I'm sorry for your unhappiness. I do hope I shan't make such an awful mess of the job as you did . . . I wonder if I could have my coat, Mrs Hammersley? Thank you for a lovely party.' And swept out.

It really was done with dignity after all, and, although when I helped her into a taxi I could feel her arm trembling, she didn't at all give way or let herself down. I expect she felt pretty bad when she got home.

After all this I went back in and found Olive too was on the point of leaving. She was aware that she'd behaved pretty badly, and she obviously preferred to leave us to talk about her in her absence. The only explanation was offered by Mary White-thorn who said she'd heard that Olive's engagement to Peter Sharble was in a shaky state, and maybe she was working something off.

My cough is better, so this is the last long letter you'll have before we meet.

Love, love,
Madge

From Holly Stafford to William Grant, at Piazza
San Borromeo, Borgo Monalieri, Rome.

Royal Avenue
6 May

Dearest Bill,

So sorry to have been such an age replying to
your last letter.

My reason for the delay, which is no excuse, is
that we have been away on a motor holiday. Last
month I caught a streptococcal throat, and when it
was better the doctor said 'a change', so we went a
tour, up through Wales and the lovely Welsh
scenery before there were too many char-à-bancs
about, through the Mersey tunnel, which reminds
me of a Bax Symphony, and then Lancashire and
up to the Lakes. Quite a few people, including a
fellow called Wordsworth, have had a go at them;
but it's hard to pin down in words what they're
really like. A first silly thing that struck me was the
lovely absence of banks. Not the sort that are
crashing in America at the moment but the common
or garden earthen ones which serve usually to
contain. In the Lake District they hardly seem to
exist: there's just green valleys brimming with clear
water, and where the water ends the trees and the
green lawns begin, sloping gently up.

I must tell you of one day. Paul wanted to
see Wastwater, which is supposed to be different
from the others, more gloomy. From Broughton-
in-Furness one takes a road north and branches
off. Well, we did branch off, but too soon, and
followed a narrowing track into an enchanted
valley.

I call it enchanted because it seemed without life,

not a bird was singing, not a house to be seen, only this narrow road winding in and out of huge lichen-covered boulders. Then a stream joined the road and went with us, bubbling but somehow hollow and not very cheering. Perhaps that was because there was no other sound; not even wind. You know how quietly our Chrysler goes. We just stole along into the quietness, up little rises and round corners among the boulders and the undulating moorland and the short stunted trees. It was the sort of experience I felt I might have after I was dead: moving along without effort and without sound through an empty moss-grown valley, not knowing what to expect round any corner, but devoid of fear. Not quite alive and nothing else alive but the stream.

At length we passed a small empty house and then came on a large cottage standing by itself where the valley broadened, among a few trees and with a stone bridge across the stream, and with mountains on either side. We were both hungry, as we'd intended getting something at Broughton, and we were also curious to know what the name of this valley was. So we stopped and went to the door. There was a 'For Sale' notice in one of the windows, but the house was occupied and an oldish woman came to the door.

Paul asked her if she could make us a cup of tea, and after an argument she gave way and we went in. In one room we could see chicken feathers scattered all over the floor, and in the kitchen there was a dirty child playing in front of the fire. The room we went into had a stone floor with one rug and grubby lace curtains at the window and a big deal table.

The woman told us that this was Crichton Beck. We were eight miles from the nearest village and there were only three ways into this valley: the road we had come on or over the two mountain passes, west to Wastwater, east to Langdale. Her husband was working in the fields; there was one other cottage three miles up the valley and the empty house we had passed; no, she didn't find it lonely, they were leaving because the child would have to get schooling and she couldn't walk sixteen miles a day. No, they'd only lived here a matter of two years, up to then they'd lived in the cottage up the valley. You couldn't farm this land. No, she didn't think much about the scenery. It was all right for visitors who saw it fresh-like, but when you lived in a place one view was much like another.

After tea we went on to Wastwater: an awful climb, then a precipitous descent in the rain with seven hair-pin bends and any number of gates and water splashes and slipping yellow mud.

Paul did nothing but talk about the valley. If only he could drop everything and go up there and paint. But I still had that first impression of *unearthliness*; the silence and the stream, then the interior of the old cottage with its dirt and its air of having been something better; the woman's rigid narrow peasant face and her story of disappointment and failure, and all round the sloping brown mountains. I'm afraid Paul wouldn't get many portraits to paint there unless they were the portraits of departed spirits.

We called to see Paul's father on the way home. He's a nice old man, fierce outside and soft in. He is coming down to stay with us next month. You must by now be wondering whether the germs have left

behind them what Daddy pedantically calls a
cacoëthes scribendi, so will finish.

Love

from

Holly

Enclosed with above a scrawled note from Paul.

What's this—a *flat* in Rome? Are you setting up
a ménage? Don't mind, except that I don't want you
to *settle* there. Come home soon.

Holly has been off colour but is fine now.

Will write *more* soon.

P.

From Paul Stafford to William Grant, at the same
address.

Royal Avenue

30 June

My dear Bill,

Again thanks for the letter. Am glad you
appreciate my offer, even if from a purely monetary
point of view; though I don't think my stuff will
fetch much in the pawnshops of the Eternal City.
So sorry, though, that I can't send you one of Holly
as requested. To tell the truth I have never once
painted her, and your letter made me face up to the
matter and ask myself why.

The only answer that seems to be an honest one
is this: Holly is the one thing in my life that has
come to serve as a sort of touchstone for the genuine.
She means something which is true and without
alloy, that is, something with which I'm not
prepared to compromise. So the two sides of

existence just don't meet at present. Do I make myself clear?

Besides, she isn't beautiful and I don't want her to be. She exists but you don't paint her. Who can put her kind of personality on canvas? I can't. There's no way of making it more clear. I know if you want to be awkward you can argue that Monet and others have painted light, and maybe air; but that's not really the point.

Am sending you the 'Head of a Parisian Girl' which you admired.

In haste,
Paul

Letter from Holly Stafford to William Grant at same address.

10 September

Dearest Bill,

A word in a hurry to say how *delighted* we are you're coming home, and especially as Lit. Ed. of the *Chronicle*. This should suit you exactly. *Con-grat-u-lations*!!!

Are you likely to be back by Thursday the twenty-third? Leo is in England and is playing his concerto at Torquay; an afternoon show, but its first performance in this country. If you can drop us a card we'll save you a seat—not that there's likely to be a crush. *Do* if you can. Looking forward to it if you are there.

Holly

Extract from the *Daily Telegraph*, 12 September 1929.

'The marriage took place at Brompton Oratory

yesterday of Mr Peter Frank Sharble, Member of Parliament for the Epping division of Surrey, second son of Brigadier John Sharble and the late Mrs Sharble, of Knowledge Court, Farnham; and Miss Elizabeth Mary Wainwright, only daughter of Dr and Mrs Wainwright, of The Grange, Abbey Road, Epsom.'

Chapter Seventeen

I

Torquay drowsed like a middle-aged prima donna in the autumn sun, its ample curves and plump little hills warm and prosperous under the ripe blue sky. People thronged the promenade and main streets, little white boats clustered in the harbour, wasps hummed and struggled about the waste-bins in the harbour car park.

The orchestra was just finishing the Midsummer Night's Dream Scherzo as I entered the Pavilion, and when it was over I squeezed up the third row and found myself sitting next to Holly. She put up her left fist and I gripped it and pecked her cheek. Paul leaned across and put his hand on mine.

'Welcome home.'

'Bill, this is *perfect*! It's Leonora next and then comes Leo. How *are* you?'

The conductor held up his baton and the Beethoven overture began. Glance sideways at Holly. Happily not too smart. Glossy hair worn rather long and turned up at the ends. Pale horn spectacles. No colour on her face; some on the lips, that was nice; thank God she hadn't mucked about with her eyebrows. Mature, though; she was mature now. Paul ... the same old Paul; an expression of inscrutable power and discontent. His skin was clearer.

I looked down at the programme. There it was: 'Concerto in D Minor for Pianoforte and Orchestra, by Galileo Lynn . . . *Allegro con brio, Andante sostenuto, Allegretto* . . . Soloist, Galileo Lynn.'

Perfunctory clapping.

'This audience!' said Holly. 'Why do they have a Municipal Orchestra if nobody wants to hear it?'

I glanced round. 'People cling to the sun. Like flies to a wall; especially in autumn.'

'No, they say it's always like this when the soloist's unknown. Even when he's better known it's not too good.'

'One thing. That won't affect Leo.'

'No,' she agreed, and broke off as a little applause rippled round the auditorium. The composer had made his appearance.

A dark morning suit, his broad face shadowed with a frown; the fingers of his right hand touched the cuff of his left sleeve as he came to the front of the platform and made a slow bow. He looked like Schubert. At the piano, he adjusted the seat, took out a large handkerchief to mop his hands and brow, nodded to the conductor and they were off.

I am an occasional concert-goer, but no music critic. I can't tell whether I like a piece of music by reading the score; I'm not always completely certain whether I'm going to like it on first hearing; I have even known my attention to wander to a fly creeping across a lady's bare back in the row in front, and that during a Bach programme. So real musicians, Leo included, will not be unduly depressed by the knowledge that I could make little of his first big work.

They'll be even less impressed when I say I don't really like a concerto with an inordinate number of fifths and I've always felt that the use of a piano as a percussion instrument is a limited one. After a while I closed my eyes and tried to concentrate that way.

For Leo was not behaving too well. At every break in the solo part he took out his handkerchief and mopped his hands and brow afresh. He frequently shot his cuffs and sometimes put a hand to his side or his forehead as if in pain. Then he waited like a hawk with hands poised over the keys for his next entry. Leo at school flipping bits of ink-soaked blotting paper at a bust of Gladstone. Leo swimming in the creek at Newton with his head under water, blowing bubbles like a codfish. I thought of him sulky and temperamental in his late teens. I remembered the look of his upturned face when we dragged him out of the gas-filled room in his Euston lodgings. I forgot the music and came back to it and forgot it again.

When it was over there was a good deal of what sounded like genuine applause. The interval followed, but Holly said: 'Sit still. He asked us not to rush round in the middle, and he's playing some preludes of his own in the second half. What d'you think of it, Bill?'

I shook my head. 'Difficult at a first hearing. Deeper than I can go.'

'Pick and shovel needed,' said Paul, who, I could see, had been much irritated by Leo's mannerisms.

'You're beastly rude,' said Holly. 'I thought at one time—'

'What's Lady Lynn doing over there?' I asked, seeing a long, pink face at the other side of the hall.

'She wanted to form an undisturbed judgement. She sent Daddy up in the circle. Are you really back for good this time, Bill?'

'It looks like it. And glad to be. You? . . .'

Her eyes met mine. 'I feel fine now.'

'You didn't take on an easy job,' I said. 'Thank God you seem to be making a go of it.'

'I do,' she said simply.

'What are you two mumbling about?' asked Paul.

'He's congratulating me on having made you a happy man,' Holly said.

'She hasn't done that,' said Paul. 'I was born with a divine unrest. There's no cure for it except the bottle.'

'Still working hard?' I asked.

'I haven't accepted a fresh commission for nearly two months.'

'What's wrong?'

'Don't look at me,' said Holly. 'It's Paul's own doing.'

Paul was studying the programme. 'Wonder who took this photo of Leo.'

'I suppose he hasn't been painting any more Diana Marnsetts?' I suggested.

'Oh, no; he's been very well behaved—'

'Like a performing seal,' said Paul.

'—But seems to be getting tired of sardines,' she finished.

The orchestra was filing in again.

'So you haven't brought home an Italian wife,' said Paul. 'Did you leave one behind?'

'By the way,' said Holly. 'Did you know Leo was married?'

'No! When did this happen?'

'Not many weeks ago. We didn't know until he arrived in England. He'd forgotten to tell us. That's his wife sitting with Mother.'

A dark, pretty girl with black hair and a sulky mouth.

'Good Heavens!'

'What's the matter?' Holly asked quickly.

Paul mouthed at me.

'Nothing,' I said. 'For a moment I thought you

meant the awful freak at this side. What's her name?'

'Jacqueline,' said Holly. 'Her name was Dupaix. She's a Belgian.'

'Nice looking.'

'Yes,' said Paul. 'If I were ever going to add to my famous courtesans, which God forbid, I'd like her to sit as Madame de Montespan.'

'Hush,' said Holly.

The second half of the concert was about to begin.

II

We had tea afterwards in the Pavilion Café, and everybody discussed Leo's concerto. Fortunately Leo was impervious to criticism.

The little Belgian sometime teacher of dancing greeted me gravely and without sign of recognition. Perhaps she didn't remember me from the brief interview we had had at her door seven years ago. Now she was the wife of a composer, the perfect young matron. Any other life was forgotten, and with the instinct of her race she would settle down and order his life and have children and save money. I wondered if they had been in touch with each other all this time.

Leo sat at her side, aloof and gloomy, deeply conscious of the pearls he had been casting before— well, the uneducated. His hair curled over the back of his collar and he wore a black cape thrown carelessly about his shoulders and fastened with a large gold clasp. The only person he listened to with any show of interest was his mother.

'It has its points,' she was saying, pulling at the brim of her disreputable hat. 'It has its points, Leo.

There's design in it. One can see the bones of a well-thought-out structure. But you must remember that a musical sentence is not a juggler's stick to be turned any way and twisted inside out. Very well in moderation, but carried too far you lose dignity and achieve only inebriety. Well, Bill, how pleasant to see you again! Why haven't you been over for the week-end recently?'

'It's a long way from Rome,' I said.

'Are you still there? Nice of you to come all this way for Leo's concert.'

I congratulated Leo. He waved my remarks aside. 'It's practice, you know. Gives one an insight into the mentality of provincial audiences.'

'Those antics,' said Lady Lynn. 'I'd almost forgotten. Most distressing. You must get out of them. Take a course of Yoga. I was afraid for you. What do you say, Paul?'

'I enjoyed the concert,' said Paul. Leo glanced at him but his expression didn't change.

'It only shows,' said Sir Clement. 'I'm not really musical so there was a lot I couldn't follow. The man I was standing next to in the gentlemen's lavatory seemed very pleased with the whole thing. Personally, the orchestral dissonances put me off.'

'Come to dinner on Saturday,' Holly said to me.

'I'd love to but I've agreed to spend the week-end with Pennington—that's the editor, you know. This is a new departure for me. From Foreign Affairs to Eng. Lit. is a jump. I'll be free by Thursday. Would that do?'

Paul frowned at me, his eyes searching mine. There was an added sensitivity, a certain look of strain. 'We've bought this cottage in the Lake District and we're supposedly leaving on Wednesday. The whole

248

thing's been badly stage managed.'

'Well, I'll still be here when you come back. It's going to be hectic for me these first weeks.'

The chatter went on around. I suddenly felt apart from my friends. Apart, a stranger and lonely. In Rome it didn't matter. Here . . . well, Holly and Paul were sufficient to themselves. So were the others. So was I for that matter. We each went our own way, bent on particular ends . . .

A few moments later I got Paul alone and said: 'What do I hear about Olive? She *hasn't* married Sharble?'

'He welshed on her. He was cleverer than I was and saw the danger signals in time. Mind you, it's hard luck on Olive in a way. She'd have made the perfect MP's wife. I gather they went on some sort of cruise, and he met this other girl, Elizabeth something, and when they got back to London it was never the same between them. Then he just wrote Olive a letter . . .'

'So now the poor little piggy got none.'

'No . . . I hear she's been ill, but whether it's something serious or just an emotional thing I don't know. Anyway I'm grateful to Sharble for making the right motions at the right time. Otherwise I would *never* have been free.'

Holly came towards us.

'What's happened to your limp?' I asked.

She laughed. 'Last year I met Dr Gorstone, the bone man, and he said half the trouble was simply habit in walking, so he sent me to a friend of his who taught me to walk. That's all. Paul was furious.'

'Not literally, ragingly furious,' he said. 'Merely irritated. I want Holly to remain as she is without surgical or other improvements.'

'In one week we go back to Paris,' the new Mrs Lynn said. 'There Leo is the great success. The French are so much more advanc-ed. We have a little apart-ament, so small, but just big enough. We sleep beside the piano. You must come and see us, Madame Lynn.'

'I hadn't thought of that,' said Lady Lynn. 'Paris is so improving. We'll go there together, Clem. I'll buy a new hat.'

'Hm,' said Sir Clement, drinking tea.

'I haven't been to Paris,' said his wife, 'since the year Eddington spoke to the Royal Society on Electromagnetic-gravitational geometry. All I remember is the policemen standing like inverted Y's blowing whistles and people rushing about in tumbrils.'

'You mean the buses,' said Leo.

'And,' said Lady Lynn, 'I remember a man in a cap stopped Clem and offered to sell him some obscene postcards.'

'Did he buy them?' Paul asked.

'I tried to engage him in conversation,' said Sir Clement, 'I was interested in his mentality. But he didn't seem to appreciate my efforts and ran down a side alley.'

'When I make some money,' said Leo, 'I'll rent a decent flat and you can stay with us. But anyway, there's a passable little hotel round the corner. Of course it isn't *fashionable* Paris.'

'Perhaps we could put off going to Cumberland,' Holly said in an undertone to Paul. 'The first week Bill's back . . . And there's no special hurry.'

'I should be very upset if you did that,' I interrupted.

Paul smiled. 'We'll leave on Saturday week instead.'

I'd given up my old place, so temporarily was in a grander service flat in Red Lion Square. There to my surprise I found Holly waiting on the following Monday evening about seven. The porter said she'd been waiting an hour, and I was apologetic as we went up in the lift. Nothing wrong, I hoped.

She shook her head.

I led her in, apologising for the mess of books, magazines and newspapers that festooned the living room. Coming back like this and being put in charge of the literary page of a daily . . . One had to take in a great deal in a short time.

'You needn't talk,' she said, 'to put me at my ease.'

'Sit down,' I said. 'Then I shall believe you.'

She obeyed, pulled off her hat, shook out her hair. We both sat quietly, waiting for each other for a moment or two, neither speaking. I went to the side table.

'Get you a drink? Excellent brand of soda water, with or without lemon barley. Or do you go in for the hard stuff now?'

She smiled across at me. 'I would have rung you, but I didn't know till the last minute. Paul began painting about five, and then I knew I could slip out without his noticing.'

'Some dread secret?'

'Not really. But I wanted to see you privately and try to explain things.'

I offered her a cigarette, but she again refused. 'Well, we're private enough here,' I said.

She seemed not to be listening. 'I only wanted to tell you that we are going away on Wednesday after all, and to tell you why.'

'Because you arranged to, presumably.'

'Yes, but we're such old friends. It doesn't seem good enough—at least not without the fullest explanation.'

I sat on the chair opposite her. 'Well, don't take it to heart, Holly. You'll be back.'

'That's the question.'

'What is?'

'Whether we shall be back.'

'Oh?'

'Yes . . .'

'I don't get it. Didn't Paul say he had bought this cottage and wanted to go up there to paint? You don't mean he wants to *stay* there?'

'That's his idea at present.'

'. . . So all the discontent has come to a head at last.'

'Yes.'

I picked up a literary weekly and dropped it on some others.

'He's had ideas like this before,' I said. 'They've been simmering for years. Don't you think he'll let off a bit of steam and then go back to his simmering?'

'You've been out of touch, Bill. He's really in earnest this time. It's quite true he hasn't painted a portrait for two months. He's refused every commission.'

'Then what is he doing?'

'Not anything really. And yet everything. His studio is littered with half-finished canvases.'

'What of?'

'Landscapes, people, faces, buildings, when you can recognise them. Often he just mixes colours.'

I moved more magazines. 'He seemed to get the same impulses after the Marnsett case. I thought he'd come to terms with them. Have you been encouraging him?'

'Not by anything I say or do! But he thinks—says—feels—I have to bear some of the responsibility.'

'That's unfair.'

'Last week he painted an interior of the studio. He squeezed the colour direct onto the canvas out of the tube. When he showed it me we nearly had a fight, like Mrs Marnsett only the other way round. I said it was marvellous. He said it was phoney Rouault.'

'Who won?'

Her lips moved. 'I did. On condition I kept it out of his sight.'

'Perhaps I shouldn't ask—but do you believe in what he's doing now?'

She got up and walked to the window. The limp really had almost gone.

'The other day an old gentleman came asking for Paul. Paul was out. Becker, he said his name was. A little Frenchman with a bald head and a big black tie. Looked like a ballet master.'

'He's head of the Grasse School, where Paul went.'

'Yes, he told me. He's just retired. That's why he thought he'd call. He hadn't seen Paul for four years. He kept eyeing me up and down, as if trying to make up his mind about me, and then he began to talk about Paul's painting. He didn't say very much but I caught the note of, well—it was the way Daddy would have spoken of a favourite physics pupil who had become a chartered accountant. After a bit I couldn't refrain from telling him what Paul was doing now. Coming from me, the news didn't impress him. He shook his head and said it was too late, one couldn't drop an acquired technique. This head-shaking went on so long that he provoked me into showing him the studio painting I've just mentioned.

'As soon as I'd shown it him I was sorry, because he

253

said nothing but just stared, and I began to be afraid Paul would come back and catch us. In the end I had to take the picture away from him. He apologised then and chatted quite brightly without mentioning the picture. I asked him to come again when Paul was in, and he promised to. I showed him to the door. When he got there he twiddled his hat and said: "The emotional vision is there. At present he's only half able to hold it and less than half able to transcribe it. It's certainly like nothing he's ever done before. If he goes on from there I shall be happy to swallow my doubts."'

Outside a taxi turned and moved down the street.

'Did you tell Paul?'

'Yes. He wasn't very interested. Other opinions don't seem to matter to him over this.'

'This cottage,' I said. 'I suppose it's the one you wrote about in one of your letters?'

'Yes. Paul bought it. He didn't tell me until last month. He's had it done up and a couple of extra windows put in.'

'I thought you didn't like it.'

Her eyes grew thoughtful. 'I didn't like the occupant of the cottage. With ourselves alone there things would be quite different.'

'You'll probably be back before the spring. This break may do him all the good in the world. Like the voyage in the *Patience*. He may need these breaks and rests. But he won't resist the lure of London for long.'

'I'm not sure I want that, Bill. I'm not sure I want to return here myself—except for keeping contact with one or two good friends. I shall be quite content to change back to a simpler life. But, now it's come to the point, I'm just a little afraid for him. Although it was not exactly intentional on my part, I've—helped him to make this move. And I'm a little afraid that he may make the attempt and fail.'

She came back and leaned her elbows on the back of the chair. 'You see, Bill, as I look at it, there's a certain secret satisfaction in discontent if it carries with it a feeling of "I really could do something else if I wanted: I despise what I'm doing because I could do *better*." But there's no satisfaction in the sort of failure which might follow the attempt. You can only say to yourself then: "I've no right to despise what I'm doing because that's all I'm good for." And painting goes so deep with Paul that I wonder what he might do if that happened to him.'

She had certainly grown up.

'I've known him fifteen years,' I said. 'He's not failed yet.'

'I said I was only a *little* afraid. But that's because so much hangs on it ... Anyway, I felt I had to come. We've been trying to get away and so many things have delayed us. So putting it off another week ...'

'Set your mind at rest. I'm content if—'

The door bell whirred. 'Hold on ... Probably someone for the last tenant.'

I went to the door and opened it. Paul was there.

IV

'I wondered if I might catch you in, Bill.'

'Yes,' I said.

He stood there, strongly built, well dressed, self-contained, the very reverse, so it seemed, of a temperamental artist.

'Lucky I remembered your number,' he said, and then he caught sight of Holly. 'Well, I'm hanged!' He looked at her quizzically. 'So this was where you went.'

'Yes,' said Holly. 'I thought of telling you, and then I thought I wouldn't.'

He came in and slipped off his coat. 'All women are deceitful. Even this one. And I suppose you came here to tell him secretly all the things I came here to tell him secretly.'

'I thought you weren't perhaps going to explain everything to him,' said Holly. 'And he ought to know.'

'You are a couple,' I said; 'both sneaking round like this. If you want to go and live in Cumberland, go with my blessing. Paint yourselves pink if you like. Don't think I care.'

Paul looked at Holly. 'He doesn't care.'

'Yes, he does,' said Holly. 'He's just on his dignity.'

'Well, have it your own way. Stop for a drink now you're here, anyhow.'

Paul sighed and sat slowly in a chair.

'So you're going to cut right away from London?' I said. 'Going to be a primitive and grow hair down your back.'

'One doesn't need to leave London for that.' He accepted the drink and looked at it until its presence in his fingers registered itself. Then he put the glass down. 'Thanks, I don't.' He looked at Holly again and smiled; then turned to me. 'I've been hunting sprats all my life, Bill. Ever since I took to fresh air in the *Patience* and met Holly I've been convinced that I ought to be a deep-sea fisherman. Well, there's only one thing to do, go out and try, even if I don't catch anything.'

I said: 'Send me down a whale from time to time.'

'When we're settled—' Holly began.

256

'When we're settled,' Paul said, 'you must come up and examine the catch for yourself.'

'Holly said you wanted to free yourself from old associations. If—'

'Don't be a fool. Come for a month to begin with. It'll be your own fault if you don't.'

His eyes were darker than usual. They looked quite old.

'What are you trying to do, Paul?'

'Do?' He put the tips of his square fingers together and stared at the cage. 'I've not done much yet. I'm a blind man trying to see, a small-time artist hag-ridden by a vision . . . I'm trying to learn to spell over again— and to forget most of the words that have come in so useful up to now. How can I say more than that without becoming pompous? It's nothing *unique*, for God's sake. Even great artists get these troubles. Renoir did. Many others.'

'At one time,' I said, 'you had another end in view.'

'Oh, I know. Every second-rate politician eats his words—and I'll bet you could quote some of mine. But that's the way it is. We live by our mistakes—and the lucky ones learn by them.' He looked at the clock. 'I must get back. Not that there's much to be done now the daylight's gone. Coming, Holly?'

'Yes.'

'All this, Bill, is for your private ear. We shelter the public from such enterprising views. Tomorrow we leave for a holiday in Cumberland. How long we stay depends on what happens there, and what happens here is nobody's business but our own.'

'And mine,' I said.

He patted my arm.

'Of course.'

Chapter Eighteen

I

I think it was Bismarck who said that military campaigns are often decided by 'the imponderables'. You can prepare for so much, plan and arrange and think it all out; but the unexpected, the unforeseen and unforeseeable, will still emerge to upset it. Burns of course had the same idea a good deal earlier.

It might be better for their reputation as thinking adults if the element that went wrong with Paul and Holly's best laid plans came into the category of an imponderable. Unfortunately not. That evening, and for many months afterwards, it never occurred to me that they had not taken into account a stumbling block which was so obvious.

Letters were desultory; and I have to admit that at this time I was more absorbed in my own work than ever before or since. To become literary editor of one of London's newspapers, a bachelor, just thirty, with the entrée of all literary and dramatic circles, was as precise a recipe for satisfaction and happiness as I can imagine.

And I was *rich* too—on an income of a thousand pounds a year. It was a time when a room at Claridge's cost two pounds a night, you could buy a good shirt for fifteen shillings, beef was sevenpence a pound, coal 1/5d a hundredweight, and certain furnishing firms advertised complete furniture for a house for twenty-six guineas.

That my contentment was not absolute was probably because at the heart of the thing, surrounded by all the hard work and the excitement, I was lonely, and though I went out with girls from time to time they never seemed to mean enough. It wasn't done in those days to live openly with a girl without marrying her, and there was none I wanted to marry.

Yet it was a lovely life, and I have often wondered since why I threw it all away. Was it for friendship, for love, or out of a sort of inverted vanity, supposing I could arrange or alter other people's lives?

Christmas came and went, and still no news of a return. People were beginning to inquire as to Paul's whereabouts. I had been given permission to provide vague particulars but no address. Some greeted the information with raised eyebrows or a cynical quirk of the mouth. At the turn of the year he had resigned from two of the three clubs of which he had been a member—his attendances had been falling off ever since his new marriage. Old friends and old members were indignant and laid the blame on Holly. These possessive women: Stafford had been specially unlucky in marrying two of the same sort. One wouldn't think to look at his second wife that she could grasp and hold the reins, especially when dealing with a headstrong man older and far more experienced than herself. It only showed.

To my suggestion that the change of habits might be Paul's own choice they adopted a wisely knowing air. After all, why should he want to go and bury himself in the country at the height of his success? When I retorted with the query: Why should she? they responded with, Oh, well, Paul was such a good-looking fellow and such a favourite with the ladies and she so ordinary, was it not fairly clear that she was determined to keep him for herself as long as she could?

In March Paul instructed a firm of auctioneers to sell the contents of his Chelsea home. In a note to me he said: 'Did I tell you that when I split up with Olive I made a deal with her father to stay on at Royal Avenue and pay a rent for it? It was a fairly civilised arrangement, except that I was paying a higher rent than he could have got from anyone else. Well, we're OK up here, and there seems simply no point in keeping a place in London. I'm not bothering to come down for the sale, as it's a melancholy business disposing of one's possessions, even though you'll find when you come to Crichton that we've brought most of our favourites with us.'

Morbid curiosity took me to the sale, but I wished I hadn't gone, for a large number of Paul's friends were there, puzzled at his move. Most things brought good prices, including twenty-three paintings and sketches. None of his ceramic ware was on offer.

Most unexpected visitor at the sale was Diana Marnsett with her new husband. She had remarried the previous month. Her second husband, a film director with a Hungarian name, was a big, dark, heavy-featured man dressed in a pin-stripe blue suit and light-topped calf-leather shoes. One couldn't see him being as indulgent towards her as old Colonel Marnsett. She herself had deteriorated in looks, and it seemed that a few more years might bring Paul's maligned portrait near the truth.

She didn't bid all afternoon.

Of that other lady who had figured so largely in Paul's past I saw nothing at all. Nor for a time did I have any news of her. Then one day I saw her maid-companion, the sullen, spotty Maud, on a bus going up Piccadilly, and took a seat beside her.

'Well, Mister Grant,' she said. 'H'm—well . . .'

Maud and I had disliked each other from the start. I asked after her mistress.

'Oh, up and down as you might say. Attacks of nerves and can't sleep. Like her mother that way. Just nerves, I say. Things upset her too easy. We came back from Cannes last month.'

'You're still in Clarendon Gardens, I suppose?'

'Oh, dear, yes. Just had it redecorated. Not before it was time, I'd say. And got rid of some of that white furniture. Shows every mark.'

'Your mistress doing any painting?'

The scornful expression on the woman's face deepened.

'Mrs Stafford ain't well enough to spend all her life before an easel. And she's plenty of more important things to do.'

'I'm glad to hear it.'

'Good life, yes; she's more invitations than she knows what to do with. What with week-ends in the country and first nights and the rest.'

'You reassure me. It needs a strong constitution to stand up to that.'

She turned her head towards the window with a sharp movement. The bus ground along.

I felt pleased at having provoked her, but a little disturbed.

'One gets out of touch with things. Is Mrs Stafford thinking of marrying again?'

She gave an irritable shrug. 'She don't confide in me. You'd better ask her about it yourself, Mister Grant, hadn't you?'

'I will,' I said. 'One never knows.'

'Once bitten, twice shy, I should say.'

'That's the way. Keep her to that view, Maud, and you're safe enough.'

I left the bus, with the satisfaction of knowing that I had rubbed her up the wrong way. But tempering that satisfaction was a sense of disquiet as to who was paying for the expensive refurnishing and re-decoration.

It was high time to take up that long-standing invitation to Crichton Beck.

II

The following week there was a chance of a break, so I set off in a little car I had just bought. It was one of the first Morris Minors, Sir William Morris's reply to the immensely popular and successful Austin 7, a direct challenge in the small car market. It seemed ideal for getting about London. It cost £125 new.

I spent a night in York and decided to go in by the Langdale road and over the Wry Neck Pass. The road past the Pikes is pleasant enough, with the sharp green little mountains rising almost from the fringe of the road. After asking several times I was directed through a couple of gates and a farmyard and began the long slow climb over a bumpy road between narrow stone walls. This goes on for some time before one reaches the pass proper, which in fact seems to be no pass at all but an ill-made track over the shoulder of the mountain. Twice my engine boiled, and once there seemed some danger of the car side-slipping on the greasy mud over the edge and into the field a few hundred feet below.

When the summit was reached, the mountain tops, so much more impressive than their real height,

262

brooded and gloomed. One didn't feel one had much right pottering about up there among the clouds and the silence. The descent was not fierce but the surface was bad and crossed a number of watercourses. One came down into a shallow cup of a valley, largely barren but with a few clusters of trees dotted among boulders and cairns. In the distance was a grey stone-built, slate-roofed cottage, with another small stone house about half a mile beyond.

A stream ran beside the cottage and several elm trees clustered behind. A woman was in the garden playing with a dog. It was Holly.

As the sound of my engine reached her in the great empty silence she looked up, shading her eyes with her hand. Then she saw the car and ran indoors. Presently she came out again with a man in his shirt-sleeves, and they both peered up. I blew my horn, with a sense of apology for the noise. The echo came back from the opposite hill. They waved.

It seemed ages then, traversing the bumpy road, before I reached the cottage. The dog ran up barking. I recognised his russet brown snout. He was Ethelred, that cocker spaniel who had disgraced himself in the drawing-room at Newton on the afternoon when I had discussed Holly's marriage with Lady Lynn.

III

They had spent money on the house, and everything was painted light to give an added sense of airiness and space and cleanliness. Some of his furniture had been brought here and also the best of his ceramic ware. Upstairs they had knocked two bedrooms into one to make a studio for Paul. The furniture was covered with chintzes and the curtains were of the same material. Whatever it had been at the time of their first visit, the cottage wasn't gloomy now.

Nor even dusty and untidy like Newton. Compelled to do her own work, Holly had developed some latent housewifely sense which kept the place neat and clean.

Of course the valley was eerie. No suggestions from Holly were needed. Spring was not far away, but one scarcely heard the song of a bird. The stream was the only commentator, the one never-ceasing voice in a vacuum of silence. The mountain slopes lay quiet and bare, ever changing in mood and colour under the ever-changing sky; cloud and sun, cloud and sun, rain and sun and mist and sun. Black specks of sheep were crumbs on a counterpane which changed patterns away in the distance; a wind now and then moved down the valley; clouds drifted with it bringing soft rain; and through all the empty silence ran the thin, brittle voice of the stream.

But they were not altogether alone. The house a quarter of a mile down the valley was still empty, but there were three farms within a radius of five miles, and milk and bread was brought to them daily from one of these. Gipsies and crofters often passed up the valley.

Paul had become a walker. Every day, in an open-neck shirt, a worn pullover worthy of Sir Clement, and old flannel trousers, he went off, pipe in mouth and satchel over his back, striding across the moors. Sometimes Holly went with him. He smoked constantly but didn't drink at all. He seemed serious, absorbed, more open of manner than I had known him.

As for his pictures, one had no need to ask to see

264

them, for they were everywhere, none of them hung on the walls, but stacked in corners of the kitchen, the living-room, the bedrooms and his studio. He had no regard for them; they were not treated as ornaments but as lumber. Much of his work had gone little further than the sketching stage. But all of it was taken from definite models and all models were recognisable for what they were. There was no question of inventing abstract forms. He seemed to depend closely on his model to help him towards the reality of what he was looking for.

I said to him: 'The more I see of art the less I'm able to judge it. A few of these appeal to me, but I don't know whether they're good.'

'They're rungs in a ladder. But all the rungs aren't a step up.'

'I've often wondered about you. Do you miss London and its excitements?'

'Not its excitements. I'm well content up here; shall be more so in another six or twelve months when I begin to get somewhere.'

'You're not thinking of returning, then?'

'What makes you ask?'

'Most of your friends think you will.'

'What *friends* have I got? Do you think I'm likely to let up at this stage?'

'Up to this visit I'd reserved my judgment. Now I'd say no.'

'The only thing which would be likely to influence me to move were if Holly were unhappy.' He turned over one of his pictures and stared at it moodily. 'You know, I can't even remember painting this one. I don't look for ideas; they just won't let me alone. Of course this has no merit; it just helped to express something, helped me on my way. That's all they do. I'm too much in a hurry to be able to stop to finish. I miss London now and then, but not often, not as often as you'd think. I've no time.'

I began again to look through the pictures.

'If you like,' he said, 'pick out a dozen and take them home. They're no use to me.'

I stared at a curious farm scene, seen through the wheel of a cart. It was all suggested rather than shown, in the way that the Japanese by painting a line of blue along a horizon suggest the sky.

'I might even try to sell them for you. No point in letting them get mildewed and dirty.'

Paul smiled. 'Would you show them if you were an art dealer?'

'Well, yes, I think so.'

'Go on: look again.'

'All dealers aren't afraid of new ideas.'

'But they wouldn't buy these. I don't think Leo is a genius, but even if he were, do you think the public would pay money to hear him practising scales? These are my scales.'

'Why not let the public judge? Your name still counts. You're not an unknown artist struggling for recognition. You're a well-known artist breaking new ground.'

'With a well-known flair for publicity,' said Paul. 'Well, take 'em if you like. Take what you fancy. Don't think I've come to despise money. I could do with some now. But it's got to be kept in its place—and its place is below stairs.'

I thought he was going on, but the dog came in and he said nothing more. The opportunity to put my questions passed. Well, I would first sound Holly.

Their day was simply planned—almost too simply for one of Paul's hitherto erratic habits. They rose at eight and he worked all day, with a light breakfast and a sandwich lunch. Holly cooked a meal in the evening, and afterwards he sat and read and smoked or dozed while Holly wrote letters or read or did some of the work her father had sent her. They had sold the Chrysler and went once a week to shop in Ambleside on a rickety old motor bicycle and sidecar.

We did a great deal of walking during the three days I stayed with them, over the moors, and sometimes we climbed to the tops of the more accessible of the strange, small, distinguished mountains. We wandered round the dew-ponds and sheltered together under hedges while showers beat on the grass and stones. Clouds followed us and hid us in their damp vapours, so that we had to wait until they were past before continuing on our way. Sun glinted through fine hazes and from sudden patches of pale washed-blue sky. We turned homewards as the sun deepened the shadows between the hills, and ate hungry meals and then sat and smoked and talked before the odorous peat fire. Whether he knew it or not, Paul was recreating as nearly as possible on land the conditions of isolation from material things he had first found in the *Patience*.

Yet to speak of a peaceful and leisurely routine left out of account altogether the ferocious concentration he put into his working hours.

Paul's attitude towards Holly, their attitude towards each other, had crystallised during the months they had been in Cumberland. Paul often wore a preoccupied, morose expression when alone or working—one was reminded of the sullen boy of Turstall days—but that expression never failed to change when he spoke to Holly. Her presence provided him with some sort of reaction which he needed and welcomed. They often joked with each other, but their fun was noticeably devoid of that sub-acid flavour which often characterises exchanges between married people.

On the morning I was leaving there was a chance at last to speak to Holly. Paul had gone upstairs, leaving us at the breakfast-table.

'You know Paul has offered me the choice of his paintings to take back to London?'

She nodded and I said: 'It's strictly a business proposition. Ten per cent on sales.'

'You'll deserve your full twenty-five,' she said, smiling.

'Well, he won't do anything himself. Someone has to look after him.'

She tapped on the table with her fingers. 'Before, he was doing something quite different: his painting was honest craftsmanship of which it was ridiculous to feel ashamed. But now . . . well, he's not painting for money and not painting to please anyone. He's just working out his own—his own future.'

'Will you help me to choose the pictures?'

'Of course.'

I swallowed my last corner of toast. 'Can you manage financially?'

'We need very little.'

'For yourselves. But Paul has commitments.'

Her eyes moved to stare out of the window at the low clouds masking the top of the opposite hill. 'Paul lived extravagantly when he was making money. And then the three lawsuits cost him thousands.'

'It's this question of Olive. Has he been able to pay her her allowance or has she been content to let it get in arrears?'

'Olive is the snag.'

'You mean he hasn't been able to pay her in full?'

'He's paid her all until this quarter. By selling up Royal Avenue furniture and the rest.'

'What is it he has to find?'

'Five hundred a quarter.'

'My God!'

'Sh! He wouldn't want me to tell you.'

'*Tell* me! But it's something that one has to *know* about! It's monstrous—far worse than I ever imagined! What sort of provision did Paul make before he left London?'

'None, as far as I can make out. He'd become so accustomed to his success that I suppose he didn't think it would end. That's silly, a stupid explanation! ... But when you've been making eight or nine thousand a year and 've got a healthy bank balance you don't quite imagine it will disappear so quickly. That's the only way I can imagine it happened. Of course in those days I knew nothing about it. Paul always tried to keep his money affairs separate—away from me ...'

'And now,' I said. 'And now?'

'Well ... Things have been made worse by claims for unpaid income tax in the last two years when he was earning so much. That's all cleared up now. Except for Olive we could manage well. But, with her, it's a hand-to-mouth existence. Very soon we shall have to start selling these.' She made a gesture towards the pieces of ceramic ware. 'But that'll be the end of our assets.'

'You *are* a couple of children,' I said. 'Paul far more than you. And *surprisingly* so! He was brought up to count his pennies ... That he should have gone this far astray ... Of *course* there must be an adjustment. I don't know how it will work, but it must work somehow.'

269

'You know ... it's funny, I was brought up very strictly—in a *way*, don't laugh, Bill, in a *way*!—but I'd default tomorrow, let Olive pursue us if she wants to. Not Paul. There's something inbred in him that makes him unable to go back on his debts. Olive is one of them. His father is another. He still allows him a hundred and fifty pounds a year, and that's something we *can't* default on; the old man has bad arthritis now.' Holly looked at me through her lashes. 'Paul told me I wasn't to tell you anything of this.'

'When did he say that?'

'As soon as you arrived.'

'Couldn't you have written me?'

'My dear, I'm inclined to agree with Paul: it's time you stopped feeling a responsibility for us. We've got to live our own life and look after ourselves. You've got to live yours. Don't think we're not grateful for your friendship, but it isn't fair that you should take responsibilities that should rightly fall on us.'

I said: 'Well, I should feel insulted if you didn't let me do something! Now will you help me choose these pictures?'

We assembled them and began to go through them.

'Have your father and mother been up to see you here?'

'They were coming at Christmas. Daddy couldn't manage it at the last moment.'

'You're able to do some work for him, though?'

'There's more time up here than in London. We hardly have any letters sent on. Vincent and Mary de Lisle came about a month ago and spent a long week-end. They liked the house and its surroundings very much and thought we'd arranged everything most charmingly; but I don't think they'll come again for some time. Paul and Vincent had a long argument.

Vincent looks on it as a retrograde step. For him the metropolis is the place for first-class artists. He says Paul could change his style just as well there. He says that to come up here is to invite provincialism.'

'What did Paul say?'

'He just said if he could attain the provincialism of Cézanne, he'd be satisfied.'

She began to pack up the pictures I'd chosen, and I watched her long fingers busy with the parcel. 'Are you going to work out your salvation as well as Paul his?'

She looked up and smiled. 'Everybody doesn't need salvation, not in the way Paul does. He's got to produce what's in him or else go to the wall. But for my part . . .'

'We all need some sort of spiritual satisfaction,' I said. 'It would be nice to feel that you are getting yours.'

Her mouth straightened. 'Now Paul's started on this track I think he'll go on painting whatever happens: he's got to. But without me the inspiration would be crooked, bent, forced out *in spite* of everything. At present it's coming in a sort of steady flood, *because* of everything.'

'Does that answer my question?'

'In a way. You see, if the trouble with Olive can be removed and Paul can be allowed to go on and find what he's looking for, then that's going to help me to find what I'm looking for too.'

I picked up the parcel and carried it out to the car. She followed me, the breeze and the sun making bright confusion of her hair.

'What will you do when you reach London?' she asked.

'About Olive's allowance?'

'Yes.'

'See Kidstone first, I expect.'

'Who is Kidstone? Does Paul know him?'

'He's the solicitor who acted for him in all the lawsuits.'

'I wonder then,' she said, 'if you could try somebody else. That's if you know of anyone. I think Paul would want you to.'

'*Why*, for God's sake?'

'You see,' said Holly, 'we haven't any money now, and Paul would feel that friends of his might undertake something for him on the strength of old friendships.'

'Well, why *shouldn't* they? They've made enough money out of him in the past.'

'I know. But we're arranging all this without Paul's consent. I know he'll be grateful to you if you're able to do anything; more than perhaps you realise. But I also know he'll feel more comfortable about it if he feels it isn't exactly a conspiracy of old friends to get him out of a tight corner of his own making. You do see what I mean?'

'All right,' I said despairingly. 'I'll do what I can.'

IV

Three days later I went to see Mr Rosse, of Messrs Carp, Cleeve & Rosse of Chancery Lane. Mr Rosse was a very bald man with a pinkish head. He had protuberant eyes, a careful smile, a wing-collar and a discreet morning suit. I had met him through a press friend and he specialised in divorce.

I put the matter to him. While I was talking he played with his pencil, rose and lit the gas fire, blinking and coughing slightly at the pop as it lit, and strolled round the room feeling the tops of his books for dust. When I had finished he came back and sat down.

Up to now he had only given an occasional grunt. At this juncture he put his finger-tips together and looked over them at me.

'My dear Mr Grant, of *course* he can do something about it! The English law was not devised as a punitive system. Too often we get it the other way round, of course. Husbands disappear without trace, leaving their first wives high and dry. This is quite the exception rather than the rule ... What your friend should do is to apply for a Summons for Variation. He'll be required to make an affidavit as to his present income, and in due course the matter will come up for adjustment.'

'One drawback remains. Solicitors are not philanthropists. My friend must have paid them hundreds while he was wealthy. But a court hearing now might cost him more than he could afford to pay.'

'Well, my dear Mr Grant, solicitors have to live. But their charges would be very much less ruinous than having to continue to pay permanent maintenance to the tune of forty pounds a week.'

'Can the first wife contest the adjustment?'

'Naturally. At the hearing her counsel will do everything he can to prove that the husband is still able to pay, if not all, then some considerable part of the original order. Your friend will have to appear in order to be cross-examined upon the affidavit he has sworn.'

'As to his present income?'

'As to his entire means and possessions. Yes.'

I said: 'He's one of those awkward devils who won't

273

accept a loan; but I've a number of his pictures, and I think I could sell them sufficiently well to make the necessary fees. Would you be prepared to take it on?'

'I'll take it on,' said Rosse. 'But it will be necessary to brief counsel. And I shall have to see your friend. Where does he live and what is his name?'

'Paul Stafford. He lives in Cumberland. I shall have to persuade him to come down to see you.'

'*The* Paul Stafford?' Rosse pursed his lips as if to whistle, but did not do so. 'As bad as that?'

'I'm afraid so.'

'Well, well. He must have been making a tidy income until quite recently. But it soon fritters away if one gets mixed up with women.'

'He's had the misfortune to become involved with two very awkward ones.'

Rosse adjusted his wing-collar in the mirror.

'Take it from me,' he said, 'ninety per cent of 'em are awkward if they don't get their own way. I should know. I live out of them.'

Chapter Nineteen

I

During the next few days I tried to get in touch with Henry Ludwig, but he was in hospital after a heart attack and was not expected home for at least two weeks. Ludwig was a man who had assistants, never a partner, so I really couldn't expect Abrahams, his second man, to take the responsibility of a decision.

I went to see Mr Farman of the Grosvenor Gallery. He and Paul had not been on the best of terms of recent years, but he was an honest man—somewhat unusual in the world of dealers—and he would have a keen eye for the market.

Farman took me into his back room and I unwrapped my parcel. He took the pictures out one by one, put each on the easel, studied it, replaced it with another.

After he had done he took off his eyeglasses and polished them. 'Certainly a great change.'

'They're meant to be.'

'If you hadn't told me they were his, Mr—a—Grant, I should have no means of knowing it. I see no resemblance—of approach, of choice of pigment, of brush-stroke. I seriously don't think I could sell them.'

'Does his name count for nothing?'

'Oh, indeed. He has a great following for his portraits—and I got good prices for some of his earlier works. But these . . .'

'You don't think they're very good?'

'I don't think they're very good. They have originality of a sort—but it's the originality of being different, not of innovation. Besides, they're all unfinished.'

'Except this one.'

He looked again at the painting of the studio. 'Yes . . . You could say so.'

'Other men have changed their styles.'

'Yes. Oh, *yes*. And I'm not infallible. It may be these represent the growing pains, the birth pangs, and that in a few years something exciting will emerge. I don't see it there yet.'

'Well,' I said, 'thank you.'

'I tell you what I will do,' he said. 'I'll take that one. And that farm scene—where is it?—ah, here. I'll take those two and put them up, for old times' sake, on the usual commission basis. They might attract someone with an eye for the unusual. No one would be more pleased than I to help him.'

I hesitated. The things might go up on the wall for a couple of weeks and then be stacked away in the basement with a lot of other stuff, to be taken out occasionally and shown to a client. They might stay in the gallery for years. That wasn't what I wanted. But could one do better elsewhere? The trouble was he'd picked on the two I thought the most saleable.

I said: 'Can I sleep on it?'

'By all means. Or you may find some other gallery more forthcoming. Sad news about Mr Ludwig, isn't it?'

II

I tried Carter & Ziesman of Bond Street, with whom Paul had done business occasionally. Mr Ziesman was tall and grey and tired, and after he had gone through the paintings he stood with his back to a magnificent Bonnard and talked about the Wall Street crash and the slump in England, the vast unemployment problem in Germany, the drop in values in the art world. After a few minutes he said: 'Is Mr Stafford happy in Cumberland?'

'He's certainly finding more satisfaction in this work than in his portraiture.'

'It's an unfortunate time to change—to make such a radical departure.'

'No doubt.'

'If he can live without his portraiture I'd say good luck to him. We are in this world to fulfil ourselves. But if he has to live by his art then I'd strongly advise him to spend a part of his year doing the work for which he's now justly famous. Then for the rest he can thumb his nose at the public and experiment as he pleases.'

'I don't think he finds it possible to do both.'

Mr Ziesman shook his head. 'That's too bad. I can see merit in some of these. A sense of power. But the public won't see it.'

'Surely the public has grown up a bit. I could pick out six paintings in this gallery now that the public wouldn't have looked at twenty years ago. Now they pay big prices for them.'

'The public has become—more educated, Mr Grant. But only in some respects. It has been taught to understand—say—a little French and Latin. It doesn't yet read Greek or Arabic. If you follow me. At the moment—though I quite admire that farm scene—these paintings are almost worthless.'

'So was Cézanne,' I said. 'And you could buy a Vermeer for eight pounds thirty years ago.'

'Of course. Of course. The history of art is littered

with examples. It's quite possible that in thirty years more some influential art critic will discover greatness in these Stafford canvases—call them unfinished masterpieces. So that farm scene might then become worth ten thousand pounds. But the chances are—the chances very strongly are—that it will never be worth more than ten.'

'Well, thanks again.'

'When this sort of thing happens,' Mr Ziesman said, helping me with the string, 'and it's not a unique occurrence by any means, I think of Simeon Solomon. Have you heard of him?'

'No.'

'Very few people have nowadays. Sixty years ago he was at least as well known as Mr Stafford. One of the most popular members of the Pre-Raphaelite school. A great friend of Swinburne and Rossetti. But he had ambitions to change his style, to begin something quite fresh, to startle the world with a new conception of life seen through the magic oil-paint of his own inspiration. So he broke away from his friends and began to paint and sketch in a new style. His money was soon exhausted, he began to drift and drink. He came to my father for help, and for a number of years my father paid him two pounds a week to keep him alive, and took the sketches in payment.'

Mr Ziesman walked with me to the door.

'We still have a stock of them in the cupboard upstairs. Very soon the money had to be paid daily, otherwise he'd drink it all and be penniless for the rest of the week. He often slept on the Embankment. He went on painting right to the end, but he died in an asylum.'

'I gather you've no wish to extend your philanthropy to Paul Stafford.'

'Good gracious, I trust he'll not need it.'

'No,' I said. 'I trust not.'

III

I left it two weeks. Ludwig was still in hospital but was much better, so I went to see him there.

He said: 'Don't show me any of them! For God's sake, I don't think they'll please me. Take them to Abrahams. Tell him I sent you. Tell him to put them in the window—three or four anyway. Put the others up inside. Make a story of it. For God's sake, you're a bit of a newspaper man, aren't you? Stafford's name is still news. Tell Abrahams to invite a few people for six o'clock Wednesday week. Champagne and biscuits. There's none of his conventional work at all, I suppose?'

'I'm afraid not.'

'Pity. Well, we'll do our best. Get the horses to the water even if we can't make 'em drink.'

IV

I wrote to Paul telling him what had occurred and urging him to come to town at the earliest opportunity to see Rosse. I did my stuff with the news editor, and sure enough we got an interesting and influential group to see the paintings on the Wednesday. Nothing sold; and then I was busy all the next week; and then Abrahams rang me to say the farmyard scene and another two had together gone for a hundred guineas. I knew Paul would be delighted, however much he might pretend indifference.

The following day Abrahams rang me asking me to come round to the Ludwig Galleries, as there was something he wanted to discuss with me, Mr Ludwig still being absent convalescing.

I got away late the following morning and parked in King Street. Mr Abrahams, who was a young scrawny Jew with a perpetually anxious expression, said: 'Mr Grant, I'm very sorry, there's been a little hitch. A little hitch, and I didn't like to bother Mr Ludwig. A firm of solicitors acting for Mrs Stafford—that's his wife, I suppose? His first wife?—they sent a man round to see me yesterday afternoon. They must have been snooping around. Couldn't believe it, but I suppose they heard of the sale. It seems Mr Stafford owes his wife money under some maintenance order. Now that this picture of his is sold they've obtained an order from the court—what's it called?—did he say a garnishee order?—to restrain us from paying the cheque to him. The money goes to her, they say. They say it's the law.'

I stared at him. I stared at the slip of paper he held in his hand. I took the paper from him and read it.

'So that's the law.'

'Yes, Mr Grant, it does seem to be, doesn't it?'

'It's time it was changed ... Anyway,' I thought quickly, 'I'm working as an agent for Mr Stafford on a twenty-five per cent commission. I'm entitled to that, and no one can deny it.'

Abrahams breathed through his nose. 'Have you—is there a written agreement?'

'No, verbal.'

'I believe verbal is legal, Mr Grant.'

'I believe it is.'

'I'll see to that, then. But so far as the rest goes, we

have to comply with the law.'

'I have a painting in Stafford's earlier style. "Head of a Parisian Girl". But that belongs to me. Think you could sell that for me?'

'Of course, Mr Grant. Mr Ludwig will be delighted.'

A letter from Paul the following week expressed gratitude for receipt of cheque for £17.10 and more particularly for all the other things I'd done to help. He concluded: 'I can't bring myself to the idea of coming to London at this stage. Remember old Clem talking of the number of hours left to him if he lived to an average age? Well, that's how I feel at present. Pompous but true. In another year or so it may be different. So I've written Rosse and suggested I visit a local solicitor—local by Cumbrian standards any-way—and make the affidavits to him. Then he can send them on.'

V

The 'Head of a Parisian Girl' fetched £150, and I contrived with some juggling to pass this on directly to Holly to pay preliminary law costs, to settle a few minor local debts, and to leave them with a little working capital. During the six months before the court case came up I managed one further visit to Crichton and was again quite impressed. It's not easy to have, one year, a luxury house, a smart American car, two servants, the membership of three good clubs and the best of food and wines, and the next year to be living as a semi-hermit on the edge of poverty. The change is hard if it is unavoidable: it's infinitely more difficult as a matter of free choice. I felt it almost certain that Paul would give way to the pressure of circumstances and return to London: a few weeks of his normal portrait work would see his position re-established. But he gave no sign.

And Holly gave no sign. She could have been his Achilles' heel, but she wasn't.

From the second visit I brought back four of the best pieces of Paul's ceramic ware carefully packed on the passenger's seat; and I was able to get rid of it without Olive knowing. But that left only eight more.

And in the law's good time, after the usual hesitation and delays, consideration was given to a variation of the permanent maintenance order by Mr Justice Pardy.

The case seemed to go on far too long. Olive's counsel put forward the plea that a man who voluntarily and deliberately ceased to earn deserved less considerate treatment than one who had ceased to earn as a result of misfortune or ill-health. There was, he argued, a definite responsibility at law devolving upon the husband to maintain a wife, and the evasion of such a responsibility by simply sitting down and ceasing to earn was a fundamental breach of the original consent order. Also Mrs Stafford, in perfectly good faith, had incurred a number of debts while waiting for her quarterly allowance, and these must necessarily be taken into account in any readjustment.

Paul had been forced to come to London at last, and he went through a cross-examination which could have been little worse if he'd been in the criminal court. He'd got a heavy cold, and for the first time ever looked really ill.

Giving judgment, Mr Justice Pardy said he could not admit the argument put forward by the counsel for Mrs Stafford. In the kind of case under review the law did not recognise intention or capacity but only the actual figures of a man's present earnings. The artistic question hardly entered into it. If, for instance, a prosperous merchant were to be divorced and after his divorce he were to give up his business and become a bricklayer at two pounds a week, then the law recognised his changed circumstances as a reason for a change in the maintenance order. No law on the statute book could make that bricklayer give up his new work and resume his business as a merchant merely to maintain his first wife, desirable though such maintenance might well be. A man's present income and realisable assets were the sole bases of assessment.

And reliable evidence had been produced to show that Mr Stafford was now living with his second wife in circumstances which, if not describable as poverty, could be called very poor indeed. Mr Stafford had equal responsibility for the maintenance of himself and his second wife. Counsel for Mrs Stafford could not seriously suggest that Mr Stafford was living in such circumstances merely to deprive his first wife of her legitimate allowance. Granted his ability to earn money on the scale of hitherto, it must surely be accepted that he had chosen such circumstances for his new home under some powerful impulse far removed from petty spite.

But far be it from him, Mr Justice Pardy continued, to encourage the belief that an order for permanent maintenance could be lightly evaded. It could not too often be emphasised that the responsibility of a guilty husband remained as a permanent charge on his income, whether that income was large or small. In making an order in this court he could only take into consideration the present income of Mr Stafford together with such assets as remained to him. If, however, his income were to improve again, Mrs Stafford had only to apply in this court for a readjustment of the amount of maintenance awarded to her, which he would now fix at one hundred and fifty pounds a year.

Chapter Twenty

I

The first two years of Paul Stafford's voluntary exile in Cumberland have been little covered by his biographers because they've found little enough to say about them. I have tried to fill in a few of the gaps; but only he and Holly could really ever have done that satisfactorily and neither chose to.

After the readjustment of the maintenance order peace might have been expected to descend on them for a while; but Paul's bad cold developed into pneumonia as soon as he returned, and he nearly died.

A month later in convalescence he wrote: 'Don't come up till the weather improves, and for Pete's sake don't feel *sorry* for me. It's all too conventional, isn't it, the struggling genius wasting away with TB and continuing his immortal battle against a cruel and unfeeling world. Feel sorry for Holly, if you like. She somehow managed to get a nurse from Broughton, and while the wind and rain raged tempestuously through the valley for five days and nights they fought to keep the genius alive.

'So now, apart from a cough that sounds like someone shovelling wet coal, he *is* alive and making rapid progress towards his usual upstanding vigour. The doctor says I'm horse-strong and will come to no harm now, except that I must take shorter walks for the time being and not actually go out when it's snowing. Also spend less time at the easel.

'This last is bloody exasperating, because just before I was dragged down to London I found some new colours—or maybe just a new luminosity in old colours—particularly in the ultramarines, viridian, raw umber and Naples yellow. I'm going all fancy, like, just for a change. In another month, if you can tear yourself away from the footlights, come and see the first snowdrops.'

Holly had added a PS.

'What rubbish! I've *picked* snowdrops already.'

When eventually I went I found Paul looking much older. His thick hair was receding from his forehead, and the frontal bones of his temples and strong cheek-bones stood out through the clear brown skin. But he looked happy. Holly hadn't changed. If it had been a horrible winter it had left no more impression than the first month of married life in fashionable London.

I thought Paul's paintings were getting stronger, more complete and probably more saleable. I took half a dozen away with me.

A trickle of money was finding its way to him from Ludwig and one or two other friends. It was just enough to make do. But in the summer he had a sudden windfall. Three of his portraits of famous courtesans had gone to De Vere's, the New York dealers, and nothing more had been heard of them. Now after this long time they all went to the same purchaser for a figure which worked out in sterling at a net £478 each.

It was a fortune, by later standards. As Paul said sardonically, if nothing else it took Olive off their hands for nine years.

At Holly's birthday party held in Crichton shortly after the sale of the pictures I wondered what Jeremy

Winthrop would have thought had he seen Paul now, obviously content with the new life he'd chosen, and not, it seemed, any longer the victim of that Merciless Lady of success. Perhaps a few of us, I thought, the lucky ones, can shake themselves free without coming too complete a cropper.

The party was half for Holly's birthday and half to celebrate the fact that they were solvent again. Sir Clement and Lady Lynn were there, and Paul's father. Paul had bought three bottles of champagne, and this was just enough to unlock tongues all round.

At the end of supper Holly gave us an impression of Sir Clement delivering a lecture to Wisconsin University when he had mislaid his notes. It was all there: she was sufficiently like her father to make the mimicry complete: the opening phrases of the lecture delivered while still searching in every available and unavailable pocket, the lecture getting under way without notes but still accompanied from time to time by a reflex groping in this pocket and that; then the hands finally getting into their proper motions, the gestures he always made slightly exaggerated, drawing an idea like a conjurer out of thin air, assembling various threads with a collective drawing up of the long fingers; the big climax larger than life, followed by the absent-minded bows to applause and the mopping of a heated brow with a handkerchief in which the notes were still tied.

Lady Lynn laughed till the tears dripped down her cheeks. Sir Clement said he had no idea his platform manner was so fascinating: this would encourage him to lecture in his own home from time to time, on the house-training of puppies and kindred subjects.

Even old Mr Stafford was more talkative than usual and sat watching the others with a good-tempered smile. Paul's giving up all he had worked for had been something Mr Stafford could not bring himself to understand; almost a worse blow than when the youthful Paul had refused to go in for a degree. This whole episode of the removal from London with its following consequences had been a sore trial to him; but he had slowly come to have confidence in his son. Paul might do strange things but it always came out right in the end.

After supper, Ethelred, the overgrown cocker spaniel, in whom, true to Lady Lynn's philosophy, the blood of some larger dog was clearly stirring, became overwhelmed with all the admiration he was receiving and upset the dining table with the remains of the meal still on it. Later we all played noisy card games until after midnight. Altogether it was one of those happy evenings which seem so commonplace to set down.

I had to leave early the following morning, and Paul gave me a letter for Vincent de Lisle which he said contained a cheque for a hundred pounds. 'That time he came here he insisted on giving it to Holly— said it was a debt he owed me. Complete lie, of course. Now I'm able to return it. I've had one or two good friends and let's hope this is the end of sponging on them.'

'You never sponged on me.'

'*All* the time. But with you it hasn't been money.'

I climbed into my car. 'I see the house down the valley has been repainted.'

Paul nodded. 'Someone's taken it, we don't know who. It's a mistake for any man to think he can get on without at least a few good friends. And Holly's been ... well ... It's a valuable lesson in humility. In a hundred years when some bone-headed dealer is

288

arguing whether such-and-such a picture is by me or by some other clown, they'll scrape away a bit of paint under my signature and find the words "Also by Holly Stafford, William Grant, Vincent de Lisle etc."'

'Remind me to ask for my ten per cent.'

'I'm getting *on*, Bill,' he said. 'You may not notice much difference between what I'm doing now and what I was doing last year, but it's *there*. And it's going to mean a lot in the end.'

II

Two months to the day from this conversation Olive issued a new Summons for Variation. She had learned of the sale of the pictures in America and wanted her fair share.

III

I decided to go and see little Olive. I owed her a call. I had no idea whether she was still living in her expensive flat, but I found she was. I wondered how it happened that she was.

I thought of ringing and decided against it. If she was in she was in.

I had a meal nearby, drinking enough to settle my thoughts, no more. I walked up the stairs to her flat, which was on the first floor, pressed the bell. If Maud opened the door I should be sure of a sour welcome.

But it was Olive herself.

She was in a peach silk dressing-gown, with a bandanna of the same colour about her bright hair. I was startled at the change in her. She was still pretty, but thinner, and her eyes were deep set, preoccupied.

I said: 'I was passing and I saw your light. It's been ages.'

'I was just going to bed.' It was not an invitation. But she stood aside to let me enter.

'You're early tonight.'

'One of my headaches.'

'D'you get them much?'

'Enough. Go on in.'

I went into that large white living-room I knew so well but which was no longer so white, having undergone the redecoration Maud had told me about. A feature of the room tonight was that all the drawers of the writing bureau were open and their contents disturbed.

'Burglars?' I asked.

She untied the bandanna and shook out her hair. 'That's what I'm trying to find out.'

'Meaning?'

'Meaning Maud. It's her night out. I've missed a few things. Now I've laid traps for her so if she takes anything more I shall know.'

'Maud's been with you for *years*. *Would* she take anything?'

'It remains to be seen, doesn't it?'

'She's so devoted. You'd have a job ever to find anyone as ... good.' I hesitated at the adjective, uncertain how to label without offence the peculiar dog-like attention of the sullen spotty Maud.

Olive sat down and crossed her legs, adjusting the dressing-gown carefully to cover them.

'I haven't seen you since you pulled down this new job. In fact, we've hardly spoken since my dear husband remarried. *That* was a shambles, wasn't it? Have you been cutting me?'

'Hardly. But you *were* a bit naughty over the divorce.'

'The divine justice of it! And Diana got it in the neck too. *Could* it have been better arranged?'

'Or more bitchily?'

She carefully licked her lips. 'If you've come here to read the lesson I have to tell you I've sold the lectern to pay my grocery bill.'

'I didn't come here for any specific purpose other than to see you. I was nearby and thought I'd like to. Do we always have this effect on each other?'

'What effect? Sort of flint and tinder?'

'If you like ... At least they often share the same box.'

'Well, from our one experience I don't think we should be too happy sharing the same bed. Do you?'

'I don't remember it with distaste.'

'Oh, no,' she said. 'Oh, no. But not to be repeated. In case you came here for that purpose.'

'No ... I've told you why I came. Though the memory came back soon enough when I saw you. What's *wrong*, Olive?'

'Wrong?'

'Yes. Wrong.'

She considered me. 'Because I choose not to fall down on my back before you? This unbearable arrogance—'

'Not *me*, Olive. Any man. Because there isn't any other man, is there?'

'What the hell business is it of yours?'

'None, obviously.'

After a moment she said: 'There's a drink on the table.'

'Thanks, I'm OK. You're not in a company mood tonight. I think I'll push off.'

'If I'd been in a company mood tonight I wouldn't have been at home when you called. I cancelled a theatre. *And* with a man, for your interest.'

'Will *you* have a drink?'

'A couple of fingers of brandy. If I take more it makes my head worse . . .'

'Seriously, Olive, why don't you remarry? There are plenty of other fish in the sea besides Paul and the Sharble fellow.'

'You want me to get off Paul's back? Is that the purpose of the visit?'

'That's the second or third guess you've made about my purpose. Can't you accept the truth—that I just wanted to see you?'

She laughed shortly. 'No. Don't you know your reputation—that you only call when you want something.'

I refused to rise to the taunt. 'Who doesn't?'

'Were you thinking of proposing marriage to me yourself?'

'As I've said before, I'm not a marrying man.'

'Where was the accent on that?'

'But since you raise the question of Paul . . .'

'Ah . . .'

'What's the point of this new summons?'

'You've heard of it, then . . . Simply to have money to pay the rent of this flat. My parents paid it for six months, but now my father has just died.'

'I'm sorry, I didn't know . . . But, Olive, anything you get out of Paul—whatever it is—will be swallowed up in legal costs. What are *you* really getting out of it? Surely revenge is pretty sour by now? Because some other woman has made a success where you failed? Dead Sea fruit, isn't it?'

'What other sort of fruit would you like me to pick?'

'Something with life and flavour in it. We've all only so many hours to enjoy the decent, warm things of the world. Why shrivel up your soul before its time?'

'My soul's well able to take care of itself.'

'Believe me, if it were only your own soul you were poisoning I'd let it rot in peace.'

'I know,' she said. 'That's what amuses me.'

I could have struck her then, because she had made me lose my temper.

I sat down. 'All right. All right. Since we're talking about Paul, let's level on that. Have you seen any of his recent work?'

'I saw one in the Ludwig window. I thought it pretty much of a daub.'

'At least you must admit he's trying to do something new. You're an artist, Olive. If you create something yourself you must surely respect the efforts of a fellow artist. Gauguin and Van Gogh were laughed at not so very long ago. Who can be certain that Paul isn't doing the same sort of thing today? Why then go out of your way to stultify his efforts and to make his life intolerable?'

She lit a cigarette, snapped out her lighter, leaned her head back. 'Gauguin, did you say? Van Gogh?'

'Well?'

'You're mentioning them in the same breath as my ex-husband? Oh, dear! Paul, the pretty portrait painter, turned genius. Did I once say you were a poor journalist?'

'What he was painting in London is gone and forgotten. He's working now on the raw stuff of life. Of *course* I can't prove to you he's a genius. Of *course* I'm not certain that his present work is going to be this, that or the other. He's only just beginning to find himself. But it's supremely *honest*. There's not a trace of the fake or the meretricious about it. And in the time he's been in Cumberland he's made big strides ... Supposing, just supposing he *is* good—so good that he'll have a biography written about him someday. D'you want the biographer to write: "The greed and malice of his first wife were responsible for the short duration of his most brilliant period. Her conduct would have been less inexcusable in a woman of mean intelligence, but having some artistic ability herself . . ."'

She drew in her cheeks over the cigarette. Her eyes looked sunken.

'He's really got you fooled, hasn't he! You don't think of my feelings! Paul, the oppressed genius. What a ramp!'

'I'm only suggesting you should give him a chance by dropping out of his life.'

'Why should I drop out? To help create a phoney legend—'

'I'm not trying to create anything. I *know* there's your side to the case. But it's time it was all forgotten, put aside. You can't go on having vendettas for ever.'

She looked me over, coolly, politely, her lips firm.

'Because you've caught me at home, you suppose I'm sitting here eating my heart out for Paul? What damned stupid nonsense! I live a good life! I live it as I please, not at the beck and call of some man who supposes he's God's gift to the world! I'm *free*, and I'm going to stay free. All I want is that Paul should earn enough to keep *me*, as well as that timid one-legged bespectacled creature who's got him in tow now. Let him come back to London and earn what he's capable of earning and pay me a fair maintenance! When he does that there'll be no further quarrel between us.'

'He won't do that. He'll stay up there if it kills him.'

'Then let it kill him! D'you think I care? He emerges from some dirty shop in Lancashire, climbs as far as he can on a trick talent for portrait painting. He battens on to Diana for what he can get out of her. But he can't marry her, so he throws her over for me. Olive will introduce him here and there. Olive has social connections and will bring him the type of client he wants! Then when he's firmly established with them Olive can go to hell! She can rot on any convenient slag-heap!' She twisted her body and stared at me with cold anger.

'Is that how you *really* see him?'

'Has he ever had a thought in his life except for himself? Name me one!'

'There's other—'

'Why should I bother to underwrite his daubs and experiments? Look at this place! Now my father's died my mother loses part of his pension and can afford little enough for me. So unless Paul does the right thing I'm going to have to give it up!'

'Why don't you work?'

'What *at*? My paintings don't sell, as you damned well know! What else am I useful for? Assistant in a ladies' dress shop? Teach the Theory of Art at a local day school? Design Christmas cards? Go and live with my mother and nurse her headaches as well as my own? . . . Not while Paul is alive, dear! Not while he's quietly putting money away and pretending to starve—'

'He's not putting money away. I can assure you of that.'

She got up and stubbed out her cigarette. 'Oh, you can throw dust in the judge's eyes, but don't try it on me! What *about* the clinging Holly? She has money of her own, and everything he makes now goes into her name. Don't think I don't know how these things can be worked!'

'They've sold practically everything to pay you,' I said.

'*They* did. Oh, I'm sure *they* did. Can you imagine dear little Holly saying in her fluty tones: "Paul, dear, we can't afford a new car this year because we have the alimony to find." Can you imagine a normal woman, let alone a scarecrow with a tubercular hip? ...'

She stopped at the look on my face. With an effort she took control of herself.

'I've told you to go once.'

'You're dying,' I said. 'You're dying of malice and envy and hate. It's killing you. For God's sake try to come alive again.'

I went then without looking at her again. I went out into the little box hall and ran down the stairs into the street.

There was no more to be done.

Chapter Twenty-One

I

In a café in Fleet Street hard by the entrance to
Chancery Lane I met the discreet Mr Rosse and took
tea with him. He ate three large muffins specially
plastered with butter, and while we talked he
delicately licked a finger-tip.

'I'm beginning to believe you, my dear Mr Grant,'
he said. 'The first Mrs Stafford has a combative side
to her nature which will be hard to overcome.'

'This maintenance business,' I said. 'There must be
some remedy to the complaint, surely. A man like Mr
Stafford may have an income which fluctuates
between very wide margins year by year. One year he
may earn two thousand, the next he may not make
two hundred, especially during this transition period.
What's to prevent the woman from bringing a
summons every time his income goes up, thereby
forcing him to bring one every time it goes down?'

'In principle, simply nothing at all.'

'But in practice?'

'In practice? Well . . .' Mr Rosse stirred his tea with
the little finger of the right hand raised. 'In practice it
wouldn't be worth her while. In practice the—lawyers
concerned do their best to save the money of their
respective clients by coming to a compromise agreement which is as nearly fair as possible to both parties.'

'Yes,' I said. 'That seems very reasonable. And in
this case—'

'Three weeks ago I proposed to the lawyers acting for Mrs Stafford that I would be pleased to submit to my client any reasonable compromise proposal they cared to send me. Their answer was that, acting on the instructions of their client, they were not prepared to submit or consider a compromise proposal. And I have since heard, strictly *inter nos* of course, that Mrs Stafford threatened to change her solicitors if they persisted in advising her to settle.'

I bit at a piece of toast with none of Mr Rosse's refinement. 'That means, practically speaking, a court case every year. The woman's beside herself with jealousy. You can't reason with her and you can't bribe her. You can't get *at* her at all. We're kicking against a brick wall, Mr Rosse.'

The solicitor nodded. 'I have only met Mr Stafford at the High Court hearing. He strikes me as a difficult man to prescribe for. One can only *offer* advice.'

'And I can only pass it on.'

Mr Rosse finished his muffins, stared at his plate. I ordered some more.

'If I were in Mr Stafford's position I'd simply come up for the next hearing and defend myself. Let him say that he cannot afford a barrister; that will immediately emphasise his position *vis-à-vis* his first wife. Then if the judgment goes somewhat against him, as it must if he has earned over a thousand pounds this year, let him default on his payments. Let him make no effort to pay. Let his wife summons him again. Let her go on issuing garnishee orders. It'll keep her well occupied. It'll keep her amused. It'll cost her a pretty penny. It's really a question of staying power. In the end she'll get tired. After all, in cases like this, it is usually the husband who comes off best in the long run.'

I nodded. 'Very good advice. The trouble is you're not prescribing for a normal man. He wouldn't come down and defend himself in court—I'm pretty sure. Nor would he tolerate bailiffs knocking on his door. Olive Stafford has more staying power than he has, and she'll last the course if it finishes her. It's much more likely to finish him instead.'

'Failing anything else,' said Rosse, 'it might be worth the trifling expense to employ an inquiry agent. One never knows what one is going to find. And naturally there is a *dum casta* clause in the maintenance agreement.'

'What the devil is that?'

'A clause making it a condition of the payment that the wife shall remain chaste. Very necessary and right.'

'I think it would be a waste of money. You could try it but I think it would simply fail. Olive is—an unusual creature. She's really very pretty, and can be charming; but she's as unlovable as granite. Even if she ever took the time in her exhausting social life she'd be scrupulously careful to cover her tracks. She's not altogether sexless, of course, but I believe she hates giving way. She resents being possessed. There are insects, aren't there, in which the female kills the male afterwards. There's something of that in her nature.'

Mr Rosse was looking at me interestedly. 'She's probably *had* affairs. But to get her re-married is the best solution.'

'No doubt.'

'Surely she would prefer some trifling loss of independence to the uneasy debt-ridden existence of a divorced wife?'

'You have to remember that until a year ago she was getting an allowance of two thousand a year.

Every prospective husband hasn't that to offer.'

'No. A reasonable view ... You say when you went to see her she was perfectly determined to go on with it, laid all the blame on her husband, I suppose?'

'Yes. All.'

Mr Rosse began another muffin.

'Well, she's not—hm—unusual in that respect anyway.'

II

For a while nothing. All this time my own life was going on, full and exacting and satisfying. In the country the financial crisis had mounted and a National Government formed under Ramsay Macdonald. Another idealist corrupted by the establishment. Or another hothead discovering the hard facts of life. Depending how you looked at it. Thank God I no longer had a responsibility to report it.

One in three Americans was out of work; six hundred banks had closed their doors; the skyscrapers were proving useful platforms for suicide; dispossessed householders camped in broken shacks on the sides of rivers; former industrialists begged the price of a meal.

I sold my Morris Minor and bought a Wolseley Hornet, the first small car brought out by that distinguished firm, the smallest six cylinder ever. One and a quarter litres. A new radical design, pushing the engine far forward over the front wheels. I didn't keep it long enough to discover all the bugs: that the valve springs were too weak, that the tiny cylinders suffered excessive wear, that its 'twin-top' gear was occasionally valuable for overtaking but was no use whatever on gradients because there was not sufficient power.

A play was in rehearsal to open shortly at Drury Lane called *Cavalcade*. St John Ervine in the *Observer* wrote of Coward that he was 'a faithful representative of the spirit of his time. If we wish to understand some of the youth that grew to manhood in the War, we must take a good look at Mr Coward, in whom the gaiety and despair of his generation is exactly mixed. He has no faith in life here or hereafter ...'

P. Steegman had just painted Somerset Maugham, a commission which almost certainly would have fallen to P. Stafford if he had still been functioning. There was talk of an award of the Nobel Prize for Literature to John Galsworthy.

I had a girl friend called Jane Bowker, with whom for a few months I thought something important and serious for us both was growing. But always I found myself not totally lost. Often I thought of Holly in Cumberland. And often I thought of Olive in Clarendon Gardens. Maybe I was always doomed to live other people's lives more urgently than my own. It is perhaps a failure of personality, which accounts for so much.

As autumn approached I had another letter from Holly.

'Paul has been away for five days. This, I know, should be in capital letters. He had a letter last week to say that old Dr Marshall, your one-time headmaster, was dying, so he packed a bag and went. I had a woman in to sleep; but I'm not in the least afraid of being alone here. When you get to know it the valley isn't eerie any longer.

'I was turning out a suit-case yesterday and came across the photographs taken in the old *Patience*. What a crazy scheme of ours to come home in that little leaky cutter!

'Do you remember a discussion we had, you and I, in the saloon of the *Patience* right in the middle of the bad weather? It was a deep one, about religion and God and seasickness, and having something to believe in, though it never really got going. But I did feel in those days that life had been examined too closely for my good. It wasn't that I couldn't see wood for trees; but I couldn't see the trees for the wood. Life in a thoroughly well-run, well-explained universe just wasn't attractive.

'Things have changed a bit since then. Not that I see things much more clearly, but the perspective is better. For a long time now I've watched a man struggling to express his personal view of life, which he alone can feel. That has knocked holes in the scientific explanations.

'*Not* because Paul's pictures are necessarily good. I wonder if you see what I mean, Bill? The man with the one talent is just as good an argument as the man with ten, so long as he uses it. If I were starting a religious revival I should put down as a first law that it is the business of all of us to create something to the very highest level of our ability, whether that something is a symphony or a cake, a home in a city or a pair of shoes, a cathedral or a field of corn. Aren't such people the people who are happy? And don't we all, by the act of producing something which has not existed before, show a sort of kinship with the Something which made *us*?

'Here endeth the first lesson. Not very impressive; but I feel there's a sort of personal truth for me wrapped up in it. Be kind enough not to laugh.

'Paul has been doing two pictures with the palette knife for a change. He uses the PK like a workman using a trowel for building a house. I want him to send you one.

'I had a letter from Bertie last week; my first this year. No thought of returning home. He seems to be the happiest of any of us.'

On the back of the letter, written in pencil was a postscript.

'By the way, I've come to the conclusion I'm going to have a baby. About March. Perhaps this fact had a hidden influence on the prosy part of this letter. After all, if a girl can't start a religious revival once in her life . . .

'So I'm going to be a creative artist in a way I hadn't bargained for. Perhaps Daddy's mathematics may yet come in useful for adding up the grocer's bill.'

III

A few days later, moth to flame, I telephoned Olive.

'This is Bill. I thought I'd ring.'

'Well?'

'Sorry about our last meeting. Afraid I was rude.'

'Should I expect anything else?'

'Well, you *were* a little provoking.'

'Flint to tinder, eh?'

'Yes . . . But I've come to the conclusion that squabbling like that is a fairly sterile occupation. It gets us nowhere.'

'D'you think we ought to get somewhere?'

'Not in those insinuating terms. But I miss you when I don't see you . . . and it seems a pity.'

'For whom?'

'Well, doesn't it? We're closer in a way than many people who don't fight. And if we agreed to cut that out.'

'Could we?'

'Once in a while, I think. How about trying?'

'In what way?'

'Have dinner with me sometime.'

A slight metallic laugh. 'Where?'

'The Savoy.'

'Can you afford it?'

'How about Monday?'

'Sorry. Can't.'

'Tuesday?'

'All right ... On one condition ... that you don't mention Paul.'

I made a face at the receiver. 'Agreed.'

'What time?'

'I'll call for you at seven-thirty.'

'All right. Thanks.' She rang off.

Chapter Twenty-Two

I

The older one gets, the further one moves from the events to be told, the more reluctant one becomes, when the memories are painful, to disturb them, to give them the benefit of an extra life by setting them down for others to see. It's like showing some stranger round your house and into a room not opened for years. You draw back the curtains, dust drifts in the pale sunlight and shows up long-remembered yet half-forgotten furniture. The eye of the memory catches sight of so much better left unseen.

I should like to make it clear that I went to meet Olive that evening with no plan of any sort in mind. None at all. I did not at the time closely analyse my motives for going, and in retrospect it's impossible to define them without confusing the intention with the outcome.

The evening was bright and fine with the first thin freckle of autumn frost on the pavements. Tyres left faint marks on the delicately powdered roads. My car was having its first service, so I took a cab. She was wearing an azure velvet dinner frock with sleeves to the elbow and a low square neck. Over it was a mink bolero. She congratulated me on finding her with a night free this week: if it had not been tonight it could not have been for twelve days. I accepted this remark in a fittingly humble spirit and took her to dinner.

I set out to please her, and under the effects of the food and the wine she began to thaw. She frequently smiled at my remarks as well as expecting me to defer to her own. I watched the small bright teeth, the small pointed eye-teeth, disappearing behind precise firm lips, the vivid painted little face changing its contours. Except when smiling she looked so much older, so much more like her mother. Some of the bloom had gone already—she was only thirty-one—but the more I watched her the more sure I was that it was not physical ill-health. Much more probably what in those days used to be called neurasthenia. The old corrosive element of self-absorption.

We had a cocktail first, a half-bottle of Puligny Montrachet, a bottle of Volnay '25, and Cointreau with the coffee. As we sipped the last I said: 'Where now?'

'Now? Home, I suppose. D'you want to go on?'

'It's early yet. You must know more night clubs than I do.'

'There's "The 77". And "The Blue Peter" which isn't far from where I live. There's "The Hungaria".'

'Let's try "The Blue Peter". I've heard of it but haven't been. Are you a member?'

'Yes.' She looked at her watch. 'But it's early yet. The place doesn't get going till midnight. I suppose we could dance here ... Or have a drink at my flat?'

I nodded. 'Let's do that.'

As we got into a taxi I said: 'What did you decide to do about Maud?'

Olive laughed. 'She's leaving next week.'

'So she *was* stealing things?'

'I never caught her out. But I'm *tired* of her. She knows me too well. Anyhow I can't afford her now.'

'Poor Maud.'

'Poor Olive. I can't even keep the flat, so that's going too.'

'What will you do?'

'Ah. That's a surprise. I'll tell you later.'

'Is Maud in tonight?'

'She's out till midnight. She's really taking it hard. You never liked her, did you?'

'I don't fancy women with acne.'

She laughed again. She was not drunk but she was more easy and friendly in her manner than I had ever known her—except perhaps in the very early days before she married Paul.

'She hates my guts, really. I believe she had a thing for me—wanted to keep me all for herself. One of those women. Now she feels she's being turned off without a thought and all her love has changed to jealousy.'

It was about ten-thirty when we reached the flat. By then ideas were moving in my head—or perhaps they were responding to physical impulses. At this distance I can't be sure. When we got in she threw off her bolero and went over to put on a record.

'Get you a drink?' I said.

'Please. Brandy. D'you know, stupid Bill, I feel better than I've done for ages. Perhaps, if you can only keep off the forbidden subject, you *are* good for me.'

'Glad to hear it.'

We drank and danced. I knew then, if I wanted her . . .

We sat for a bit, sipping brandy. I leaned over and kissed her gently, experimentally. She didn't resist.

She said: 'I'll tell you sometime. I'm sure it'll amuse you—if it doesn't infuriate you. Will it infuriate you? I expect so. So I'll say nothing now.'

'You *can't*,' I said. 'Not after that!'

307

'I'll do what I damn well please!'

I kissed her again. 'Give.'

She licked her lips. 'Perhaps "The Blue Peter" isn't such a good idea after all.'

'Carried without a vote. What were you going to say?'

'Nothing. Not now.'

'Is Maud ever back early?'

She laughed. 'Never.'

I looked at the clock. 'So we've rather more than an hour.'

'All of that. Can you keep me interested?'

I kept her interested.

II

An odd thing about love-making is that it unlocks the tongue. Or perhaps it isn't odd. And perhaps love-making is an old-fashioned expression—anyhow for what happened between Olive and me. In spite of her obvious sexuality, there was something spinsterish about her which resisted self-surrender until almost too late. But when it came, there were no restraints then.

And when it was all over, although her cool wits and sharp tongue were soon in evidence, they were not for a while in such control. And of course we had drunk quite a bit.

'Did I spit at you?'

'Not exactly.'

'Well, you smacked my face.'

'A love tap.'

'The old male assertion, you bastard. But I must say it's better that way—fighting.'

'Do you behave so with your other lovers?'

'I haven't any—as you know damned well.'

'Oh, come. With all your social life, there must be occasions which lead invitingly up the stairs.'

'My social life!... What sort of social life d'you think I really have? Did you really fall for that hokum of tonight being my only free night in two weeks?'

'Then why say so?'

'To impress you, I suppose.'

'To impress me? You don't need to do that. Anyway, you must be in great demand.'

'Demand!' she said vehemently. 'D'you know any single divorced woman who's greatly in demand? *Do* you? Not in this society, not with half the men killed in the war! It's all right for a man—there's always room for him—the odd one at the dinner table, someone to make up numbers for a week-end. How often does a *woman* get an invitation like that?'

'You have friends—'

'Of *course* we had friends! But those who didn't take Paul's side, well, they asked me out a few times and then conveniently forgot about it. There's no room for a single woman in this society! You're just an odd one out, a left-over, a has-been ...'

'At your age, with your looks?'

'Of course I could have a life of a sort, if I were prepared to be a tart. There are always men looking out for that. But as for marriage ... Oh, I know I'm pretty and still fairly young ... but d'you think I get worthwhile offers every week? Or every quarter? Or every *year*? Even if I were willing to consider any of them.'

'You did with Peter Sharble.'

Her eyes went hard. 'Men are such suckers for flattery, for appeals to their protective nature. Although they'd deny it, most of them don't really want an equal—they want a little woman they can keep at home and *patronise* ... Peter was bright enough—we could have made something of life together—but he chose to fall for that little creep he met on the cruise ... I often wonder if Paul poisoned his mind against me.'

'*Paul*? Whatever d'you mean?'

'Peter was a member of the Hanover. No doubt they met and talked.'

'You can set your mind at rest on that! Paul was only anxious to get a divorce. Sharble was his one chance. He wouldn't have been such a fool.'

She glanced at the clock. 'Maybe. But after the divorce...'

'It's not like you to think so unclearly. If you'd married Sharble Paul would have been free of alimony. That's the thing he wanted most—wants most now in all the world.'

She sighed. 'So we're back on the forbidden topic, aren't we? My fault this time, was it? Bill ...'

'Yes?'

'I don't feel like "The Blue Peter" now. It's time you went.'

'Yes...'

'God, you're good for me! Pity *we* couldn't marry ... But it would be hell in a week.'

'I know.'

'But once in a while like this.'

I moved to get up. 'Olive, what were you going to tell me before this happened?'

'Oh ... that.' Her eyes grew amused. 'Guess.'

'Can't.'

'It'll bring up the *verboten* subject.'

'Does it matter now?'

'It matters that it's twenty to twelve. Buck up.'

She gave me a push.

'When you've told me.'

'Well ... you know I'm leaving this flat—can't afford it. The expense is crippling. I'm going to be able to afford precious little. My mother hasn't much to spare... So I've taken a house—a small house— guess where.'

'I've no idea.'

'Cumberland. I'm going to paint there. Seeking freedom for my artistic soul.'

I peered at her. 'Rubbish. I don't believe you... Where in Cumberland?'

'Place called Crichton Beck.'

I licked my lips. 'Near *Paul*?'

'Why not? Two can play at the same game. I've taken a little four-roomed house that's been empty for some time. The owner is having it repainted and decorated. The rent is peanuts—unbelievable.'

I took a deep breath. 'You'd die of boredom, Olive.'

'D'you think I don't sometimes nearly die of boredom *here*? There's nowhere lonelier than London. Can you imagine me in a bed-sitter? Not damned likely. Anyway, I've only taken it for a year. Apparently it's very close to Paul and his little lame duck, so I shall be able to keep an eye on them. Call round to borrow milk or a pinch of tea. Drop in and see his latest painting. Sure he'll be glad of my advice. If I get on his nerves he can always decide to pay up and get me something better in London.'

I still stared at her. 'You don't really mean this, Olive.'

She moistened her lips and gave a little smile. 'You see if I don't.'

I lay back, thinking of it all. I thought a lot. This was the last straw. I began to think of Mr Rosse. I thought of a *dum casta* clause. Wise Mr Rosse. An hour ago I had speculated as to what would come of the evening. I hadn't supposed this.

'Go on,' she said. 'We don't want Maud to catch us.'

'Is she usually prompt?' I asked cautiously, thinking all round it.

'I'm often asleep. But more often than not it's about twelve-thirty when I hear her key.'

'Oh, there's plenty of time, then.'

'We can't be *certain*. Her stupid sister may have toothache or something.'

I moistened my own lips. 'But she doesn't come in here when she comes home surely?'

'Oh, yes, she does! Puts her head round the door to see if I'm asleep or want anything. Wouldn't be Maud if she didn't. Me, the ewe lamb.'

I sighed. 'You'll miss her.'

'Oh, God, yes in a way. But now I want to miss you.'

I listened to the ticking of the clock.

I said: 'I'd like to stay the night.'

She stared. 'Well, you *can't*! Don't be utterly ridiculous.'

'D'you think she'd notice if the light was out?'

'Of course she'd *notice*! Bill, don't be damned silly. It's ten to twelve. Get dressed!'

'All right,' I said. 'On one condition.'

'What are you *talking* about? I don't make *conditions*! What condition?'

'That you don't go and live in Cumberland.'

There was quite a long silence. She sat up very slowly and I watched her naked back disappear into a white knitted jumper.

'Get out!' she said.

'Olive, I don't want tonight to end in a free-for-all. Believe me. It's been—good. But I'm making a condition about leaving, and I mean to stick to it.'

She pulled on a skirt and stood up.

'Get out!'

I said: 'Control yourself. You won't get me out by force. I'm stronger than you—as you know... If you go up and live as Paul's neighbour you'll drive him out of his mind! Or certainly you'll ruin his work. You can only be doing this out of pure malice. Forget it! Let me pay you something. I can let you have two hundred and fifty a year. That, with what you're getting now, will maybe enable you to keep this flat. At least you can live a decent life in London. We can—perhaps—have other evenings like this.'

She said: 'Has the whole thing been a trick? Just to get me in this situation so that Maud will come home and find us, and then ...' She glared. 'There's some *clause*, isn't there, about the wife? By prying on the wife the husband can prove she's immoral and save his maintenance. That's it, isn't it? Did Paul put you up to it?'

'D'you think if it had been a put-up job from the start it would have happened between us as it's happened tonight? Don't be a fool!'

'*You're* the fool,' she said, 'supposing Maud will tell on me.'

'We'll have to see, won't we?'

She glared at me again, her puckish face looking like the Devil.

'*Get out!*'

'No...' I shook my head at her.

Her hands clutched and unclutched. She stared again, and then swung on her heel, padded like a fury to her dressing table, wrenched open a drawer, fumbled, took something out, came back. She pointed a revolver at me.

313

'Now go!'

I put my hand slowly on the side of the bed, needing stability.

'Where the hell did you get that?'

'I bought it after the divorce. To defend myself against unwelcome intruders. London is becoming lawless. Well, you're an unwelcome intruder. Now go.'

I looked into a little round hole, no bigger than a sixpence, from which, presumably, death or injury in the form of a small lead bullet could emerge. Her hand was trembling. Suddenly everything was out of hand. Life, ordinary life, goes on, and then the skin breaks. Clearly she didn't mean it. Clearly the thing was not loaded. And yet . . .

'Olive,' I said. 'Don't be quite such an idiot.'

'I give you two minutes to get dressed.'

I couldn't tell whether the safety catch was down. I saw her thumb moving on the little revolver and thought she was cocking it.

'Really,' I said, 'does one *have* to be so melodramatic? Don't we have *any* common ground between loving and killing? Listen—'

'Get dressed,' she said.

'What time is it? It's scarcely twelve yet.'

She glanced at the clock, and as she turned her head I jumped her. It was an insane thing to do, of course; but hers had been the first hysterical move. Neither of us perhaps was sober. My own move was a compound of lust (still) and hate. Perhaps it was not only hatred of her. Knowing her body and its soft firmness inside the knitted jumper and the disarrayed skirt; seeing the bitter rancour in her eyes; it was suddenly necessary to subdue them both. Also for the over-all intent. If her malice was going to those lengths

314

I would stop it *now*. And enjoy stopping it. Calling her bluff.

So I called her bluff.

III

There might have been a moment when she could have pulled the trigger, but in the two seconds of hesitation my hands were on her right hand, clutching it so tight that her fingers were jammed. She hit me in the face with her left hand, jarring my teeth; we fell together across the bed; I wrenched at the revolver but she would not let go. She raked my right forearm with her long nails; blood began to start; I released my left hand in time to catch hers as it went for my eyes. We rolled again and the gun went off.

I had no pain, no sense of injury or loss. She was obviously aware that something terrible had happened because she relaxed her grip and was watching me. I could feel the warm blood on my leg. Still there was no pain. She sighed and said: 'Damn you.'

The blood ran down my leg. She was pressing me down, determined I should not move.

I said: 'Olive, for Christ's sake!'

And then her eyes fluttered and turned up.

Sickness in my throat; I struggled and wriggled to be free of her. I got myself free, looked down at my leg, which was thick with viscous blood. I looked at Olive. She wasn't moving. I turned her over. The revolver was still in her hand and pressed into her abdomen, just below the navel. That was where the blood was coming from.

For a moment or two I passed out. The next thing I remember is swallowing the vomit in my throat as

I crawled towards the door to reach the telephone. Telephones were not so common in bedrooms in those days. But at the door I stopped. A doctor. A doctor at once. I pulled myself slowly upright and looked back. She was lying across the bed, her golden crown a little tarnished with time, her left arm raised provocatively, lying across the pillow, one leg folded. Must get a doctor. Get to the telephone. The room was still quavering. I came unsteadily a few paces back, gripped the corner of a chair, stared. Her eyes were open. But they didn't see me. Gone was the malice, the rancour, the envy, the hate. Only the beauty remained. But it was an empty beauty . . .

A doctor. The first thing. A doctor. Must get one soon. Quickly, quickly. . .

Three more steps back towards her. Fingers to her wrist. Nothing. Effort now. Great effort now. Put hand slowly under her slight breast. Nothing. Watch the mouth . . . Her eyes were staring at the ceiling . . . A doctor.

It was *impossible*.

I stared down at my own leg where the thick blood was congealing. Her blood. Not mine. Her blood. Get a doctor. Then the police.

I turned away and fell on my knees and retched. I knelt and held my head in my hands and retched.

A bell. Not a doorbell but a clock bell, a chime, coming from the open door of the living-room. Midnight.

All in ten minutes. Ten minutes ago we had still been lovers, just breaking into the fatal argument. *Fatal?* Get doctor, to be *certain*. But wasn't one . . . certain already?

A doctor and the police.

Could it happen as quickly as this? All the incredible

and intricate mechanism of a human body with its marvellous secretions, nervous impulses, muscular adaptability and sensory sagacity and discrimination, *all* stopped, permanently put an end to by a small discharge of cordite and lead from a machine only a few diameters larger than a pea-shooter? Virtually in *seconds*. And her blood—on my *leg*. First, I must be rid of *that* . . .

I somehow got into the bathroom, turned on the shower, sluiced my body of its stain. When I began to dry myself I kept dropping the towel, picking it up with trembling fingers, dropping it again.

When Maud came . . . Any time now. She would go for a doctor, know who to ring. And the police . . .

Maud of course would say I'd killed her. Was it true? Some urge in me wanting to destroy her when I leaped at her across the bed. For years attraction-repulsion working in the subconscious. Tonight the two impulses had polarised. In sex there is always conquest—carried to excess it produces the urge to destroy. Notable syndrome among criminal lunatics.

I began to pull on clothes. At least I must be dressed to face Maud and the others. My forearm where she'd scratched me was still oozing blood—it stained my shirt. Tie wouldn't tie. Struggle with it. Too preoccupied staring at the ashen man in the mirror. Shoes . . . where were my shoes? I was not a criminal lunatic. And, however one might pile up the responsibility, the moral guilt, it was *she* who had produced the revolver, *she* who took off the safety catch, and an accident had caused her death. An *accident*?

Who'd believe that? Not Maud. Certainly not Maud. The Police? Well, Olive *was* holding the revolver. But how had it come to turn upon herself and fire? The result of a struggle? What were we

fighting about? Why should she threaten me with a
revolver if I constituted no threat to her? Probably I
had intended rape. She had clearly not committed
suicide. Or *had* she?

Who knew I was here tonight? Maud might have
known Olive was going out with me; but in view of
what Olive said it was unlikely they were any longer
on those confidential terms. I had no car and we had
come by taxi. But what taxi driver would remember?
Would anyone even know Olive had been out tonight?
Could she have become intensely depressed in her
loneliness and walked into her bedroom and committed suicide? Or she might have been out with me and
I had left her at her door? Who was to say I had ever
been in her flat tonight? Only Maud, due back soon.

It was seven minutes after midnight.

Somehow the watch got back on my wrist, the tie
tied, the hair straightened over the drawn and bitter
face. Already fifteen minutes had passed, and no
police called, no doctor summoned. Get out. Those
were the words Olive had used. Get out. Good advice.
I'd brought no coat and hat. Leave now—let Maud
find what I'd left—slip out of the flat—look each way.
Clarendon Gardens was still lighted by gas, and there
were shadows to cling to. Get out. Get away.

But with returning nerve came returning sanity. I
was not such a fool. Panic must be controlled. The
police would come, would find. Fingerprints everywhere, glasses, door handles . . . Well, not everywhere,
but plenty in this room.

A decision to be made. Almost guiltless, I could
stay and see it out. Or a guilty flight?

But a battle's to fight ere the guerdon be gained, the
reward of it all. Browning a bad counsellor?

Oh, Christ, what was I to do?

318

Start in the living-room. Two glasses. Wash one, leave the other with the dregs from both. Unscrew cap of brandy bottle. Wipe cap. Wipe door handles. Anything else? I had not handled the gramophone. The only other thing I'd touched in this room was *her*. Use my handkerchief as a precaution down the cushions and the back of the settee. All clear. Back to the bedroom. Dead silence. *Dead* silence. Clock ticking. A creak somewhere. Maud back, door opening? No. Only my foot on a carpeted floorboard.

Olive stared fixedly at the ceiling. She was paling now. No blood in the lips. It had all oozed out onto the bed.

And on me.

Bedrail. Had I touched it? Handkerchief over to make sure. Bedside table ... Chair ... Clock? No ... No finger-prints possible on bedclothes. Twelve twenty-two. Any other hard surfaces? Bathroom door. Bathroom towel rail. That was it.

Finally the revolver. This was the vilest part. Though I'd never wrenched it out of her grasp I had clutched it. What risk of marks here? Gently I touched her hand, half expecting it to react. It didn't. Gently I rubbed the corner of my handkerchief round the barrel, dabbed the butt. That was all. That really was it. Time to *go*. To go.

I left the light on. No one ever committed suicide in the dark. Twelve twenty-seven. I might just make it. Now all the panic signals were out urging *flee—flee—flee*.

Stumble into the little hall. Listen. Nobody coming up the stairs. Handkerchief round the knob, open, slide out. The stairs were lit but empty. Two seconds to bolt down.

But with handkerchiefed hand on door I stopped.

319

Oh, *God*! What was the use of any of this without ...
Nails had scratched my arm. Any pathologist would
see. Time? Was it better to check and away? The
blood could belong to anybody ... But she had no
scratches to suggest she had been inflicting wounds
on *herself*. It proved conclusively that someone else
had been with her and that they had been *fighting* ...

Twelve thirty-two. Where was Maud?

So back into that bedroom I'd hoped never to see
again, with its occupant sprawling and glaring. 'And
her eyes close them, staring so blindly.' I could *not*
have touched the lids. It was bad enough to take the
cool left hand in mine; she might have been out in the
frosty night.

Take out that used handkerchief, moisten it with
my tongue, go carefully under each nail. Yes, there
was something under them: pink particles of skin;
careful to gather them, not drop them on bed. A few
flakes of dust floated down, and I dabbed at them
with my finger and tried to put them into the loop of
the handkerchief. Perhaps at this stage it was luck
how far an investigating detective might go; but at
least her nails were clean.

Click ... I swung round, nerves stammering. The
door, which had been ajar, had tapped to. There was
no wind tonight. Errant breeze? Someone had opened
the front door? Hair literally raised, I went to the
door. If Maud were there, what did I do? A clean
admission? With a corner of the towel I pulled the
door slowly open again. There appeared to be no one
in the hall. It was a quarter to one. Perhaps she had
come quietly in while I was cleaning up and was
sitting in the living-room enjoying a last cigarette.
But there was no light on in there. Perhaps Maud was
sitting in the dark. Perhaps she was sitting in there

with her throat cut, the blood staining the big white settee.

Last control snapped; I clutched at the front door, opened it clumsily, just remembered to wipe the catch, pulled it to after me with a thump, went down the stairs. Knees were without joints. I leaned against the wall, gasping for breath. The outer door.

I opened it, turned up the collar of my jacket, walked out into the street.

Chapter Twenty-Three

I

There was a half gale blowing the next morning. Heavy rain in the night had washed away the hoar frost, leaving this legacy of wind.

About eleven the telephone went.

'Hullo,' I said, licking a swollen lip.

'This is Osway, Grant.' Osway was a news editor on the *Chronicle*. 'Pennington tells me you're off work.'

'I rang him earlier. It's only a chill. I'll be OK tomorrow.'

'Bill, what was the first Mrs Stafford's christian name?'

'Stafford?'

'Paul Stafford's wife.'

'Olive.'

'That's the one then. I thought there couldn't be a mistake. She lived in Clarendon Gardens, didn't she?'

'Yes. What of it?'

'You know them both pretty well, don't you? She shot herself last night.'

'Good *God*!' I said. 'Shot herself? Are you sure?'

'Beasley's come in with the story. Her maid found her late last night.'

'Oh, my God . . . This *is* a shock! Thanks for letting me know. I suppose it couldn't have been an accident?'

'It doesn't sound like it. Beasley's going back again to see if he can get more details.'

'D'you—I suppose you don't know yet when the inquest will be?'

'No . . . I'll let you know when we hear.'

'Thanks.'

I hung up.

II

At twelve Jeremy Winthrop rang. He had been back from Washington six months.

'Is that you, Bill? I telephoned the *Chronicle* but they said you were sick. Nothing serious, I hope?'

'A touch of flu. I'll be about again tomorrow.'

'Good man. I phoned you about Olive.'

'Yes?'

'Haven't you heard? It says in the early edition of the *Standard* that she's been found dead in her flat. Shot apparently.'

'One of our staff gave me the news an hour ago. An extraordinary thing to happen.'

'I agree. Though if it's suicide I wouldn't be *very* astonished. From what I saw of her she was very much the neurotic type.'

'Living on her nerves,' I said.

'Maybe she's been living on other things as well.'

'It's possible.'

'I really rang you to know if you could give me any more details. I gather not.'

'Not yet anyway. I missed the full story with being sick. Though I believe not much is being released yet.'

'When's the inquest?'

'I haven't heard.'

'Let me know when you do, will you? If I'm free I'll pop in.'

'Of course. Goodbye.'

I hung up and then rang the local newsagent to ask him to send me copies of the evening papers.

III

The *Standard* headed its paragraph: 'Society Woman Found Shot.' The *News* said: 'Tragedy of Artist's Ex-wife'. The *Star* put it: 'Death in Mayfair Flat'. The bare details were there but nothing more. The later editions might fill it out. There would be pictures.

I tried to work. At ten past two the telephone rang again. It was Vincent de Lisle.

'Is that you, Bill? Have you heard about Olive?'

'Yes ... A real shock ...'

'I should say so. What d'you think can have happened?'

'No idea. I suppose some sudden impulse.'

'There isn't any suggestion of foul play, is there?'

'Not as far as I know.'

'Have you seen her lately?'

'... About a fortnight ago.'

'As recently as that? Did she seem all right then?'

'Sane enough. Rather bitter still.'

'About Paul? Well, this will certainly ease things for him.'

'I hadn't thought of that.'

'*Hadn't* you? It's the first thing that occurred to me.'

Careful; it should have been the first thing that occurred to *me* too.

'In a way,' he said, 'it's a good thing Paul lives in Cumberland.'

'Why?'

'Well, if anyone had an excuse for bumping her off it was Paul. *I* would have felt like murdering the woman.'

'I don't think there's any suggestion of foul play at all!' I said shortly. 'But perhaps you're right: it's better he should be out of reach of any whisper of suspicion.'

'As you know,' said Vincent, 'I've always felt it a mistake of his going up there and burying himself. One doesn't—or shouldn't—need to do that. Every artist, wherever and however he lives, has to come to terms with life.'

'I think he's doing that,' I said, 'but he's worked it out so that they're nearer his own terms.'

We rang off and again I tried to work. My right forearm was still burning. There was a bruise on my cheek-bone. My head felt as big as a football. The deeply reminiscent sound of the wind pushing among the houses made me think longingly of that solitary trip in the *Patience*. To feel the sun and the salt spray on one's face, to hear the creak of tackle and the drum of canvas and the never ceasing babble of water under the keel. It was not only Paul who needed isolation, who wished to withdraw from the world.

Half an hour later the phone rang again. I wished to Heaven and I wished to God that people did not keep ringing me up to talk about Olive. Little glaring silent Olive with the blood-red finger tips and the revolver pressed into her abdomen.

I took up the receiver. But this time it was only Pennington.

IV

Two days later I slipped into a seat in the coroner's court. Proceedings were already under way. Evidence of identity had been taken and a police constable was

325

in the stand giving his account of finding the body.

It seemed that he had been patrolling Curzon Street at 1.14 a.m. on Wednesday morning the fourteenth instant, proceeding in a westerly direction towards Park Lane when a woman approached him who appeared to be in considerable distress and asked him to accompany her to Clarendon Gardens, because, she asserted, there had been 'a dreadful tragedy'. Accordingly he made a note of the time and accompanied her some five hundred and fifty yards to the first floor of a block of modern flats leading out of Shepherd's Market. Here he mounted the stairs, and entered the bedroom of the flat where he observed the deceased lying on the bed. The bed was stained with blood and there was a wound near the navel, some two inches below and to the left. Life appeared to be extinct. The woman's head was towards the pillows and a pocket size .32 Colt revolver was clasped in her right hand. One chamber was discharged. Deceased was attired in a white woollen jumper and grey serge skirt. She wore no underclothes and was barefoot. She was wearing diamond stud earrings, and a diamond bracelet watch was on the table by the bed. The bed appeared to have been occupied. The windows of the room were shut and the light was on. There was a damp towel on the floor between the bedroom and the bathroom. The woman who had summoned him gave her name as Brade, personal maid to the deceased. After satisfying himself that the recumbent person was beyond his aid, he had proceeded to . . .

I wondered where the police were taught the English language and why some of them seemed to think it wrong to use one syllable where three would do. The court was crowded. Olive's mother was there and apparently her uncle, a man who looked so much like the recently deceased Sir Alexander Crayam that he could have been mistaken for him. One or two others I dimly remembered from the wedding. And Vincent de Lisle and Jeremy Winthrop. And a fair gaggle of reporters. I thought of Paul and Holly in Crichton. They would have heard by now, but neither had come down. Why should they? On a bright cold morning like this the air would be fresh and sweet and the hills a special shade of gold-brown.

The police surgeon had taken the stand. Death, he said, had been caused by a bullet from a Colt .32 revolver, and he held up a small flattened piece of lead for the court to see. The bullet had been fired with the barrel of the revolver pressed hard against the abdomen but pointing upwards in a peculiar way, as if the wrist holding it had been bent. The bullet had lodged in the spine, severing the spinal cord, and death had been instantaneous. When he reached the dead woman the time was 1.52 a.m. and he doubted if she had been dead much more than an hour. There were no other marks on the body except a slight abrasion on the left wrist and another on the right upper arm. These had occurred before death.

The coroner said: 'Could the wound which caused death have been self-inflicted?'

'It could.'

'In your opinion is it such a wound as might in fact result from an attempt to destroy one's own life?'

Little spiteful golden-haired Olive ... clinging to me ... clinging ...

The surgeon said: 'Except for the unusual angle, quite consistent. Possibly one might suppose she fell forward on the bed before she pulled the trigger.'

'There is no evidence of foul play?'

'No, sir.'

327

Maud Brade was called. A different person from the timid little maid the court might have expected to see. No snivelling into a handkerchief for Maud. Dry-eyed and tart, she gave her evidence as if holding a grievance against the coroner.

Yes, she was Mrs Olive Stafford's personal maid, her only maid, and had been with her four years: though she had actually been in the employment of the Crayam family for nearly twenty-five. Tuesday was her evening out. She usually left the flat about one o'clock and returned soon after midnight. On this Tuesday she went to see her mother, who lived in Shepherd's Bush. She had tea there, and then she and her sister went to the pictures. She came out at ten-thirty and went back to her mother's for a cup of coffee. She stayed a bit later than usual discussing family matters, including her own future, so it was midnight before she left home. She took the tube to Bond Street and walked down from there. It was just a minute or two after one o'clock when she reached Clarendon Gardens. She had her own key, of course, and let herself in. The only unusual thing she noticed was that she always had to put a tea-tray with a spirit-lamp etc. ready in the living-room before she left, and this hadn't been used: instead there was a used glass on the table and a brandy bottle without its top. As the light was on in Mrs Stafford's bedroom she thought she might still be awake, so she tapped and went in, and that was what she found.

'Did Mrs Stafford tell you her plans on this particular evening?'

'No, but I thought she was going out. She was always better tempered when she was off out.'

'Was it not customary for her to give you some idea of her movements?'

'Sometimes. Not this week.'

'Why not this week?'

'We wasn't on the best of terms this week,' said Maud. 'A month's notice after years of looking after her like a mother. It wasn't fair.'

'You were leaving Mrs Stafford? For what reason?'

Maud glanced spitefully round the court. After fumbling with her bag, she said: 'She had to economise; couldn't afford to keep me, so she said.'

'Was Mrs Stafford in reduced circumstances?'

'Yes. Her divorced husband hadn't paid up.'

'Was she, do you think, worried over money matters?'

'Well, if she wasn't she ought to have been. There was nothing but bills in the post.'

'Can you tell us if she did anything unusual on Tuesday?'

Maud thought. 'Can't say as I can.'

'Nothing which might give us reason to believe that your mistress was specially worried or upset or suffering from, say, an attack of nerves?'

'Can't say as I can. Of course, she was under a doctor with her nerves.'

The coroner said: 'Do you know if she had anything else to worry about except money?'

'Well, isn't that enough?' said Maud. 'She'd a case comin' off against her husband next month. She was all nerves. Her husband—'

'Did she ever speak as if she were contemplating taking her own life?'

'Not except once, just after she'd left her husband, she said she was sick of life.'

'But that was some years ago?'

'Yes. She was mad enough for anything then.'

The coroner held up something in his hand. 'Do

329

you recognise this weapon, Miss Brade?'

'Yes, sir, it belonged to Mrs Stafford.'

'Did she ever say why she had a revolver?'

'She was nervous. She had expensive jewellery. And the flat's easy to break into.'

'How long has she had this weapon?'

'Since her divorce. Soon after.'

'Where did she keep it?'

'In the middle drawer of the dressing-table in her bedroom.'

'To your knowledge, had your mistress any special enemies or people from whom she might fear harm?'

'Yes,' said Maud. 'She was at daggers drawn with her husband. He deserted her and married another woman.'

'I understand that her late husband lives in the north of England. Have they met or corresponded of recent months?'

'I don't know about met. They've corresponded.'

'Did he have a key to this flat?'

'No-o,' said Maud reluctantly. 'Well, not as far as I know.'

'Did anyone else possess a key?'

'The janitor.'

'When you came in there was no sign of any letter, any suicide note?'

'No, sir.'

'Thank you, Miss Brade.'

Olive's solicitor was called briefly to give evidence about the divorce and her dispute with Paul about maintenance. He was followed by Brigadier Crayam, whose testimony did not seem to have much value except to fill in the details of Olive's life. When he got in the box he looked plumper and younger than his brother, and something in his manner suggested he had not had to carry the burden of Lady Crayam for forty years.

Proceedings were taking their humdrum and most desirable course. Beasley, who was covering the case for the *Chronicle*, caught my eye and winked. He was obviously bored and thinking if I would stay for the verdict he might cut and run.

Olive's doctor gave a Wimpole Street address. Mrs Stafford had first come to him three years ago, suffering from severe headaches and sleeplessness. There was nothing organically wrong with her but she was potentially a neurasthenic. He understood there was a history of it in the family. He had given her treatment and she had seen him from time to time since then and had seemed generally to improve under his care. There was, of course, no doubt that she all the time made too many demands on her nervous energy.

'Would you say,' the coroner asked, 'that Mrs Stafford in your experience was the sort of woman who would be likely to take her own life?'

The doctor took off his glasses.

'In my experience . . . I should say, no.'

There was a brief stir in the court.

'Would you kindly explain what you mean?'

'I understood you to ask me if in my experience Mrs Stafford was the type of woman who would be likely to take her own life. I can only answer, no. The neurotic class to which she belonged has a very low rate of suicide.'

'We have heard in the evidence of Miss Brade,' said the coroner, 'that Mrs Stafford spoke of ending her life.'

'She did so to me once,' said the doctor. 'I naturally spoke to her very sharply; but I did not take her seriously. Since you asked my opinion, I wished to make it clear that this was the exception for her type, not the rule. That type of hysterical, nervous woman, of whom I may say I have had some experience, often comes to the point of talking of suicide, indeed of threatening suicide if it will gain her any point. It might, indeed, be that such a woman would go to the extreme, *before a witness*, of pointing a revolver at her own breast; but that is a condition far removed from pulling the trigger—and *when alone*. For that reason I was surprised to hear of Mrs Stafford's death.'

'Was Mrs Stafford's condition, generally speaking, better or worse on the last occasion you saw her?'

'In my opinion it was better. But the human mind is unfathomable.'

There was a pause before the next witness came to the stand. The clerk of the court was consulting with the coroner. Presently the coroner looked up and nodded.

A man with thin brown hair and protuberant eyes was seen making his way towards the stand. He gave his name as Inspector Priestley.

'You are in charge of this case?'

'I am, sir.'

'You wish to give evidence at this juncture?'

'I am here at the moment, sir, to ask for an adjournment of this inquest until after lunch.'

'On what grounds?'

'We have further medical evidence which will not be available until this afternoon. Then I wish to call a fresh witness who has just come in and is at present only just making his statement.'

The coroner looked at the clock.

'Very well. The court is adjourned until two o'clock.'

V

I pushed my way out, anxious to get a breath of fresh air and also to avoid the people who would be issuing from the court behind me. A hand touched my arm. It was Beasley.

'Hullo, Grant, you going my way?'

'Depends which way that is,' I replied, not graciously.

'Well, I was off to the pub round the corner. It's a decent little place, and not many of the Press go there.'

'You're staying for this afternoon, then?'

'I am *now*. Don't know what the police have got on to but Priestley was breathing through his nose, which is always an interesting sign.'

Perhaps talking would help to pass the time more quickly than sitting alone. I fell into step beside him.

'This is quite a new line for you, isn't it?' he said. 'Are you looking for a new angle?'

We went in. The place was pretty full.

'I knew Olive Stafford well.'

'Oh, sorry. I'd no idea.'

We ordered drinks and sandwiches.

'Now I remember,' said Beasley. 'You were a friend of her husband's. I'd forgotten.'

I nodded.

'Does he never come to Town nowadays?'

'No.'

'I suppose that's why he wasn't there today. But he should have been, shouldn't he?'

'They were nothing to each other.'

'Well, this should rather turn out a blessing in disguise for him. If all the lawyer said is true. I mean it'll make a difference to his finances with no divorced wolf to keep from the door.'

We found a table.

'Evidently no love between Paul Stafford and that serving wench. She'd make trouble for him with her "daggers drawn" if she could.'

I said: 'A man who's in Cumberland . . .'

'Oh, yes, of course. Naturally.' Beasley went on with his mouth full: 'I was pretty tired of the whole thing until Priestley asked for an adjournment.'

'I wonder what they're driving at.'

'There was a rumour current that Bernard Spilsbury has been called in.'

It was a long time before I spoke.

'Whatever for?'

'What? . . . Oh, it's not unusual, I suppose. Maybe the police pathologist is dissatisfied with something.'

'We shall see.'

'Paul Stafford,' said Beasley. 'What's the idea, d'you think, going off to Cumberland and hiding himself there? A fellow who knew him at the Hanover Club said he was never quite the same after those lawsuits.' Beasley helped himself to the mustard. 'But there we are: it's happened before. Man gets to the top, can't stand corn, kicks over the traces, gets himself in a mess and goes all to pieces. Look at Oscar Wilde. D'you think drink's had something to do with it?'

'As a matter of fact, no,' I said.

Beasley looked up at me. 'You still see him? What's he doing?'

'Painting.'

'Ah? Portraits?'

'No. Advanced stuff.'

'Oh . . . He's been bitten by that bug. D'you think there'd be a story in it for me if I went up and saw him some time?'

'No,' I said.

'Um. He was always pretty helpful to us fellows in the old days.'

'I think you'd find him changed.'

'Oh, well, in that case ...' Beasley sighed. He glanced at my plate but didn't remark on the fact that its contents were slow to disappear.

VI

I had refused Beasley's offer of a seat on the Press bench and slid into my old position on the back row. There I waited.

This adjournment ...

The court was stuffy and cold.

'Call Mr Bernard Sparks.'

A little anaemic man in a blue suit, with a brown moustache slightly browner in the middle.

A harmless little man.

He was sworn in and gave his name and address. He was, he said, employed by Messrs Glebe & Hunter, private inquiry agents, of Wardour Street. His firm had been instructed to keep a watch on the movements of Mrs Stafford. They were acting on the instructions of Messrs Carp, Cleeve & Rosse, of Chancery Lane. At 7.30 p.m. on Tuesday last, he had been standing outside No. 3, Clarendon Gardens ...

With a great effort the court came singing back, back out of a distant dome of time ...

So Mr Rosse had been too clever ...

... when a gentleman drove up in a taxi.

'Can you describe this man?' asked the coroner.

'Yes, sir. He was above average height, about five feet ten or eleven, about thirty years of age, and rather thin, with a tendency to a slight stoop. Grey eyes, good teeth, and wearing a dinner jacket evening dress, no hat, fair hair, silk scarf . . .'

With a black monogram.

Mr Rosse had been too clever. Wise Mr Rosse.

I had been too clever.

' . . . And what happened after they left the Savoy?'

'They drove back to Mrs Stafford's flat, sir; at which they arrived at ten thirty-five. They went into the flat laughing and talking, and presently a light came on in the window which I had previously ascertained was the sitting-room.'

Mr Sparks had a thrice damned habit of closing his eyes while he spoke and then opening them very suddenly to stare at his notebook as if he expected his notes to have changed their significance. But they had not. Nothing now would ever change their significance.

'This light remained on for about fifteen minutes, and then a light came on in the window which I had previously ascertained was the bedroom. Both lights remained on, sir. At eleven-fifteen exact I went round to the back of the flat, where there is a bedroom window looking upon Carlton Mews, hoping that I might be able to see something more, but the curtains of the bedroom were drawn. I then returned and took up my position in Clarendon Gardens again.

'At midnight thirty the light in the living-room went out, but the bedroom light remained on. I continued observation until midnight forty when the man I had seen entering the flat with Mrs Stafford came out and walked rapidly into Curzon Street.'

Mr Sparks closed his eyes again and coughed into his fist to show he had finished.

The coroner said: 'Did you not follow the man?'

'I did, sir. But as he came to the corner a taxi

happened to be passing and he hailed it and drove away. I tried to follow, but couldn't get a taxi for myself in time.'

'What was your exact purpose in keeping this watch on Mrs Stafford's movements?'

'I had been instructed to make a report on her moral character.'

'Did this man when he left the flat show any signs of emotion or distress?'

'As I've said, he walked very quick, sir. In coming out of the doorway he looked both ways to make sure no one was about. But he didn't see me, sir.'

'During the time you were watching, did you hear any explosion which might have been a shot fired?'

'I did not, sir. But, then, a pocket Colt don't make a big noise and I was on the other side of the street.'

'Did you know the identity of this man you saw with Mrs Stafford?'

'No, sir; but I'd know him again anywhere.'

'How long had you been keeping a watch on Mrs Stafford's movements?'

'Fourteen days, sir.'

'Had you seen her in company with this man before?'

'No, sir.'

'Very well, Mr Sparks. Don't leave the court. You may be needed again.'

I watched him leave the box and take a seat at the end of the third bench from the front. A harmless little man.

'Call Miss Mary Oakley.'

A tall, thin, pleasant-faced spinster took the stand.

She lived by herself, she said, and occupied the flat below Mrs Stafford's. She had been in bed for several days with bronchitis. On the night of the nineteenth she had been in bed reading and listening to the wireless when she heard what she took to be a car backfire. She had not looked at the time and had only recollected the noise when interrogated by the police. But one thing she did remember: she had been listening to the third act of *Aïda*, and had switched off at eleven-fifty, immediately it was over. 'And the noise I heard was soon after I switched off.'

'You heard nothing else unusual?'

'Nothing.'

When she was gone it was observed that Inspector Priestley was again standing up in the well of the court.

'In view of the evidence which has been given this afternoon I wish to apply for an adjournment of this inquest for one week.'

The coroner consulted with the clerk of the court, but I knew his answer was a foregone conclusion. I rose, slid across the man beside me and pushed past the policeman at the door. I had no wish at all to encounter Mr Sparks on his way out.

Beasley must have noticed my movement and had also slipped out, just as quickly aware that proceedings were over until the police chose to have them resumed.

'Developments, what?' he said. 'This is a question of *cherchez l'homme*. It'll make a story. Are you going east, old boy?'

I tried to think of an excuse, but he talked on until we reached my Hornet. I made a motion towards it, and he got in. We drove off in silence. I wanted to think.

'You don't look well, Grant. Feeling all right?'

'I've had flu.'

'Ah. It's no good getting up too soon.'

There was silence again.

338

'Tell me what you think happened,' I said suddenly.

'What, in this case?'

'In this case.'

'Well, that's a tall order, isn't it? Still . . . OK. I think . . . I think X, this unknown man, had a crush on Mrs Stafford—they say she was a good looker—and they made a date to spend the evening together. Off they went and had a good evening, and back they came to the flat full of drink and high spirits. They fall for each other in a big way, but afterwards, ah, afterwards, they come back to earth with a bump and they quarrel over something. Maybe he asks for money. Anyway, she takes the revolver from the drawer and threatens to shoot him. Or maybe she merely gets histrionic and threatens to shoot herself. Anyway, he grabs the revolver, they struggle and off goes the gun.'

'I notice,' I said, 'that you give this man credit for not doing the job deliberately.'

'Well, obviously this wasn't a premeditated act or he'd not have taken her to a fashionable restaurant beforehand to advertise himself, would he? Then he'd probably have brought his own weapon; it's hardly likely he'd know she had one handy.' Beasley grunted and filled his pipe. 'Of course, if it was a long-standing liaison and he was tiring of her, that puts another complexion on the matter. But I don't feel that that was it.'

'Why not?'

'Wouldn't the inquiry agent have seen him before? And wouldn't the Brade woman have dropped some hint? She'd no reason to love her mistress.'

We drove for some minutes.

'Anyway,' he said, 'she didn't take out the revolver in the first place to protect herself.'

'Why not?' I said again.

He looked at me. 'Well, women don't discard their underwear to defend their virtue.'

We came to a stop. 'This is as far as I go. I suppose,' I said, 'there's just a chance they may still find the man had nothing to do with it.'

Beasley got out of the car. 'The evidence was pretty conclusive, wasn't it? Miss What's-it heard the shot about midnight, and the inquiry agent saw the man leave at twelve-forty. Do you know what I'd be inclined to do if I were the man?'

'No.'

He waved his pipe. 'Come forward and give my version. He might get away with accidental death. After all, there can't have been witnesses to what happened. *She* can't deny what he says. Verdict at a trial might hinge on the strength of his motive, on how much the man stood to gain. It's a moot point. Don't you agree?'

I said: 'But men who do that sort of thing don't usually have the guts to come forward until they're found by the police.'

'Quite,' he said. 'So long. And thanks for the lift.'

I watched him lope swiftly away.

Chapter Twenty-Four

I

I drove to my flat, threw pyjamas and a few accessories into an attaché case and took it out to the car. At a nearby garage I filled up with oil and petrol.

As I left London a few lights were already winking through the early dusk of the late October afternoon. Rain-clouds blew across the smoky sky. Buses roared and grated down the narrow, busy streets, swinging in and out like galleons on an asphalt sea. Milestones in every suburb, the white granite pillars of 'The Tailor of Taste' and the scarlet and gold façade of the sixpenny stores; or the monstrous shape of some local super-cinema thrust itself out, electric lights already glinting a spurious smile of welcome. The pavements were crowded. The world was full of anonymous little egos each jostling with the others, each talkative but secretive, self-assertive but self-afraid, free to go as it wished but a prisoner within its own ivory tower until death brought release, death coming unobtrusively and gently with old age or striking swiftly and unnaturally as it had done with Olive Stafford.

The afternoon advanced and one town succeeded another, each with the same scene to print on the memory so that there was no memory; lights flickered and multiplied; the few but increasing stretches of unlighted road were a rest to aching eyes. I stopped again for petrol, but not for food, being conscious only of the hunger to get on. I drove clumsily, without consideration for the car.

Can love turn to hate while the minute-hand of the clock moves an inch on the clock's face? But love had never entered into it: attraction and aversion had been different sides of the same coin. And all in a way actuated by the feelings I had for the couple I was now going to visit.

Yet one could not unload the final responsibility on them. Certainly they had provided—their problems had provided—the seed bed from which had sprouted this abnormal, divergent relationship between Olive and me. The crisis of Tuesday night could not be called a catharsis for there had been nothing vicarious about it. But it had been a purging, a resolution, the climax of a conflict that had been deep-rooted in my nature and in Olive's too.

It was one of those intense, cloudy, English nights when there is no wind and no light, when there is nothing but an abyss of darkness between the great nebulae of the towns and the small star clusters of each succeeding village. You journey through spaces of night between steep walls of trees, and the approach of another car is like the moon rising below the horizon.

As hours went by the villages began to wink out and the towns to become less garish. A thin freckle of rain set the screen-wipers to work. The car was running well despite its treatment. I was conscious for the first time of a sense of discomfort which suggested hunger. A snack-bar was still open in a town whose name I never knew and some sandwiches were available. The bright light of the bar was distasteful, as also was the sleepy barman talking and yawning with the solitary customer in the far corner. Keep away from other human beings; keep away while I think what is to happen next.

Strange that Mr Rosse had ruined everything by putting the idea of the *dum casta* clause in my head, and then acting on it himself. Yet but for the revolver all would still have worked out. Mr Sparks's testimony would have confirmed Maud's. If Maud had refused to tell on her mistress his alone might have sufficed. Olive in any case was likely to have been powerless—as she had seen in a flash. The one incalculable—the imponderable of *this* situation—had been her possession of a revolver. Would she have used it on me? I thought so.

The night turned more chill as I began to thread a way through the Lancashire mill towns. Here again lights winked afresh. Here again big multiple shops and super-cinemas and rows of poor houses, and the occasional clanging tram.

In Lancaster I stopped to fill up again, and waited long enough to drink three cups of strong black coffee. As I climbed back into the car the first streaks of dawn were splitting the night clouds of the east. Light came slowly, and when I ran over the border into Westmorland there was just sufficient daylight to see the landscape sprinkled with snow. To have gone round and into Crichton Beck by way of the road Holly had once described would have been a sensible precaution; but impatience insisted on the direct route over the Long Neck Pass.

Past the Langdales the snow showed signs of thickening, but at the beginning of the climb over the shoulder of the mountain it disappeared. The wind had been blowing from the north, and if further snow was to be found it would be on the other face.

The car was already hot with its long, hard drive.

As we climbed the clouds began to clear and a desolate sun stared over the top of the mountains. Boiling, the car reached the top. I stopped and lifted the bonnet; steam simmered from every joint of the cooling system. I walked ahead a few yards, and peered down into a valley of deathly stillness and virgin snow. When the water had stopped boiling I filled the radiator with some scrapings of snow from the ditch and went on. Some guiding providence—whose help I should have appreciated more often during the previous week—avoided a skid, and the valley was reached.

There had been quietness on my visits before, an all-embracing, all-powerful silence which incidental noise could no more penetrate than a fish breaking the surface can disturb the deeper quietness of a lake. But all previous silences were fussy and commonplace before the supreme quiet of this autumn morning. Even the sputtering of the engine was at once absorbed. A phrase came into my mind and kept recurring: 'The peace that passeth all understanding.' Well, you couldn't get more inapt than that, so far as I was concerned.

Slipping and sliding, I came to the floor of the valley. Low cloud had drifted across again to obscure the sun. I drew up before the cottage and switched off the engine. Now the true weight of the silence fell on me like darkness on a snuffed candle. There was no movement about the cottage. The gaunt branches of the trees showed black against the snowy hillside. Into numbed ears crept the faint whisper of the stream.

Climb stiffly out, tired now, and chilled and hungry and afraid. Go to the door and knock. An outrage in breaking this peace.

The door opened and Holly stood there in a

dressing-gown. Her face lit up and she uttered a squeak of pleasure.

'Bill!... I thought you were Mrs Dawson with the milk. Come in, come in. How did you ... In that car? Was the snow bad? It's *so* unusual so early. Paul's still asleep. Paul! Paul! Why didn't you wire us you were coming?'

She kissed me and I went in and sat back in an easy chair while she bent to set the fire in the grate and chattered.

'Where did you spend last night? Could you drink a cup of tea? I was going to make one. Paul usually comes down, but he was working late, so I've stolen a march on him. How long can you stay?'

I stared at the pleasant room, at the morning light striking a glint from Holly's hair. She bent prayer-mat fashion before the fire and began to blow through the bars.

'Let me do that,' I said, going down beside her.

'Where did you stop the night?'

'Lancaster.'

'And why so pale and wan, young lover, prithee why so pale? Did they turn you out without breakfast?'

'I was afraid of further snow. I was afraid the pass might be impracticable.'

'You came over Long Neck? You might have been stuck there all day!' She leaned back on her heels. 'You look *tired*.'

'I've had a touch of flu, so took a couple of days off. I thought the drive would do me good. How are things with you?'

She smiled. 'I never felt better, Bill. Paul is still painting as if he hadn't a moment to lose, painting as if ... What a tragic end for poor Olive ... I *was* sorry.'

'They wired you, then.'

345

'Yes. I told Paul he ought to go to the funeral. He said he couldn't.'

'It wouldn't do any good.'

Their mixed-up cocker spaniel, Ethelred, came bounding into the room and, finding my face accessible, licked it with enthusiasm.

'It'll make a big difference to us, but one tries not to look at it that way.'

'There's no reason why you shouldn't look at it that way. There's no reason not to be thankful.'

She looked at me. 'It wasn't about that that you came? Has the inquest been held?'

'It'll be just a matter of form . . . I think I would like a cup of tea, Holly. Can I make it?'

She scrambled to her feet. 'The kettle's on the oil stove. Let's go and see if it's boiling.'

'It's boiling and I've brewed the tea,' said Paul from the door.

It was interesting to note the way in which he was recalling North-country phrases into his speech.

II

That was perhaps the strangest day of my life.

We were happy together, even high-spirited, while the shadow of little Olive hung over us.

Or rather it hung over me, not over them. *Their* concern with her had ended.

After lunch Paul asked me the same question as Holly had. Both of them in their hearts perhaps had a feeling that my visit to them in this hurried manner was not purely a chance impulse. Mr Rosse's telegram had stated that Olive had shot herself; but Paul at least was not satisfied with the bare statement; when we were alone he began to question me to find out all

346

I knew. Parrying his questions was a difficult matter, for we understood each other too well.

At length he seemed satisfied that I was as ignorant as I seemed.

'Well,' he said, 'I can't begin to pretend I'm sorry. Why be a hypocrite? It was my fault in the first place for marrying her; but we can't go on for ever paying for our mistakes. I can't believe yet that it's all over. I can't get away from the feeling that wherever she's gone she'll contrive to send me a solicitor's letter.'

'Are you still talking about that?' said Holly, coming in. 'It's past. Now you've only me to maintain. Isn't that enough to talk about?'

'Indeed, yes.' He laughed and stretched his legs to the fire. His eyes followed her. 'When I can believe it's true I shall feel like a millionaire. No, that's wrong. I shall feel like myself, but twice as free.'

'You look like a tramp,' said Holly.

Paul laughed again. 'That's part of the fun.'

I eyed him, and wondered whether some of his old companions of the successful years would have identified their friend. His cheeks were thin and tanned and sallow; clothes hung loosely on him; his hair needed cutting; his speech was a natural compromise between its too-rough origin and its too-smooth cultivation. His hands were stained with pigment, he looked worn and tired.

Paul noticed my scrutiny and turned his head and grinned. 'Don't quote myself against me.'

'I wasn't going to.'

'It's been a devious route, I admit. And not yet ended. But it looks a bit straighter from now on.'

'Not so many of your pictures about.'

'It's all upstairs.'

Some of his work, when I saw it, still looked

347

unfinished, tentative. But I was much struck by the colours, which had suddenly released themselves from the occasional muddiness of the past and become altogether brilliant.

One of the paintings that impressed me that morning was of a spinning wheel and an old cane armchair, done in a farmhouse down the valley. It is now in the Guggenheim Museum, New York, and I have in front of me an early gallery note about it written by Anthony Pride White.

'One has to examine this picture at a distance, for its strength at close quarters is a little overpowering. The cane of the chair looks as if it has supported all humanity, and grown sere and yellow with the passage of so much time and stress. The colour of the shawl hanging over its back makes ordinary crimsons anaemic: there never was such a shawl in Cumberland. The sunlight falling through the window is butter yellow, as if coming from a warmth and radiance unknown to ordinary men.'

It is of course the function of the critic to express himself in language of this sort, but for once I would not quarrel with the sentiment.

Of another I saw that day, of two mackerel on a plate, now well known, and now in Cardiff in the National Museum of Wales, A. H. Jennings writes: 'The blues and greens of this picture are more alive, more radiant than that of almost any painter since Vermeer. His use of white pigment is particularly impressive. Two fish on an old kitchen plate, glinting luminously as if still dripping from the sea. That is all. Yet one imagines that in the dark the painting will be phosphorescent.'

A third, of which nobody has written, and the one I found most illuminating of a change in development and mood, was a large canvas of Holly standing by the window in his studio wearing a grey woollen frock. She had her back to the painter and the light shone through her hair. Her slim, tall figure was painted in soft, very heavy strokes of grey and green. The figure is too simplified to be a likeness, yet it is unmistakably Holly. Paul has painted the essence of her more than just her physical form. He seems to have seen her with the half-blindness, the half-clairvoyance of a lover and in so doing to have expressed both the individual and the universal.

I have to write about this painting myself, for it has never been exhibited and is still on the wall of my bedroom.

We left Paul pottering with some canvases he had primed, deciding whether they were fit for use, and returned to the sitting-room with the welcome warmth of its peat fire. Ethelred lay nose on paws against the fender. Outside the sky had cleared and the sun, less etiolated than at dawn, glistened over the thin white landscape.

'This snow,' she said. 'We've *never* had it so early.'

'It'll pass,' I said, 'like everything else.'

'That's rather a depressing remark.'

'Think nothing of it.'

'His work,' she said. 'It's different, isn't it? I believe he's happy for the first time in his life.'

'And you?'

She stooped to fondle Ethelred's ear.

'Women are primary producers, aren't they? Great discovery of mine. Now I'm going to have a baby everything seems more complete. Old and puzzling pieces have fitted in. I've done the jig-saw.'

'Any plans yet?'

'About? . . . I think we may go a bit nearer civilisation for the Event. Where we haven't decided. I thought I'd stay with Ma, but Paul thought she wasn't the type to have the responsibility put on her.'

'Thank God for that,' I said.

'Well, we might have had to. But now—with this happening to Olive . . .'

We listened to the wind moving down the valley. She was sitting on the window side of the fire so that her face was in shadow. The light struck the curve of her cheek. Her long fingers clasped and unclasped.

'And you, Bill?'

'What?'

'What about you? Are you happy? Or at least content?'

'. . . I'm always more content for seeing you.'

'Is that an answer? . . . I see it's the only answer I shall get.' She leaned forward and poked the fire. Sparks and a blaze broke reluctantly from the peat. Ethelred cocked a bloodshot eye. 'Anyway . . . it's nice to chatter.'

'Chatter on.'

The invitation brought silence. I thought of men in London painstakingly reconstructing the events of a crime.

'Tell me, Bill: when I married Paul, did you think the marriage would be a success?'

'If you must know,' I said, 'no.'

'And have I given you the impression that it is a success now?'

'You have.' I shifted in my seat. 'It wasn't unnatural to feel at first . . .'

'Yes, I know. Well, that's all right. It's because I'm happy now and begin to see things more straightforwardly, and because of everything, that I'd like to tell you more than you already know. I—hope it won't spoil anything. I expect I should really keep my mouth shut.'

She got up and stood by the fire. Under her light and casual manner she was finding it difficult to express something. For a few moments I forgot the patient men.

'I married Paul,' she said, 'not at the time because I was fearfully in love with him, but because his feeling for me was stronger than anything I could work up in myself either for or against. And he needed me: I knew that, could feel that. All the time he has needed me. It's funny how things work out, isn't it? For these three years of our marriage there's been that in addition to my affection for him to keep me—in contact. It's kept me content. I've been happy in all sorts of things—in his feeling for me, in the knowledge that I was indispensable to the creation of something greater than either of us. Isn't that enough for anyone?'

'But . . .'

She looked at the door to make sure it was shut.

'And now I feel in a short time he'll have begun to do what he set out to do. I may always be necessary to him, but not to the same extent. If I were to die tomorrow he'd still go on painting like this. So, in a way, feeling that, I might have begun to—to slack off. Is that the way to put it? Do you see what I mean? But this year I've felt more—and now there's this. There have always been two Pauls I've been concerned about: the ordinary human Paul who is just as weak and easily disorganised and responsive to praise, and generous and fractious and fallible as any of us; and the creative, slightly more than human Paul who is prepared to ride roughshod over anything and everything in pursuit of his aims, and can be quite a devil to live with. Now I feel that one, the second one,

351

can get along on his own; but instead I've got a young Paul to think of and to care about. It's a fair exchange and I'm more than content.'

I rose too and went to the window. The brilliance of the sun dazzled my eyes. I had hardly slept for three nights. I couldn't be concerned with the finer shades of phrasing.

'Do you mean you don't love Paul?'

She made a brief gesture. 'It isn't as simple as *that*. I've always been fond of him. From the first, something . . . But it wasn't more than that at first.' I caught the gleam of her teeth again, but wasn't sure if the glint betokened amusement. She had obviously begun with the intention of speaking lightly, objectively. But every now and then something else crept into her voice. 'At the start—you see, I was—it seemed such a tall order. The idea of being the wife of a fashionable portrait painter didn't attract a bit. Yet I knew—I felt he'd never get where he ought if I said no. And he seemed to love me—with such intenseness and such restraint. But I was scared. That seems funny now. I think Lady Jane Grey must have felt like that when someone went in and told her she was going to have to be a queen. Those months while we were waiting for the divorce—they were a bit wearing to us all, but they were trying to me in a way no one suspected. D'you know what I used to do? We can both laugh at it now.'

'No,' I said.

'I didn't say any prayers. It didn't seem quite fair to make a convenience of somebody I wasn't sure about. So every morning I used to cross my fingers and make a wish that before the day was out you'd ask me to marry *you* instead.'

There was a pause.

'Oh?' I said.

'Yes. It does seem pretty quaint now, doesn't it? But it was very much in earnest then. And even afterwards for a time . . .' She bent again to the fire. 'Fortunately you didn't guess. You see, I wasn't a bit ambitious in the sense of wishing to paint London red or see the lights till the small hours every morning. I just wanted to get married in a quiet way and settle down in a quiet way, and a journalist's income would have done.'

'I suppose,' I said. 'I suppose it was a case of any port in a storm.'

She moved somewhere behind me. 'Dear Bill. Always so modest. If it won't embarrass you to know it now, the answer is, no. For two years I'm afraid I felt rather badly about you. If you had felt the same, things would have turned out different; but who's to say they would have turned out better? I suppose you never suspected anything?'

'. . . Why are you telling me this?'

'Well, obviously I couldn't until I'd got over it—or nearly over it. Lucky you didn't ever receive that letter I wrote you.'

'*What* letter?'

'. . . When I was at Oxford working, and waiting for Paul's divorce, things seemed suddenly to get me down. I had the mad idea that perhaps you really felt the same as I did, and I had to make sure. You know the funny ideas schoolgirls get. So I cut everything and came up to London to see you. But you were in Geneva . . .'

'So? . . .'

'So I went to a hotel nearby and ordered tea and wrote you a letter, telling you exactly how I felt.'

'I *never got it*,' I said. 'How did it—'

She laughed apologetically. 'You couldn't have,

because I never posted it. When I'd finished writing I realised how stupid it all was. Just putting it on paper was enough to purge me of these—feelings. By setting them down I'd—relieved the pressure, and I could see how foolish I was being. Funny ... I've never felt quite so badly about you since.' She jabbed at the fire again, which had gone to sleep. 'Perhaps I shouldn't have told you this now ... but now that things are coming right for us all, I thought I'd like to tell you. Sorry if it embarrasses you. Confession's good for the soul.'

Good for the soul. I said at last: 'I suppose Paul ... knows nothing of this?'

'Naturally not. If I didn't tell him when I didn't—feel a great deal, I obviously shouldn't tell him now I feel so very much more ...'

'Whatever happens you mustn't tell him, Holly.'

'What could happen?' She sounded surprised. 'I only felt I wanted to tell you today. I only felt ... I suppose it might have been better not said.'

'Holly ...'

'Yes?'

I didn't speak.

'Go on,' she urged.

Damned banalities. Say something. Get away ... No sleep ... Quiet Bill never had any troubles. God's in his heaven, all's right with the world.

'I'm sorry too,' I said.

She uttered a breathy sound which this time was half a laugh and half a sigh.

'That's the big statement of the morning. I believe I've embarrassed you after all.'

'Of course you have,' I said. 'Who wouldn't be? ... It's a pretty compliment ...'

'Oh, well. Now I've told you, let's forget it. Don't

354

think me a fool. But it's funny the way things seem to be going the opposite to the way you want them, and then in the end you find that they've been going the right way after all.'

A pretty compliment. That was just right. How cleverly the mind worked under stress. With what coolness and judgment. I couldn't see through the window at all. I couldn't see where the window was. I couldn't hear what Holly was saying. Fear death?— to feel the fog in my throat, the mist in my face . . .

Dear old Browning, always came in helpful. One effort more.

'Let's go for a walk,' I said. 'This sun's beautiful and I must start back soon. Let's interrupt Paul and take him for a walk . . . Let's go for a walk, Holly.'

Chapter Twenty-Five

I

They tried to keep me, but I wouldn't stay. I left soon after five, so as to be out of the valley before dusk. I went by the valley road, which avoids the mountain passes.

It's a beautiful road, just as Holly once described it to me. It follows the shallow bubbling stream. Fine hoary rocks cluster. Small trees dot the route, but mostly the land is barren and silent. Few birds or animals live here. There is a house to be passed half a mile down the valley. It has been repaired and repainted, but now its new tenant will not come.

This evening the thin snow was already melting, and the damp earth smelt fresh and autumnal.

As I turned out of the valley into the main road to Broughton a flurry of snow beat on the windscreen, and the screen-wiper began patiently to brush aside the soft silent flakes, but soon the snow turned to sleet and the sleet to rain.

. . . It was strange, but I found I couldn't feel any more. I could remember everything that had happened in my life. I could think it all out. But I couldn't feel any more.

I thought of Paul and his painting. I had seen him begin to paint this afternoon. Of course a lot of nonsense was always talked and written about artists, blowing up the fashionable man of the moment. The function of the critic was to rend to pieces what he didn't like and to discover unimaginable virtues in what he admired. Either attitude was exaggerated, slightly hysterical. Yet I could not believe that what Paul was painting now was not of lasting value. It spoke for itself. And, as such, justified the sacrifices he had made to achieve his ends.

They justified *his* sacrifices. Did they justify other people's, those within his orbit whose paths were pulled off their proper course by his gravitational pull? Who knew? A man of genius—or even high talent—must subordinate ordinary considerations to it. So must his friends. All *ordinary* considerations. But how far did that go?

I thought of little Olive, whom I had at last got out of his life and out of my life in the most costly and preposterous way possible—but costly only to me. I thought of her glaring at me from the bed, as if even in death she was fulfilling her resentment and her hate. I thought of Holly, gifted, brainy, eccentric, unperceptive as myself, but lovable beyond price. I thought of what she had told me this afternoon.

I thought of Lady Lynn, tall as a fir-tree, dressed like a gipsy, red-cheeked and preoccupied, lavishing on her puppies the attention her daughter might have found of greater value. I thought of Clement Lynn and his pencils and his ill-knitted pullovers and his growing paunch and his long jaw and his brilliant brain.

I think of Bertie finding his own happiness among the scarred and diseased natives of Africa; of Leo playing the piano, without humour, punitively, and with all the ego of the merely talented. Of Diana, tall and graceful and spoiled and consumedly selfish, and needing admiration as a flower needs sunlight. I think of my life over the last two years in theatrical and

357

literary London, stimulating, demanding, rewarding; and of my future.

Westmorland disappears into the darkness, drawing its curtains behind me. Lancaster will soon be here.

I must stop at Lancaster.

II

I enter the telephone booth and give a London number. After a bit of argument I put in enough money for a six-minute call and the girl reluctantly—it seems—agrees to try to connect me. In the intervening gap before she does so she tells me three times that she is doing this. The position is quite private, the phone being in a recess beside the post office. Outside my little car waits, dripping, to continue its journey. I think now it will probably rain all night.

It is cold waiting.

A voice comes through. The wait has not really been so long.

'Is that Scotland Yard? I want to speak to Inspector Priestley.'

'I don't think he's in,' says the voice. 'I'll inquire. What name is it?'

'Never mind that. It's important.'

A wait. The dark shadows of stray pedestrians stretch and restretch beneath the light of the lamp outside.

'Hullo.'

'I want to speak to Inspector Priestley.'

'Speaking.'

'Oh... You're the man engaged on the investigation into the death of Mrs Olive Stafford? Is that correct?'

'It is. Who's that speaking?'

'At the inquest yesterday, I think you came to the conclusion that some man was in her flat at the time of her death. You want that man. Am I right?'

'Perfectly.'

'I'm that man,' I say.

There is a pause at the other end of the wire. Then the voice comes very casually.

'Who are you? Where are you speaking from?'

'Some distance away. My name doesn't matter. You'll know it very soon.'

'Well?'

'I'm returning to London by car tonight. I'll call at your office in the morning at ten. Will that be agreeable?'

'Is this a hoax?'

'No hoax. I'm prepared to make a full statement. The inquiry agent will be able to identify me. I'll call at ten.'

'Where are you speaking from?'

I hang up the receiver.

I leave the telephone box. Someone is waiting to use it after me. A tall, fair girl with full lips and large prominent breasts. No doubt she is going to ring up some boy friend or tell her husband she's going to be late. Or both.

I climb into the car and start the engine.

I drive out of Lancaster and take the road south. A long night ahead. The road glistens like wet coal.

I have to make the move at this stage, with its irreversible consequences, while the decision is clear cut, before the anaesthetic wears off, before the doubts and the regrets begin. There's no place now for second thoughts.

Now those patient men will turn their attention on what I have to say, listening to it gravely, sifting through it for the truth and the lies. What is the truth but the opinion of a majority when only one man knows it and his integrity is suspect? But if I tell the absolute truth, the whole of it and nothing but it, how shall I come to greater harm than if I attempt any subterfuge?

I wonder then—and have wondered since—what took me to Crichton Beck before deciding on any other action. I suppose I wanted to see Paul and his paintings again and I wanted to see the girl I loved. There might be some justification for the mess and the tragedy that had occurred if as a result of it I could consider them so much the better for it.

That no doubt was a consolation I would have come away with—if Holly had not spoken. But there's a limit to the extent to which one can put other people's happiness first. And I have reached it. Fortunately I cannot yet feel the extent of the personal loss. Emotion is played out.

I drive all through the night without apparent fatigue. This is the fourth night I haven't slept. Lack of sleep is like lack of food, it induces a high sense of physical perception. Towards dawn my screen-wipers pack up, but fortunately the worst of the rain is over and soon it stops altogether. I draw up beside the road and get out and feel the cool breeze on my face and eyes. I stand beside the car and watch the canopy of cloud begin to lift from the east like a roll-top desk. After a few minutes the desk jams and the brilliant sky shows only for a few inches above the horizon. Then as the sun rises the whole of the desk top catches fire and crumbles into crimson ash.

Red sky in the morning ... I get back into the car and drive on. My finger tips are sensitive to the thin rim of the wheel. The speedometer in this car is not by clock face and needle but by a moving tape that slides behind a window. It is showing sixty miles an hour, which is a fair speed for this car, and on roads still wet. But somehow I'm convinced I'll not have an accident. That wouldn't please the fates.

And presently as I near London I realise I'm becoming myself again. Sensation is being unfrozen. I'm almost out of the chloroform. There is pain again. But not much fear. And not much remorse. Something after all has changed, and I wonder what is the difference.

I look back on what has happened with an eye still detached, and with a cool mind. I look back on what has happened and find that there is little room or time for regret. I look forward into the future and find there is little to be afraid of. For the worst has happened. And once the worst has happened there is nothing more to fear.

By the time I reach London the buses are out in the streets, the workers thronging along drying pavements, the newspaper posters flapping. What news will they have tomorrow? I say it over to myself as I drive through the traffic: once the worst has happened there is nothing more to fear.